TALES FROM
THE BOTTOM
OF MY SOLE

Essential Prose Series 182

 Canada Council **Conseil des Arts**
for the Arts **du Canada**

ONTARIO ARTS COUNCIL
CONSEIL DES ARTS DE L'ONTARIO

an Ontario government agency
un organisme du gouvernement de l'Ontario

 Canadä

Guernica Editions Inc. acknowledges the support of the Canada Council
for the Arts and the Ontario Arts Council. The Ontario Arts Council
is an agency of the Government of Ontario.

We acknowledge the financial support of the Government of Canada.

TALES FROM THE BOTTOM OF MY SOLE

DAVID KINGSTON YEH

GUERNICA EDITIONS
TORONTO • BUFFALO • LANCASTER (U.K.)
2020

Michael Mirolla, general editor
Lindsay Brown, editor
David Moratto, interior and cover design
Guernica Editions Inc.
287 Templemead Drive, Hamilton, ON L8W 2W4
2250 Military Road, Tonawanda, N.Y. 14150-6000 U.S.A.
www.guernicaeditions.com

Distributors:
Independent Publishers Group (IPG)
600 North Pulaski Road, Chicago IL 60624
University of Toronto Press Distribution,
5201 Dufferin Street, Toronto (ON), Canada M3H 5T8
Gazelle Book Services, White Cross Mills
High Town, Lancaster LA1 4XS U.K.

First edition.
Printed in Canada.

Legal Deposit—Third Quarter
Library of Congress Catalog Card Number: 2019949232
Library and Archives Canada Cataloguing in Publication
Title: Tales from the bottom of my sole / David Kingston Yeh.
Names: Yeh, David Kingston, author.
Series: Essential prose series ; 182
Description: Series statement: Essential prose series ; 182
Identifiers: Canadiana (print) 20190175990 | Canadiana (ebook)
20190176008 | ISBN 9781771835411 (softcover) | ISBN
9781771835428 (EPUB) | ISBN 9781771835435 (Kindle)
Classification: LCC PS8647.E47 T35 2020 | DDC C813/.6—dc23

For my family and my friends

*No need to hurry. No need to sparkle.
No need to be anybody but oneself.*
—Virginia Woolf

CONTENTS

PART I

CHAPTER ONE

Somewhere Down the Crazy River

Christmas Eve. The one-year anniversary of Grandma's death. My brothers Pat and Liam and I were coming back from the farmhouse of a tattoo artist named Denis out on Old Highway 69. Denis worked by appointment only and had a five-week waiting list. In October, Pat had booked us three sessions back-to-back. The story was we'd be gone the whole day volunteering with Conservation Sudbury, fixing up the boardwalk on Ramsey Lake. Pat did the fast-talking; Liam and I were never much good at pulling one over on Grandpa. This was also my first tattoo.

"Yah, Denis and I go way back," Pat said during the drive home. "Check this out." In the backseat, he unzipped and pulled his pants down low over one hip.

"What," I asked, "is that?"

"This," he said, beaming, "is a rocket ship."

"Denis did that?"

"Yeppers."

"It's upside-down."

"I've got another one on the other side."

"Why, Pat, do you have two rocket ships tattooed on your hips?"

Pat arched his back and pulled up his jeans. "Because Blonde Dawn calls me her space cowboy? Because she's got these shooting stars all around her waist and we figured I'd get something to match?"

Once I asked Blonde Dawn how many tattoos she had. She said that if you counted her sleeves as one piece each, then under a dozen. Pat's second tattoo had been Blonde Dawn's name over his heart.

"Trust me," Pat said, crowding forward between Liam and me so he could change the radio station, "I'm just getting started."

Sloan was singing about the good in everyone when Liam pulled into our drive, parking his Jeep next to Grandpa's pick-up. The front curtains were open and the Christmas tree inside all lit up. Gingerly, I checked the sterile bandage on my upper arm. When it came to Liam's turn, he'd said he wanted it done on his chest. Pat got his behind his shoulder. "So she can always watch over me," he explained.

"David's here," Liam said.

"What?"

Liam stood with his hands on his hips and pointed at tracks in the snow. "That's a taxi. Those are a man's size nine-and-a-half prints. Here's where he knelt to pet Jackson."

"Seriously?"

Betty stuck her head out the front door, wearing a reindeer sweater and a gold-frosted crimson bouffant. "Hello boys!" She raised a martini glass garnished with a candy cane. "Welcome back." She leaned forward con-spiratorially. "So, how'd it go?"

"Sugar crispy." Pat grinned. "Where's Grandpa?"

"In the kitchen."

"Does he suspect anything?" I asked.

Betty winked and shook her head. "Come on in, wash up. Dinner's almost ready. Oh and by the way, Daniel, you have a visitor."

We'd officially met Grandpa's lady friend Betty back in September up at the Good Medicine Cabin. But the truth was we'd known her for years as the head nurse at Grandma's nursing home.

Inside, the rich aromas of cinnamon and cloves, pine and meat pies filled the house. In the kitchen, David and Grandpa were wearing aprons, wrapping freshly-baked tourtières. There must've been a dozen already stacked on the counter.

"David," I said from the doorway, "what are you doing here?"

"Hey." He was wearing a Santa hat and had flour on his nose. "Your grandpa invited me."

"Surprise!" Grandpa said, clapping David on the shoulder.

David was supposed to be spending the holidays with his family in Toronto.

"When did you get here?" I asked.

"This afternoon."

"What about your mom?"

"I'll catch a bus back tomorrow morning."

"What about Midnight Mass?"

"She's got company. My aunts are visiting from

Palermo, remember? Trust me, it's all good. I'll spend the whole day with them tomorrow."

"You're sure about this?"

"I'm here, aren't I?"

"Holy shit."

"So?" He raised and dropped his arms. "Do I get a hug or what?"

I crossed the kitchen and gave David a bear hug. "I can't believe you're here."

"What are boyfriends for?" Grandpa said, elbowing me in the side.

"Thanks for coming."

"Thank your grandpa. He paid for my ticket." David whispered in my ear: "I love you."

Later that evening, after Grandpa and Betty had retired for the night, Liam, Pat and David stepped out back for a smoke. I stayed behind to tidy up and wait for my best friend Karen whose adoptive parents, the Miltons, lived just across the street. Near midnight, wearing a fuzzy toque with a skull-and-crossbones pattern and a ginormous pompom, she let herself in the front door, stamping the snow off her boots.

"Where's Anne?"

Karen tossed her ski jacket onto Grandpa's deer antler coat rack. "She went out back."

"They're smoking up."

"Why do you think she's out back?"

"Okay." It was time I stopped thinking of Karen's sister as a little kid. Anne was nineteen. "Okay. You want a drink?"

"No thanks." Native artwork decorated Karen's T-shirt:

abstract, Picasso-like figures. She brushed tinsel and playing cards off the living room couch and plopped down next to me, pulling a dented flask out of her snow pants. "You want a drink?"

"Sure." I took a swig.

"Fireball," Karen said.

I coughed, nearly choking, and took a second swig before handing it back. "That's a cool shirt."

"Thanks. My aunt's friend Daphne did this."

The backdoor banged opened and the others trooped into the living room. Jackson thrashed his bushy tail, licking Karen's face and clambered up next to her.

"Hey, Anne," I said.

Anne waved. "Hey." When she was little, she'd started wearing her hair short and looked just like a boy. Now, her hair was still buzzed short, but she wore expertly applied mascara and her nails were painted emerald and electric blue. The last four months at the Ontario College of Art and Design had changed her.

"Okay, let's see 'em," Karen said. Anne perched crossed-legged on the patched arm of the couch. David slid down to the rug at Karen's feet.

Liam, Pat and I exchanged glances. Taking off my flannel shirt, I rolled up the sleeve of my tee and carefully peeled away the square bandage on my arm.

"Wow." Karen sat up. "Definitely."

"You like?"

"It's beautiful," Anne said.

"It's big," Karen said.

"It had to be," Pat said, "to get all the details in."

David whistled. "Nice work."

"Swelling's gone down," Liam said.

"It looks just like her," Anne said, eyes wide, chewing on her lip ring.

"Denis is an artiste," Pat said. "My man knows what he's doing."

"So, let's see all of them," Karen said. Obligingly, Pat yanked his shirt off over his head and Liam did the same. We crowded into each other, lining up our new tattoos side-by-side. Anne glanced up the stairwell. "You sure your grandpa's sleeping?"

"I wouldn't say Pépère's sleeping," Liam said. "But they're not coming back down."

"I gotta get a picture of this," Karen said. "Hold on, don't move."

As a surprise gift to Grandpa this year, the three of us had gotten matching tattoos of our grandma, Josette Garneau. It hadn't taken long to agree on the image we'd use: a photo of her taken just after they'd gotten married. In the end, they'd stayed married fifty-nine years. Denis had done a bang-up job. He'd gotten her dimples just right, and the beauty mark on her cheek. Back in the day, Grandma had been a glamorous gal. She always had the look of a Hollywood starlet.

Karen had her phone out and was lining up a group shot. "These are awesome, guys."

"Merry Christmas!" Pat said over his shoulder. "It's midnight. It's Christmas."

"What about Betty?" Anne asked. "What will she think of this?"

"This," Liam said, "was Betty's idea."

The flash went off. "Oh sweet Mother Earth," Karen said, studying the image on her phone, "your grandpa is so totally going to absolutely love this."

And he did.

⌒ New Year's Eve, Pat drove me back into Toronto. My tattoo was starting to itch and peel. Pat assured me that was normal and told me to make sure I kept it clean. He insisted on dropping me off downtown before heading back out to the airport to pick up Blonde Dawn. At Spadina and Dundas, he leaned out the driver's window and gave me a high five. "See ya tonight!" Their band Three Dog Run was playing at Graffiti's down the street and David and I had promised to attend.

Shouldering my backpack, I headed into Kensington Market. It was late in the afternoon, and the ramshackle neighbourhood was bustling with last-minute shoppers searching for that special sequined choker or one-of-a-kind velvet jacket. Vintage clothing stores lined Kensington Avenue with names like Courage My Love, The Fairies Pyjamas and Eye of Shiva. Crowded cafés and eateries offered everything from Tibetan dumplings and Jamaican patties to samosas and Salvadoran pupusas with generous portions of spicy curtido on the side.

I paused in front of the window display of Orbital Arts where luminous buddhas, Eyes of Horus, angels and Indian gods decorated refurbished furniture. Inside, two coiffed boys in skinny jeans held hands, admiring a crystal paperweight. It occurred to me that, when I was their age, I was still closeted in Sudbury, sporting a mullet, and jacking off to secret fantasies about my assistant hockey coach, Stephan Tondeur.

Turning down a shovelled alleyway, I keyed into my building. Someone had freshly Febrezed the lobby in an attempt to cover up the odour of mouldy carpeting and wet dog. Our building manager Rick stomped down the stairwell hefting a monkey wrench in his hairy paw, looking even more pissed-off than usual. When I asked him what was up, he told me the water heater was down again and he was working on it. I turned sideways to let him pass and called out politely: "Good luck."

At the top landing, David was waiting for me. "Happy New Year's Eve, mister."

I slung my pack off my shoulders. "Happy New Year's Eve." There was a funny look on David's face. I gave him a hug and stood back. "What's wrong?"

"It's good to see you."

"Okay."

"My sister's here."

"Your sister? Alright. Is she here right now?" He nodded. "Is everything okay?"

"No, not really."

In the two years I'd known David, I'd yet to meet his sister. All I knew was that, when she was seventeen and David was twelve, she'd run away from home, and that I had strict instructions to avoid mentioning her in front of David's mom. "Lucy, right?"

"Well ..."

Behind him, a slim, angular guy stepped out of our loft. He was barefoot, wearing a pair of David's old jeans and towel-drying his hair, with a scruffy goatee and a thin dusting of hair on his narrow chest.

For one second, a sharp knot of confusion and jealousy tightened in my throat.

"Hey, you must be Daniel." His voice was a scratchy tenor pitched slightly higher than David's. He slung the towel over his shoulder. "I've heard a lot about you. I'm Luke." I stared at his outstretched hand, and then at the horizontal scars just below his nipples. Still, it took me another second to put all the pieces together.

"Luke." I cleared my throat. "Pleased to meet you." His grip was firm, his eyes big and steely grey, just like David's. The resemblance was uncanny. I couldn't help but notice he also had a six-pack.

"You two have special plans?" he asked, looking from one of us to the other.

"Plans?"

"New Year's Eve?"

"Ah. My brother's band is playing tonight," I said, "just a couple blocks from here."

"Sounds like fun." Luke tousled David's hair. "Hey, thanks for the clothes, kiddo. I'll be out of your way in a minute." He winked and disappeared back inside.

"Luke?"

David leaned back against the wall. "She was Luciana, growing up."

"Whoa."

"The last time I saw her was three years ago. I'm sorry, I had no idea she was coming by."

"You always said you had an older sister."

"Half-sister. Look, this is all new to me."

"What do you mean?"

"I mean," David said, "I just found out."

"You mean about Luke?"

"She's never said anything to me about this."

"Shouldn't you, like, be using 'he' and 'him'?"

"Sure. Easy enough for you to say. You didn't grow up with her. Him. Lucy, Luke. Whatever."

"No, I didn't. Where's he been?"

"Out west, Vancouver mostly. Working in some boxing gym."

"How long has he been gone?"

"Twelve years. I wouldn't hear from her for months at a time. When I did, she'd usually be hitting me up for money."

"You really had no idea?"

"Daniel, I just found out like two friggin' hours ago, okay? She calls me this morning, says she's coming into town and asks if she can drop by and take a shower and borrow some clothes."

"Whoa, okay. Relax."

David paced the hallway. "And she wanted to pay me back."

"For what?"

"Like I said, she'd borrowed a lot of money from me over the years."

"How much?"

"Apparently, four thousand dollars."

"Holy shit."

"I never kept track. I never thought I'd see any of it again. She paid me in cash."

"Cash?"

"You don't think it's stolen, do you?"

"Well, if the RCMP comes banging on our door, we'll know for sure, won't we?"

"Daniel, Lucy spent a year in juvie back in the day. Kids in our neighbourhood were scared of her, Luciana Moretti. Everyone called her the Boss."

I raised my eyebrows. I'd never seen David this unsettled, not by a long shot.

"Sorry, but I am so fucking gobsmacked right now."

"It's okay."

"It's just a lot to take in."

"Of course!" I tried to imagine how I'd feel if one of my brothers turned up in a dress, with cleavage. Liam was a two-hundred-pound farmhand with a black belt in kung fu. Pat had a whole alphabetized roster of affectionate nicknames for his penis. "I get it. Kinda."

Dull banging echoed up the stairwell from the boiler room. David massaged his face. "Batman and Robin."

"What?"

"Halloween. We'd go as Batman and Robin, or the Lone Ranger and Tonto. Once she made us up like Ziggy Stardust and the Thin White Duke. Lucy taught me how to ride longboard, and then BMX. She'd always be hanging out with the guys. When she got older, she had this whole posse going. For a while there, us kids ruled the neighbourhood. They'd put up with me because I was her kid brother. I idolized her. We all did."

"What happened?"

"She got caught, B&E. After juvie, she got into dealing.

Ma found her stash and kicked her out. She took off, left town. And that was the end of it, until now."

"She never came back?"

"She came back, once. But she was drunk and Ma wouldn't let her in the house." David buried his hands in his pockets. "After that, no, she never came back."

"And now he's Luke."

"Shit."

"Where's he staying?"

"I dunno."

"Look, if he's passing through Toronto, he can crash here if he wants."

"I wasn't going to ask."

"You weren't going to ask him or me?"

"He probably already has plans. It's New Year's Eve. We really don't have the space. What? Why are you smiling like that?"

"You said 'he.' Look." I picked up my bag and pointed at our loft. "I'm going in now. Is that okay?"

"You live here."

"I know. So do you. C'mon. I need to put Grandpa's tourtières in the freezer. I also want to get to know my boyfriend's big brother."

"Right."

"Before he disappears for another three years."

"Take your best shot."

I rested my hand on David's shoulder, straight-armed. I leaned in close. "He's also pretty hot, you know."

"Fuck you."

I wrapped my arm around him. "Fuck you too."

⌒ Graffiti's Bar and Grill was a local watering hole on Baldwin Street, two blocks from where we lived, in the heart of Kensington Market. New Year's Eve was Three Dog Run's first professional gig. They were lined up as the opening act for an out-of-town headliner called Accursed Spawn and Pat was thrilled. Most of the regulars were paunchy metalheads like Rick, middle-aged hippies, and aging rockers.

It had started to snow late in the afternoon and hadn't stopped, huge fluffy flakes drifting straight down out of a silvery-grey sky. Over dinner they announced a severe weather alert. By the time David and I arrived, they'd cancelled most flights at the airport.

My friends Charles and Megan had saved a table for us. Tonight, Charles was sporting a flat cap and a grey wool cardigan, while Megan had on bright glossy lipstick that matched her blouse.

"Well," I said, "you two look spiffy."

"Charlie and I are going to another event later," Megan said, nervously fishing a maraschino cherry out of her cocktail. "We're here for the count-down and everything but then we have this other invitation." She fussed with an enormous silk neck scarf. "Tell me, honestly, does this look okay on me?"

"It looks very nice."

"Thank you, Daniel. I can always count on you."

Charles sipped from his Guinness. "We're going to a sex party."

"Really?"

Megan clutched his hand. "It's for couples."

"Sounds like fun."

"I hope so," Charles said. "The last one we attended was a little too advanced for us. Wouldn't you say, sweetie?"

Megan downed her drink and nodded in agreement.

I wondered what that meant, picturing all sorts of acrobatic equipment and yoga poses. Years ago, Charles and I had dated until he left me for Megan. Now the two were into a five-month engagement. They'd yet to set a wedding date, but I'd agreed to be their best man.

"I'm wearing a new harness," Charles said.

"Oh?"

"It seems to be chafing a little."

"You mean," I asked, "right now?"

Megan patted him on the knee. "You just need to break it in, poopsie."

"Megan helped me pick it out."

"That's great. Alright." I gave a thumbs-up sign. "Okay." I was afraid to ask what else he might be wearing. As Charles reached under his cardigan to adjust some strap or buckle, Megan whipped out a tissue and dabbed at the foam on his upper lip. I searched for David who'd joined Pat and the rest of the band up at the bar. "I'll be right back."

Pat's girlfriend and band manager Blonde Dawn was blonder than ever and tanned from her annual family trip to Florida. Even in a plain black tank-top, she looked like a rock goddess.

"Blonde Dawn," David was saying as I walked up, "you know you look like a rock goddess?"

Pat draped himself over David's shoulder. "She is a

rock goddess. She's my rock goddess. I worship the drum she beats. Hallelujah!"

"Daniel," Blonde Dawn said, "I hear you met Denis."

When I showed her the tattoo on my arm, she pursed her lips approvingly.

"Now that," she said, pointing with the drum stick she was twirling in her hand, "is why I have him do all my ink."

Three Dog Run had arrived early and already finished their sound check. The other members, Bobby and Rod, sat in the corner hunched over their glowing phones. I waved at them. "Hey guys." They glanced up and waved back.

Someone tapped me on the shoulder. It was Parker Kapoor dressed like one of Santa's elves.

"Daniel," he said, clearly out of breath, "we got here as fast as we could. Did we miss it?" He shook his head, scattering snow into people's drinks, bells tinkling in his red and green cap.

I stared at the candy cane stockings stretched tightly over his knobby knees.

"They're not up for another half-hour. Parker, why are you dressed like an elf?"

"It's the Christmas spirit, I can't help it, it's not going away. I know I'm Hindu, but that's beside the point. It's here, it's all right here." Parker splayed his hand over his heart. "The spirit of the season, goodwill and joy. Who says we're only allowed to celebrate these things once a year? Who says I can't be an elf tonight?"

"Parker, have you been drinking?"

"Daniel, you know I don't drink. Well, maybe I had

a little eggnog, but that doesn't count, does it?" His eyes bulged and swivelled in his head. "I don't know what's come over me. I'll have to write about this in my memoirs. Daniel, you remember Kyle, don't you?"

Parker's friend Kyle had appeared at his side, also dressed like an elf. There were sparkles on his rosy cheeks, and he'd even waxed his blond moustache.

"Yo, dudes, love the threads!" Pat said, fist-bumping Kyle. "Thanks for coming out, guys. How's your mom? How's the Kandy Factory?"

"Sweet, man," Kyle said. "Sweet."

"Right on." Pat slapped Kyle on the chest. "Parker, don't let this one get away. He's a keeper."

Later in the washroom, David asked: "Hey, are those two together?"

"Parker and Kyle? I'm not sure. Parker says they're just friends."

"What's the Kandy Factory?"

"Kyle makes fudge and peanut brittle out of his mom's kitchen. He sells it at the café out on Ward's Island."

"Oh, I get it." David zipped up his fly. "Sweet."

The cracked soap dispenser wasn't working, no matter how hard I pumped it. The door swung open and David's brother walked in bundled up in a leather bomber jacket.

"Hey, Luke," I exclaimed, "you made it!"

"Yeah." He took off his toque and shook out his hair. "It's a fucking blizzard out there."

"You're right on time."

"Thanks again for inviting us."

"Your girlfriend was okay to come?"

"Yeah, for sure. Absolutely. Like I said, we had no plans.

Hey, do me a favour and introduce yourselves? She's the chick in the Helix shirt. Her name's Ai Chang." He stepped up to the urinal and unbuckled his belt. Upstairs, I could hear Pat greeting the festive crowd. Luke glanced over his shoulder. "Guys. You mind?"

"Sorry." I opened the door and pushed David out of the washroom ahead of me.

"How does she do that?" David asked as we manoeuvred past empty beer kegs and climbed the narrow stairs.

"Do what?"

"You know what, back there, like that."

"I dunno," I said. "Ask him."

"Are you kidding me? I'm not asking her."

"David, you're doing it again."

"What?"

"Calling him her. There she is."

"Who?"

"Luke's girlfriend, over there." A short Asian girl in a metal shirt was paying the bartender for two beers. When she glanced at us sidelong, I waved.

"This is too weird."

"David, c'mon. It's your brother's girlfriend. And I want another drink and you need another drink."

"Fine."

We made our way over. The girl was wearing Amy Winehouse-styled mascara, with at least a dozen piercings in her ears and face. "Hey, hi." I cleared my throat. "I'm Daniel."

The girl turned her shoulder to us. "No."

"Hold on," David said. "You don't understand—"

"No." She studied a drinks menu.

"But I'm—"

She raised a finger. "No."

"Wait," I said. "This is David, Luke's brother. I'm David's boyfriend."

Her heavy-lidded eyes widened. "Oh. You're Luke's brother." When she spoke, she didn't exactly mumble, but her lips weren't moving either. "I thought you were … I mean, you don't look like you're boyfriends."

"That's alright."

"I'm Ai Chang Cho."

"Daniel."

"Sorry about that." She shook my outstretched hand. White skulls adorned each of her black fingernails. "You know how it is."

"Don't worry about it."

"No," David said. "No, I don't know how it is. Tell me how it is."

"Well." Ai Chang's eyes narrowed. "Let's just say it's a straight guy thing."

"Oh, so." David pointed between us. "You thought we were …"

"Let's just say I'm not into playing games."

"And you're not into straight guys?"

"Hey," Luke said behind us, "I see you've met. Ai Chang, this is my little brother David I've been telling you about."

Ai Chang handed Luke a frosty beer. "He's all grown up."

"There," David said. "It's official. I'm all grown up. I'm a big boy now."

"I hope so," I said.

"What's that supposed to mean?"

"It means," I said, stepping up to the bar between the two, "we need drinks."

Up on the low stage, Three Dog Run launched into their opening number. Rod was wearing a trench coat, bent over his bass guitar, and Bobby was playing a gigantic sparkling-blue accordion. David hollered and clapped a little too loudly. Tonight, Pat was wearing a Stetson and a plaid shirt opened at the collar. Blonde Dawn had a big black feather stuck in her cowboy hat. The band sounded great. Pat looked like he was having the time of his life.

After the first song I noticed Luke talking into David's ear. David scowled, his arms crossed. I sipped my beer. I knew better than to get involved.

"I'm going out for a smoke," David said. He shouldered his way toward the door. Luke ordered a shot, threw it back and followed him.

I glanced at Ai Chang, but her expression was unreadable.

After the second song, she leaned into me. "Just in case you were wondering, I know about Luke, okay?"

We both kept our eyes on the stage. "Um. I wasn't wondering."

"I'm not a dyke."

"I never said you were."

"His brother's pissed, isn't he?"

"David? I think he's still just getting used to all this. Up until this afternoon, he thought he had a sister named Lucy."

"Lucy's a dead name. You call him Luke."

"Hey look, I'm on your side here." I drew a breath. "David's a good guy. Just give him some time."

"Sure, you'd say that, you're his boyfriend."

"Luke's his family."

"Is family that important?"

"Of course, it is."

"Families are fucked."

"I never said they weren't."

One corner of Ai Chang's mouth turned up. It was the closest thing to a smile I'd seen yet. Then I noticed she was wearing a full set of metal braces. She raised her beer and we knocked bottles. "Cheers to that."

More people were coming in the front door. It was standing room only and the windows were steaming up. Twinkling lights framed the tiny stage. Pat was in his element, working the crowd, introducing the band members and cracking jokes. To my horror, he began telling a story about the Three Amigas, international students we'd met years ago. It was the only time I'd ever had sex with a girl. It was also the only time I'd ever had sex in front of one of my brothers. But before the details got too sordid, the band launched into a mash-up of "La Bamba" and "Twist and Shout." Bobby had swapped his accordion for a trumpet. By then I had to shout into the bartender's ear to order another round.

People were up on their feet dancing. Nobody ever danced at Graffiti's. Now I could spot two elves pogoing up and down in their own little mosh pit. Outside, the snow was coming down harder than ever. I was just starting to have visions of Luke and David frozen somewhere in an alleyway clutching six-guns, with bullet holes in each of their hearts, when I saw them wedging their way back to the bar.

"Sorry we were gone so long," Luke said, wrapping his arms around Ai Chang. "You okay?"

"Fuck your hands are cold," Ai Chang said. But you could tell she was happy to see him.

"Sorry, kiddo." He nuzzled her ear.

David gave me a *we'll-talk-about-it-later* look, signalled the bartender over and slapped a fistful of one-hundred-dollar bills down on the bar. "Round of whiskey shots for everyone!" He turned to me and grinned. "I've always wanted to say that."

An hour later, the manager announced Accursed Spawn was stuck at the airport and their show was cancelled. Of course, after that, it was Three Dog Run all the way, stepping up to cover New Year's Eve at Graffiti's Bar and Grill. Complete strangers kept buying David drinks, Pat's shirt came off at the stroke of midnight, and Charles and Megan never did make it to their special event. By closing time, the band had sold all its EPs, Charles' assless chaps were the surprise hit of the evening, and Luke and Ai Chang were sharing pitchers with Pat and the rest of the band.

"Parker and Kyle are mackin' in the basement," David said.

"You sure about that?" I asked.

"Yep."

"Well, I guess that answers your question. Good for them."

"Good for them. Good for the band."

"Yeah, they were amazing tonight."

David tossed his bottle aside. "Here." He rummaged in the pocket of his jeans and pinned a Three Dog Run button to my T-shirt. He'd designed the band logo himself back in the summer: three puppies silhouetted inside a spiral circle. Then he hiccoughed, gripped my face between his hands and planted a kiss on my mouth. His breath smelled like Jägermeister, cigarettes, and cinnamon chewing gum. "Happy New Year, mister. I love you, Daniel Garneau, you're the best. You are a very very kind soul, did you know that?" He poked me in the chest. "And you are a very very fuckable man. I mean it. I love you. Did I say that already?"

"Yes, you did, but that's okay."

"I love you."

"I love you too, David Gallucci. Happy New Year."

CHAPTER TWO

The Limit to Your Love

Early in February, I was getting take-out at Big Fat Burrito when my old acquaintance Marwa walked in carrying a shopping bag full of posters. She was dressed in a fitted white pea coat, a white Russian hat with dangling pompoms and matching fur-lined boots. When I commented on her outfit, she spun coyly and struck a pose. "Zo you like zees, comrade?" she said in her best Soviet era accent. "I win ushanka in vodka-drinking contest."

"In Siberian prison," I said.

"Against toothless babushka," Marwa said, "of Mongolian warlord."

Marwa explained she was helping to promote a Valentine's Day burlesque show at the Revival Bar. Her catering company, Cherry Bomb Bakery, was hosting a booth at the event. As it turned out, my ex-boyfriend Marcus Wittenbrink Jr. was scheduled to make a guest appearance. "Marcus," Marwa said, stapling a poster to the wall, "he's like a surprise celebrity performer."

"What? Is he going to jump of out of a giant frosted cupcake or something?"

Marwa giggled. "I offered to bake him one, but he turned me down. Truth is, I don't know what he's planning. He says he's choreographing something special. It's all very secret. He won't even let me see. He insisted his name stay off the bill. Don't tell him I told you. Daniel, you and your boyfriend should come. David, right? It'll be fabulous."

"And delicious?"

Marwa pinched my cheek. "And delicious."

A boy with neon-blue hair called out my number, and I retrieved my big fat burrito wrapped in foil. "It sounds fun, Marwa but to be honest, I'm not really sure it's my thing."

"It should be your thing," Marwa said. "Burlesque is all about playfulness and subversion and feminist empowerment."

"Maybe you should be performing."

"Me? I'm just a reformed goth girl from Burlington, remember? I channel my inner goddess into baking. It's Skin Tight Outta Sight teaming up with Boylesque."

"Boylesque? There are boys in this show?"

"Marcus eez boy, isn't he? But yes, comrade, are boys in zees show. Aha ..." She stroked my burrito with a pom-pom. "Now, Mr. Garneau, I haf your attention. Now you must come zee fabulous Valentine's cabaret. I bake special cupcake just for you."

Marwa's Russian accent was awful. I laughed, despite myself. "I'll think about it."

"Here." She handed me a glossy, heart-shaped postcard. "Take this. Promise you'll think about it?"

"I'll think about it."

"Good boy."

Later when I mentioned it to David, he was more than enthusiastic. "Of course, we should go," he said, running the hot water, clutching a towel around his waist. "I've always wanted to see burlesque. It'll be fun."

"You just want to see twirling pasties."

"Yeah, and?"

Before moving into David's Kensington Market loft, I'd never lived with a boyfriend. David was messy and played his music too loud. But I loved that he collected old LPs and Scott Pilgrim books, and had over two dozen spices in his spice rack (all of which he actually used). It was cramped for two (especially with my giant palm taking up half the living room area), but somehow we made it work. This evening we were sharing a bubble bath. Back in the fall, David had come across a vintage claw-foot bathtub abandoned in an alleyway. It took a week for him and Rick the building manager to find the parts to install it properly in our bathroom. When they were done, we went into Chinatown and adopted two rubber duckies we named Sam and Dean and popped a bottle of Asti Spumante.

"Did you know Marwa's hired a second part-time assistant to help with her company?" I said. "She's doing really well for herself."

David leaned back into me, lighting half a joint. "Good for her, she deserves it. She works really hard. Maybe Cherry Bomb Bakery could team up with Kyle's Kandy Factory."

"I could introduce them."

"It's all about who you know, networking, strength in numbers. Teamwork."

"Marcus is helping out with Boylesque. Marwa says he used to date one of the performers."

"Oh?"

"Joseph."

"The Joseph who was in that threesome?"

"With Marcus and Fang, yeah."

"Didn't we bump into them at Inside Out last year?"

"Yeah, we did."

David reached out and carefully ashed his joint in a Pop Shoppe bottle. "That didn't last too long. But it's good they can still stay friends."

I stroked David's shoulders and limbs. "Marcus stays friends with all his exes. He never said anything to you about this show he's doing?"

"Nope. He hasn't mentioned anything on Facebook either."

I rested my chin on top of David's head. "Don't you think it's weird?"

"What?"

"Us going to see him perform in a show he hasn't told anyone about?"

"Daniel, he's just making a guest appearance, right? He's probably only going to be on stage like five minutes."

"Probably."

"So I doubt it's any big deal at all."

"Karen says he's a narcissist."

David butted out his roach. "Marcus? He's a theatre artist. Hell, he's a three-ring circus. It's how he makes his living. He's allowed to be a narcissist."

"You just want to see him do a striptease."

"Of course, I do. And so do you." David craned his neck to look back up at me. "Are we okay with that?"

"Yes, we are okay with that."

"Spiderman kiss."

I kissed him, open-mouthed. After that, David reached for his wineglass. "And I also want to see twirling pasties."

"Apparently there'll be a lot of boys in the show."

"Very inclusive. Very avant-garde. Now I'm definitely getting excited."

"Are you?" I reached forward under the bubbles and palpated. "Uh-oh. Young man, it does feel swollen. Is there any tenderness?"

"Oh, yes, sir, there is. I think it needs medical attention."

"Or maybe just a little TLC."

"Maybe."

"Like this?"

David bit his lower lip. "Mmm."

I took his glass and set it aside. "Or like this." I pinned him against me with one arm across his chest. Water sloshed onto the bathroom floor. He gripped the edges of the tub. I ran my mouth over his jaw and neck, careful not to break the skin. Sam and Dean bobbed up and down with surprised expressions. After a while, I could tell he was getting close. David's hips arched. Then I kissed him hard just as his toes clenched and a muffled groan escaped his lips. It was always easy with David. Afterwards, he sank back into me. We ran more scalding water and took our time finishing the wine.

"So," I said, "should I tell Marcus we're coming?"

"No, why should we?" David said drowsily. "It's our date night, not his."

"Well, we'll just surprise him then."
"Perfect."

⌒ One week before Valentine's Day, David and I went shopping for outfits. I was never a fan of shopping (despite Parker Kapoor's best efforts) but David insisted. The Saturday afternoon was brisk and sun-drenched, with sparkling flecks of snow blowing off the rooftops. We strolled down Queen Street West, coffees in hand. Past MuchMusic and the Black Bull Tavern, we hugged the big colourful tree stump on the north side. I was ready to look into The Gap, but David made a face and the sign of the cross and hurried us past. He knew exactly where we were going and I eventually followed him down a short flight of stairs into a store called Borderline Plus.

"Welcome," he said, holding the door open for me, "to Toronto's gothic and alternative retail boutique."

I'd never seen so much lace, leather and rubber in one place. The store was narrow and long, with red-painted walls. A Chinese woman hunched behind the counter hand-stitching ostrich plumes into a top hat. David led me into the back, which was crowded with ornate dresses and luxurious, Victorian-tailored jackets. The aesthetic inspired but my jaw dropped when I checked a price tag.

"I fucking love this place," David said, holding up a crushed velvet frock coat. "How decadent is this? Just feel it."

I closed my mouth. "No thanks."

"C'mon. Touch it."

"Okay. Very nice."

"But do you like it? I think it's absolutely brilliant. *Rocambolesco*! That's what Ma would always say."

Life was *rocambolesco* for David's ma. I'd never met a more passionate or opinionated person. The few times I'd actually been in her presence, she never failed to terrify me.

I rolled my eyes. "*Rocambolesco*."

"Ooh, look at this, way too steampunk."

I followed David around as he admired one item after another—this was no Fabricville. Black boots of all shapes and sizes lined one section of wall. Tacky accessories featured skulls and pentagrams but there were also beautiful, one-of-a-kind pieces. Others just confused me. David held up what looked like a flak jacket constructed from vacuum hoses and industrial-grade Saran Wrap.

"Now you would look hot in this," he said.

"Are you kidding me?"

"I know, a little more apocalypso than *rocambolesco*, I get it. Oooh, wow, check this out. For your friends Charles and Megan?"

"What are they?"

"Matching corsets, his and hers."

"David, we can't afford any of this stuff."

"Daniel, people dress up for these burlesque events. I've still got that money from Luke. Let's have some fun here. I'm paying." He peered at me through a pair of aviator goggles. "Whatever we pick out, it'll be our Valentine's gift to the both of us."

"Shouldn't you be saving that money?"

"For what? Our kid's college fund? We still got time for that. C'mon, show me something you like."

Reluctantly, I let myself stray through the aisles as

David tried on half-a-dozen items. While I waited for him, two big girls in Hello Kitty fanny packs walked into the store. David drew back the change room curtain and stepped out wearing a dark brown cotton kilt trimmed in leather.

"So," he said, "what do you think? I'm not sure about all these chains and pockets here. Is it too much?"

He was holding up his T-shirt, exposing half his torso. I'd never looked twice at a man in a kilt before, but on this occasion, I couldn't help but stare. The truth was, it was sexy as hell.

"Wow."

David grinned at me. "You think?"

"Definitely."

"That works on you," one of the girls said, peering down the aisle. She pointed with a lollipop she was sucking. "Except you're wearing it backwards."

"Oh shit." David laughed. "Oops."

"Here, can I help you with that?" Lollipop Girl got down on one knee and expertly rearranged the kilt over his hips, loosening and cinching buckles and straps.

"Your boots rock," David said. "They look like the Full Metal Alchemist boots."

"Oh, thanks man. That's awesome." She got up and stood back. "There, how does that feel?"

"Great," David said.

She nodded in approval, arms folded, and waved her Chupa Chup at me like it was some sugar fairy wand. "Now you try one on."

"Oh." I backed away. "No thanks."

"Not everyone can pull off a kilt."

"Precisely."

"I think," she said, "you two boys would look awesome in kilts."

"What are you, some kind of fashion designer?"

Lollipop Girl glanced at her companion who was talking to Top Hat Lady up at the front counter, then adjusted the thick glasses on her snub nose. "Mm-hm. We are." She pulled two kilts off a rack, examined them both, and held one out for me. "Here. Try this one. Go on, it won't bite."

"C'mon, Daniel," David said, massaging my shoulders (and keeping me from escaping). "Resistance is futile."

Resistance *was* futile. While I was in the change room trying to remember which way was front, David poked his head through the curtains. "Remember, no underwear."

"What?"

"You can't wear underwear with a kilt."

"I don't think so."

"Daniel, c'mon, it's tradition. You can't mess with tradition."

"Tradition? These aren't even real Highland kilts. No way, man."

"Trust me, you'll be way more comfortable."

"Are you," I asked, "wearing your underwear?"

David shook his head. "Nope."

"Really?"

"Dude, when in Rome."

"Fine." I pulled down my underwear. "Happy?"

David's eyebrows rose. "Very."

I pulled up my underwear. "Seriously, I'm not going without my underwear. It's unhygienic."

"Aw, Daniel, c'mon."

Lollipop Girl stuck her head through the curtain. "Excuse me," I blurted, clutching my kilt. "I'm changing here."

"Your boyfriend's right," she said. "It really is a lot more comfortable if you go regimental."

"Regimental?"

"She means," David said, "going without your underwear."

"I'm not," I said, "going regimental."

"It frees your base chakra."

"What?"

Lollipop Girl thrust out her Chupa Chup, waving it in little circles. I stepped back, unsure if she was channelling Glinda from Oz or more Bellatrix Lestrange. "It allows for more flow down there."

"Definitely." David nodded. "More flow."

"If you don't mind me saying so," Lollipop Girl said, "your aura could use a little more flow."

I was being double-teamed here and my back was against the wall. This was not a contest I intended to lose. I'd show them flow. "Look, do you want me to wear the stupid kilt or not?"

David folded his arms. "Daniel, it's not stupid. It's *rocambolesco*. It's for Valentine's Day. You and I, we'll be the hottest couple there. And," he said, rocking forward on the balls of his feet, "it'll make Marcus jealous."

⌒ That next weekend, David and I arrived at Revival Bar's Valentine's Day burlesque show wearing matching kilts, vintage dress shirts and old combat boots we'd polished up. I'd agreed to go regimental and we did turn heads. On more than one occasion, people even asked if they could take our pictures. I had to confess, it was incredibly comfortable, even liberating, to just let it all hang out. A couple shots of Crown Royal from our hip flasks didn't hurt.

As David had promised, we weren't the only ones dressed up. The audience included an elegant older couple in a tuxedo and evening gown, and a host of others in costumes from the Victorian period through to the Roaring Twenties. No one seemed out of place, and everyone looked like they were having a great time. By the end of the first act, Marcus had yet to appear on stage. It was a sold-out show, and the performances had been cheeky, raunchy and over-the-top. When the last dancer soaked her tassels in lamp oil and set them on fire, all the while gyrating to Alannah Myles' "Black Velvet," the audience rose to its feet, whooping and hollering.

During intermission, David lined up at the bar and I made a point of searching out Marwa. Tonight she was looking coquettish in a hip-hugging Chinese dress, sequins glinting beneath the glowing chandeliers.

A gold and crystal candelabra drew a small crowd to her table featuring a decadent display of Valentine's-themed cupcakes and confections. To my surprise, her assistants turned out to be two awkward-looking boys with rouged cheeks, wearing togas and fuzzy angel wings, handling the cashbox and doling out free samples of Nipples of Venus.

"You've got to give it to Marwa," David said as we stepped outside for a smoke, "when it comes to promoting herself."

"Actually, the shorter one's her cousin and website designer," I said. "The other one's studying culinary arts at George Brown College."

"No kidding. And I thought they were just actors she hired. Her cousin's kinda cute."

"David, the kid's still in high school."

"I'm just saying."

"Here." I handed David a piece of Turkish Delight dusted in sugar and wrapped in red foil. "Compliments of Cherry Bomb Bakery."

A gong rang to signal the start of the second act, and we hurried back to our seats. The emcee introduced the next number only as, "A Somnambulistic Soldier's Soliloquy." Music was cued and a nurse pushed an old man in a wheelchair on stage. Dim, watery light flickered. I didn't even recognize Marcus until he lifted his head. Five minutes later, the song was over. After a second of silence, uncertain, scattered applause arose. Then someone called out: "Bravo." It was the white-haired gentleman in the tuxedo. "Bravo!" He started clapping, methodically and clearly. I quickly joined in and within moments, thunderous applause and whistling shook the house.

A bawdy act followed involving a girl dressed like a lobster, and the evening careened on toward its end. There'd been pole-dancing, circus-sized props, opera singing, and even an aerial silks act. At the final curtain call, all the performers crowded the stage, including Marcus leaning on his cane. He'd washed off his make-up, but the grey colouring remained in his eyebrows and hair.

Afterwards, chairs were cleared, and the floor swept of glitter and feathers. While people loitered at the bar and in small groups, I recognized many of the performers who'd come out to share a drink, but there was no sign of Marcus. It was Marwa who eventually pulled me aside to say Marcus had left already.

"Marcus Wittenbrink Jr. has left the building," David intoned in my ear. In his normal voice he added: "That's too bad. What'd you think of his performance anyway?"

"It was alright."

"Just alright?"

"It was very Marcus."

"You okay?"

"Of course, I am. How are you?"

"Daniel, I'm good. I had a great time tonight. I actually had an awesome time."

"Me too."

"You want a drink?"

We'd both finished our flasks long ago. "Sure, why not."

I looked for Marwa but she was busy packing up her booth. The truth was, Marcus's performance had been unlike any of the others. It had been hallucinatory and sensual. Its bittersweet tone only added to the rich flavour of the evening. I was proud of Marcus, in awe and envious of him at the same time.

I spotted Tuxedo Man leaning over two champagne glasses at the end of the bar. He was a strikingly handsome gentleman in his sixties, poised and unselfconscious, observing his surroundings with an air of detached curiosity. Then I recalled where I knew him from, approached and introduced myself.

We were still chatting when his wife joined us.

"Rebecca," he said, "you remember Daniel, don't you? One of M's old friends."

The woman's silver hair was drawn up in a severe bun, but her smooth features were warm and inquisitive. "Why yes, from M's New Year's Eve party. You took our coats and served us Marwa's special meatballs."

"Yes, I did." The truth was, I was shocked she remembered me. There had been a lot of people at that party and it'd been over three years ago.

"You were one of M's lovers at the time."

"Um, I was his boyfriend."

"Yes, of course you were. You meant an awful lot to him."

David appeared at my side and handed me a pint.

"Hi," he said. "I'm David."

The woman's gaze lingered over us. "So very pleased to meet you, David. Now, you two young men look dashing together."

David raised his glass. "Why, thank you, ma'am."

"Please, call me Becky."

"Becky and Frederic are friends with Marcus," I explained.

"Frederic," Becky said, "was one of Marcus's lovers, a long time ago."

David coughed, spilling his beer. I handed him a crumpled napkin. "Frederic was Marcus's semiotics professor."

"I suppose," Becky said, "I risk sounding salacious. This younger generation remains puritanical in so many ways. Frederic and I have kept many lovers over the years."

"And shared a few," Frederic said.

"So very true, dear."

"Rock on," David said.

Frederic smiled. "Rock on."

"Tell us," Becky said, "what did you think of M's performance tonight?"

All eyes turned to me. David poked me in the side. "What did you call it earlier?"

"I said it was very Marcus."

"Well that about sums it up, doesn't it?" Frederic said. Then he and his wife both laughed as if I'd told the funniest joke in the whole wide world. I fixed a smile to my face and bowed my head.

"This was our first burlesque," David said. "We really enjoyed it."

Becky tilted her glass flute toward him. "And what part did you enjoy the most?"

David opened and closed his mouth. I mentally prayed as hard as I could he wouldn't mention Lobster Girl drizzling her tits with melted butter. Another second passed and I was just about to intervene when David replied: "The characters, the story-telling, the parody. Take that act with the opera diva and the maestro. It was clearly a commentary on the intersection of racism and patriarchy." I stared at my pot-smoking, bike mechanic boyfriend but he wasn't done yet. "Does a woman's body have value only before a man's gaze? Or can she step outside the script that's been assigned her? Can she have her own voice? When she hit that high note and blew off that guy's pants, that was freakin' brilliant. Society codifies and commodifies sexuality and beauty. But tonight was a celebration of the human form in all its shapes, colours and sizes."

Rebecca's gaze narrowed. "Some would say it's still exploitation. It's still women being paid to remove their clothes."

"But for whom? How many straight men do you think were in the audience tonight? Very few, I'd say. If these dancers are doing burlesque to feel joyful and subversive and defiant, and if it's in front of an appreciative and supportive audience, then that's real empowerment. The truth of it is, burlesque isn't inherently feminist or anti-feminist any more than any other art form. But like any art form, it can be used for good or for evil."

"For good or for evil?" Becky said. "How terribly romantic."

David emptied his pint in one slow, unhurried quaff. As I watched his Adam's apple bob up and down, framed by the rough, unshaven curve of his jaw and the musculature of his throat and neck, I realized with the inexorable and elemental force of a glacier calving that, after two years, I was just beginning to know this man standing next to me with no underwear on and his balls hanging out, that I'd just scratched the surface of everything he was, and everything he was capable of. Reaching between Frederic and Becky, he set his empty pint glass on the bar, shrugged and knuckled away the moisture on his upper lip.

"I'm Italian," he said.

At the far end of the room, a small circle of friends sang in perfect, three-part harmony "Happy Birthday" while sparklers illuminated all their faces in an ephemeral, golden light.

"Viva l'Italia," Frederic said.

Becky leaned forward and kissed David on both

cheeks, right to left. In that moment, it seemed the most natural, warm gesture possible. The top buttons of David's dress shirt were undone, exposing a glinting crucifix. Frederic's hand rested on the back of my neck. I couldn't recall when he'd actually placed it there, but it also seemed more than okay.

"It is getting late, dear," Becky said. "Will you fetch us our coats?"

"Of course," Frederic said. Then, as a kind of afterthought, he squeezed my shoulder and glanced sidelong at David and me. "Why don't you two join us a for a nightcap?"

"We don't live too far from here," Becky said, adjusting her shawl. "A ten-minute cab ride. I'm afraid our glorious M has abandoned us all tonight."

I was just about to politely decline when Marwa approached with a tiny, red-ribboned jewellery box, just large enough for cufflinks or earrings. "Here you go." She handed it to Becky. "Everything's in there."

"Thank you, Marwa. You're a sweetheart. You'll put this on our tab?"

"Daniel." Marwa looked from one of us to the other with a furrowed pixie smile. "Do you know Freddy and Becky?"

"Yeah, we're old friends," David said.

"Any friends of M are friends of ours," Becky said. "We were all just about to come back to our place for a drink. Marwa, your little wingèd helpers will join us tonight, won't they?"

"My cousin's just finishing packing the van. Sure, I can ask them, if that's okay."

"I insist. Marwa, you did a splendid job this evening. Congratulations. If you young people are hungry, perhaps we can call ahead and have something delivered?"

"I'm hungry." David nudged me in the arm. "What about you?"

"Perhaps something from Terroni?" Becky said.

"Oh. Fuck me sideways." Marwa's big eyes grew bigger. She clasped her hands beneath her chin. "We have to order their C't Mang."

I looked at Marwa. "What's *see-tay-mon-jay*?"

"Just the pizza version of crack cocaine. It's mozzarella and gorgonzola, with smoked prosciutto and sliced pear and walnuts, all drizzled in honey." Her eyes rolled back in her head like she was having an orgasm. "I know the combination sounds crazy, but trust me, it's absolutely to die for."

"Then it's settled." Becky unsnapped the razor-mouth of her taloned purse. "A nightcap and a midnight snack. Marwa, remember to order extra this time, so people can have something to take home with them."

Marwa already had her phone out. "Roger that." She took the credit card Becky handed her and retreated to a quiet corner.

"Frederic, sweetheart. The coats, please."

"Yes, of course, dear."

After that, there was no off-ramp in sight. If life was a highway, we were careening along at breakneck speed. Before I even realized it, we were getting into a cab with Frederic and Becky; Marwa and her two assistants would meet up with us in their own van. I clutched my coat in my lap. The truth was, I had a semi-hard-on, and I was scared to even begin to think why.

Becky had somehow ended up sitting in the back between David and me. As we skated north-by-west through residential side streets, David expounded on Venus figurines and Renaissance art while Becky listened attentively with one hand resting on top of my knee.

After ten minutes I asked, trying not to sound too pathetic: "So, are we almost there yet?"

"Not far," Frederic said.

"Almost there," Becky said. Then she squeezed my knee and winked at me.

I entertained a vision of the two of them snapping the cabbie's neck before turning to plunge their fangs into our jugulars, or maybe once we were alone they'd calmly reach behind their heads and peel off their faces revealing themselves as grey-skinned, double-jointed, prostate-probing aliens. No wonder they liked prosciutto on their pizza; hadn't I read somewhere that human flesh tasted just like pork?

Finally, after what seemed like hours driving through the night (but which in reality was probably less than fifteen minutes), we arrived at our destination. Their vine-covered, Tudor-styled home in The Junction looked deceptively modest and just a little bit sinister, set back from the road. As we stepped out of our cab, Marwa's van pulled into the drive. Once inside, Frederic gave us a tour of his newly-renovated, glass-walled, climate-controlled cellar, reconstructed entirely from reclaimed lumber and Ottawa Valley river rock. Back upstairs, we settled on plush cream-coloured couches in front of an enormous gas fireplace. Marwa strolled comfortably in her bare feet and cheongsam between the living room and the kitchen, replenishing our glasses and helping Frederic in the pantry.

Marwa's cousin was a nervous teenager named Youssef who relaxed after his first beer and passed out after his second. Then I wondered what might be in the gazillion-year-old Scotch Frederic was serving the rest of us (although that didn't stop me from drinking it). Marwa's other assistant was a loud, talkative redhead named Brody who apparently owned a proper, authentic kilt, and whose family boasted its own clan tartan. I started eying a soapstone beaver on the mantel, thinking I could use it to club him unconscious, but thankfully the conversation moved on to other topics. As promised, when it arrived, Terroni's C't Mang was truly fabulously delicious. While Youssef snored, curled up like a puppy in his love seat, we stuffed ourselves with gourmet pizza, washing it all down with heady bottles of Pinot Noir and Chardonnay.

A little after 2 a.m., the six of us gathered around Youssef and woke him gently. We said our goodbyes and Frederic and Becky hugged each of us in turn. Before we left, they made us promise we'd come back to a proper dinner party which they'd host in the spring. Then Marwa, who hadn't been drinking, drove us all home, dropping off David and me last.

As we stood outside our building in our kilts and blowing snow, Marwa called me over to the driver's window. "I almost forgot." She presented me a small box sealed with a Cherry Bomb Bakery label. "Something special, just for you."

Inside our loft, David and I flung off our coats. I accidentally tore his shirt wrestling it over his head, but neither of us cared. David's back was against the front door and I had him in my mouth when he came. I swallowed all of it, deep-throating him, one sweaty hand splayed over his crucifix, while jacking off furiously on my bruised knees. After that, I felt a whole lot better. I felt so much better I was laughing from relief. Then we cracked open some beers and ate the leftover pizza Becky had insisted on sending home with us, standing around the kitchen table wearing nothing but our combat boots. Inside Marwa's box, we discovered a single fancy cupcake decorated with the letters "D&D" in pink icing.

So, we were alive and we hadn't been eaten by aliens or roofied (and sold into the white sex slave trade) after all. I was embarrassed and immensely gratified, and I was also feeling full and drunk, and grateful, and exhausted in the best way possible, which was a good thing because I was looking forward to spooning David naked and passing out, and then waking up in our own familiar bed and under our own warm blankets, in the cool and hazy, dawn-bright February morning.

CHAPTER THREE

Magic Carpet Ride

On a Sunday early in April, David and I took the 506 streetcar east across Toronto's Don Valley to The Rock Oasis climbing gym where David's friend Arthur worked part-time. During the trip the morning drizzle turned into a steady downpour and, although the stop was only two minutes from the venue, by the time we arrived we were both soaked through. (I also realized we were up the block from where Marcus lived, but neither David nor I commented on that fact.) The space was suitably cavernous, with vertical and canted walls covered with thousands of holds. David Usher was playing on the sound system, and framed prints of ecstatic climbers haloed in lens flares decorated the snack bar.

Arthur was a friendly, lanky guy who could've been Vince Carter's kid brother. He met us at the registration desk, gave us towels and waivers to sign. By the time we'd dried off and changed, he was already speaking in front of a small group of beginners, three other couples in addition to ourselves.

Obediently, we lined up in front of a training wall

where Arthur talked us through harnessing-up and tying ourselves in. I had on my regular mesh workout shorts, but when I tightened my straps I was shocked at how noticeable my junk was. It wasn't so bad for David who was wearing black.

"Gee willikers," he said.

"Don't," I said.

He started to giggle. I gave him the finger. I pushed my leg straps down on my thighs and did my best to keep my back to the others.

It came time to practice belaying and I went up the wall first. It was an easy enough climb to the top. When I let go and swung free, I was acutely conscious of the taut, creaking rope bearing my full weight, and of my harness riding up higher than ever. As David lowered me down, I slowly revolved, my bulging crotch on display to the world like an overstuffed piñata.

Then it was my turn to belay and the first thing I noticed was how the equipment gripped David's ass. I didn't recall ever seeing him from this particular angle before, and never strapped in like this. If women had Victoria's Secret push-up bras, then gay guys had climbing gear. What with all the ropes and harnesses and grunting and straining, I was discovering rock-climbing was one step sideways from a Folsom Fair smackdown.

David's legs were his best asset, so I shouldn't have been surprised when, gawking up at him open-mouthed, I felt a swelling tension inside my shorts. I was mortified. Both my hands were full, and there was no way I could adjust myself. When Arthur called out to me to take in the slack, others turned to look. One girl glanced down in my direction and just plain stared. I wanted to say: "Excuse me, my eyes are up here."

The group lesson went on for another ten minutes. After that, thankfully, we were on our own and each couple wandered off to explore the gym. At that moment a noisy birthday party of prepubescent girls arrived with their parents in tow, and Arthur hurried back to the front desk.

"So," David said, "what do you think?"

"I think," I said, "let's do this."

Our passes were good for the day and we took our time trying out the beginner routes before moving on to more challenging ones. David was more agile than me, but I had the longer reach. After a couple hours, our forearms aching, we took a break. That was when we spotted a guy climbing on his own (what Arthur later told us was solo top-roping). He was thin with a scruffy beard, wearing a bandana and denim shorts. He was also shirtless and sporting a farmer's tan, which (according to David) no respectable gay guy would ever do. He was taking his time, hanging one-armed off a steep overhang, dipping into his chalk bag, and checking out his course, the muscles of his body standing out like an anatomy textbook diagram. As we watched, he launched himself through the air, caught onto another hold with both hands and dangled for a second before wedging in one knee and digging in his other toe.

"That's impressive," David said.

I reluctantly agreed.

"He knows people are watching him." David sipped from his Gatorade.

I looked around but there was no one else in the area. By "people" he meant us, but that didn't stop David from

keenly observing. At the far end of the gym in the boulder-
ing area, the birthday girls were shrieking and laughing.
We finished our Clif Bars and I went to the washroom (an
unexpected ordeal in my harness), and by the time I got
back, Shirtless Guy was on the ground chatting with
David. He nodded in my direction, stretching his shoulders, one elbow in the air with his hands locked behind
his back.

"Hey."

"Hey," I replied, trying not to stare into his bushy pit.

"Daniel, this is Joshua," David said. "He's from Mel-
bourne. I was just asking him for some pointers."

"Right."

"Look," Joshua said, shaking out his shoulders, "why
don't you go up this wall here and I'll watch what you're
doing. That's the best way to learn." His hands were taped,
and he had scabs on his knuckles and chalk on his nose.
His torso was also gleaming with sweat. He pointed at
David's Gatorade. "You mind?"

"Sure." David handed it over, Joshua took a thirsty
swig and passed it to me.

"Daniel," David said, "you'll belay?"

"Okay." I pushed my leg straps down on my thighs,
and clipped myself in.

"So, you always want to do a partner check," Joshua
said, tugging hard on David's belay loop and then on
mine. "Check the knot, check the harness. All tied in?
Then she'll be right. Before you go up, previz your route,
know where your hands and feet are going. Keep your
centre of gravity balanced, good job. Keep your body close
to the wall. You got it. You're a natural. Relax your grip.

You always want to hold yourself in place with the least amount of force. Push up with your legs, arms are for balance. Too many blokes try to muscle their way up, pulling with their upper body but that's bad form that'll just wear you out."

By this point, David was already about three metres off the ground.

"Belaying," Joshua said, leaning into me, "is the most important, sacred job we have as climbers. You've got your mate's life in your hands. Give him just a little more slack, that's right. You wanna give a good belay, stay focused, anticipate his next move. Don't be afraid of getting closer to the wall. You got, what, ten, twelve kilos on your mate? That works in your favour. But if you're lighter and he takes a fall, you don't want to get pulled into the rock. Keep your knees bent. 'David, you got it!' Make sure his leg doesn't get behind the rope." His mouth turned to my ear. "Behind every great climber is a great belayer." He clapped me on the shoulder. "Real nice job." He folded his arms. "That's a ripper. You're both doing great!"

I was trying my best to listen to what Joshua was saying. I could feel the heat radiating from his body and smell his crisp B.O. I half-expected a halo of lens flares to appear around his beatific, upturned face. I wondered how his beard would feel if I turned and kissed him. I also wanted to tell him I was only nine-point-five kilos heavier than David.

"Actually," I said, "I'm only nine-point-five kilos heavier than he is."

He gave me a sidelong glance and flashed a crooked smile. "Funny guy. Eyes up."

Back home that evening, we agreed the experience had definitely been worth the trip.

"Yeah, I think you and I could really get into this," David said, scrubbing a casserole dish. "Arthur said if we wanted to buy our own gear, he could get us a discount. I think we should at least get our own shoes. And he said if we ever wanted to try outdoor climbing, he could take us."

I was only half-listening, leaning against our kitchen counter, admiring the way David's jeans hugged his butt.

"Did you know," I said, "behind every great climber there's a great belayer?"

David set the casserole dish into the rack and dried his hands. "Is that right?"

"Oh definitely. Although, a good belayer these days is hard to come by."

"I see. Well." David turned to face me. He flipped his dish towel over his shoulder. "Let's do a partner check then." He wrapped his fists around my belt buckle. "Are we all tied in?"

"I'm just doing a previz," I said, "on where my hands are going to go."

"The trick is to keep your grip relaxed and your body close."

"I'll keep that in mind. So, you ready to do some top-roping?"

"Maybe I am."

"How about some jugging?"

"How about some boinking?"

"Sure, but only after a nice soft catch."

"What if I want a nice hard catch?"

"Well, then I'll give you something harder."

"Bring it."

"I will."

And we did.

﹏ Early that spring, Karen and I were surprised to receive wedding invitations from our old friends, Melissa and Mike. We'd met them during our first year in Toronto, after moving into a house in Palmerston-Little Italy. After a Canadian Tire shopping spree, Karen and I had just finished hauling everything up the narrow stairwell, including a gigantic potted palm. A few minutes later, a tall blonde in cut-off jeans and abalone-rimmed glasses knocked on our open door.

"It's the welcome wagon, woohoo," she said, handing off a basket. "Bienvenue, neighbours! Now, you'll want to pair that Havarti with this Pinot Blanc, it's from our favourite vineyard out by Niagara-on-the-Lake. Maybe smoke up a bit first. Here, I rolled a joint for you both, I hope that's okay. Michael and I don't really partake, hardly at all anymore. If you do smoke, just please keep the windows open. Mind you, that *Dypsis lutescens* of yours will help clean the air. Now, my therapist recommended this organic fertilizer to me. I swear, she keeps ten dozen plants in her office, it's a veritable boreal forest in there, you can practically spot David Suzuki lurking behind the couch. Those are gluten-free peanut butter chocolate swirl, by the way. You're not allergic, are you? I can just imagine Michael coming home and me telling him: 'Michael, honey, you know that student couple who moved in downstairs? Well they just dropped dead from anaphylactic shock because I fed them the cookies you baked this morning.' Oh, my name's Melissa by the way. Michael and I, we're your neighbours upstairs."

Two years later, Mellissa and Mike moved to North York and had a second baby. After that, Mike quit his job to become a stay-at-home dad. Their wedding would take place downtown, at an event space called The Burroughes. When I asked Melissa via Facebook why they'd decided to get married at this point in their lives, she said: "Well, Benjamin's old enough now to be our ring bearer. Michael's always wanted to get married. Me, I'll have just finished breastfeeding Klara (thank god!), and frankly it's a great excuse to get drunk." After I congratulated Mike, he promptly replied with a cheerful thumbs-up emoji.

When I told Karen she and Liam were welcome to stay at our place, she told me she wasn't going to be coming with Liam, but she had another date.

"Daniel, I told you, Liam and I aren't together anymore. We're really close, but that's it. We're both okay with it. And even if we were still together, I doubt I'd be able to convince him to come all the way to Toronto for some hipster wedding."

"Melissa and Mike aren't hipsters."

"Sure they are."

"Hipsters don't live in the suburbs."

"In Toronto, Daniel, they don't live north of Bloor Street, but there are always exceptions."

"Really?"

"Didn't Melissa just get promoted at the CBC?"

"Yeah."

"And is Mike still rockin' that beard of his?" I had to agree that was the case. "Weren't they the ones who introduced us to the Brickworks and to that organic co-op?"

"Sure."

"And," Karen said, "they vote NDP."

"Yeah."

"I rest my case."

It was our monthly Sunday-evening-ice-cream-Skype-date, and we'd decided on President's Choice Red Velvet Cake. Karen had to drive all the way into Sudbury from Manitoulin Island to acquire hers at the Superstore, but the trip had been worth it. After the first three spoonfuls, we both agreed there could be more cake chunks, but we weren't complaining.

"I didn't mean hipster in a bad way," Karen said, poking at the inside of her tub, "I admire them a lot. In fact, I'm really flattered they even thought of inviting us. I mean, how long has it been? All I'm saying is that this wedding is going to be exactly the kind of thing that Liam hates. You should know that."

I did know that. Liam's idea of a good time was ultra-light backpacking in the deep bush and spit-roasting bull-frogs. As far as he was concerned, *Survivorman*'s Les Stroud was the greatest Canadian who ever lived.

"So who," I asked, "are you bringing?"

"Someone I've been seeing for a few months. His name's Bob."

"A few months? Why haven't you mentioned him?"

"I'm mentioning him now."

"Bob."

"Don't make fun of him."

I rearranged the pillows on my couch and lay back. "I'm not making fun of him."

"Yes, you are."

"Karen, how can I be making fun of him? I don't even know the guy."

"That's exactly right."

"Right."

"But you don't approve."

Passing by with his ironing board, David leaned over my shoulder and waved. "Hey Karen."

"Hey David."

He helped himself to a spoonful of Red Velvet. "Daniel, you need any shirts ironed?"

"No thanks."

"Mmm, not bad. So what's the score on this one?"

"Three-point-five," we replied in unison.

David kissed my laptop's camera and walked away. I pulled out a napkin and wiped the ice cream from the screen.

"C'mon, Karen," I said. "You've always had a good head on your shoulders. If you see something in this guy, well, then, then that's something. You're my best friend. I'm really happy for you, okay? I'm looking forward to meeting him. Bob."

Secretly, of course, I was already harbouring a deep-seated resentment toward Bob, if not outright antipathy. I'd always hoped Karen and Liam would get back together. I'd lost track of the number of times they'd broken up over the years. Karen was in love with Liam, probably ever since high school. But Liam wasn't easy to get along with at the best of times. Antidepressants had helped somewhat but they didn't change his basic nature. It was unfair to expect Karen to put up with him just so I could call her my sister-in-law.

"You think Liam and I should get back together again, don't you?" Karen said.

"I never said that."

"He's been doing a lot better lately."

"I agree."

"Bob's nice."

"I'm sure he is."

"He's stable." Karen's face loomed on my computer screen. "Did I mention he's stable?"

"So, what does he do?"

Karen sat back cross-legged in her swivel chair. "He runs a tackle shop in Little Current. And sometimes charters out fishing tours."

"That doesn't sound so bad," I said, licking my spoon.

"He's thirty-seven, separated, and has two kids."

I blinked. "Okay."

"He's missing one eye, and half of two fingers on his right hand."

"Really?"

"Ice fishing accident, when he was twelve."

"Okay."

"He's really looking forward to coming to Toronto. He says he hasn't visited since he was in high school."

"Okay."

"He just needs to find a babysitter."

"Okay."

"Okay? Daniel, is that all you can say?"

I shrugged, at a loss for words. "Look, okay."

Karen sighed, and scraped the bottom of her ice cream tub. "I just really hope," she said, "it's an open bar at this wedding."

⌒ The Burroughes turned out to be a century-old refurbished furniture warehouse: stripped hardwood floors, exposed venting, brick and concrete, spacious enough for the hundred or so guests. The building even boasted its own old-fashioned freight elevator with a wooden grate sliding door. Karen wore the pearl-drop necklace with matching earrings I'd gotten for her graduation three years ago. Bob turned out to be a big guy, bigger even than Liam, built like an enforcer, sun-weathered and scarred, with a patch over one eye. He wore a classic, perfectly-tailored, vintage suit. When I shook his deformed, callused hand, it was all I could do not to call him "sir." The conversation moved to family and he pulled out pictures of his daughters, seven and nine, photographs he kept in a thick, grease-stained wallet. (The older girl was all decked out in hockey gear.) After that, I could see what Karen saw in him.

"So," Karen said just before the ceremony, following me into the men's washroom and locking the door behind us, "what do you think?"

"He seems like a nice guy."

"He is, Daniel. He's a little nervous being here."

"Him, nervous? Seriously."

"This is the first time he's ever been away from his kids overnight."

"Oh, right. Where are they now?"

"With one of his neighbours. Be nice to him, okay? He's a little rough around the edges, but he really is the sweetest guy."

"Rough around the edges? He looks like he just stepped out of a GQ fashion shoot."

"He does look good, doesn't he? Would you believe that's his grandfather's suit? We found it in his attic. I got it dry-cleaned and retailored for him."

"That eye-patch thingy of his is pretty cool. Very *Pirates of the Caribbean*."

"Daniel." Karen poked me in the chest. "You promised."

"I did."

"You wouldn't joke if you knew what happened."

"You said ice fishing."

"That was his fingers."

"Right. So, how'd he lose his eye?"

"I'll let him tell you that story."

"Well, he seems like a gentleman."

Karen, who almost never wore make-up, carefully folded a tissue and dabbed at her mascara.

"He is a gentleman, and he's an amazing dad. You should see him with those two girls. They're really amazing kids. He also makes me laugh like nobody can. Daniel, I know it's only been a few months but, I dunno. It's crazy, but I think I really like him."

"You really like him?"

"Yeah, I do."

"Okay. Okay, Karen Fobister, let's make this happen. You alright?"

"How do I look?"

"You look beautiful. You look perfect. C'mon, c'mere." I gave her a hug. "You've got this. Look, this guy came here all the way down from Manitoulin just for you. He didn't have to come, right? But he's here now, with you. And he really likes you."

"You think?"

"Yeah, it's pretty obvious. And, he's a Habs fan. That's gotta count for something."

Someone rapped loudly on the door. It was David warning us the guests were already seated. We hurried back and had barely taken our places when the processional music was cued.

Because we were in the last row, we were the first to witness the wedding party enter in pairs and trios, grooving and boogying to what I later learned was a popular Raffi tune. After the initial shock, the guests cheered and laughed. Cameras flashed, and people started clapping along. Melissa appeared last, clutching her wedding dress, dancing down the aisle hand-in-hand with her four-year-old son Benjamin who was sporting a miniature tuxedo and fauxhawk. Up at the front, Mike stood beaming, surrounded by family, looking like the happiest man alive.

The ceremony itself was brief, almost perfunctory. The officiant was a pepper-haired woman with a zesty Jamaican accent who quoted Kahlil Gibran and Dr. Seuss in a stentorian voice full of humour. Benjamin offered up the rings while his baby sister watched, wide-eyed and drooling, from the front row. The wedding couple kissed and hugged and the whole business was over.

Later that night, after the reception and speeches, David and I found ourselves on the rooftop admiring the view of the city. Parker Kapoor always professed May as his favourite month, and tonight I felt why, filling my lungs with the moist spring air. Toronto was a lake fed by countless waterways, cataracts and springs, with convoluted banks, rapids and shadowy pools. Constellations of light shifted and spiralled, near and afar, buoyed by the rumble of streetcars, the sounds of conversations and laughter, the thumping bass of the live band below. Someone stepped up between us, one hand in his pocket, a Pabst Blue Ribbon in the other.

"Hey, Mike," I said. "How're you doing?"

Mike regarded us calmly, clear-eyed. He was a short, matter-of-fact kind of guy, the kind who partnered well in science lab, or was a good sport at the end of an evening's poker game; the kind of guy who'd actually stop and have an intelligent conversation with those people carrying clipboards on street corners.

"Good," he said. "Really good."

"This is my boyfriend David."

"Hey, thanks for coming."

"Thanks for the invite," David said. "This is one awesome wedding. That speech your father-in-law gave was hilarious. It was like a whole stand-up routine."

"Yeah, he's great."

"Congratulations, by the way."

"Thank you."

"You shaved off your beard," I said.

"Yeah." Mike looked mildly surprised. "I suppose I did."

"You look good."

"Thanks. Melissa loves it. I hadn't planned it. I was just trimming it this morning, then one thing led to another.

I guess I wanted my kids to see my face, y'know? It actually took a minute before Benjamin recognized me."

"Yeah, I saw that video Melissa posted. It was super cute."

"You and Karen were living downstairs when we got pregnant the first time. You helped me carry Benjamin's crib upstairs."

"That's right! It was the same weekend we hosted that dinner party, the six of us with Charles and Megan."

"That was the night they met, right?"

"Yeah."

Mike squinted at me. "And now they're engaged?"

"That's right."

"Wow, good for them. A lot of good memories in that old house."

"You ever miss living downtown?"

"Sometimes."

"You two," I said, "were at that address a while."

"Seven years, including our first year with Benjamin."

"So how is family life?"

"You mean, what's it like raising two kids out in the burbs?" Mike folded his arms. "Truth?" A cool breeze rustled the huge bouquets of chrysanthemums set about the terrace. "I love it. I really, absolutely love it. It's like it's something I was always meant to do, y'know? I baked banana bread with Benjamin the other day. I'm teaching him yoga. He helps me change Klara's diapers. The three of us go biking together. I just started this blog for stay-at-home daddies. I've got almost a hundred readers already. My in-laws live ten minutes away. Melissa loves her work and she's making really good money. It's great."

"Well, here's to fatherhood," David said.

"Here's to family," I said.

"Cheers," Mike said. He emptied his beer and studied the label. "I don't know why I ever started drinking this stuff. I think we just wanted to be hipster, y'know." He laughed. "Well. I better go back in. My mom-in-law wants a dance. Thanks again for coming."

As Mike departed, a small crowd spilled onto the rooftop, four couples along with a half-dozen children. One last final look at the Toronto skyline before bedtime, that was the deal. Mike high-fived one of the dads who had a toddler passed out over one shoulder.

David and I drifted to the other side of the terrace. "Lot of kids here tonight," he said.

"Yeah."

"Daniel, have you thought about having kids?"

"Me? I'm still in school, I can't think about that. I mean, I dunno. Mike makes it look easy. But it's not easy. It's a helluva job."

David retrieved a plastic squirrel from his pocket. "This was fun. Show me yours again?"

I showed him mine, a little raccoon with my name handwritten on its side with a Sharpie. Toy animals had been used as place markers at all the tables. "You think Benjamin had anything to do with planning this wedding?"

"Ya gotta wonder."

"There you guys are," Karen called out, crossing the rooftop. Bob's bowtie and the top two buttons of his shirt were undone, and Karen was barefoot with her shoes in one hand. "I think we're going to head back to the hotel. We're pretty tired and we've got an early start."

Karen didn't look tired, but she did look pretty cozy with Bob, one arm wrapped around his waist.

"You two driving back home tomorrow?" David asked.

"Yeah, we have to pick up the girls."

Bob nodded toward the CN Tower. "I remember when they built that back in '76."

"My ma's second husband worked on the construction three years," David said.

"Her second husband?"

"Michele Moretti. Died of a heart attack last week on the job."

"Oh, I'm sorry to hear that," Bob said. "Was that your dad?"

"What? Oh no, my pa was this hotshot researcher in the classics department, Tony Gallucci. Story goes, he attended one of Ma's workshops and fell in love during her lecture on Caravaggio and Artemisia. Of course, she thought he was way too young, but he wouldn't let up. Finally, she agreed to go out with him. She always told me I was the most beautiful accident that ever happened to her. After that, well, she got hitched a third time."

Long ago, David had told me his dad had died from an aneurysm. But I'd never heard this story before. "She said you were an accident?"

"Life's full of accidents, Daniel." David set his raccoon on the edge of the railing, gazing down at the bustling street below. "Making great art is staying open to them. Ma always says: Life is art."

"What does she do?" Bob asked.

"She's an art historian and critic. She's curated a few shows. These days, she mainly writes for the *Globe & Mail*."

"Wait a second," Bob said, "your mom's not Isabella De Luca, is she?"

David blinked. "Yeah, that's her."

"My daughters have all of her children's books. They love them. Their favourite is *A Pretty Girl's Encyclopedia of Pretty Awesome Women Artists*."

"Oh yeah, that one. It's funny, she writes all these serious books and essays, but it's her kids' books that everyone knows about."

"David," Bob said, "your mom's been awarded the Order of Canada. She's really famous."

I didn't know what the Order of Canada was but it sure as hell sounded impressive. "You never told me this," I said.

David shrugged. "Yeah, well. Isabella De Luca's been around a while."

"I always called her Mrs. Gallucci."

"That's okay. She just writes under her maiden name, De Luca. My sister's named after her side of the family. I mean, my brother."

"How many siblings do you have?" Bob asked.

David pulled out a cigarette pack. "Just one, actually, my brother."

Karen squeezed Bob's elbow. "I'll explain later." She hugged David and me. "It was good seeing you both. You should come up to the Island sometime. We'd love to tour you around. We could go horseback riding. I could show you boys how to milk a cow."

David and I looked at each other and silently agreed: *Not-in-front-of-Bob.* "Sounds fun."

Bob shook our hands. "Well, Karen's been talking about you both for a long time. I'm really glad to have finally met."

David poked me in the side. "Wait until you meet his brothers."

"Oh, Liam and I have met," Bob said. "He's a good guy."

"He's a great guy," David said.

"He is," Bob said.

David folded his arms. "One-of-a-kind."

"Liam is a good guy," Karen said. "We all love Liam." She hooked Bob's arm in her own. "But this is my guy. Come on, daddy-o, you hungry? I know the best poutine place right across the street. Have a safe night, boys. Be good."

David waved and called after them: "We always are!" He glanced at me. "Hey, you hungry for poutine?"

"Did it look like she was inviting us for poutine?"

"Right."

I stifled a yawn. "Well, Karen seems happy."

"What's with the Nick Fury eye patch?"

"I never got a chance to ask."

"If there ever was a zombie apocalypse," David said, "Bob's on my team."

"What about me?"

"You can be on my team too. We'll need a doctor."

"Oh, gee, thanks."

David tucked a cigarette behind his ear. "Here, give me that." He snatched up his squirrel and took my raccoon. "Follow me."

"Where are we going?"

"You'll see."

David led me down three flights in the stairwell and stopped mid-way between floors. "Right here."

"Right here where?"

"Right here, Daniel. Look at this." He pointed at the bannister.

"What?"

"Look."

The dark brown paint was chipping away, exposing purple underneath. "I don't get it."

"Daniel, this used to be the stairwell for the Big Bop next door, before it closed. It was your birthday, we saw Alixisonfire at the Kathedral main-stage. This spot, right here, this is where you and I first kissed."

"Oh my god, you're right. That was three years ago."

"Yeah it was. Then I took you home and we had crazy sex. We broke my futon."

"Shit."

"You just figured it was a one-night stand."

"I'm afraid I did."

David winked at me. "Little did you know."

"Did you think otherwise?"

David bit his lower lip and cocked his head to one side. "Yeah, I did. The moment I kissed you, I knew."

I couldn't tell if he was joking. I hadn't known. It was David who texted me three days later to ask me out on a "real date." The truth was I didn't think I'd ever see him again.

David weighed the plastic animals, one on each palm. "I think," he said, "Benjamin got these backwards. I think you're the squirrel and I'm the raccoon."

"Why do you say that?"

"You're more organized, you plan for the future. You're not the kind of guy to go rummaging in garbage cans."

"Oh and you are?" I laughed.

"Here." David set the raccoon and squirrel on the bannister post and took out his phone. "Selfie time, mister." I knelt beside him and he wrapped an arm around my shoulder. "Here's to Art." He pressed his scruffy cheek against my own. Someone opened a door and a wash of live music flooded the stairwell, a swirling, booze-soaked cover of Steppenwolf's "Magic Carpet Ride." After that we went and danced with the newlyweds Mike and Melissa and all their hipster friends, until our ties were undone and our hair was messy, well on into the deep-lake night, long after all the babies and the kids had gone home and been put to sleep.

CHAPTER FOUR

Lovers in a Dangerous Time

For close to a year-and-a-half, I'd been meeting my friend Nadia for coffee and cake. Our paths had crossed at the U of T bookstore where she worked part-time. On that occasion, she had to remind me the actual first time we'd met was at Sneaky Dee's, at which point I was on a drunken rebound from my break-up with Marcus. Nadia called that initial meeting "inelegant" and we both agreed it wouldn't count toward the history of our relationship.

Our first proper date took place on a Sunday in the Library Bar of the Royal York Hotel where Afternoon Tea had been traditionally served since 1929. The fine china, artisanal sandwiches and pastries were a far cry from Sneaky Dee's cheese and chili-smothered nacho plates. When I took her to Future's Bakery in the Annex, she observed how the chaotic traffic of bohemian scholars and artists reminded her of the market of Marrakesh. Had she actually been to Morocco? Yes, in fact, she had, with her father as a young girl.

Then she folded her hands on the stained tabletop,

leaned forward and quoted an entire song by Loreena McKennitt. For our third date, she took us to the sacred source itself: Dufflet Pastries on Queen Street West, founded in 1975 by Dufflet Rosenberg the "Queen of Cake," where we enjoyed a cup of her famous Extra Brut Hot Chocolate. It was an unspoken agreement that we'd not visit any place twice. Every few months, one of us would text the other with a lead for a cake-tasting experience, and a date would be arranged. On each of these occasions, we went Dutch, and upon conclusion, we'd always offer each other a simple handshake in parting. Once I told Nadia if I were straight and my mother was Isabella De Luca, she was the girl I'd bring home to her. She thought that was a lovely compliment.

I never spoke of Nadia to Karen.

Today Nadia and I were to meet at the Flying Elephant Bakery in Toronto's east end. It took close to an hour to reach by bike, but it was well worth the journey. It was a bright day in June and I'd taken the Martin Goodman Trail along Lake Ontario's waterfront, past the boardwalk by the Beaches where people played volleyball, pushed strollers, and sunbathed. The bakery itself was a cheery, family-run business, with the walls painted red-and-white like the inside of a big-top tent. The Venezuelan owner had infused many of the baked goods with a Latin American flair. The bathrooms were labelled "donikers" which I learned was circus slang for "toilets."

"So, your boyfriend David is going away for the summer," Nadia said, "and he's wondering if it'd be okay if his brother shared your loft with you?"

"That's the gist of it," I replied. "His mom has been planning this trip for a while."

We both reclined on a couch scattered with colourful pillows. Nadia appeared relaxed and poised in a cool teal dress and Grecian sandals. Her pale blue eyeliner accented the beauty mark on her cheek. "How long are they going away for?"

"Two months. They've got relatives all over Italy and his grandparents are really old. This is probably the last time he'll get to see them."

"His nonna and nonno."

"Luke remembers them a lot better than David does."

"But Luke's not going."

"Well, Mrs. Gallucci really wants the three of them to go together, except she and Luke aren't on speaking terms."

"Oh?"

"They haven't been for twelve years."

Nadia took off her glasses. "That," she observed, "is a very long time."

"Yeah, I know. But last fall, she asked David to pass on the invitation."

"She's holding out the olive branch."

I plucked cake crumbs off the coffee table and carefully rearranged our empty plates and silverware. Sunlight glowed on the hardwood floor. "This trip is really important to Mrs. Gallucci. She's ready to pay for everyone's tickets."

"Except she doesn't know her daughter Luciana is Luke now."

"No, she doesn't."

Nadia sipped from her espresso, saucer in hand. "And does she know David is gay?"

"No. And she doesn't know I'm his boyfriend."

"You've met his mother?"

"Yeah, a few times. She just thinks I'm David's roommate and best buddy, his *gumba*. She's kind of an intimidating woman. She's not someone I'd ever want to argue with."

"She doesn't suspect anything?"

"I don't think so."

"You two have been together a while."

"We just celebrated our three-year anniversary."

"Already? Congratulations. Did you do something special?"

"We went rock-climbing. There's an indoor gym we really like. David says I should bring Luke this summer."

Nadia studied the vintage images of carnival performers decorating the walls. A large chalkboard behind the counter listed dozens of customized cake ingredients: chocolate ganache, orange marmalade, tequila buttercream.

"So, Luke's definitely staying behind."

"It's complicated. Last year, when his girlfriend moved back from Vancouver, they decided they'd break up. But now they both want to try to make it work. Luke's plan from the beginning was to spend the summer in Toronto."

"With his girlfriend."

"Ai Chang Cho. Last fall she won an apprenticeship here with the National Ballet of Canada's costume department."

"So why doesn't he stay with her?"

"That's impossible. Ai Chang went to fashion school in Vancouver but now that she's back, she's been living with her family, at least for the time being. They're from Taiwan, and pretty traditional. They wouldn't approve of him."

"Because he's transgender."

"Oh no. Because he's white."

Nadia smoothed the fabric of her dress. A plump, freckled woman in a wheelchair sat close-by, texting on her tablet. Two bearded men in silk turbans reposed by the window playing a game of chess.

Nadia rested her hands on her knees. "I think, Daniel," she said, "you and I should go for a walk."

When we asked the cashier to split the bill, the woman in the wheelchair clucked her tongue. "A young man like you," she said mildly, glancing up, "should be paying for the young lady. Who knows? She could be the mother of your children one day."

Nadia and I only smiled and blushed. We left the Flying Elephant Bakery, agreeing it'd been a successful venture. In the end, we'd shared three different desserts new to both of us. Nadia had also come on her bicycle, a classic, moss-green cruiser, all sleek chrome with a rearview mirror and a woven basket secured to the front. We walked our bikes south toward the lake, along a quiet side street beneath a canopy of century-old maples and oaks.

At the grassy waterfront, half-a-dozen dogs were running off-leash, their owners assembled with coffees and plastic baggies in hand. Further along the shoreline, we leaned our bikes against a wooden bench and sat facing the lake.

"So, it's settled, then," Nadia said. "Luke will be living with you while David's away."

"I think so. He says he's happy to stay on the couch."

"And what about Mrs. Gallucci?"

"Well, David's going to tell his mom he hasn't heard back from his sister. It's a lie, but it's probably better for everyone this way."

"From a certain perspective, there is truth to that statement."

"Mrs. Gallucci's pretty Catholic. I think it'd turn the woman's life upside-down if she ever found out one kid was gay and the other one trans."

Nadia sat straight-backed, observing the sailboats slipping past, chaperoned by raucous gulls. Her thin nostrils flared.

"'I am made and remade continually,' " she said. "'Different people draw different words from me.'"

When I glanced at her, she said: "Virginia Woolf."

I recalled the name from high school English but that seemed like a hundred years ago. When I confessed as much, Nadia drew a breath. A jewel-like dragonfly settled on her foot, iridescent and quivering, before abruptly flitting away.

"She was someone who understood gender long before anyone else. She was a writer. She loved her husband passionately. She also had an affair with a married woman, her best friend. Have you ever heard of *Orlando: A Biography*?" I shook my head. Nadia put on her glasses and turned her face to the sun. "Let's just say, upside-down is not always a bad thing."

"You think Luke should go, don't you?"

"I think," Nadia said, "Mrs. Gallucci has a right to know the truth."

David once jokingly described Nadia as my mistress. It was such an old-fashioned, Old World term. It evoked Victorian intrigue, clandestine trysts, sword duels, horse-drawn carriages surging through the mist. My encounters with Nadia were never comfortable. I found myself regularly sharing secrets with her I'd not shared with anyone else. This bright day in June was no different.

"Do you think," I asked, "David should come out to her?"

"What do you think?"

"I do. I think both of them should."

"Well, it is easy for people like us to judge. I never had to come out to my family. You were welcomed when you came out to yours."

That was true, more or less, but I hadn't known for sure I'd be welcomed. I was eighteen and home for Christmas. When the news broke, Liam had a harder time than Pat, but it'd all turned out well enough in the end. Grandpa acted like he'd known all along. Neither David nor Luke seemed so concerned by their secret. But appearances were just that. My closeted years were painful, shame-filled, and confusing. How could I be gay if I didn't love Barbies or musical theatre? I grew up playing hockey, rough-housing with my brothers and blasting Bryan Adams on the car stereo. Hell, I had a mullet and got drunk at bush parties.

Nobody, I figured, was really how they seemed. There was always something surprising to discover when you looked under the hood.

Nadia stood and retrieved her bicycle. She extended her hand. "I've enjoyed our time together today, Daniel. I've stayed longer than I meant to." She smiled wistfully, the way someone else might shrug. Then, to my utter surprise, she rested one palm against the side of my face. She stroked the stubble on my cheek. "You and David are lovers already. There's no need to hurry." The lake sparkled behind her, drifting beyond. "No need to be anybody but oneself."

⌢ Three Dog Run was heading down to Burning Man.

"It's in Black Rock, Nevada," Pat explained, wolfing down his enchilada. "It's like this radical gathering of artists and free thinkers out in the desert, fifty thousand people camped out for a week. There's going to be this whole convoy of us driving down. Rod's just bought this used Winnebago, he's organizing everything. It's going to be the awesomest road trip. He calls all of us his baby proto-Burners."

"His baby what?" I asked.

"Here, check this out." Pat propped his crooked leg up on the corner of the table, displaying the Three Dog Run logo the size of a hockey puck, emblazoned on his shaved calf.

"Is that new?" I asked.

"We all got it done last Friday. It was Rod's idea. You should see where Bobby put his." Pat took in a huge mouthful of baked beans and fries and washed it down with a gulp of black coffee. "And you won't believe, Daniel, who I'm hooking up with while I'm there: Carolina Sanchez from Colombia!"

"Pat, can you please take your foot off the table?"

"Roger that."

I sat back in our graffiti-stained booth at Sneaky Dee's. I wished Pat wouldn't talk with his mouth full. He was wearing a faded Bruce Lee T-shirt and high tops. The colourful ceiling mural blazed down over the bustling Sunday brunch crowd. It was the beginning of Pride Week, and someone had stuck a little rainbow flag in the famous "Bonehead" cow skull over the bar framed by jalapeño lights.

"Does Blonde Dawn know you're meeting up with Carolina?" I asked.

"No, not yet, but I'll tell her. She knows how you and I hooked up with the Three Amigas, she knows all about that."

"What? Pat, I asked you not to tell her about that."

Pat waved his fork, speckling the tabletop with *mole* sauce. "Daniel, so what? You worry too much. Seriously, dude, you can't go through life worrying all the time what other people think." He put down his fork, stood upright and shouted: "Hey, everybody, my gay brother here had sex with a girl!"

Heads briefly turned towards us, then everyone turned back to their own business.

"See?" Pat said. "Nobody cares." He sat back down. "In any case, it's Blonde Dawn. She definitely doesn't care. It's no big deal."

I stared at Pat. I wondered if he'd care if I stuck my fork in his forehead. I wanted to say: "But I care. And if it was no big deal, then why'd you have to tell her at all?" But I kept my mouth shut. There was no use arguing with

Pat. He'd always find some way to make it seem like he was right. But the drug-fuelled debauchery we'd shared was years in the past, and I wanted to keep it that way. Claw marks bloodied Bruce's cheek and chest, but his fist was raised and his expression was one of arrogant resolve.

"So Rod's been to this Burning Man thing?"

"It's not a thing," Pat said. "It's a spiritual experience. People come from all over the world to Burning Man. Black Rock City, man, that's mecca for the psychonaut. There's like this whole temple they build every year. It's brilliant. Liam's lending me all his tenting gear. He's going commando again this summer."

Since he was a kid, Liam's passion had been the outdoors. For years, every summer, he'd disappear into the bush with a bivouac sack and a knife and be gone a week or longer. I was just surprised Liam actually trusted Pat with his gear.

"Oh, holy bejesus, you gotta be kidding me. Oh shit. Aw, no way." Pat rummaged through his paint-stained cargo shorts. "As if. I think I left my wallet at home." He stared at me. "Daniel, I don't suppose you could spot me breakfast, could you? I'll pay you back, honest, I promise. Did you know that at Burning Man they don't use any money at all? Everything's like run on a gift economy, can you believe it? Whoa, hey, you know what I can do? I'll bring you back a vial of playa dust, how about that?"

Pat and I rarely spent one-on-one time together. He was always busy, tearing around with a dozen projects on the go. Pat and Blonde Dawn had taken over the lease on my old apartment, where Karen and I'd lived three years. Even now, it wasn't entirely clear to me how he covered his portion of the rent. I knew he was certified as an ESL instructor. Did Pat just say he'd pay me back in dust? I sighed. "Sure, no problem. You have a good trip. Be safe. Tell Carolina I say hello."

After that, Pat had the rest of his breakfast put in a doggie bag and ordered another coffee to go. When we stepped out onto the sidewalk, he gave me a bear hug. "Happy Pride, man! You hitting the big circuit parties?"

"What? No. It's not really my thing."

"C'mon, really?" Pat crouched, moving his elbows in circular motions. "All those hot, sweaty, naked guys?"

"Really," I said. "David and I might check out the parade Sunday. What about you?"

"We have front row seats to The Hip, Saturday down at Fort York."

"How'd you manage that?"

"Blonde Dawn knows someone who knows someone and scored two VIP passes. It is going to rock. Oh shit, gotta run, late for class, thanks again for breakfast. I love you, big brother."

A busboy strolled out of the restaurant and held out a battered scrap of leather. "Excuse me, I think this is yours."

"Holy shit, dude, are you kidding me?"

"It was on the floor."

Pat clutched his wallet. "This is amazeballs. This is fucking awesome." He stared at me. "This is an omen. This is the spirit of Burning Man manifesting, moving through this spot, right here right now. Yo, buddy, hold on, wait a second wait a second!" Pat pulled out all his bills, three crumpled fivers, and pressed them into the busboy's hands, along with all the change in his pockets. A loonie fell and rolled over to my feet. I picked it up and handed it to Pat, who thrust it at the kid. "Here, cheers, take it take it. Thank you, can't thank you enough. You are awesome. You are a sacred being." Pat beamed at me. "Gotta keep the channels open, keep the spirit flowing. Karma, man, it's all karma."

⌢ Later that night, I climbed the stairs to our bedroom. My feet ached and I wondered if it was time I invested in orthotics. I stepped over David's half-packed suitcase at the foot of the bed.

"So, look," David said, sorting through travel documents, "Luke doesn't do small talk and he's allergic to shellfish. I doubt you'll see him around much. He's here to spend time with his girlfriend. If things work out between them, he might move back to Toronto."

"He uses an STP device, by the way."

"What?"

I flopped down on our bed. "You asked me," I said, "how your brother pees standing up. He uses a stand-to-pee device."

"He told you this?"

"He didn't have to. It's obvious." I didn't mention how we'd recently covered a section on trans health at school. Nobody in our class knew what an STP packer was, and the guest instructor had to explain it to us like we were three-year-olds.

"Okay, well. Good for him. Whatever it takes."

"David. Are you sure this is the best thing?"

"What?"

"That Luke doesn't come with you."

"Yeah, this is the best thing. You don't know my ma. She's lost three husbands already. Here, check it out." David's new passport had just arrived in the mail. He handed it at me. "Do I look like a Mafioso or what?"

"What do you mean?"

"I mean, do I look like some hardened criminal?"

"No. What did you mean about your mom?"

David frowned, breathing through his nose. He took back his passport. "Nothing," he said.

"Well, you meant something."

"Forget about it."

Between us, David was usually the bolder, more self-assured one. He'd let his close-cropped hair grow out and it had started to curl. He also hadn't shaved in over a week. Somehow, it made him look wilder, more European. "You're happy with me, right?"

"Being with you?"

"Yeah."

"Daniel, I love you. I'm in love with you. Yeah, I'm happy with you."

"Then I think you should tell her. Tell your mom now, before this big family reunion in Italy."

David's face darkened. "Tell her what?"

"Tell her that I'm your boyfriend." I sat up. "Look, Luke can decide whatever he wants. But David, why don't you tell her about us? We can tell her together."

David put down the Italian phrase book he'd been studying. By the dim light of the bed lamp, his features were still, his lips compressed. "You know," he said, "I've been with girls."

"I know. Your mom thinks her son's a womanizing Don Giovanni."

"Yeah."

"She's always hoping you'll fall in love and settle down."

"So she says."

"Don't you think she'd want to know you are in love? Don't you want to tell her that?"

"You don't know my ma."

"So enlighten me."

"She can be really stubborn. When she gets an idea into her head, there's no discussion."

"Okay."

"Remember I told you how Lucy came back? Don't correct me, Daniel. She was Lucy Moretti at the time, okay? My big sister, five months after she ran way, she came back. She came home on Christmas Day. It was late in the evening, she'd been drinking. She had this brand-new car and new clothes and presents for both of us. They were big presents, shiny with huge bows. Except my ma wouldn't accept any of them. I was thirteen years old, and I was begging my ma to just let her in the house. But she wouldn't even listen to me. She'd already had the locks changed. They were arguing, shouting at each other. Then Ma, she shut the front door, right in her face. It was awful. It was humiliating. By the time I got outside, Lucy was gone. I ran three blocks after her, but she was gone. I wanted to run away myself. But I didn't. How can any mother do that to her own child?"

After a moment, I asked: "What were they arguing about?"

"I don't know, they were speaking Italian. If you ever want to get into a screaming match with someone, Italian's the way to go. Look at me, reading this. It's so fucking embarrassing." David threw his phrase book across the bed. His eyes were wet. "Do you get it? Sure, everyone loves Isabella de Luca, famous Canadian art critic and philosopher, woohoo. But there's another side to her. There's this other side. I just don't think Luke could take another door slammed in his face. I don't think I ever could."

"Okay. Okay. I get it."

"Can I tell you something else?"

"Sure."

"This whole trans thing. That afternoon, on New Year's Eve, when I opened our door and saw him standing there like that, her, Luke, it was like he did it on purpose. He could've phoned to warn me but he didn't. It was planned, like it was a test. He said he wanted to surprise me. Yeah, right. What an asshole thing to do. What a fucking asshole thing to do, Daniel. And you know what the craziest part was? The honest truth was, I wasn't even that surprised. I mean, the Boss is still the Boss, right? He hasn't changed, whether he calls himself Lucy or Luke. He still acts and talks the same. He's older now, maybe with more muscles and hair all over, but you look in his eyes and he's still the same person."

"That's a good thing, right?"

"All I'm saying is, he could've told me sooner. But he kept it to himself, he kept it secret. Even after I told him I was gay."

"When did you tell him that?"

"I dunno, three years ago. Someone he knew actually

spotted me kissing some guy. Holy shit, Daniel, I think it was your brother Pat. Remember Pat and I made out once at a party?"

"Sure. You've both told me this story."

"Okay. Well, we were just messing around, right? But someone must've seen us, and somehow word got back to Luke. He made a trip all the way back to Toronto just to ask me about that."

"And?"

"He was cool. He said he didn't care. He said I was his kid brother, and he'd always love me no matter what."

"David."

"Yeah?"

"On New Year's Eve, that night the two of you left the bar and went for a walk, what did you talk about?"

"That night at Graffiti's? Hell, we didn't talk about anything. I mean, we talked about bikes and soccer; what the old neighbourhood gang was up to; you, I talked a lot about you; he told me how he and Ai Chang were still in love, even though they'd broken up because she'd moved to Toronto. You know the rest of that story. We just talked and walked. We were looking for a place where we could light a cigarette but it was blowing snow so hard it took us forever and our hands were freezing. We found some corner behind a dumpster and he got me to open my coat, but then he accidentally lit my scarf on fire. After that, well, everything seemed okay. Everything seemed right, after that."

I took David's passport and opened it to his picture. He did look different. In real life he smiled easily, his mouth wide, his whole face alive and bright. He and Pat were alike in so many ways. Pat and Blonde Dawn seemed made for each other. If I'd been straight, Karen and I always figured we'd be together, maybe even married with kids and settled down like Melissa and Mike. I always thought Karen and Liam would marry one day, but now Karen was with Bob and his two daughters. Even Grandpa was seeing someone new, Betty from the nursing home. Apart from Karen and Anne and the Miltons, Betty was the probably the person who knew our family better than anyone in the world.

"Everything is okay." I closed David's passport. "I'm sorry."

"About what?"

"About asking you to come out to your mom, I'm sorry."

"Don't be." David bowed his head. "You know, she really likes you."

"Does she?"

"She thinks you're a good influence."

"She just likes that I'm in med school."

"And she likes you because you eat second servings of everything she puts in front of you."

"That's easy, she's an amazing cook."

"If she had her way, she'd have the both of us eating there every night."

That wasn't so hard for me to imagine. So why was it for David? "I wouldn't mind."

"Your waistline would. You know I once caught her serving coffee for four? She had a setting out for each of her husbands. She was talking out loud and going through her old photo albums."

"I think your mom is a very special woman."

"Thanks for taking in Luke."

"He's family, right?"

"Yeah, he is."

"David, are we going to be okay?"

"You and me?"

"Yeah. I mean, you're going to be away for two whole months."

"Of course we're going to be okay. Time's just going to fly by. Trust me, we're good."

"You promise?"

"I promise."

"I'm going to miss you."

"I'm going to miss you too."

⌒ The night before David was to catch his flight out to Europe, we had sex. I was on my back and he was straddling me, and I was gripping his thighs, and I was moving inside of him. We took our time, sharing an unspoken agreement to make it last as long as we could. He arched back, hands braced against my knees. His teeth were parted, his brow furrowed. The tendons and muscles of his neck stood out in sharp relief. A single line of sweat ran from the hollow of his throat down his chest and stomach. Once David had shared a fantasy with me, imagining himself a Roman legionary and prisoner of war, and me a Celtic chieftain. At another time he'd described us as David and Jonathan, from the Bible. I hadn't known what he meant, and he told me the story of how Jonathan son of King Saul of Israel, had fallen in love with David who had slain Goliath. The Israelites were at war with the invading Philistines. David had been considered too young to go into battle at the time. When presented at the royal court, he still carried Goliath's severed head in his hands. Prince Jonathan, standing at his father's side, was so awestruck, he stripped off his robes, his armour and his weapons, and gave them to David. After that, the two youths pledged their devotion to each other and became lovers. But the bloody war continued, and shortly after their pledge, Jonathan and his brothers were killed on a mountainside, and King Saul, pierced with many arrows, took his own life.

David's fantasies were always dark, violent and tragic. A framed poster of Zeffirelli's *Romeo and Juliet* hung in our bathroom over the claw-foot tub. More than once he'd cheerfully recited Mercutio's dying speech to me. David bent forward, lifted my head in the palm of his hand and pressed his lips against mine. "I love you, Daniel Garneau," he whispered.

I didn't have David's vivid imagination. But I had learned long ago to stay present in the moment, to breathe and to keep my eyes open. When David straightened, I poured more lube into my hand and took him in my fist, and he quickened the muscular motion of his hips. I timed it so that, in the end, we came together. After that, he collapsed on top on me and we breathed in unison until I thought he might have fallen asleep. Then I drew myself out of him and gently pushed him off. I showered quickly and returned to bed where he still lay curled on one side. I'd brought a hot face towel which I used to wipe him clean. We'd both been tested and had stopped wearing condoms months ago. Some part of me remained inside of him.

After that, I spooned him from behind and pulled the thin sheet over us. It was a warm night, and his skin was hot, damp and salty to the taste. I held his thick wrist and pressed my cheek against the side of his head, breathing in the familiar smell of his hair and the back of his neck. I roused enough to kiss the base of his skull. Then I reminded myself I was no longer in love with Marcus Wittenbrink Jr., but I was in love entirely with this man I held in my arms, David Gallucci son of Isabella de Luca. And in that numinous, liminal space, halfway between wakefulness and sleep, halfway between sense and imagination, it wasn't hard to convince myself at all that this was the truth.

CHAPTER FIVE

The Spirit of Radio

Marcus was on CBC radio.

He was being interviewed by Sook-Yin Lee on her show, *Definitely Not the Opera*. I'd been lying in bed masturbating, when my clock radio alarm went off. I listened in shock to the sound of my ex-boyfriend talking right next to my head. It occurred to me he had the perfect radio announcer's voice: a resonant bari-tenor, thoughtful and modulated, authoritative yet playful. There was also the tiniest hint of a European accent which I happened to know was utterly affected. Marcus was, after all, the third generation son of white-bread lawyers from Burlington, Ontario. He was describing Tuvan throat singing, providing instructions on technique and encouraging Sook-Yin to give it a whirl, which the radio host was more than game to do. The two were clearly flirting. When she commented on the prevalence of nudity in his multimedia art projects, he reminded her (and their millions of listeners) of her last day as a MuchMusic VJ, when she and her co-host had mooned the Canadian audience on live television.

After a few minutes, I realized the theme of this DNTO episode was "The Art of Noise," inspiring a rambling discussion ranging from Tanya Tagaq to beatboxing to Glenn Gould's experimentations with musique concrète. It was like listening to a friendly tennis exhibition match, as each player made witty, entertaining points with increasingly acrobatic aplomb. Inevitably, the reflections turned to noise as metaphor: the works of Jean-Paul Riopelle, graffiti in the urban landscape, the state of media technologies. "But tell me," Marcus said, "what's the one signal our human sensorium tunes into, listens for, desperate to receive, more than anything else?"

"Sex!" Sook-Yin exclaimed.

"And?"

"Love."

"Precisely."

Sook-Yin rallied. "Except even here, there's so much white noise getting in the way."

"Especially here," Marcus said. "A cacophony of distractions."

"Perverting the original flow."

"Literally!"

"So," Sook-Yin asked, ever mindful of her listeners, "what exactly are we talking about here?"

"Take for example," Marcus said, "who we think we're attracted to …"

I reached over and turned off the radio.

Marcus and I had been together only five months and that had ended three years ago. But he'd been my first serious boyfriend and, as much as I hated to admit it, the time I'd spent with him had changed my life. Marcus had introduced me to more than the arts and culture of the city. He'd constantly reminded me how the brain was the largest sex organ in our body. Stimulate the brain, he'd announced in his Dora-nominated one-man show, *Philophobia*, and the whole world would rise glittering like Venus on a shell.

I pulled up my underwear and tossed my Kleenex box aside. The truth was, I'd been fantasizing about Marcus and Fang again. During my final month with Marcus, the three of us were lovers, until I finally broke it off. I'd thought we'd been discreet, but I found out later that pretty much everyone knew. I was embarrassed and I was angry. Personally, I had nothing against Trevor Fang, part-time DJ and full-time party boy. But Marcus's insistence that he and I open up our relationship had marked the beginning of the end for us. If it wasn't Fang, it was going to be someone else.

I rolled out of bed and took a cold shower.

It'd been a week since David left for Italy. Tomorrow, Luke would arrive from Vancouver. At the end of the day, I borrowed a hospital privacy screen, carrying it home precariously on my bike across the U of T campus. If Luke Moretti was going to spend the summer sleeping on our couch, the least I could do was give him some personal space. I rearranged the furniture, moved my giant palm, and cleared out a shelf in our medicine cabinet. For two months, I figured, it'd be a liveable arrangement.

A week later, I met Parker Kapoor for sushi next door to the Carlton Cinema. We'd come to see *Kaijuly: A Midnight Japanese Monster Movie Marathon*, but as usual, our conversation took on a life of its own and we'd ended up passing on the kaiju fest. On this occasion, Parker was wearing a bright orange, short-sleeved, buttoned shirt decorated with baby blue robots. He'd just come back from a week in Montreal and was effusing over his evening with Mado Lamotte, the owner of a local drag cabaret. "She's an icon in Quebec," Parker said, "a living legend." He brandished a piece of ikayaki with his chopsticks. "She's a DJ, MC, author, raconteur. She's been performing for twenty years. She usually lip-synchs, but sometimes, if you're really lucky, she'll sing live. I, Daniel, got to sit in her lap."

"Wow. That sounds awesome."

"She smelled like cherry blossoms." Parker's eyes rolled back in his head. "It was heavenly, you have no idea. She called me up on stage, draped her arm over my shoulder, and sang 'Little Man' entirely in French. Can you believe it? I still haven't washed that T-shirt."

"'Little Man'?"

"By Sonny and Cher. Daniel, it's a classic, better than 'I Got You Babe.'" Parker bopped in his chair, humming the opening refrain.

"Well, I'm happy you had a good time."

"So." Parker sipped from his tea. "How's your boyfriend doing? Have you heard from him?"

"David called when he got to Rome. They were just about to catch a connecting flight to Palermo."

"And now?"

"Well, from Palermo they took a train to this village near his family's farmhouse. Except they have no Wi-Fi so, no, I haven't heard from him."

"You said it's his aunts' place?"

"His grandparents own an olive grove out in the

country, but they're pretty old, so it's his two aunts and a cousin of his who run the place now. It's where his mom grew up. They're getting ready to host this family reunion."

"And how are you doing? How are things with his brother? He's staying with you, right?"

"Luke? Alright. He's been here a week, but I hardly ever see him. He comes home really late and he sleeps in. He's super tidy. He eats out most of the time."

"Sounds like the perfect houseguest."

"I guess so."

"You look disappointed."

"I just thought we'd hang out more, you know? He's polite and everything, but it's pretty clear he's just not interested in connecting."

"Maybe he's just trying to stay out of your way."

"Maybe."

"He's also here for his girlfriend, right? Isn't that the main reason he came all the way out here?"

"True. He's been busy helping her get ready for some fall art show she's in."

Parker's ears perked up. "Art show?"

"Something hosted by the Toronto Fashion Incubator."

"The TFI? Not everyone gets into the TFI. What did you say her name was?"

"Ai Chang Cho."

"Was she that Chinese girl with all the piercings, from New Year's Eve?"

"Yeah, that's her."

"I remember her. She was shy but really sweet."

"Really?"

"She complimented me on my outfit."

"You were an elf."

"I was."

"Well, I'm glad you connected."

"Daniel." Parker gripped the table edge. "I have the most fabulous idea. Why don't I host a tea dance?"

"A what?"

"An afternoon cocktail party. I can book the rooftop patio in my condo building. I'll bring in a couple DJs. I have all this fresh mint growing on my balcony. We can serve mojitos!"

"And invite Luke and Ai Chang?"

"I know people in the fashion industry. She'll thank me before it's over. Who knows? She could be the next Lida Baday! What do you think?"

"Sounds fun?"

"It will be fun. You just have to confirm they can both make it. Ask them first and let me know, then I'll do the rest."

"You sure about this?"

"How long have we known each other, Daniel?"

"Four years?"

"Have you ever known me not to be sure about anything?"

"Um, yeah, lots of times."

"Okay, well. This time I'm sure. I need to do something, I need a project to keep myself busy. This will be good for me. It'll be good material for my blog."

"You have a blog?"

"Oh, I didn't tell you. I'm serializing my memoirs. I've been thinking to myself, when am I wrapping this thing up? I've been working on this for years. Then it occurred to me, it's not wrapping up. Of course it's not. I mean, it just goes on, right? There's no end to it. It's life! So I'm launching a blog site, I'm going live: *The Misanthropic Misadventures of Parker Kapoor.*"

"You're really calling it that?"

"Yes, Daniel, you gave me the idea. Don't you remember? Are you going to have that last piece of sashimi?"

"Go for it."

"Mmm, I love Japanese food, it's so fresh and clean and beautiful. Aaah!"

"What is it?"

Parker clutched his mouth. "Wasabi, doo butch wasabi." He slurped from his tea cup.

"That's not going to help." I handed him my bowl. "Here, try some plain rice. Is that better?"

"Bedder."

"You okay?"

Parker chewed and swallowed. "I have a sensitive palate. That was intense."

"I look forward to reading your blog."

"If I ever get around to launching it."

"You will. You have to promise me I get to be your first reader."

"I promise," Parker said, his eyes watering. "Look, I bought this shirt just for tonight. I'm still up for a kaiju all-nighter if you are. Everyone's a fan of Godzilla, but Mothra's my favourite. I love her two fairy companions, and how she metamorphoses into something so celestial. Who's your favourite?"

"I'm not sure. King Kong, I guess?"

"Doomed love, epic tragedy. Fay Wray was inimitable.

Classic Hollywood cinema. That," Parker said, wagging a finger, "is an excellent choice. Thank you for coming out, by the way, it means a lot."

"Thanks for inviting me."

"Don't forget to ask Luke and Ai Chang about the tea dance."

"I won't."

"You promise?"

"I'll ask them."

"So, Daniel, are you ready for a mega-mania-monster-movie-mashup-marathon?"

I'd realized long ago that Parker Kapoor and I had absolutely nothing in common. We had completely different sets of friends. Our tastes and interests barely overlapped. But neither of us seemed to care in the least. And none of it made any difference in the end.

"Parker," I said, "I'm ready whenever you are."

~ One morning a few days later, I woke up to find Luke Moretti doing bicep curls in the middle of our living room area. "Hey, I hope you don't mind," he said. "I found these under the couch. Crazy thing is, these used to be my dumbbells. I had no idea David kept them. You know, I actually won these on a bet?"

"Oh?" I tried not to stare at his perfect, muscled frame. In the last six months, it looked like he'd put on five kilos.

"Yeah, we were drinking and smoking-up in Doug Romano's garage. He wouldn't believe I could bench my own weight. So I bet him my hockey jersey I could."

"This was when?"

"I must've been fifteen, I think. Thing is, I actually had no idea if I could really do it or not. But Romano was being such a dick, I couldn't help myself."

"You were the Boss."

Luke laughed. "David told you about that, eh? Yeah, I was the Boss."

I poured myself a cup of coffee. "David mentioned you used to work in a boxing gym."

"In Vancouver, for a couple years there, yeah, in the Downtown Eastside." He widened his stance and started to do standing shoulder presses. "I've also worked as a contractor, mostly drywall and stairwell carpeting. And I've been a competitive oyster shucker, a professional dog-walker, and a part-time model. You know what the trick is to walking dogs?"

"What?"

"Be the first out the door, and always walk in front. That shows them you're the pack leader. Always keep 'em on a short leash, beside you or behind you."

"I'll try to remember that."

"It'll save you a helluva lot of trouble."

"You were a part-time model?"

"Oh yeah, that's how I met Ai Chang. She spotted me in Steveston Village, walked right up to me and asked me to model for her. It was for her graduate fashion show. We hit it off the second we met."

I poured myself a bowl of cereal. "You're both still coming to Parker's party, right?"

"Yeah, for sure. We have a photo-shoot scheduled the next day. But we'll be there." Luke put down the weights and shook out his arms. "Hey, can I ask you something?"

"Sure. Ask away."

"Well, we're scouting locations for this shoot, and I was thinking of this space. Your loft."

"You want to do a fashion shoot here?"

Luke got down on the floor and started doing stomach crunches. "Not a full-out fashion shoot. But Ai Chang's being featured in this spotlight on young designers, right? And they want her to submit a couple prints of her latest work."

"In a magazine?"

"A city blog, the *Torontoist*."

"Okay."

"We're looking for an indoor location: someplace masculine with character, but also unpretentious, real, lived-in, y'know what I mean?"

I looked around the loft. I'd never thought twice about how it might look to others. Board games, DVDs and medical texts crowded the shelves and stacked milk cartons. When friends came over, I'd throw magazines and all our junk into the battered steamer trunk that doubled as our coffee table. Our two bikes were mounted under the staircase leading to our bedroom. A tandem bike frame hung over David's workstation littered with rims, chains and bike gears.

I pointed at the framed print of Che Guevara. "You don't think that's too pretentious?"

I was half-joking but Luke regarded it critically. "Yeah, now that you mention it, it probably is. We might want to move a few things around. We'll be in-and-out, just a couple hours. Whadya say?"

"I mean, if you think it'll work."

"Awesome! We owe you one. It'll be fun. We are going to have a good time."

I studied the postcards from Italy on the fridge. I wondered if David was having a good time. I knew better than to bring up the family reunion again with Luke. The few occasions I had mentioned it, he'd walked away from me. Luke Moretti didn't spend time on small talk, or on anything he'd decided wasn't going to be part of his life.

Luke jumped to his feet and strode over to the mirror by the front door. He flexed his biceps, one after the other. After that, he lifted his thin shirt and examined his midsection.

"Looking good," I said.

"Getting there. I moved into a new weight class this spring. We should work out sometime, you and me."

"Um." Milk dribbled down my chin. "Sure."

"I could use a spotter," Luke said, crossing the room, "and you could use some gym time." He picked up my cereal bowl and helped himself to a generous spoonful. His cologne was subtle and musky, or was that just the guy's natural scent? He stood back and munched while looking me up and down. He pointed with the spoon. "You kinda got this dad bod going on there." He winked, took another mouthful before handing back my bowl. "But don't worry. It's all about getting onto a compound exercise circuit and cross-training. I can whip you into shape in no time. Mind if I take a shower?"

"Go for it."

I poked at my cereal, pretending to read a *NOW Magazine*, while Luke rummaged through his duffle bag and headed to the bathroom. The door shut only partway behind him. If I leaned forward just enough, I could catch a glimpse of his reflection in the medicine cabinet mirror. He peeled his shirt off over his head, the muscles in his shoulders and arms flexing. Luke was definitely in a lot better shape than either David or me. He drew the shower curtain and turned on the water.

Glancing up, he caught me watching. He smiled and winked again, before reaching over and pulling the door firmly shut.

∿ Sunday night Skype date with Karen.

Central Smith's Algonquin ice cream (French vanilla maple with chocolate ripple and caramel chocolate canoes). Rating: three-and-three-quarters.

"He said," Karen exclaimed, "you had a dad bod?"

"Yeah, not in a mean way, but it was just, I dunno. Still, I mean what the fuck? What do you think?"

"Well. Let me see."

I got up and positioned myself in front of the camera. Karen squinted. I raised my arms and let them fall.

"This," I said, "is humiliating."

"Move back," Karen said. "Take off your shirt."

I backed up and reluctantly pulled off my T-shirt. Karen twirled a finger and I turned on the spot.

"Stand up straight. Are you sucking it in? Don't suck it in."

"Okay!"

"Hmm. Daniel Garneau, you've been sneaking a few extra Creamsicles, haven't you? Have you weighed yourself recently?"

"Karen, seriously?"

"Daniel, you're in med school. You're not playing hockey anymore. It only makes sense you'd pack on a few pounds. Don't worry about it, you're still hot. Girls like a dad bod. Anyway, since when did you ever worry about how you looked?"

I flopped back down on the couch. "I'm gay, remember? Gay guys are supposed to look like fucking Calvin Klein models."

"Ah, welcome to my world." Karen poked at her ice cream, smacking her lips. "Anyhow, you're with David now. You don't need to impress the boys."

"I'm not trying to impress anyone. I just want to be in shape."

"Really?" Karen cocked her head and licked her spoon. "Because it seems like you're trying to impress someone."

"What's that supposed to mean?"

"So, have you done it with anyone yet?"

"What, had sex?"

"Yeah."

"No. I mean, of course not."

"You have permission, right? You said you and David discussed this: while he's away in Italy, you're both allowed to have sex with other people."

I cringed. "I guess so."

"You guess so?"

"Yes," I said. "We discussed it." I pushed aside my half-empty bowl. "Yes, I have permission."

"So why 'of course not'?"

"I dunno, Karen. It just seems weird."

"Daniel, you and David have an open relationship.

Some people would give an arm and a leg to be in an open relationship."

"Karen, you make it sound like we're Pat and Blonde Dawn. Those two hook up with random people all the time. That's not us at all. I mean, for starters, this is just while David's away for the summer."

"Has he met anyone?"

"David? Karen, the guy's travelling around Italy with his mom."

"He'd tell you if he did?"

"David tells me everything. Look, all I'm saying is, I just don't think what we're about counts as an open relationship."

"But you're not monogamous."

"We're monogamish."

"Oh. Monogamish. Okay. I get it."

"Do you?"

"I do. So." Karen picked up her laptop and strolled with it into her kitchen. "Have you thought about doing it?"

"Not really." I folded my arms. "I dunno. Maybe."

"Are you going to hook-up with Marcus? You've told me you still want to sleep with him."

"Absolutely not. Definitely not. I mean, just because I think about sex with someone, doesn't mean I want to have sex with someone."

Karen set dirty cups and dishes in the sink and headed down a hallway. "There's a difference?"

"Of course there's a difference."

"Please clarify."

I flipped through a mental rolodex. "Mr. Arbuckle."

Karen drew a breath and made a face. "Right." Our former high school art teacher might've been Ryan Reynolds' better-looking kid brother. In pottery class he'd put on a smock and roll up his sleeves, working the wet clay with his big hands. All the girls loved pottery with Mr. Arbuckle. After his daughter died of cancer, he'd cried in front of the whole class. "Gotcha."

"Also, like. I mean, take Luke."

"Luke? Oh my god." Behind Karen, I caught a shaky glimpse of a shower curtain with a colourful forest print: pine trees, cardinals, raccoons and foxes. She set the laptop down. "Daniel, are you attracted to Luke?"

"Karen, I'm attracted to pretty much any guy who walks around in ripped jeans with his shirt off. But Luke. He's, I dunno. Luke's a sexy guy. He also wears this amazing cologne. I think it's his cologne. Fuck. But he's also David's big brother. So there you go. And he likes women."

Karen's face bobbed in and out of the camera frame. "He has a girlfriend."

"Yeah, a scary ass rocker chick girlfriend. David says if Ai Chang Cho was a Final Fantasy character, she'd be lopping off heads with a vibranium battle-axe. Karen, what are you doing?"

"I'm peeing." Karen rested her chin in her hands and regarded me thoughtfully. She reached out and adjusted the angle of her laptop. "Daniel, are you okay?"

"What do you mean?"

"You just seem distracted."

Karen could always do this: Tell me what was going on with me before I knew what was going on with me.

"I'm okay." I sighed. "I mean school is really busy. It's

a lot of studying. It's tough. I get these headaches. I haven't had a chance to get out much."

"You miss him, don't you?"

"Yeah, I suppose I do. This is our first time apart."

"Daniel, you spent the first twenty-one years of your life apart from each other, and you were just fine. David will be back before you know it. Time apart can be healthy for a relationship. Just picture meeting him at the airport."

"How are things with Bob?"

"Things with Bob are good. Bob's my big daddy-o teddy bear. I know he doesn't look it, but he's really a sweet, fun-loving guy. He's a lot different."

"You mean different from Liam."

"Yeah."

"I'm happy for you."

"Thanks." Karen crumpled up a handful of toilet paper. "Daniel, you should take a break. Spend a day on the Toronto Islands or something. Go for a walk in High Park. Will you do that for me?"

"I'll think about it."

"Hey." Karen peered into the camera. "This is me you're talking to. You look tired. You've been working too hard. I know school's important, but you need to get out of the house. Get reconnected with nature. You'll feel better when you do."

"Work on this dad bod?"

"Get outdoors. You promise you'll do that?" Off-screen, Karen wiped herself, and flushed. "Do something to help your body feel healthy and good. Trust me, your mind and spirit will follow."

"Yes, Karen, I promise."

⌁ The next Saturday afternoon, I went for a bike ride to Riverdale Farm in Cabbagetown. Behind wooden fences, well-fed cows and horses lounged in the hazy, mid-July heat, switching their tails at the flies. Hefting my bike, I descended a hill to an expansive field where a softball game was in full swing. After that it was only a short route up to an overpass where a metal staircase led down into the Don River Valley Trail.

David had shown me this path last summer, winding from the Portlands up to Taylor Creek Park, mostly hidden by dense valley foliage, set apart from the nearby parkway. Passing joggers and dog-walkers, I eventually approached the mammoth concrete foundations of the Prince Edward Viaduct, where I stopped for a water break.

The sun was blazing hot and my pit-stains were showing. Far overhead, a subway train rumbled past. Sycamores and sugar maples overshadowed swaths of sumac. I took off my helmet and tied my bandana around my head. After that, I hit a long stretch parallel to wetlands and shallow rapids where trout lilies and dogwood crowded the riverbank. The lazy buzz of cicadas filled the air. If Liam were here, I was sure he could identify every living thing in the valley. I stopped again for a drink by a half-rotten cedar, then retreated further into the underbrush to relieve myself.

I'd finished my business and was just about to leave, when a flash of colour caught my eye. Through the green branches, I spied a man at the river's edge in a riding helmet. I recognized the tattoo across his broad shoulders, REBEL HEART. It was Trevor Fang. I was about to call out when I realized he wasn't alone. Another man was kneeling in front of him. As I watched, he pulled Fang's shorts down around his ankles. Fang kicked them aside, and gripped his companion's head, pulling him close. Then I backed away as discreetly as I could.

I got on my bike and rode on. After five minutes, I slowed and stopped. A rabbit hopped across my path. I turned around and headed back the way I came. When I approached the cedar, I spotted Fang and his companion sitting on the grass, sharing a tallboy.

"Yo, Dan-the-Man!" Fang called out as I flew by at high speed.

I braked and swung back around. "Hey, Fang."

"I thought it was you. You're looking fit."

"You too."

Trevor Fang was looking fit, his cycling shorts hugging his hips. He always was the poster boy gym bunny.

"Daniel, this is Jonathan."

I took off my sunglasses and mopped my face with the bottom of my T-shirt. "Hey."

"Jonathan, Dan-the-Man."

Jonathan smiled up at me, shading his eyes. He was a pale, curly-haired boy with angelic features (what David would call a Botticelli face), the opposite of Fang in every way. The kid might've been nineteen or twenty, wearing a pink tank top and flip-flops. Two expensive-looking road bikes lay next to them. Jonathan held out the tallboy.

"You wanna sip?"

"No, thanks. I'm good."

Fang shook his head. "Daniel." He reached into a cooler pack and lobbed me a beer which I fumbled and almost dropped. "C'mon, take a break. You know you want to." He slapped the ground between them.

The can was ice cold. "Alright." I dismounted and sat down. "Thanks."

Jonathan finished his beer and the three of us shared the one I had. Two crew-cut women in Birkenstocks hiked past, red-faced with legs like tree stumps, each with their own lethal-looking pair of walking sticks. Eventually, I asked: "So how's Marcus doing these days?"

"I dunno," Fang said. "I don't think he's seeing anyone, if that's what you're wondering. But I haven't talked to him in a while."

"Oh?" I plucked a blade of grass. Secretly, I resented Fang's assumption, even if it was true. I wondered if the two had had a falling out.

"Well, I was in New York all of June," Fang said.

"What were you doing in New York?"

"DJing, helping to produce a friend's music video."

"That's cool."

Fang was a lot older than Marcus or me. For some years now, he'd been slumming it in Toronto on his Hong Kong parents' trust fund. I also knew that his favourite ice cream flavour was tiger tail, his grandfather was a centenarian, and that he liked having his nipples and balls played with during sex. I wondered if, by the riverbank, Jonathan knew to play with his nipples and balls.

"That's new." Fang nodded at my tattoo.

"Is that your girlfriend?" Jonathan asked.

"No. This." I pulled the sleeve of my T-shirt up higher. "This is my grandmother."

"She's really pretty."

"Pretty rockin'," Fang said.

A red-tailed hawk circled far overhead. "So, Fang, how's your grandfather doing?"

"He died last spring."

"Oh shit. I'm sorry to hear that."

"Yeah."

"He was like over a hundred, right?"

"He was one-hundred-and-four."

Jonathan sat up cross-legged. "No kidding?"

"That's a long life."

"It was." Fang handed me the beer. "Jonathan, I think you're starting to burn."

"Uh oh. I think I am."

"Here." I rummaged in my bike pack. "I have some sunblock."

"Gee, thanks." Jonathan pulled off his tank-top and turned his back to me.

"What are you looking at me for?" Fang said.

"You need any?" I asked.

Fang's thick torso and limbs were dark golden-brown. "Does it look like I need any?"

"Just asking."

As casually as I could, I applied sunblock to Jonathan's pink shoulders.

"Trevor," Jonathan said, "you've never told me about your grandfather."

"He was a wise old man, Jonathan. You would've liked him. He used to fix watches for a living. He was also a musician, and an inventor."

"Neat. What did he invent?"

"Nothing to make him rich or famous. But he liked making things with his hands."

"Me too."

"Now his grandfather," Fang said, "was the first person in his village to own a bicycle."

"Let me think. That's your great-great-grandfather, right?"

"That's right. All the villagers came out to see this strange, new-fangled machine. He sat my grandfather on the handlebars and they rode around like rock stars. All the villagers were just amazed by it."

"That's funny."

"Pretty much everything's amazing, Jonathan, if you've never experienced it before."

"That's true, I guess. I've never thought about it that way."

"Take tacos, for instance. I didn't have my first taco until I was half-way through university. I still remember the first time I tried one."

"How was it?"

"It was amazing."

"Was it delicious?"

"It was amazing delicious, just like you, Jonathan."

"Done," I said.

Jonathan turned around to face me, wiggled himself closer and extended his arms. "Trevor, when was the last time you were amazed?"

"The last time I was amazed?" Fang scratched the back of his head. "I'll have to think about that."

I squirted sunblock onto Jonathan's forearms. A flock of red-winged blackbirds settled into the nearby shade.

Jonathan regarded Fang expectantly. I rubbed the lotion into Jonathan's arms.

"I suppose," Fang said, "the last time I was amazed was when you and I first had sex. You were beautiful. You know that, right?"

"I didn't know that," Jonathan said.

"Well, you were. Your ass was beautiful. I loved fucking it. It felt amazing."

"Thank you."

"So, Daniel," Fang said, "do you think Jonathan's beautiful?"

I was massaging the lotion into Jonathan's hands now. First the right, and then the left. There was dirt under his fingernails. I was surprised at how callused his palms were. I regarded Jonathan's Botticelli face.

"Sure," I said. "Yeah. He's beautiful."

"His ass is amazing. Would you ever want to fuck Jonathan's ass?" Overhead, the sun was relentless. All the clouds in the sky had disappeared. "Daniel, I think I'd like to watch you fuck his ass." Jonathan smiled and blushed.

"Jonathan," Fang said, seeing that I was obviously at a loss for words, "would you like Daniel to fuck your beautiful ass?"

Jonathan held both my hands in his and looked me in the eyes. "Only," he said, "if all the villagers can come out and watch."

"We can serve them all tacos," I said.

"Wow," Jonathan said, grinning from ear to ear. "That would be amazing."

"I think so," I said.

Jonathan laughed. I passed him the bottle of sunblock.

"Don't forget to do the tops of your feet," Fang said, "and your ears."

"Yes, Trevor."

"Daniel." Fang held out the tallboy.

"No thanks."

"Suit yourself." He drained the can and crushed it in one hand.

"Is there any more?" Jonathan asked.

Fang shook his head. "No, Jonathan, I only brought the two. You know that."

The boy looked crestfallen.

"Hey." I drew a breath. "Look, thanks for sharing." I cleared my throat. "I've got some water if anyone …" Both of them regarded me blankly. A bumblebee, laden with pollen, droned past. After a minute, I got up. "Well, I should be heading off."

Fang stretched out his legs, leaned back on his elbows, and squinted up at me. "Daniel, you've got a hard-on. Look, why don't the three of us take our bikes and go down by the river."

"Yeah, Fang, now that you point it out, I guess I do." I thrust my hand into my shorts and adjusted myself. "I'm going now. Seriously, thanks for the beer."

"Jonathan, did you know Daniel pre-cums more than anyone I know?"

"Really?"

"Really, he does. He's like this pre-cum machine. That's a spot on his shorts right there, if I'm not mistaken. How would you like to taste Daniel's sweet pre-cum?"

"Fang," I said, "we're done here. I'm leaving."

"That's right, I forgot. You have a boyfriend. What's his name?"

"It's David."

"And where is David?"

"Right now, he's in Italy."

"Your boyfriend lives in Italy?" Jonathan asked.

"No, he's just visiting with his mom."

"His mom lives in Italy?"

"No, he and his mom are both from here. The two of them are travelling together. They're visiting relatives in Italy."

"How long are they gone for?"

"Pretty much the whole summer."

"Do you miss him?"

"Yeah, I do."

"They took a plane, right?"

"Yes, they did."

"I've never been on a plane. I'd like to fly on a plane one day."

I rested my hands on my hips and studied the tree line. "You know what, Jonathan?"

"What?"

"I've never been on a plane either."

"Really? Maybe we could fly on a plane together one day."

"Maybe."

He smiled at me. "It'd be amazing."

"Yes, it would be."

"Trevor, when was the last time you went on a plane?"

Fang lay back in the grass and put on a pair of gun-metal Ray-Bans. "When I visited New York."

"And before then?"

"When I flew to Hong Kong for my grandfather's funeral."

"Was that a long fight?"

Fang folded his hands over his stomach. "Yes, it was, Jonathan. It was a very long flight."

"Hong Kong, that's farther away than Italy."

"That's right."

"Daniel, do you want to smoke a joint with us?"

"No thanks. I really should get going."

"Daniel doesn't smoke-up," Fang said. "It makes him sick."

"Is that true?" Jonathan asked.

I nodded.

"Alright. Well, it was nice meeting you." Jonathan held out his hand.

I shook his hand. "It was nice meeting you too."

"Wait." He plucked a dandelion and held it out. "Here. This is for you." He pointed. "You can put it in your bandana."

"Okay." Carefully, I tucked the dandelion over one ear. "How's that?"

Jonathan beamed. "Now you look beautiful. Now you look amazing."

"Fang," I said. "It was nice seeing you."

"Don't be a stranger," Fang said.

"I'm sorry again about your grandfather."

He waved goodbye.

I got on my bike and rode away. When I glanced over my shoulder, Jonathan was bent over a plastic Ziploc in his lap, rolling a joint.

A single white heron crossed the sky. I rounded a bend in the path and cycled on for another ten minutes before pulling over. I carried my bike into the dense bush, found a secluded spot and jacked off. For a long minute, I observed my glistening cum on the tree roots and moss.

After that, I pulled up my shorts, and headed back home.

CHAPTER SIX

The Grand Optimist

On the morning of Parker Kapoor's rooftop party, the sky was overcast and windblown, threatening rain. A silvery-grey veil speckled with seagulls swept across the lake. But by noontime, the clouds thinned and scattered, and the early August sun broke through. In Parker's Art Deco lobby, I provided the password "There's No Place Like Home" to the building concierge, a short, balding gentleman in an emerald blazer. He pointed me in the direction of the brass-framed elevators.

The gathering was a BYOB potluck, but at Parker's request I'd only brought a 26er of Bacardi. I stepped out onto the rooftop, expecting a dozen or so guests. To my shock, there were closer to fifty people milling about, chatting and laughing, cocktails in hand. We were twenty storeys up, and the view was spectacular. I could easily spot the U of T campus to the east and City Hall to the south. The lake between Harbourfront and the Toronto Islands was a sparkling ribbon of blue, stitched with scores of sailboats. Cotton ball clouds tumbled across the sky, and women's summer skirts kept flying up like colourful flags. Parker jogged up to me and exclaimed: "Daniel, isn't it delicious?"

"What?"

"I invited my musical theatre friend Adam, one thing led to another, and now practically the entire ensemble from the Mirvish production of *Mamma Mia!* is here. I honestly can't personally be held responsible if they burst into song. Xavier, Xavier! I want to introduce you to my good friend Daniel." A scruffy-looking teenager in a black T-shirt and baseball cap shook my hand.

"Xavier does the Québécois voiceover work for Ron Weasley in all the Harry Potter movies," Parker said. "How exciting is that? Xavier, please tell your father that Lissa has his mixtape all ready for him." The boy saluted and sauntered off. "Lissa's one of my DJs, the one over there in the fabulous shoes. If you want to know anything going on in Toronto's music scene, she's your go-to-girl. Daniel, walk with me, let me fetch you a drink. My friends Grant and Harvey run a micro-brewery out in Dufferin Grove and they've been stocking the bar all day. Here, try this." Parker plucked a bottle out of a shining tub of ice, uncapped it and stood back expectantly. "It's their signature craft ale."

I read the label. "Beaver Bum?"

"I'm told it has undertones of caramel and mocha, with just a hint of vanilla. Hence, the moniker. Apparently, someone discovered if you pair it with Kyle's sea-salt peanut brittle, the combination is to die for."

"Thanks. Cheers." I handed him the Bacardi. "This is for you. Parker, what are you wearing?"

"Daniel, OMG." Parker clutched the rum as if I'd just

handed him baby Jesus. "Your timing is impeccable. My mojitos are a huge hit but I was just beginning to worry we might run out. What am I wearing? This is a traditional, straight-cut Punjabi kurta. My mother made it for me for my high school graduation. I've worn it twice in my life, this being occasion number two. What do you think?"

"You look great."

"Thank you. Peacock blue was always my favourite. It's just a shade darker than cyan, which of course was Audrey Hepburn's favourite colour. Your boyfriend's brother and his girlfriend are by the buffet table, by the way, over there." He hefted the rum. "Let me spirit this to my mixologist right now."

"Parker, are you okay? Do you need any help with anything?"

"I," Parker said, backing away, "am divinely and utterly okay." A gust of wind sent floral napkins flying into the air. He peeled a sunflower from the side of his cheek and waved enthusiastically. "Enjoy!"

In one corner of the rooftop, a small group of guests gathered by a DJ table, tapping their toes to bright, gambolling jazz. I caught a glimpse of the DJ bent over his turntable and made a point of turning my back. Luke Moretti and Ai Chang Cho were poised over a hummus platter talking with two big girls wearing matching, black-and-white party dresses: one in polka dots, the other in stripes.

"Daniel!" Luke said. "How're you doing? We were starting to wonder if you would make it."

"I know you," the first girl said, pushing her glasses up her nose. "You're the Reluctant Kilt Boy."

"And you," I replied, "are the Lollipop Girl."

"I suppose I was. Very good memory. And how was your Valentine's event?"

"Our outfits were a hit."

"I'm glad to hear that. And is your cute boyfriend with you today?"

"David's travelling in Europe right now."

"How debonair. Well, I am Jen and this is my partner-in-nefarious-crime, Tracey."

Tracey was platinum blonde and Jen was a russet brunette. Otherwise the two might've been sisters. But their ornate, matching wedding rings indicated otherwise. Tracey was wearing a veiled pillbox hat secured with jewelled pins. "You're both designers, right?" I asked.

"We're JT Jewellery," Tracey said. "Borderline Plus carries our whole line."

"I see you've met Luke and Ai Chang."

"Ai Chang," Tracey said, "is a very old friend of ours. Isn't that right, Ai Chang?"

Ai Chang blinked. "Oh yeah, we met minutes ago."

"Reluctant Kilt Boy?" Luke said.

Jen raised one perfectly manicured finger. "Fashion is the armour ..."

"... to survive the reality of everyday life," Tracey concluded.

I wasn't sure what to say. I was wearing jeans and a polo shirt from Mark's Work Warehouse. "Luke's my boyfriend's brother."

"There is," Tracey said, "most definitely a family resemblance."

"Although," Jen said, "I suspect you're the big brother."

"Is it that obvious?" Luke asked.

"Not precisely," Tracey said, leaning in with a studious expression. "But one can always spot the older souls."

"Bill Cunningham," Ai Chang said.

Jen peered over her glasses. "Very good."

"What?" Luke and I said.

Ai Chang folded her arms and pointed. "They just quoted Bill Cunningham."

Jen and Tracey regarded each other, nodded once, and took Ai Chang by the elbows.

"Why don't we leave you two boys for a moment," Jen said. "I think we girls may have a lot to talk about."

"Ai Chang's wearing one of their chokers," Luke said as we watched the two escort her away.

"That's a coincidence."

He poked at the hummus with a carrot stick. "Not really. She's a big fan of designers. She spotted them earlier and introduced herself."

"A big fan?"

"Ai Chang's a fashion maven, it's her life. She's been following their blog for a while. It's not my thing, but I get it. It's what she's passionate about."

"What's with everyone and blogs these days?"

Luke shrugged. "People like telling their stories, and people like reading them. It's a way to connect. It's what social media is all about: contact without intimacy. Personally, I prefer connecting face-to-face." He threw a jab-cross-hook combo.

"And how are you two doing?"

"Ai Chang and me? Great. We're officially back together again. But you figured that out already."

"I'm happy for you guys."

"Thanks. So are we." Luke put on a pair of aviator sunglasses and leaned against a planter, his slicked back hair unruffled by the breeze. He was wearing buffed leather wingtips, his sleeves rolled up, and the top three buttons of his silver shirt undone.

"You look good," I said.

"Thanks." Luke nodded toward the DJ. "He seems popular with the ladies." We both observed the laughing women gathered around the slim, curly-haired man behind the console.

"Yeah," I said. "He's a charmer, alright."

Luke regarded me sidelong. "What's up?"

"I used to date him."

"No kidding."

"It was a long time ago."

"Your friend Parker says he's one of the house DJs at the Drake Hotel."

"Is Sean still doing that? Good for him."

"I think he's looking this way."

I sipped from my beer. "I'll say 'hi' to him later, alright?"

"Remind me," Luke said, "how long have you and my brother been boyfriends?"

"Three years. I moved in with him two years ago."

"And things are good?"

"Yeah, they are. I mean, your mom just thinks I'm David's roommate, right? But that's okay for now. It's not like we're getting married or having kids or anything."

"No such plans?"

"No, not yet."

"That's too bad."

Behind his sunglasses, Luke's expression was unreadable. I asked, mainly to be polite: "What about you and Ai Chang?"

"Definitely, it's in the works. We've been talking about marriage and parenting. We have a plan. All in good time. She's got a lot on her plate right now." He took out a cigarette case. "So, how is David? You hear from the kiddo?"

Now I was definitely taken aback. This was the first time Luke had asked anything about David, specifically.

"Well," I said, "we actually haven't had a chance to talk much. He's only called a couple times. They've been travelling around Sicily doing the tourist thing, but now they're settled back on your grandparents' farm. Your mom's thrilled to be there. David says it's like her whole personality has changed. He's never seen her this happy before."

"Good for her."

"David's been helping out the neighbours with their almond harvest. He's also found a couple broken bicycles he's been fixing up. He's having a good time."

"The Sabatinis."

"What?"

"The neighbours are the Sabatinis. They're really old friends of the family."

"Okay."

Luke slipped a cigarette between his lips. "By the way, I'm going."

"You're leaving?"

"I've been thinking about this a lot. After the shoot tomorrow morning, I'm going to Italy."

"Italy. As in Palermo, Italy?"

"As in, yeah, I'm going to meet up with David and my ma."

"Holy shit. Luke."

"You sound surprised."

"Shouldn't I be?"

"Daniel, c'mon. You've been on my back about this reunion thing ever since I got here."

"On your back?"

"Yeah, going on and on about your grandparents and brothers, and sticking those Palermo pics on the fridge where I had to look at them every day. Christ, you wouldn't fucking let up."

"Those were postcards from David."

"It's all good." Luke lit his cigarette and snapped shut his lighter. "You actually got me thinking. I'm thirty years old already, y'know what I mean? What have I got to be afraid of anymore? I mean, go big or go home, right? Also, Ai Chang, well, she convinced me I was making a huge mistake."

"How'd she do that?"

"See, a few years back, she won this grant to Canada's top fashion school in Vancouver. But she almost didn't go because her family didn't approve."

"But she did go."

"That's right, she went anyway. Her parents still don't get it. They still think she's throwing her life away. Did you know she used to work as a dental hygienist?"

"That's a career change."

"Yeah, I mean, who would've thought? The point is, she took a chance and grabbed life by the balls. So I started thinking, what if she's right? What if not going to Italy turns out to be the biggest chicken shit mistake of my life? I'm good to travel. I changed up all my I.D. long ago. I've worked all my life to be Luke Moretti, y'know what I mean?"

"You're the Boss."

"I am the Boss. So I figured, what the hell."

"You only live once."

"Damn right."

"Your mom left you a ticket?"

"No. But I went ahead and bought one anyway."

"Do they know you're coming?"

"Nope."

"When are you going to tell them?"

"I'm not."

"What do you mean you're not? You're going to crash this family reunion?"

"Well, technically, you can't crash something you're already invited to. But yeah, I'm going to crash this party. If things go south, then I walk away. Then I've got the rest of Europe to explore. Truth is, Ai Chang's busier than ever right now, and I've got the time." Luke rested a finger against my chest. "Don't tell David."

"You like surprising people."

"I've been known to raise a few eyebrows. By the way, we just signed a lease for an apartment. After I come back from Europe, we're moving in together."

"Congratulations."

"Thanks."

"Luke, you know," I said, "some people don't like surprises. A lot of people."

"Does it look like I give a fuck?"

"How's your Italian?"

"*Eccellente. Parlo italiano da quando ero un bambino. Le ragazze lo adorano.*"

"Okay, then."

"Ai Chang loves it when I talk dirty. You wanna know how to say, 'Suck my cock'?" Luke took a drag off his cigarette, rested a hand on my shoulder and drew me close. "*Succhiami il cazzo.*"

When I repeated it, he shook his head. "No, listen. You have to draw out the A, like this. Try again. Not bad. Hey, look at me." He pursed his lips, then grimaced, showing his teeth. "Better. Again. *Succhiami il cazzo.*"

I put down the Beaver Bum and mimicked his gesturing with both my hands, fingertips to thumb. "*Succhiami il cazzo. Succhiami il cazzo!*"

He patted me on the cheek. "*Perfetto.*"

Across the rooftop, Lissa dropped an ABBA track and half the guests burst into song. The wind picked up, upsetting even Luke's pomaded hair. A flock of pigeons blossomed across the sky. Through the crowd, I caught Parker's eye and pointed accusingly. He gesticulated in denial, elbows raised: *It wasn't me!*

But, of course, both of us knew that it was.

∩ "You're telling me," David said, "that Ai Chang's morning photo shoot in our loft turned out to be all trans men modelling underwear?"

"Yeah."

"And Luke didn't warn you?"

"Hold on a sec." I sat up in bed and turned on my

side lamp. It was 2:06 a.m. David was calling from a pay-phone in a supermarket in Palermo, where it was eight in the morning and pouring rain.

"Well, I guess he just didn't think there was anything to warn me about," I said, rubbing the sleep from my eyes. "I mean, this was Ai Chang's latest project, right? She likes to use transgender models. She also likes to photograph them in motion."

"In motion?"

"It's more dynamic, more natural, she says. Jumping around, dancing, doing *parkour*. She showed me her portfolio, it's pretty amazing. She does all her own photography. Except they broke the couch."

"What?"

"They were going at it on the couch and the frame collapsed. Don't worry, no one got hurt."

"Great. I'm glad no one got hurt."

"It did get a little weird at one point."

"Oh?"

"Well, see, Ai Chang had brought this whole assortment of underwear, along with three guys who'd volunteered to model for her."

"And Luke?"

"Yeah, he was also part of the shoot. Anyway, so she was getting them to try on different pairs, right? Just so she could see who looked best in what. And of course all the models were different sizes. So then she got them changing up their, well, you know. At one point, all these packers were lined up on our kitchen table, and a few really realistic looking dildos as well. Then these guys started asking my advice about which ones looked better on them."

"Why you?"

"Well, they figured since I was in med school. I mean, it was really important to them to get a naturalistic look. Don't get me wrong. Ai Chang was really professional about everything."

"I'm sure she was."

"David, are you okay?"

"I'm fine, alright? I'm just sorry Luke pulled this kind of stunt on you."

"Hey David, I didn't mind. Really. I just said it was weird. Weird is not a bad thing. We all had a good time. Ai Chang's boxers were really cool, colourful with all these funky prints. It's like her personality suddenly comes out in her work. It was really amazing seeing her do what she really loves. Luke got coffee and donuts for everyone. The shoot lasted a few hours. Afterwards, Ai Chang took all of us out for lunch at Sneaky Dee's."

"Good for you guys."

"David, there's also something else you should know. Luke told me not to tell you." I drew a breath. "But this is important."

"If you mean him coming to Italy," David said, "he already told me."

"He did?"

"Yah. He pretty much had to. He needed directions and the family's itinerary and everything."

"Then everything's settled?"

"He's on a plane over the Atlantic right now, isn't he?"

"And how," I asked, "are you feeling about all of this?"

"Well, he told me not to tell anyone. So now I'm the one with this secret. I'm not sure what to think of it.

They've got me pretty busy here, helping out getting everything ready."

"Is everything okay?"

"Besides me not speaking Italian, and everyone asking about my sister, and when am I going to get married? Yeah, sure everything's fine."

"What do you tell them about your sister?"

"I tell them what Ma tells them, that Luciana's out west in Vancouver and couldn't make it."

"So what are you going to do when Luke shows up?"

"I don't know, Daniel. I haven't thought that far ahead, okay? All I know is this reunion is way bigger than I thought. There's going to be close to a hundred relatives coming to this thing."

"What? Are you kidding?" I sat up straighter in bed. "Who are all these people?"

"Mostly cousins. A lot of them. Nonno was the youngest of five kids, four of them boys. So the De Lucas are everywhere over here. They're flying in from all over Europe and the States. I had no idea. My aunts are hosting a dozen of us, their neighbours are putting up a contingent at their villa, most are staying in Palermo and Torretta. They've got ninety acres here. The big gathering is this coming long weekend. It's the *Ferragosto*, which is a popular vacation time. They've rented two party tents. Daniel, it's going to be a three-ring-circus."

"Who's in charge of all of this?"

"My cousin Carina. Her ma, my aunt Bianca, is the family genealogist. But Carina's the person who's actually organizing everything."

"And where's Luke going to stay?"

"He says he's going to check into a hostel in Palermo."

"David, do you ever wonder where he gets the money?"

"What do you mean?"

"I mean, Luke pays you back in cash, right? Then he decides to spend the summer in Toronto with his girlfriend. He eats out all the time. Now he decides last minute to buy a plane ticket to Europe, just like that. I'm just wondering, how's the guy actually affording all of this? I mean, I doubt he's made his fortune shucking oysters."

"Luke worked at a boxing gym."

"Precisely."

"So, what are you saying?"

"David, you were the one who thought that money might be stolen."

Three seconds of silence. "I was joking."

"You didn't sound like you were joking."

"Maybe not stolen."

"But?"

"But I never asked him, okay?"

"David, I'm not trying to cause trouble, honest. I've actually really gotten to like the guy. I know you two have a history together. You told me Luke used to deal drugs, right? That's what you told me."

"That was a long time ago. We'd sell pot and M to the rich kids in the neighbourhood. Every school has its supplier, Daniel. Back in my day, it happened to be my big sister, Luciana Moretti, alright?"

"What do you mean 'we'?"

"What?"

"You said, 'We'd sell pot.'"

"I'd help out sometimes. It was no big deal."

"How old were you?"

"Like, in middle school. She'd get me to pick up and deliver packages for her, and sometimes store stuff. She leased me this brand new Stinky 24 just so I could get around."

"Stinky 24?"

"It was a bike, silver-and-black, with a Shimano 1x9 drivetrain and a RockShox 100mm fork. It was sick. I loved that bike. I was a little shredder."

"David, you'd help Luke deal drugs? You were, what, like twelve years old?"

"Daniel."

"Look, I'm not judging."

"It sure as hell sounds like you're judging."

"Well, I'm not."

"Then what?"

"Nothing, alright. Forget it. Like you said, it was a long time ago."

"Yeah, it was."

"Alright."

Silence on the line. Finally, I heard David clear his throat. "Well. I'm sorry I woke you. I just really wanted to call and say hi."

"David. I'm really glad you called. I don't mind. Call anytime, okay? I miss you."

"I miss you too."

"I love you."

I could picture David hunched against the payphone, one arm draped across his knapsack, wearing my old Blue Jays cap which he'd insisted on taking with him. "Wow."

"What is it?"

"You know," he said, "that's the first time you've ever said that to me?"

"I've said 'I love you' lots of times."

"That's the first time you've said it without me saying it first."

"Really?" I drew my knees up to my chest. "Okay. Well, I love you. I'm saying it."

"When was the last time you came?" David asked.

"You're always asking me that." I smiled. "When was the last time you came?"

"I jacked off last night."

"What were you thinking of?"

"You mean what was I fantasizing?"

"Yeah."

"Well, I was fantasizing," David said, "that you and I were having a threesome."

"Oh, is that so? Who with?"

"You really want to talk about this right now?"

"Yeah, I do." My hand slipped inside my underwear. "You woke me up, I'm hearing your voice, and now I'm horny."

"You know," David said, "I'm using a calling card right now."

"I know."

"And I'm in a supermarket in downtown Palermo."

"Is that a problem?"

"Okay, well. Listen. I can tell you, there are five farm-hands who work on my aunts' property. They're all these older men, except for this one younger guy, Antonio."

"Oooh. Antonio."

"He's missing his left arm above the elbow."

"Oh."

"Yeah. He wears a prosthesis with a kind of double hook thing on the end. He's around our age. He's actually really cute. His uncle Nicoli's the boss farmhand. The other day, I walk into the barn and Antonio's hauling bales of hay by himself. It's really hot, but he's in great shape, a lot stronger than he looks, and he's working really fast. His hook's perfect for the job. When he sees me, he takes a break and pulls up his shirt to mop the sweat from his face. His jeans are riding low and it looks like he's not wearing any underwear at all, and I notice his treasure trail goes down to where I can just see the top of his bush. Then he asks me in his broken English if I ever get so horny I just have to jack off right then and there."

"No way. You're making this up."

"Honest to God, I'm telling the truth. This really happened. He tells me how the neighbour's granddaughter has been cock-teasing him all summer, this girl Silvia who's back home from college. So then we get to commiserating. He asks me about Canadian girls, and I tell him they're from all over the world, right? I tell him how they're independent, athletic, and super sexy. That seems to get him excited. He's pacing and adjusting himself while we're talking. He tells me he's been studying English so he can move to America one day. It turns out this guy's never left Sicily and grew up in the village down the road. Then he holds up his fist and starts singing 'California Girls' by the Beach Boys. He's got this amazing voice and I'm totally blown away.

"So I jump in, grab his wrist, and start singing along

with him, and he thinks this is brilliant. It's his favourite song, and he's never met anyone who knew the lyrics. After that, I ask him how to say blow-job in Italian. He doesn't understand so I mime it for him, and he says it's 'pompino.' I ask him when he last had a pompino, and he laughs and actually blushes. But he tells me it's been a while, and I notice he's glancing down at my crotch too. Of course, I've got this massive boner standing so close to this guy in this empty barn with all this sunlight lighting up the hay dust like sparks in the air. I can practically smell the sweat coming off him and the fresh straw on his skin, and bits of it in his hair and on his cheek. Then he looks kinda nervous but asks me if I can maybe do a favour for him, and I say sure. Uh-oh."

In the background, I could hear the sounds of a PA system and rattling grocery carts, sifting across six thousand kilometres of fibre optic cables at the bottom of the Atlantic Ocean. My own underwear was already down around my ankles. "What is it?"

"I think my calling card's about to run out."

"The hell it is! David, finish the story."

"Alright. But don't be upset if we get cut off. So this guy, Antonio, he asks me to help him with his prosthetic. We have to get his T-shirt off of him first. Then there's a leather strap that goes over both his shoulders which he needs me to unbuckle. I discover this thing is a lot heavier than I thought. It's definitely not state-of-the-art, you can tell it's been MacGyvered a million times over. I help him out of it, and he shakes out all this straw and dirt from the inside of it, including a dead moth. It's a huge relief for him. He tells me his uncle got the prosthetic for him second-hand years ago, and it really doesn't fit so well any-more. The stump of his arm's all calloused and chafed, and there's a torn blister just below the base of his neck. When I point this out, he gives me a Band-Aid, and I put it on for him. Half his upper back is covered in old burn scars.

"I ask him how he lost his arm, and he tells me it was in a motorcycle accident five years ago. It wasn't his fault, there was a drunk driver who ran a red light. His mo-ped was completely wrecked, torn right in half. It made the front page of the local newspaper. From the way he's talking, it's obvious he's told this story to a lot of people already.

"For a second he's lost in thought. Then he tells me he was riding with his little sister at the time and that she died in the crash. I'm shocked, and I don't know what to say. He says he still visits her every week in the cemetery close to his home. He's also sorry for the driver's family, because of course they lost a husband and a father. So I assume the driver also died in the accident, right? But Antonio says no, that man was killed six months later in prison.

"He doesn't say anything more after that. I help him back into his arm, and he's able to put his shirt on by himself. Right about then, the other farmhands show up, including his uncle. The old guy starts yelling at him, something along the lines of: 'Why's he sitting on his ass?' And Antonio's yelling back and everyone's waving, but it's all in good humour, and he takes a second to smile at me and says, *grazie*."

Faintly, across the city, I could hear the thin wail of ambulance sirens in the night. "Wow."

"So, I've been hanging out with this Antonio guy," David said. "I mean, he's someone I've gotten to know."

"He sounds interesting."

"Yeah, he is."

"Should I be jealous?"

"What do you think? He says he wants to show me the Capuchin Catacombs in Palermo before I go. Apparently, they've got nine thousand corpses and mummies on display to the public. It's a famous tourist site. That's where, Antonio says, he kissed his first girl."

"I'm not sure whether that's romantic or macabre."

"I'd say opportunistic. He was twelve, on a school trip. He also says if he ever comes to Canada, he wants to meet Avril Lavigne."

"Why Avril Lavigne?"

"He thinks she's really hot."

"Okay. Well. I'm glad you made a friend."

"I suppose I have."

"Does he know you're gay?"

"I don't think so."

"Are you planning on telling him?"

"I dunno. I'm not sure. Are you okay with that?"

"I get it. You don't have to, only if you want to. Would you have sex with him?"

"With Antonio?" David laughed. "Absolutely. But the guy's totally one-hundred percent straight."

"But you fantasize about him."

"Yeah, of course I do. I've fantasized about the three of us. I'm a horny little bastard. I've also fantasized about having a foursome with Sam and Dean Winchester. Listen,

I've really got to go. I've got the van this morning and I have all these errands to run."

"Alright. Well, thanks for calling."

"I'll call again."

"Okay."

Our connection abruptly ended. David's card had run out. I put away my phone and got up to get a drink of water. After that, I turned off the side lamp and lay back down. The sheets on David's side of the bed were cool to the touch. I thought about Antonio's first kiss when he was twelve, how he might've held this girl's hand, inhaling the subtle perfume of her, the blood rushing in his temples as she pressed her lips against his. I imagined his body crushed and torn, splayed on the black asphalt starry with shattered glass, aflame in burning gasoline. I wondered what the Sabatinis' granddaughter really thought of him, this scarred, one-armed farm boy who still loved American music and dreamed of foreign girls. I thought of David and Antonio driving through the hilly countryside into the medieval heart of Palermo, where I waited in a café overlooking the Tyrrhenian Sea. Greeting each other, we'd embrace and kiss, once on each cheek. Then the three of us would visit the Catacombs together, pay our admission, and step out of the sunlight into the cool darkness, descending the earth, our arms draped over each other's shoulders and around each other's waists, the ancient stone beneath our feet worn smooth by lost centuries of passage.

In the resting chambers of the dead, we'd pass the bodies of Capuchin friars and virgin women richly dressed in embroidered clothes, pausing by the chapel of the children, before entering finally the timeless and labyrinthine corridors of men. "*Viva l'Italia*," David would say, the voice of my lover echoing, intimate but also faraway, like the wing beat of a moth crossing an ocean from the far side of the world. "*Viva l'Italia*."

CHAPTER SEVEN

Where Have All the Good People Gone?

O n the day after Pat and Three Dog Run left for Burning Man, I got a text from Charles Ondaatje. He didn't sound well and when I asked him if everything was okay, he said, no it wasn't and that he and Megan had broken off their engagement. Charles met me after my last class and we walked my bike into the Village, ending up on the crowded patio of The Churchmouse and Firkin. It was a warm Friday evening and the neighbourhood was bustling with tourists and locals. Across Maitland Street, beneath an expansive maple tree, a drag queen in a sparkling pantsuit shared a smoke with two shirtless dancers from Flash, a private men's club. An elderly couple strolled past walking a Jackapoo, pausing to read the menu posted in a nearby restaurant window.

Charles appeared oblivious to our surroundings. He sipped from his Guinness, looking morose. His black bean veggie burger had arrived ten minutes ago, but he hadn't taken more than one bite. His big frame was slumped over and his large arms draped in his lap.

"She thinks I'm having an affair," Charles said, "with the Duchess of Grey."

A sparrow landed on our table for a second before flitting away.

"And who is that?"

"A woman I've been interviewing for my doctoral research." Charles sighed. "I've never even met the Duchess! I can't believe this is happening."

"Is she really a Duchess?"

"She's a madam famous for her sex parties. I was telling Megan about my latest interview and she accused me of cheating on her."

"Charles, if you've never even met this woman, it's obviously just some big misunderstanding."

"I'm not so sure it is."

"What do you mean?"

"Well, at first, of course, I refuted Megan's accusations. The Duchess lives in Sussex, England. We've been conducting our sessions by Skype."

"Does Megan know this?"

"Of course, she does. But you know how Megan and I have been exploring our sex life by including other people?"

"Sure."

"Well, we have rules, arrangements we've agreed upon. It's important for maintaining trust and fidelity."

"Okay."

"Well, the Duchess and I began corresponding just after Valentine's Day. In hindsight, Daniel, I think there might have been a few indiscretions."

My eyebrows rose. "Charles, you've been interviewing this woman for six months?" I imagined all the possible permutations of cybersex, especially if Charles and this Duchess had been Skyping in real time.

Charles buried his face in his hands. "I kept telling myself I was interviewing her. I've catalogued all my transcripts. There was just so much material I kept uncovering, I think I could write a whole book about her life. She started as a cabaret singer before becoming a club owner. For decades, she entertained an exclusive clientele: politicians, aristocrats, celebrities. She was the only one Freddie Mercury allowed to call him by his real name. But then she started to ask me questions, personal ones about my own life."

"Charles." I sat back. "How old is this Duchess?"

"She just turned eighty this year, on June second."

"Holy shit."

The waiter paused by our table, one arm loaded with dirty plates. "Can I get you boys another round?"

"No," Charles said.

"Yes," I said.

"Yes, I know," Charles said. "Her birthday falls on International Whores' Day. But that's just a coincidence."

"There's an International Whores' Day?"

"It originated in France. In Germany, it's called, *Hurentag*. In Spanish-speaking countries, it's the *Día Internacional de la Trabajadora Sexual*. The word '*trabajadora*' is feminine of course, since most sex workers have historically been women."

The Flash dancers had finished their smoke and were heading back to work. When the shorter, hairier one winked at me in passing, I blushed and looked away. I'd never actually been in a male strip club. Trevor Fang always insisted that most of the dancers were in fact straight. Apparently, a good quarter of them also had college degrees. Fang often liked to tell the story of how he'd worked briefly as a go-go dancer in Montreal, not because he'd needed the money, but just for the sheer hell of it.

Charles was talking and I realized I hadn't heard a word he'd said, something about the modern sex worker rights movement. "So after they'd barricaded themselves inside for a week," he said, "the police threatened to take away their children. When the regular housewives of Lyon heard about that, they were outraged and many of them actually joined the sex workers in solidarity. Then the police weren't able to tell the difference between one mother and the next."

"So, how did it end?"

"The way it usually does," he said, "in police brutality. They tricked the priest into unlocking a door, broke into the church in full riot gear, beat and arrested all the women. But by then, their protest had made international headlines, and sparked a sex workers movement across Europe and North America. You might think of the Church of Saint-Nizier as their Stonewall Inn. The Duchess remembers precisely when she heard the news. That same year, she helped form the English Collective of Prostitutes."

"The Duchess was a prostitute?"

"Oh no! One would never call her that. She preferred the term courtesan. Then she was a dominatrix, holding ceremonies for special guests by invitation only. Officially, she's retired now. But she still regularly receives proposals. You'd be surprised."

"Proposals? From whom?"

"The Duchess of Grey is legendary. Even now she keeps an inner circle, a coterie of admirers, men and women. But she insists she hasn't accepted money for years, not since Thatcher became Prime Minister."

"Really?"

"She says if someone pays, then they are in charge. The Duchess needs to remain free. It's important to her that everyone involved knows that she does what she does now strictly for her own pleasure."

"Right on."

"Daniel." Charles leaned forwards. "The Duchess rarely grants interviews. But her mind is as sharp as ever. She's the most intelligent and knowledgeable woman I've ever met in my life. She's invited me to visit her."

"You're kidding."

"And my fiancée too, of course. Which is the main reason I brought up the Duchess of Grey with Megan. I thought she'd be pleased. Of course, we could never afford to travel to England. But you'd suppose one would be flattered, right?"

"But Megan wasn't flattered."

"No, she wasn't. Honestly, I never saw this coming. She accused me of having an emotional affair."

I thought of all my cake outings with Nadia. "And you think …"

"I know I am guilty, Daniel. In hindsight, I realize what I've done. I do take full responsibility. I expressed remorse to Megan, I did. I said I'd break off my relations with the Duchess immediately. I even said I'd remove any reference to her from my research. But she still had me sleep on the couch last night. This morning, I sent a dozen roses to Megan at work, but I haven't heard from her. I don't know what more I can do."

Charles' face was puffy and red. It looked like he hadn't slept at all. "You said the Duchess had started asking you personal questions?"

Charles nodded. "At first she was just inquiring about Canadian society, our attitudes toward sex, the BDSM culture here in Toronto." He blew his nose, folded the napkin and set it aside. "But then she started asking about my own social circle, details of my own sexual proclivities."

"Ah. I can see how that might upset Megan."

"Yes, I told her about my relationship with Megan, our toys, the little role-plays we'd script, other couples we've met. Once, when I mentioned how our neighbours had complained about the noise, she offered the most brilliant exposition on cross-species female copulatory vocalizations. I told her how Megan and I first met, at a dinner party you and Karen hosted. I told her about you."

"Why would you mention me?"

"Early on, during our tea-talks, she'd asked if I'd ever had relations with a man."

"During your what?"

"Oh, every Friday at noon, we'd meet for tea over Skype." Charles' face softened. "I could always see the dusk seaside behind her, and hear the gulls crying. We'd take exactly two cups of Fujian white tea with just a drop of honey. She insisted I have the same and instructed me precisely on the proper method of brewing. The Duchess would call these meetings our tea-talks. They made quite an impression on me."

"I get it. So what did you tell her about me?"

"Just that we used to date. That you were pleasant to be with and that the sex was adequate. But that I needed something more."

"Okay." I'd gotten used to Charles' detached, analytical manner long ago, or so I thought. I folded my arms. The truth was, my relationship with Charles had always been too comfortable and safe. If he hadn't left me for Megan, I would've ended it myself. This was before he'd gotten involved in BDSM.

"I told her how your boyfriend has a transgender brother."

I unfolded my arms. "You told this woman about Luke?"

"She wanted to know who else I was speaking with as part of my research. At the time, Luke Moretti was my most recent interview. She was quite intrigued."

"Hold on a second. Charles, you've interviewed David's brother? How do you even know Luke?"

"We all met New Year's Eve, remember? Luke and I talked for quite some time. He even bought me a beer. After that, I asked if I could interview him."

"Why Luke?"

"I was interested in his perspective as a trans man." Charles straightened, looking alarmed. "Daniel, you do know he's transgender, don't you? Luke told me you knew."

"Of course, I know that." I looked for my drink but it was nowhere in sight. "What did you talk about?"

"Masculinity, male privilege, sex toys. Oyster shucking.

At first I thought he was employing a thinly-veiled metaphor, but then, after ten minutes, I realized he literally was talking about oyster shucking. Did you know Luke Moretti was the Fanny Bay Oyster Shucking Champion two years running?"

"No, I didn't know that."

"After that, he suggested I interview his girlfriend, Ai Chang Cho."

"Why would he want to interview Ai Chang?"

"She's a costume designer for the National Ballet of Canada. You knew that, didn't you?"

"Yes, Charles. What's your point?"

"He thought I might find interesting her insights on the culture of ballet and body dysphoria. He was quite right about that."

"Charles." I leaned back and picked at a remnant of a sweet potato fry on my plate. "How come you've never asked to interview me?"

"Well." Charles rested his hands in his lap. "Well, you know I have been conducting ethnographic research on sexual and gender diversity for some time now."

"Yeah."

"And it's been important for me to secure as broad a sample size as I can."

"Okay."

"Well. My impression, Daniel, has always been that you are rather normative."

"Normative?"

"Establishing, relating to, or deriving from a standard or norm, especially of behaviour."

"I know what normative means, Charles. You don't have to spell it out for me."

"Most people's behaviour is normative, Daniel. There's no judgment here whatsoever."

I smiled tightly and nodded, just as the waiter brought my drink. Of course, deep down, I knew the mortifying truth: normative equalled "boring." I might as well have had a rusted neon sign blinking over my head: B-O-R-I-N-G. When I'd been with Marcus and Fang, I was sure they both thought I was boring. They never said it outright, but I knew it was what they were thinking. I'd never been a go-go dancer or a music video producer or a burlesque performer or best pals with Sook-Yin Lee on national radio. I was perpetually-exhausted med student Daniel Garneau, neck-deep in debt, who wore a mouth guard at night and orthotics in his shoes.

On the day we broke up, Marcus had described me as, "simple, like a glass of water." I'd heard it as a put-down, spoken calmly, even lovingly. In fact, Charles was the one who'd actually introduced me to Marcus Wittenbrink Jr., having already interviewed *him* for his doctoral thesis years ago.

"Look, Charles." I drew a deep breath and focused on the soggy black bean burger on his plate. "Were you ever trying to keep anything secret from Megan?"

"What? No, never."

"Did you ever talk badly about her?"

"To the Duchess? No! On the contrary. Megan's beautiful, she's wonderful. I'd tell the Duchess all the time about how wonderful she was. Megan's the best thing that's ever happened to me. She truly is. I know we've had our difficult moments, but our relationship is better than ever. At least until yesterday."

"Well, then. I really don't think you did anything wrong. I mean, when it comes to this Duchess of Grey, it sounds like you've just made a really good friend. You're allowed to have friends, Charles. You're allowed to be intimate with others. Megan only wants to be close to you. She loves you. I think she just got jealous of how passionate you are about your work. Your work brings you into contact with some really interesting, sexy people, right? I think maybe part of her was just feeling threatened."

"I never thought of it that way."

"I know, Charles, you're crazy in love with Megan. Megan's smart. She'll understand this. She just needs some time."

Charles' face tightened. "Do you really think so?" His phone buzzed and he took it out. "It's Megan," he said, head bowed. "She's just texted me."

I waited five minutes while Charles sat hunched in his chair exchanging texts. I observed how his ears were like jumbo pasta shells, and that his hair was starting to thin on the top on his head. Once, I'd thought of Charles as having all the sex appeal of IKEA furniture. But now I saw him more deeply than that. I wanted to get up and give him a hug. Finally he set down the phone.

I peered at him. "And?"

When Charles looked up, tears had welled in his red-rimmed eyes. "She said she loved the flowers."

"That's a start."

"And she apologized. She said she'd gone over the transcripts I'd given her."

"Your interviews with the Duchess of Grey?"

Charles nodded.

"Okay. And?"

"And she just realized the Duchess is older than her grandmother."

"Megan didn't know that before?"

"I guess not."

"Seriously?"

"I don't think I ever mentioned it." Charles blinked owlishly. "It never came up."

"Charles."

"She says she feels like a complete fool."

"Charles."

"Yes, Daniel?"

I compressed my lips. Finally, all I said was: "This is good. This is good, right?" The sparrow had returned, perched on the patio railing, observing us with one sharp, bright eye. "You two are going to be okay."

"She wants me to come home. I think I'm going to go home now."

"I think that's a good idea."

"You haven't finished your drink."

"That's alright. You should head home. I'll settle up here."

Charles took out his wallet and handed me a bill. "Is this enough?"

"Plenty."

"Thank you, Daniel."

"Go. Megan's waiting for you."

Without another word, Charles got up and walked away. Halfway down the street, he broke into a run. He rounded the corner and was gone.

A flock of sparrows settled in the nearby maple tree. Often, I'd wondered if I was having an emotional affair with Nadia. David joked about it. I'd told Nadia things over cake I wouldn't think to tell Karen or David. Nadia was classy and beautiful. I dressed up for her and liked being seen in her company. More than once, we'd been mistaken for a straight couple, and some small, secret part of me enjoyed it. I knew if Karen ever became close with another gay man, I'd be jealous. Hell, I was jealous of Bob for replacing my brother Liam as her boyfriend. Of course, David didn't count. I wanted Karen and David to be friends, for the same reason Karen wanted me to like Bob. David's family reunion in Italy was just about to start. Luke would've arrived in Palermo by now. I considered ordering another drink.

"Charles is lucky," someone behind me said. I turned, squinting at a figure sitting alone at a high-top table. Closing his silver laptop, he stepped off his stool and picked up a glass of pale, white wine. "To have you as a friend." He rested his fingertips on my shoulder. "Fang tells me he bumped into you. May I?"

When I didn't say anything, he eased into the chair Charles had vacated, set down his glass and rested both palms on the tabletop. The warm sunshine bathed his face, illuminating the flecks of gold in his hazel eyes. He regarded me thoughtfully, with a kind of shy bravado, the way a magician might modestly perform some inexplicable sleight of hand. "It is good to see you, Daniel," he said. "You look well."

"So do you, Marcus. So do you."

∽ The first time I'd let Marcus fuck me was on our very first date. I hadn't meant for it to happen, and I hadn't been prepared for it. It wasn't because I was against sex on a first date (I'd had enough casual hook-ups by that time to blow that ideal to smithereens), but in hindsight, I supposed it never occurred to me that someone like Marcus Wittenbrink Jr. might conceivably be attracted to someone like me. The only reason I had asked him out was because Karen made me promise I would. Even after he'd taken up my offer to meet for a drink, I was convinced it was out of boredom or pity or a sense of humour. Later, I found out he'd been a sickly, eccentric child growing up. During high school, Marwa had been his only friend. Now Marcus was an award-winning multimedia artist, poet and performer. Like the Duchess of Grey, he was surrounded by a coterie of admirers, men and women from every walk of life. Marwa called him Max, King of All Wild Things.

For our first official date, Marcus suggested meeting Saturday night at the Green Room in the Annex. I was twenty years old and had been in Toronto two years. It took a while for me to find the dark entranceway, tucked away out of sight in a graffiti-stained back alley just east of Honest Ed's. The candle-lit interior was cluttered with mismatched tables and chairs, colourful couches, and rustic chandeliers. Bookshelves and artwork adorned the walls. Pierced and bespectacled students lounged in noisy packs, The New Pornographers playing in the background. I spotted Marcus at the bar wearing a burgundy dinner jacket, chatting with a slim, pale guy with a receding hairline whom he introduced as Will.

"Will's throwing a party later," Marcus said. "Just around the corner."

Will's thin brown hair was spiked up and he was wearing eyeliner and glitter. He hefted a heavy canvas army-issue knapsack, kissed Marcus on the lips, and smiled at me. "Nice to meet you, Daniel." He squeezed my arm, backing away. "You should come to my party." He handed me a black-and-white flyer before vanishing down the stairs.

Gay men kissed on the lips, I reminded myself. It didn't mean anything.

"Sorry I'm late," I said. "I had a hard time finding this place."

"It was always kind of a secret hangout," Marcus said, looking around with an expression that was simultaneously affectionate and aloof. "When I first moved to Toronto, I used to love coming here. Daniel, I took the liberty of ordering us a pitcher of white sangria. I hope that's alright."

If I had to pick a favourite hangout for Karen and myself, I supposed it would've been Sneaky Dee's. I had no idea what sangria was. I shrugged, trying to look casual. "Sounds great."

In the half-hour it took us to finish the sangria (which turned out to be the most delicious drink I'd ever had in my entire life), three separate people paused to greet

Marcus in passing. Without needing to be prompted, I ordered a second pitcher. Later we found a small wobbly table for two with worn velvet chairs and Marcus ordered the avocado salad and veggie rolls. My vermicelli with lemongrass pork came with a crispy spring roll on top. This was exotic fare for me, and I did my best with the chopsticks I'd been given. "Here," Marcus said, after watching me struggle. "Like this." He reached over and took my hand in both of his. His touch was electrifying. Carefully, with the precision of a jeweller, he repositioned my fingers and the angle of my wrist. "Better?" I was conscious of how we were two guys sitting together on what was obviously a date. "Now try." After a few more minutes of coaching, I did get better at it. After a third pitcher of sangria, I really didn't care anymore what anyone thought of us.

The Green Room was packed by then, and we had to lean into each other to be heard. I couldn't actually remember what we talked about, except that, to my surprise, I didn't feel at all nervous. Marcus was like the handsome, charming game show host who put an arm around your shoulder, guiding you along every step of the way, making you feel right at home in the dazzling spotlight. Toward the end of our meal, I poked at the flyer Will had given me. "We should go to this," I said. "It's a party, right? You said your friend lives close by?"

"Well." Marcus sat back, wiping his mouth with a napkin, and draped one knee over the other. "It is just around the corner."

I downed the last of the sangria and studied the scrap of paper. "Vazaleen. That's the name of his party? What kind of a name is that?"

"He used to spell it Vaseline, like the petroleum jelly. But then lawyers from Unilever came after him and he was obliged to change the name."

"Unilever?"

"That's the company that makes Vaseline."

I'd imagined gathering in a student apartment with someone's scratchy mixtape playing on a boombox. Maybe we'd all hang out on the fire escape, or play drinking games in the living room, or Truth or Dare (which I'd reluctantly join only after some cheerful cajoling by my newfound, super-cool best friends). That would be fun. "How big," I asked, "is this party?"

Marcus smiled. "You'll see."

⌒ Saturday night. It was the *Ferragosto* in Italy and David's family reunion was in full swing. In Toronto in our loft, I sat alone on our broken couch in the half-dark, finishing a lukewarm beer. I hadn't heard from David, but he'd told me already he probably wouldn't be in touch until the whole thing was over. Pat and his band were somewhere in the Midwest by now, road-tripping in a Winnebago across America to Burning Man. Liam was either on Manitoulin Island or up at our family cottage. Bumping into Marcus yesterday was a bit of a shock, although I couldn't really say why. Maybe it was because in that moment I was feeling particularly lonely or horny or inadequate or all of the above. We hadn't talked long. Marcus was meeting his stage manager to discuss final details of his new show which had been in development for over a year. It was already slotted as the Mainstage

Season premiere for Buddies in Bad Times Theatre's new program.

"Congratulations," I'd said. "What's it called?"

"*Face.*"

I tried not to look confused. But Marcus knew me too well.

"Just *Face*. As in, giving face, or in-your-face, or turn-to-face. *Face.*"

After that, Marcus's stage manager showed up and we parted ways. Marcus gave me a hug and a kiss. I reminded myself it didn't mean anything. I tasted white wine on his lips.

Before he left for Italy, David and I agreed it'd be okay if we fooled around with other people. Still, I hadn't been about to go cruising for a hook-up the moment he left. I'd told Karen we were monogamish. But after seven weeks, I was starting to get tired of surfing porn on the Internet. I'd cycled away that day in the Don Valley because Trevor Fang was too close to Marcus. Fang had also annoyed me, the way he'd talked in front of that kid Jonathan, even though I knew it was pretty much the way Fang talked all the time. Jonathan also hadn't been my type, although that thought just made me feel shallow as hell.

I finished my beer, got up and tossed the can in our recycling bin. In the washroom, the toilet flushed. A moment later, Sean the DJ walked out.

He was naked and so was I, expect for my socks.

"Hey," he said.

"Hey," I replied.

"Romeo and Juliet." He pointed back into the washroom. "You a fan of William Shakespeare?"

"No. That's just my boyfriend's print."

"Is he an actor or something?"

"No, he's not an actor. He's a mechanic."

"That's hot."

"Yeah." I massaged the back of my neck. "I suppose it is."

Sean was about David's height but thinner, his body pale like cream, speckled with tiny brown moles, the bones of his wrists and hips standing out in sharp relief. Before Parker's rooftop party, I hadn't seen Sean in five years. The truth was we'd dated only briefly for about a month. When Sean showed up tonight, he'd wanted to bottom. But that was off limits. Instead, we took turns blowing each other on the couch. His uncut dick was bigger than David's. It was different and strange having it in my mouth. The inside of his thighs smelled like cut grass. In the end, Sean had jerked me off. After that, he got himself off. As a courtesy, using spit for lube, I slipped my finger inside of him just as he was getting close. Then he made a kind of strained wailing sound, and almost shot himself in the eye. Later, I remarked on the cum on his cheek the way one might point out spinach in someone's teeth. At no point did I invite him to the bedroom. That bed belonged to David and me.

"Here." I handed him his underwear and put on my own. I considered offering him a second beer, but that would just mean more small talk. I sat on the arm of the couch, watching as he put on his clothes. Corduroy pants, a rose-patterned belt buckle. Electric blue tank-top. "Thanks for coming over."

"Yeah." He nodded, tying his shoes. Purple Vans. No

socks. A leather bracelet with a Celtic medallion. "It was nice. I'm glad you texted."

He still spoke with a faint Dublin accent. You'd think after twenty years in Canada he'd have lost it by now. I handed him his grey flat cap.

"Thanks." Sean straightened and regarded me with his big seal pup eyes. "Your mechanic boyfriend, he's back in a week?"

"In six days."

"How long have you been together?"

"A little over three years now."

He looked past me. "It's a nice place you have here."

"Thanks. It's his."

"He fixes bicycles?"

"He works in a bike shop. He just got promoted to assistant manager."

"You two pretty serious?"

"Yeah, we are."

"Well, Danny. Good for you. I'm glad for you."

He picked up my T-shirt. "You know," he said, "every time I have a gin and tonic, I still think of you. Do you remember, from our first date at the Poetry Jazz Café?"

"That was our second date."

"I believe you're right. You loved jazz."

I didn't love jazz. I was just in love with the idea of being in love. Sean of all people should've understood that.

His face was earnest, his lips parted. There was a time when I thought Sean was the most beautiful boy in the world.. He'd taken care of himself and he looked better than ever. But he was the one who'd ghosted me. I heard later he was a playboy who strung along half-a-dozen guys at any time.

"That," I said, "was a long time ago." I took my T-shirt back from him.

"That it was." The wrinkles showed around his eyes. "I guess I better be going."

"I guess so."

"Okay, then."

We hugged and I patted him on the back.

Gently, he bit my ear lobe. "Take care."

"Yeah," I said, pushing him away, without making it seem too obvious. "You too."

"You should come by the Drake sometime."

"Sure."

"I'll see you around."

"Okay."

I closed the door and locked it behind him. It wasn't quite midnight yet. I could've asked him to stay for another beer. I rested my hand on the door knob, considering chasing after him, but I was still in my underwear. Then I thought to text him and call him back. But that would've just been pathetic. There'd been a time when I had the hugest crush on Sean. That was before I bumped into his jealous boyfriend. Karen and I had shared a tub of ice cream then too. I peered through the peephole but the hallway was empty.

I imagined myself telling David about what had just happened. If David ever hooked up with another guy, I'd want the truth, I'd want to know all the details. We weren't jealous boyfriends. I decided I didn't regret inviting Sean over. Up until that moment, I hadn't been so sure. David and I had stayed monogamous more by accident than anything else. Now that I'd actually had sex with someone else, I didn't feel any different. I didn't feel subversive or delinquent or unfaithful. I still loved David as much as I ever did. Couples managed open relationships all the time, didn't they? Most people just didn't talk about it. Did this mean David and I were officially open now? We'd agreed there'd be no fucking and I'd stuck to that. When Sean came up to me at Parker's party, he'd made a point of telling me he wasn't seeing anyone. Although that was what he'd told me the first time we met. But people change, I figured.

The truth was, even after five years, every time I had a gin and tonic, I did still think of Sean.

But I'd never told that to anyone. Some things you just keep to yourself.

I went to wash my finger.

CHAPTER EIGHT

You Ain't Seen Nothing Yet

On the day David was to fly back to Canada, I received an email from him. His mom had decided to extend her stay and wouldn't accompany him home. Their three-day family reunion had included a seaside excursion, one marriage proposal, a mad truffle hunt, and an apparent heart attack that paramedics pronounced was heartburn. In the end, there'd been four generations in attendance, the youngest being ten days old, and the oldest eighty-three: David's nonno Pasquale De Luca, the last surviving De Luca brother and patriarch of the family. There were also a handful of boyfriends and girlfriends, fiancés and fiancées. The neighbouring Sabatinis were considered honorary family. The farmhands' families had also been invited. All in all, close to one-hundred-and-fifty guests passed through that weekend. Most of the food had been prepared outdoors in a wood-burning oven and on two barbecues. The weather had been magnificent, and the whole affair was a rousing success.

David ended by saying he was boarding his plane in five minutes, and that he was bringing back a surprise.

He hadn't mentioned Luke, and I had to wait another eighteen hours before I could ask him about it.

David was scheduled to arrive at Pearson Airport close to midnight Friday. Our neighbour Liz insisted I borrow her car to pick him up. Liz was a divorced, middle-aged hoarder with a tiny dog named Lucille.

"It's so much nicer now that he has you living with him," she said, when she dropped off her keys. "You know, David used to have all sorts of strange visitors, at all hours of the night. Honestly, I feel so much safer now that you're here."

Lucille crouched in her arms staring at me like a piranha. "Um, I'm glad you think so," I said. "And thanks again for the car."

"Oh, puh-shaw!" Liz flopped one hand, plastic bracelets jangling. "Think nothing of it. After you're back, just slide the keys under my door. You two boys have a good time tonight. I'm sure you have a lot of catching up to do." She poked me in the chest. "Don't let the bed bugs bite!"

Liz's car turned out to be a rusted, lime-green Volkswagen stick shift, that smelled like Pomeranian piss and pot smoke, with a potpourri of candy wrappers and scratch tickets littering the dashboard. An Elvis air freshener dangled from the rearview mirror, and the backseat was stuffed with easels and shoeboxes of old oil paints and tarps.

I'd never taken the Gardiner Expressway to the airport, much less driven a stick shift before. I finally reached my destination in one piece, grinding the gears only about half-a-dozen times, just as David's plane was touching down. It took me another half hour to find parking and make my way to the Arrivals level. Even at this hour, travellers with strollers, briefcases and luggage carts passed by in a never-ending ebb and flow.

I didn't realize how much I'd missed David until I saw him. He emerged with his suitcase in tow, wearing a plain white V-neck and jeans. The Sicilian sun had baked him dark as a nut. His curling hair was tucked behind his ears, and he'd grown a short, untrimmed beard.

I waved until he saw me making my way through the crowd. In the last moments I broke into a jog. When we crashed together, I found myself hugging him as hard as I could. He'd only been gone two months, but his body felt leaner, harder. When I inhaled the smell of him, I imagined knotted wood smoke, fresh-baked olive bread, and rich caked earth. Eventually, it was David who broke away.

"Daniel," he said, wrinkling his nose, "have you been smoking up?"

"What? No! Why on earth are you asking me that? Oh, I think it's Liz's car."

"Who?"

"Liz, from across the hall. She loaned me her car. I think she uses it to hotbox. I drove here tonight."

"You did? Okay. Wow, thanks for doing that. I've really missed you. It's great to see you."

"I've missed you too."

David stepped aside.

"Look, Daniel, there's someone I want you to meet."

Startled, I noticed for the first time the individual hovering a few steps away.

He was a young, wide-eyed guy with thick eyebrows and lashes, and a camera dangling around his neck. He

was sporting an Avril Lavigne concert T-shirt, and a prosthetic arm.

He was also wearing my Blue Jays cap.

David clapped him on the shoulder and drew him
close.

"Hallo!" Antonio exclaimed, tucking my ball cap under
one armpit. He thrust out his hand, grinning from ear to
ear. "You are David's boyfriend. I am Antonio Nicoli
DiAngelo Badalamenti. It is so good to meet you."

⌒ I'd assumed Antonio was going to be sleeping at our
Kensington market loft, like Luke had for a month. But
the arrangement was for him to stay at David's mom's
house in Little Italy. David's aunt Bianca was a midwife
who had helped give birth to Antonio twenty-two years
ago. Antonio's own uncle had worked for David's aunts
even longer than that. Antonio also had a cousin in Baghe-
ria who was childhood best-friends with David's second
cousin's half-sister. Like the Sabatinis, it turned out, this
guy apparently was practically family.

This was all explained to me enthusiastically during
the drive back into the city, Antonio squeezed between
me and David in the passenger seat with Elvis' pineapple-
scented crotch bobbing in his face. As we approached the
city, he kept taking pictures of the Toronto skyline. At one
point, he launched into an *a cappella*, hip-slapping rendition of "Hound Dog." Then it was all I could do to keep
one hand on the wheel and his butt from knocking my
stick shift into reverse.

It was after 2 a.m. by the time we arrived at Mrs. Gallucci's home. This was the house where David had grown up, a Victorian semi-detached with a curving paved walkway flanked by stone lions. David unlocked the stained-glass front door, deactivated the security system, and handed Antonio the keys. The house was in impeccable order, with a gleaming Steinway in the front parlour (where David and I had moved it three years ago), and a gold-framed portrait of Pope Benedict XVI over the china cabinet.

I remembered the first time I'd met Mrs. Gallucci, sitting on the settee while she served us coffee and biscotti. I was covered in fall leaves, having just cleaned out her gutters, and had a hole in my sock which I tried to hide by pinching it between my toes. Her narrowed eyes seemed to see right through me. Of course, I thought, she must know I was fucking her son. When she instructed both of us to stay for lunch, I was sure it was to interrogate me further. After dessert, she pulled out her sewing kit, unsheathed an evil-looking needle, confiscated my sock and stitched it up in two minutes flat.

"Antonio, you'll sleep in the guest room," David said. "That used to be my old bedroom. Here, c'mon, let me show you."

Antonio was already halfway up the stairs like a puppy off its leash. David grabbed Antonio's suitcase and winked at me, before chasing after him.

While David gave Antonio the upstairs tour, I waited self-consciously in the foyer, listening to the ticking of the grandfather clock. With Mrs. Gallucci away, I felt like I was trespassing. I wondered if she had security cameras hidden in the chandeliers.

I observed the framed print of Michelangelo's *David* in the hallway, his threatening expression and tensely muscled torso, his oddly small package.

Standing in this spot, Mrs. Gallucci once explained to me, with her thin arms folded, how the classical Greeks actually preferred small phalluses, how it was the idealized look for the civilized alpha male. Small phalluses were associated with moderation, a key virtue of masculinity. Only those who were undisciplined, vulgar, or grotesque had large penises: old men, drunkards, manbeasts. The Renaissance artists weren't Greek, but their convention for male beauty was classically inspired. Did I know Michelangelo was only twenty-six when he began work on David? No, ma'am, I did not.

I became aware that it was unusually quiet upstairs. I ascended the lower landing and was just about to call out when David's head appeared over the bannister.

"Hey, Daniel," he said, "Antonio wants to celebrate. Can you open a bottle of wine?"

"Where do I find that?"

"Just grab one from the kitchen. And three glasses."

I took off my sneakers. Hesitantly, I ventured down the shadowy hallway. No Doberman Pinscher rounded the corner, nails clicking on the hardwood parquet. No poison darts came shooting out of the wainscoting. When I flicked on the kitchen lights, everything glared at me, polished and spotless, from the copper pots and pans to the wall-mounted knives. I retrieved a bottle of wine from a small rack on the counter, a corkscrew and three glasses.

When I turned around, David was standing in the doorway with Antonio's prosthetic arm in his hands.

"Holy shit," I said.

"Look, I need to find a screwdriver and tighten something up for him," David said, setting the arm on the table (where it sat like some post-apocalyptic steampunk artifact). "I'll meet you guys in two minutes." He started rummaging in the kitchen drawers.

I stood dumbly for a moment, debating whether this was the right time to ask about Luke, or at least crack some lame Edward Scissorhands joke. I didn't think it was. I headed upstairs.

When I arrived at the top landing, I discovered Antonio in his undershirt peeing into the toilet with the washroom door wide open.

"Daniel, Daniel!" he called out, compelling me to pause outside. "All three of us, we will go out tomorrow Saturday night. We will go meet Canadian girls, yes?" He was still pissing vigorously, his dick in his hand. I tried not to stare at the stump of his left arm. I glanced down, just for a second, I couldn't help it. The guy was huge.

"Canadian girls? Um, yeah, definitely."

Antonio bent his knees and shouted: "Avril Lavigne!"

"Avril Lavigne," I said, taken aback.

He shivered, swinging his snake around, shaking off the final drops, before stuffing the monstrosity back in his boxers. "Alanis Morissette!"

"Alanis Morissette," I said.

He flung out his arm. "Celine Dion!"

"Celine!" I said. "Yay, Celine!"

He flushed the toilet. "My heart will go on!"

"I'm sure it will," I said.

"David (pronounced 'Dah-vee-day') says Canadian girls are very beautiful. Daniel, is this true?"

"Yes." I nodded. "Yes it is. It's very true."

"You know, some Canadian girls are Italian girls."

"We come from all over."

"Italian women," he said, gesturing emphatically, "are the most beautiful women in the world."

"I'm sure they are."

"Do you have a girlfriend, Daniel?"

"Do I have a girlfriend?" I blinked, confused. "No, I don't have a girlfriend. I'm with David."

"Yes, you are with David. You are together."

"That's right."

"But do you have a girlfriend to show your momma and papa?"

"My parents died, a long time ago."

"Ah! I am so sorry to hear." He rested his urine-stained hand on my shoulder and peered earnestly into my face. "But you have family, yes?"

"I have two brothers and my grandpa who raised us."

"Do you have a girlfriend to bring home to your two brothers and your grandpa?"

"What? No. No, I don't. They've met David, lots of times. They know he's my boyfriend. I'm out to my whole family."

"Your whole family," Antonio said in a hushed tone, "they know you are *omosessuale*?"

"Yes. My whole family, they know." I opened my arms. "I'm a homosexual. That's me."

"And they are at peace with this?"

"Yep."

Antonio's brow furrowed. "David, he is not at peace with this. He has not told his family."

"Well." I drew a breath and studied the gleaming ceramic tiles. The floor was immaculate. A person could eat off that floor. It was strange to think that someone like David had grown up in a home like this. "We've talked about him coming out to his family."

"Not to his momma or to his brother."

"His brother?"

"His brother. You know his brother?"

The hairs on my arm prickled. "You mean Luke?"

"Luciano, yes. He has not told, I think. But he has told me. I understand why he has not told his brother. Luciano Moretti is a good man, but he is very traditional. I do not think he would understand. You and David are boyfriends, I understand. I am very fine with this. My mind is very open. David, he is like cousin to me. We are *famiglia*. So Daniel, you and I, we are like cousins too, yes?"

"Sure."

Before I could retreat, Antonio launched forward and gave me an impassioned, fraternal hug, his hand between my shoulder blades, pressing his torso hard against me. "I am unbelievable I am in Canada," he exclaimed, stepping back. "I am so happy to be here."

"I'm glad you could visit."

"I wish to eat your poutine."

"What? Oh, okay."

"We will drink your maple tree syrup?"

"For sure."

"We will go see your hockey game?"

"Antonio, you're only here two weeks. The hockey season doesn't start until next month."

"No hockey game?"

"No hockey game."

"Aah."

"But," I said, "we can visit the Hockey Hall of Fame, if you want."

"Yes?"

"And we are going to celebrate."

"Yes!"

David climbed the stairs and looked from one of us to the other. "What's all the shouting?"

I raised the wine bottle in one hand and the three glasses in the other. "We're celebrating."

Tears of joy welled in Antonio's eyes. "Viva Canada!" he cried.

David clapped both of us on the shoulders. "Welcome to Canada."

⌁ On the day Antonio was to fly home, I was genuinely sad to see him go. David and I were able to take some time to show him the city. The three of us went to Wonderland together, and the Toronto Islands. But for someone who'd never travelled outside of Sicily in his life, Antonio was surprisingly skilled at finding his own way around. He went up the CN Tower (taking a selfie jumping on the famous glass floor) and visited the Toronto Zoo (where his favourite animals were the penguins). Toward the end of his stay, he even took a bus on his own and made a day trip to Niagara Falls. His only disappointment came when he discovered Avril Lavigne had moved to Los Angeles and was newly married to the lead singer of Sum 41.

"Now," he said sadly, "she is California Girl."

The day of Antonio's departure, David was tied up at work. But I managed to clear my morning and volunteered to borrow Liz's car and drop him off at the airport. I pulled up to the busy departures terminal and hauled his luggage out of the trunk.

Standing on the curb, Antonio handed me my Blue Jays cap.

"At customs," he said, "David welcomed me to Toronto with your baseball hat. I wear it every day I am here. Thank you. Now I give it back to you."

I took my cap, rumpled and faded, and examined it in my hands. He had worn it every day he was here. Grandpa had bought me this ball cap when he'd taken Pat, Liam and me to a game at the SkyDome on our sixteenth birthday. If Antonio hadn't returned it, I would've asked for it back.

"You're welcome," I said. "Here." I reached into the glove compartment and retrieved a brand-new blue and white Jays cap. "This is for you."

Antonio's eyes widened. I put it on his head for him, squeezed his shoulder and stepped back. "Now you have your own."

After that, Antonio hugged me, kissed me on both cheeks, shouldered his backpack and picked up his luggage.

The truth was, he was starting to miss his family back in Sicily, especially his three-legged dog Pepi. He'd be home just in time for the start of the olive harvest. In a few days, David's mom would be returning to Canada. The summer was all but over.

"Daniel?" Antonio said. "You have never travelled away from Canada?"

"No. I've never had the chance." I shrugged. "I guess I've just been too busy."

"Ah, yes, you are in school. You will be a good doctor one day and you will help others."

I stared into Antonio's face. "Thanks." I wanted to add: med school was expensive, I was perpetually broke, I couldn't afford to travel. But just beneath the surface I knew the truth: I was afraid. I was afraid to leave grandpa, afraid to leave my brothers. What if something happened to them? In Toronto, I was just a few hours' drive from Sudbury. If I went away, who would watch over the family?

"It is a good thing, to travel," he said. "You must try." We observed the taxi cabs and shuttle buses rolling past. "I hope one day you and David will come to Torretta. It is not Toronto. It is very small village in the mountains. But it is my home."

"I'd like that," I said. "One day."

"Now you say to me, '*Bona partuta.*'"

"*Bona partuta.*"

"That is how you say bon voyage!"

"*Bona partuta*, Antonio."

Backing away, Antonio began to sing in a clear, strong tenor, "Leaving on a Jet Plane." I'd never been serenaded before, much less in such a public space. Passers-by stared.

Two teenage girls took photos. Just before vanishing into the terminal, Antonio shouted: "Daniel! I leave gift for you and David. It is inside coffee table." Then he was gone, buoyed away by the endless tide of humanity.

On the drive back down the 427, I managed to grind the gearshift only once. After high school, Pat had spent six months backpacking across Europe. A few years later, Liam drove his Jeep to the west coast and back. When Grandpa was younger, he'd sailed as far as Russia in the Canadian Merchant Navy. I'd yet to even step outside the province.

Back in the loft, I looked inside our dented steamer trunk and found a manila envelope. I debated whether I should wait for David to open it. But the envelope was unsealed, so I slipped out the contents.

It was a thin photo album with a dark blue cover. Since returning home, David had shared with me dozens of stories, facts he'd learned about Sicily, his family, and the farmhouse where his mom had grown up. He'd also shown me hundreds of photographs he'd taken, many of which he'd posted on Facebook. But these were different. Each page held only one 5×7 image, carefully mounted and captioned in thick black ink. For a long time, I sat on the couch, passing from one to the next.

Davide con Tintin e Milu. The first was a photograph of David, sunburnt and squinting in a wide straw hat, his face speckled with points of light. He was holding two baby goats, one under each arm, brown and white, with big floppy ears and dangling little hoofs. Behind him, past a stone cistern, rose his grandparents' two-storey manor, a traditional *masseria*, bordering the banks of a dry stream shaded by a citrus grove. Paths led under ivy-wreathed archways through the vegetable and herb gardens. On the far side of the farmhouse, I could just make out the many rows of olive trees. Here they were three kilometres from the nearest village, and twelve kilometres from the sea. David had told me the farm had been in the family five generations. David's grandparents Pasquale and Sia still lived on the property with two of their daughters, Bianca and Romy, and their granddaughter Carina. Pasquale De Luca had been going deaf and blind now for many years, but every day he still ventured out for his morning walk around the boundaries of the farm.

Davide e Silvia, San Vito Lo Capo. A photograph of David and a girl in a black bikini, posing hip-to-hip on a sand bar, sparkling wet, holding out a crimson pebbled starfish. Someone outside the frame was pointing, a blurry hand with a wedding band. I recognized this girl as the neighbour's granddaughter Silvia Sabatini. She clutched David's shoulder, her eyes dark as almonds, her other hand cupping his wrist. Rose-coloured light washed their half-naked bodies, flinging long shadows across a rocky beach. Silvia had appeared in many of the photos David had taken. The friendship between the De Lucas and the Sabatinis dated back to the Second World War, during which time both their farms had been destroyed and then rebuilt. Silvia's breasts were small like apples, her legs long and her shoulders broad. She might have been a track-and-field athlete, or a mountaineer. As it stood, she'd just completed her final year as a student in the Department of Agriculture and Forestry Science at the University of Palermo.

Davide con Nonna e Nonno. David in the vineyard holding a basket while his grandma Sia cut a bunch of grapes from the vines. Her eyes were hard and bright, deep-rooted in a driftwood face. This woman rarely ever spoke about her past. Hers was a family shrouded in mystery, gossip and precipitous flirtations with scandal. Now days would pass before she might speak aloud at all. She was nineteen when her entire family was killed during the Allied invasion of Sicily. It was a well-known story how a wounded soldier from the 1st Canadian Infantry Division encountered her tending the chickens in the bombed ruins of her father's farmhouse. That soldier was an Italian-Canadian named Pasquale De Luca. After she'd nursed him back to health, he swore he'd return after the war to marry her. When he kept his promise, he was shocked to discover he already had a two-year-old daughter named Isabella. In Biblical times, an unwed mother might have faced death by stoning. Sia managed to keep her firstborn by posing as a war widow, an elaborate and dangerous deception in which the Sabatinis were complicit. It was Sia's own grandfather who had planted the olive trees, but it was her "second" Canadian husband who planted the vineyard. Far in the background, I could see Pasquale De Luca, in round dark glasses and a buttoned vest, walking arm-in-arm with another man with an enormous moustache, Salvatore Sabatini. In the photograph, Salvatore's head was turned, his left hand resting on Pasquale's forearm, his mouth bent intimately to his companion's ear.

Davide con le Zie. David with his two aunts Bianca and Romy in the manor kitchen. Blue ceramic tiles armoured the walls beneath shelves brimming with jars, spices and colourful cookware. The three stood at a wooden table, their faces flushed from the heat, grinding parboiled tomatoes in two food mills. At any moment, zia Bianca, with her heavy-set jaw, unibrow and booming laugh, might serve up espressos thick as crude oil, or grilled swordfish crusted in pistachios, or deep-fried *arancine* stuffed with *ragù*.

As a midwife, she'd helped deliver almost one thousand babies in the course of her career. Not only was she the family genealogist but she was the local historian. It was Bianca who pointed out to David how Palermo was considered by many the most conquered city in the world. "Ours is an island shaped by a dozen cultures over three millennia," she explained. "Sicilians are African, Greek, Arab, European, Italian." She clasped his face in her hands. "It makes us who we are, never forget, this openness to whatever may come our way. As your nonna used to always say: *Vivi e lascia vivere!* Live and let live!" Zia Romy was the younger of the two, soft-spoken, willowy and fair. Fresh basil and onions harvested from her gardens spilled from baskets onto the counter. Romy once was a school teacher, born and raised in the northern heart of Verona. Children were drawn to her like bees to bougainvillea. Eighteen years ago, Romy and Bianca adopted their newborn daughter Carina. But for the last twenty-one years, the pair had shared the same queen bed on the De Luca farm.

Madre e Figli. For many minutes, I studied the face of a woman I knew to be in her sixties, except in this image she looked twenty years younger, barely recognizable, wearing a strapless blouse, her un-pinned hair falling in silver waves about her bare shoulders. She was laughing open-mouthed, her head flung back, her arms around the waists of Luke and David on either side. Each man had a different father, but the family resemblance was still uncanny. Both had their mother's broad mouth and patrician nose, their dark features limned in white gold. I knew this woman as Mrs. Gallucci, but in this photograph she was Isabella De Luca, philosopher and feminist, Officer of the Order of Canada, returned to her childhood home near Palermo by the sea. Many family secrets had been unearthed in the time since her return. Only this summer, she had learned that Pasquale De Luca

was in fact not her stepfather. It took many days
for Isabella to fully understand and accept this
revelation. In the background, glistering dawn
fountained through the century-old olive grove,
casting a lens flare over their heads, three numinous spheres of rainbow light.

I sat back in the couch and closed the album in my lap.
I rested my palms on its cover.

I thought back two weeks to the first night of David's
return. After we'd gotten Antonio settled and parted
ways, I asked David about Luke. He didn't answer right
away, but sat in the passenger seat of Liz's car resting his
arm outside the open window. It was late, the bars and
restaurants had closed long ago and the city streets were
mostly empty. A luminous rain blurred the cool skyline.
Darkened storefronts gleamed beneath the street lamps
and scattered neon signs.

When I glanced at David, he nodded. "He showed
up," he replied. "Like he said he would."

Luke Moretti had in fact joined the De Luca family
reunion hours before David realized he'd even arrived.
David told me how he first spotted Luke Saturday mid-
day grilling beef skewers, a glass of beer in hand, assembling an enormous platter of smoky meat from which
passers-by helped themselves. Two swarthy men, one fat
the other skinny, stood close by smoking cigarettes, observing Luke's technique. As David watched, Fat Man
clapped Luke on the back and sauntered away, while
Thin Man refilled his tumbler. Luke glanced up, caught
David's eye, winked and waved. He pointed at Thin

Man, who was now sampling some breaded veal skewered on the end of an ivory-handled switchblade. "Cousin Vito," Luke shouted across the sun-drenched terrace. He gestured and said something to cousin Vito who nodded in David's direction, displaying a mouthful of crooked gold teeth, and raised his grease-stained knife.

By the time we'd arrived home at our loft the rain was coming down harder and we hurried inside. I hauled David's luggage out of the trunk and carried it ahead of him up the darkened stairwell. After he emerged from a long shower, I towelled him dry and welcomed him back into our bed.

Sex was gratifying and quick. His tongue in my mouth, his lips warm against my stomach, the way his fists gripped my wrists — all of these sensations were familiar to me.

Afterwards, David lay spent with his head resting on my chest. Even now, he kept his side lamp on as if he didn't care yet for darkness to come. Its muted golden glow cast his features in a chiaroscuro light.

This summer, David told me, his brother and his mother did reconcile. Luke himself had little to say on the matter. But it was David's mother who had told him, over a glass of Sangiovese during his last hours in Sicily, the intimate details of that reunion.

Even as David first laid eyes upon Luke, she had felt from afar the presence of her eldest child.

On the opposite side of the farm, while touring a noisy flock of relatives from Dijon through the modest vineyard, Isabella De Luca heard how her son Luciano had been so helpful earlier that morning changing the flat tire on cousin Stefania's husband's Fiat. Later in the day, someone remarked how it was Luciano who had prepared the *involtini alla messinese* and had scored the winning point in the afternoon's bocce tournament. You must mean my son, David, she'd replied. No, no, they meant her eldest boy, Luciano, the stylish one who actually spoke Italian.

Then Isabella put down the potato she was peeling at the kitchen sink. Outside the window, children with sparklers were enjoying a festive birthday celebration. Her niece Carina and others were lighting lanterns illuminating the curving path to the party tents. In that moment, at the farthest edge of the field, she spotted David walking with a strange yet startlingly familiar man. For minutes she stared, long after the two had vanished into the twilit shadows of the olive grove.

Antonio's uncle, Nicoli Badalamenti, who'd been stacking crates of cucumbers in the adjoining pantry, wiped the dirt from his hands and spoke her name, asking what was wrong. Then Isabella turned and regarded Nicoli's broad face as if seeing him for the very first time: this man who'd been her childhood best friend, and the secret, first great love of her life.

"My eldest child, the one I had with Michele Moretti," she said in Sicilian, "has always been a *furbo*."

"Being a *furbo*," Nicoli declared, thrusting one thick finger heavenward, "is not such a bad thing." After that, the half-dozen other women in the large kitchen, chopping eggplants, onions and celery, launched into a fiery discussion of the art of *furbizia*. Within a minute, every person was shouting over the other.

During this melee, Isabella De Luca slipped away unnoticed, still in her apron, still gripping her sharp paring knife. By the glowing tents, Carina called after her, but Isabella was already halfway across the field, walking steadily. Firelight washed her set features, reflecting in her steely eyes. Trembling, she reached the edge of the olive grove. Four figures stood closely, talking among the low, gnarled trees. They turned, one by one, at her approach. Her son David was the first among them, supporting the arm of his nonna Sia, while his nonno Pasquale exchanged words with the strange man.

"Mamma?" Isabella said. "Papa?"

Despite his cataracts and the twilight hour (and the rundown battery in his hearing-aid), Pasquale De Luca perceived his eldest daughter's presence, leaned forward on his cane, and beckoned her closer. "*Bella*," he said, "look who has joined us after all. It's Luciano, all grown up."

For one heartbeat, Isabella saw her second husband Michele before her. She'd often had visions of him since his death, but never so clear or so youthful. But in the next heartbeat, she realized this stranger was slimmer than Michele, and not a vision at all. Michele had been a bull of a man who would haul cement bags on his shoulders two at a time. That man had rudely dropped dead from heart failure, abandoning her to raise a one-year-old child alone. Her third husband Anthony Gallucci couldn't have been more different: a bipolar, self-medicating postdoc who'd accidentally overdosed on a lethal mix of heroin and gin. No one in Isabella's family knew this horrible secret, not even her *lesbica* sister Bianca. She'd told everyone David's father in Toronto had died from an aneurysm in the brain. When Michele's seven-teen-year-old daughter recruited Tony's twelve-year-old son into dealing drugs, it was too much, more than even she could bear. In that singular, terrible moment of Isabella's long and complicated life, she had the strength to save only one of her children.

"Is it," she said, "really you?"

"I've changed, Ma," Luke Moretti said in his grand-parents' olive grove.

"You have," Isabella whispered.

"I'm a different person now."

"Are you?"

"I promise I am."

"Are you ... happy?"

"I am. I'm a lot happier now."

Twelve years had passed since she'd laid eyes on this face. "Luciano."

Luke shrugged. "Or Luke. I prefer Luke."

"You are different."

"You always taught us," he said, "to work hard, to take things into our own hands, to get the job done. That's what I did. I did that. I did everything you asked me to that Christmas Day. I've remade myself. Things are dif-ferent now. Things are better."

"You look like your father."

"Do I?"

"I've missed you so much."

"Well, thank you for the invitation."

"Your brother told me he couldn't find you."

"David and I thought it was for the best, that I should stay away."

"I see."

"I changed my mind. I want … I want to be part of this family again. I'm sorry for everything I put you through."

"I'm sorry too."

"Ma."

"Not a single day has gone by when I haven't thought of you, when I haven't prayed for you."

"Ma"

"I promise."

"Well. I'm back now." Luke drew his knuckles across his cheek. "All grown up."

"But still my child."

'Really, Ma?"

"Yes, Luciano. Always."

"*Vivi e lascia vivere*," Sia De Luca said.

PART II

CHAPTER NINE

Miasmal Smoke &
The Yellow-Bellied Freaks

On the last Thursday of September, while leaving the gym, I noticed Marcus on the cover of *NOW* Magazine and almost rode into a parking meter. I retrieved a copy from its metal box, and walked my bike to a nearby bench, limping only slightly.

It was a special themed issue on communications technologies, spotlighting the world premiere (seriously?) of his one-man-show, *Face*. On the front cover: Marcus crouches naked, his hair spiked up in a mohawk, his war-painted features distorted in a primal scream. He holds an open laptop in front of his crotch, his own blandly surprised face peering from the glowing screen. The headline read: "A View from the Wittenbrink: On Queer-core and the Cyberpunk." The *NOW* writer had attended a preview of *Face*, and was clearly a fan, enthusiastically referencing Marcus's dense CV, and extolling him as the wunderkind *enfant terrible* of Canada's arts and literary scene. The article ended with a quote from *Tales From the Bottom of My Sole,* Marcus's award-winning book of poetry and prose:

Might I be simple
a glass of water
a pane of glass
a drunken satyr
bent leaves of grass.

The words sounded strangely familiar. All the way home, they repeated themselves in my head. When I woke up the next morning, my eyes fell onto my own slim copy of Marcus's book. I retrieved it from the shelf and flipped through the pages until I found the same passage. Only then I remembered where I'd heard these words before. The night we'd broken up, Marcus had quoted his own poem to me. Even in that moment, his art had gotten between us. The title piece was a lengthy ode to stepping into other people's cum in a bathhouse (which he'd later adapted into a short film). Like the mythological Midas, the *NOW* writer gushed, Marcus Wittenbrink Jr. transformed the crudest materials into precious illuminations. As it stood, *Face* was a "vertiginous descent into the nihilism of social media and the contemporary Canadian psyche." I wasn't surprised at all to read the production had a "Sexual Content/Nudity" warning. I would've been surprised if it hadn't.

On our very first date, Marcus had set the tone of our relationship, bringing me to a dance party called Vazaleen. He made it seem like an accident, but in hindsight, I was sure he'd planned it all along. The venue was Lee's Palace, a concert hall up in the Annex, its façade covered by a two-storey mural of bizarre cartoon creatures fornicating, fighting, dancing across a psychedelic landscape. "Yeah, my friend Alex painted that," Marcus remarked as he by-passed the line-up, fist-bumping the bouncer. He reached for my hand. "C'mon. I think you're going to like this."

It was just after midnight when Marcus drew me in. The packed, sweaty space buzzed and vibrated with a carnival atmosphere. Sheets billowed from the ceiling, flickering with kaleidoscopic projections of blurry porn. The floor was a spectacle of hardcore punks and rockers, tattooed dykes, boys wearing underwear and mascara, girls decked out in platform shoes and roller-skates. Someone in a full-body chicken suit pogoed up and down in one corner. A rock 'n' roll band was playing, people climbing on and off the stage, everyone interacting and dancing.

"What is this?" I asked.

"It's where people can be," he said, "as perverted or crazy or queer as they want to be."

"This is your friend Will's party?"

"This party, Daniel, belongs to all of us."

"Is that guy naked?"

"There's always The Naked Guy." Marcus laughed. "But it's not always the same guy. Look, stay right here. I'll get us some drinks."

Marcus vanished before I could think to reply. Colourful spheres glowed over the bar in the back. Two go-go dancers, a black girl and a white boy, joyfully leapt about the stage. A sudden surge in the crowd pulled me down toward the front. Three glittering drag queens stalked past, effusing an aroma of cotton candy, poppers and cloying pot smoke. I half-expected flowers to bloom in their wake out of the stained and pitted hardwood floor. The biggest one stared in my direction.

To my horror, she whispered in her companions' ears, turned back and walked right up to me. "Daniel Garneau," she said in a booming basso.

I was utterly at a loss for words. She adjusted her boobs and her fox stole, then rested both hands on her hips, licking her gleaming upper lip. "You don't recognize me," she said.

"No. Sorry."

"Well. I suppose, I can't say I blame you."

"Really, I don't think we've met."

She lay one finger alongside her enormous, bent nose. "Do you recognize this?" She leaned into my face.

I shook my head.

Her nostrils flared. "The last time we met, Garneau, you broke my nose."

I gawped at him.

"It's been bent ever since."

She arched back. I was vaguely aware that a small group of onlookers had begun to gather. Incredulously, past the glare of sequins and pasty foundation and DIY glamour, I did begin to recognize her. The set of her eyes, the voice, her five-o'clock shadow and the squareness of her jaw. She smiled knowingly, observing the changing expressions on my face.

"Gary Kadlubek?"

She raised her finger. "Tonight, sweetheart, it's Pussy Pierogi."

"Holy shit."

She thrust out her chin and batted her eyelashes. "It's an homage, to my Polish ancestry."

Gary Kadlubek had been the enforcer on my midget

AA hockey team back in Sudbury. He'd also been the head coach's son, and the all-around number one douchebag bully in high school. It'd been years since I heard anything about Gary Kadlubek.

"You," I said, "were an asshole."

Her fierce eyes widened. She straightened, pursing her lips. She plucked a single pink hair off her arm and flicked it aside. "I was."

"You used to steal Ann Fobister's lunch money."

"Who?"

"You got me kicked off the team."

"I guess you and I are even then."

"Even? I was going somewhere! I was going for team captain! Where were you going? What were you going for?"

For two heartbeats, she looked as if I'd just punched her in the face. Again. But there was no blood running down her chin and no one was tackling me to the ice and I wasn't landing blows with my fists like they were sledgehammers because that's what I needed to do when the walls came crashing down and it felt like the end of the world.

Kadlubek (or was it Pussy Pierogi?) drew a breath and rested his hands on his padded hips.

"Look, Garneau. I just have one question."

"What's that?"

"Back in the day, when we were both stuck in that miserable little sweaty armpit of a town, did you ever fuck around with that assistant coach, the new guy, Tondeur? Truth."

Stephan Tondeur. Real estate agent. Doting husband and new father. That beautiful man who'd been the spitting image of Justin Trudeau. I'd lost track of the times I'd jacked off to fantasies about the second assistant hockey coach. I still kept a stained photo of him in my shoebox of high school memorabilia. Truth? I was seventeen when I lost my virginity to Stephan Tondeur, when he gave me a condom and a packet of lube, pulled down his pants and bent over the steering wheel of the Zamboni.

"Yeah. I did."

"Well. Lucky you." Pussy Pierogi whistled and shook her head. "So, I was right, after all. Daniel Garneau, you really actually were a closeted, fudge-packing creampuff."

"You always told everyone I was."

"Yeah. But I didn't believe it. Not really. I just liked getting a rise out of you."

"So now you know."

"Do your brothers know?"

"Pat and Liam? They know. They're good."

"Of course, they'd be. You three boys always had each other's backs. I envy you."

"Why?"

"My folks threw me out on my ass the day they found out. Nobody in my family talks to me anymore."

"I'm sorry to hear that."

"Oh, trust me, it's for the best. But like I said, lucky you." She extended her hand. I stared at it for two seconds before taking it in my own. "I know I gave you a hard time, Garneau. I was a royally fucked up kid. My dad was one helluva bastard. He treated me like a shitty doormat and I took it out on everyone around me. If you don't love yourself, how in the hell you gonna love somebody else? I know that doesn't excuse anything. But I do want to let you know, I'm sorry. The truth was I wasn't going any-where. I figure you and I both are making up for lost time now."

"It seems that way."

I couldn't let go. I felt locked to her somehow, electri-fied, connected like two train cars. Her grip was a life-line. Just as she was starting to notice, I released her with an effort.

"Hey, so, look, Kadlubek, I mean, Pussy Pierogi?"

"Yeah?"

"I'm sorry I broke your nose."

"Ha! Don't be. Truth? I deserved it. But you didn't deserve to get kicked off the team." She turned toward the radiant light, snapping open a flashing compact, and examined her profile. "It gives me character, don't you think? I wouldn't trade this beautiful schnoz now for the world. After all, we're all freaks one way or another, every goddamn one of us. Some people are just more honest about it than others. Stick it to the man, I say. Power to the people. Look around you, Garneau. We're an army of lovers. If we can just let all of it go, we can do whatever the fucking hell we want."

⌒ That September, when David's mom returned to Canada, she announced she was engaged to Nicoli Badalamenti, Antonio's uncle, and that she'd be selling her home in Toronto and moving to Sicily permanently. Three Dog Run had also come back from Burning Man, but without Pat, who'd taken off to New Mexico. When I asked Blonde Dawn if she and Pat had broken up, she said she wasn't sure, but had to think about it. Apparently, Pat was now in the outskirts of Roswell helping to build an orphanage. Pat had tried to convince the entire band to join him, but he was solo on this one. Luke Moretti had also returned on the same flight as his mom, just in time to model in Ai Chang Cho's fall Toronto Fashion Incubator show. When David and I helped Luke and Ai Chang move into their new apartment up by Ossington and Dupont, I heard her underwear designs had caught the attention of none other than fashion maven Jeanne Beker.

It was Sunday evening, and I was on the couch relaying all this news to Karen over Skype while sampling a Chapman's Peanut Butter Ice Cream Cone. David walked by with the ironing board and helped himself to a bite. "Mm. And the score on this one?"

"Four," we said.

"Impressive. Better than a Creamsicle?"

"Not quite."

David planted a kiss on the laptop's camera before strolling away.

"And who's Jeanne Beker?" Karen asked.

"The host of *Fashion Television*," I said, wiping the chocolate-y smear from the screen. "It was a whole forty-nine seconds of air time. This could be Ai Chang's big break. She's playing it pretty chill, but Luke's super excited for her."

"And Luke, what's his plan now that he's back in Toronto?"

"I'm not sure. Right now he's helping his mom pack up her home. He's started volunteering with this youth helpline. Last I heard, he had some lead with GoodLife Fitness."

"He interviewed with them yesterday," David said, ironing his pants. "They offered him a job. He starts next week."

"Really? Wow, good for him. Look, Karen, the next time you come to Toronto, you can meet him. We'll all hang out."

"So, explain to me again," Karen said, "what a *furbo* is?"

I looked to David, but he was busy laying out damp T-shirts. The dryer in the basement was broken again, and we had laundry strung up all through the loft.

"A *furbo*," I said, "is that person who gets things done because he's a fast talker, a kind of con artist. Some people might consider him a cheating sneak. But lots of Italians admire him, and think he's just being really clever or smart. *Furbizia* is the art of being a *furbo*."

"Oh, like Coyote or Raven."

"Meaning?"

"He's a trickster."

"Sure, you could say that."

"Pat's a trickster."

"Blonde Dawn says Pat's an immature man-child."

"Yeah, well." Karen nibbled the edge of her sugar cone. "Sometimes he's that too."

David shouted from the kitchen: "Your brother's Han Solo."

"What did he say?" Karen asked.

"David says Pat's Han Solo."

David draped himself over my shoulders. "And Daniel and I are renegade Jedi Knights."

"Renegade?"

"Jedi are sworn to celibacy." David stuck his tongue in my ear. "We're secret lovers."

"I see," Karen said. "Well, I did not know that. I suppose that makes me Princess Leia?"

"Oh no," David said. "You're Mon Mothma."

"Who's Mon Mothma?"

"'Who's Mon Mothma'? Karen, are you kidding me? What kind of rebel living under a rock are you?"

I leaned into David. "And your brother?"

"My big brother, Luke Moretti, is a goddamn Gallifreyan Time Lord."

Karen blinked. "A Californian what?"

"Whoa." I nodded. "Good one."

"And Blonde Dawn," David declared, "is Barbarella." Then I had to laugh out loud.

"Who?" Karen said.

"And Liam," he said, "he's like the Road Warrior. He's Mad Max."

"Guys," Karen said, "I have something to tell you."

"Oh my god," I said, giggling, "that's so true. Liam's totally Mad Max. Then maybe that makes Blonde Dawn Aunty Entity?"

"Awrh, perhaps," David said, "right you are."

"I need your advice," Karen said.

"Yes Karen," David said, "yes, I think you should definitely use the Force."

"I'm pregnant."

Ice cream dripped onto my chest. David and I stared at the laptop screen. Karen popped the last piece of her sugar cone into her mouth and munched methodically.

"What?"

"You heard me," she said. "I'm pregnant."

"Karen."

"I want to know what you think I should do."

"Wait." I sat up on the couch. "Karen, I mean. What does Bob think about this?"

"I haven't told him yet."

"You didn't plan this."

"Are you kidding me? Of course not. I've been on the pill since high school."

"So you weren't using condoms?"

"No. Sometimes. No, not every time. Ever since Mike and Melissa's wedding, things have gotten pretty serious. Sometimes we just wouldn't have one handy."

"Alright. Well, I mean, these things can happen."

"Obviously."

"How pregnant," David asked, "are you?"

"Three maybe four weeks. Look, David, do you mind if I talked to Daniel in private?"

"Um, sure. No problem." David glanced at me and backed away. "I think, look, why don't I go for a walk." He grabbed his wallet and put on his shoes. "Text me," he mouthed before closing the front door behind him.

"Is he gone?" Karen asked.

"He's gone."

"Daniel. Look." Karen drew a breath. "I'm not sure it's Bob's."

"What?"

"I fucked up."

"Oh Karen. Hey. It's okay. Hey, you're okay."

"No. No, I'm not okay. I'm not. I absolutely do not want this baby."

"It's your body, Karen. It's your choice."

"Is it?"

"Yes. It is."

"I'm not sure it's that simple."

"Karen, you think, you said it might not be Bob's?"

On the laptop screen, she leaned back, arms wrapped around herself.

"Labour Day," she said, "my aunt hosted this barbecue. It went really late and Bob needed to take the girls home, but I was having a good time, and wanted to stay. Liam said he'd drive me home, or we all figured I could just sleep over in my cousin's bunk bed. I've done that lots of times."

"Okay."

"Liam, he's in a really good place. He was smiling a lot, even laughing. Did you know he's off his meds now? He hasn't had a drink in almost a year. It was a really hot night, and we were hanging out on the dock. We decided we'd go for a swim in the pond. Then, I dunno." Karen shook her head. "One thing just led to another."

"So, what now?"

"Now, I don't know who the father is."

"Whoa." I sat back. "Karen."

"Yeah. Exactly."

"Shit."

"I am so totally not ready for this."

"Maybe you should talk to a counsellor."

"I've talked with my aunt. Now I'm talking to you."

"So, you're not going to tell Bob or Liam?"

"What do you think?"

"I think, Karen, you should do whatever's best for you."

"That's not helpful."

"Karen, all I'm saying is, I'll support you, whatever you decide, okay?"

"Daniel, you might be an uncle. Have you thought about that?"

I had thought about that. It was the very first thought that entered my mind. But I was also thinking there was no way Liam was ready to be a dad. He could barely take care of himself.

"That's not," I said, "what this is about."

"I hate this. This is such a fucking soap opera." Karen pressed the heels of her hands against her eyes. "I can't believe this is happening. I mean, what was I thinking? I moved back to Manitoulin so my life would be simpler."

"We'll get through this."

"I hate living with secrets."

'We all live with secrets, Karen."

"Daniel, I can't have this baby. I can't. I'm going to make an appointment in Sudbury. I have to."

"Are you sure?"

Karen nodded.

"I'll come with you then."

"Did I mention, Liam wants to get back together? He says he misses me."

"And how do you feel about him?"

"I just want to move on with my life, y'know?"

"And how are you and Bob?"

"Bob and I are really good. He treats me amazing. He's a fantastic cook. Sky helps him out in the kitchen. Zephyr and I have been going on walks with Gracie. We talk about boys and clothes and stuff. And Sky, well she just loves music and art. She drew me this picture of the four of us." Karen shook her head. "And we all looked so happy. We are happy. Liam knows that. He knew that! Bob and I were doing great. Oh, shit, why am I even blaming Liam? I just wish he'd find someone else."

"You and Liam have been together since high school."

"Since grade school, Daniel. Since I gave him that baby deer skull. Do you remember that?"

"Up in our tree house."

"Yeah. And it's never worked, right? It's never worked out between Liam and me. Sometimes I'd think things are so good between us. Then he just lets go, like something short circuits inside him, and I watch him falling away, like he's sinking into this bottomless black lake. And I can't follow him, and there's nothing in the world I can do about it. Sometimes it's just for a few days, but other times it'd be for months. I can't deal with that anymore, I can't. Remember when my dad died and Liam took off to Vancouver?"

"Yeah."

"I tried to convince myself that was okay. But it wasn't. It really wasn't."

"I'm sorry that happened."

"I've always been the one taking care of him. I've always been the one adjusting my life to fit his. I can't do it anymore."

"You said he's different now."

"Yeah, for now. But for how long? If Liam really has changed, then that's wonderful. That's fucking miraculous. And I'm happy for him. But I've moved on."

"With Bob?"

"With me, Daniel. My life needs to be about me. Anne's all grown up now. She's finished her first year at OCAD. She's doing great. This is my chance now to make a life of my own."

"And you are, Karen."

"But can I tell you something? And this is the crazy part. Sometimes when I look at Bob's daughters, when I'm helping with their breakfast or giving them a lift to school, I wonder if I could be their mom. And I can see it, y'know? I can see myself doing it. I could be a stepmom. I've been sleeping over a lot. They've gotten used to me. Bob, he hasn't asked me to move in yet, but I know he's going to."

"Is that what you want?"

"I dunno. I see his girls every day. Bob's got them enrolled in my afterschool program."

"How is work going for you?"

"Work? Amazing. I love it. The Ojibwe Cultural Foundation just got this big grant. They've asked me to curate the upcoming winter exhibit. They've put me in charge of the whole thing. You'd be proud of me."

"I am proud of you, Karen. I've always been proud of you."

"Even now?"

"Hey, this is me you're talking to."

"You'll come with me, right?"

"Of course. I already said I would."

"Please don't tell David."

"I won't."

"You can't tell anyone."

"I won't."

"You're in med school. You're sworn to these kind of things."

"Karen Fobister, I'm not your doctor. I'm your best friend. I love you. We'll do this, we'll get through this together."

"You and me?"

"You and me."

∽ "Buddies in Bad Times Theatre is on the traditional lands of the Mississaugas of the New Credit First Nation, the Haudenosaunee, the Anishnaabe and the Wendat. We acknowledge them and any other Nations who care for the land as the past, present and future caretakers of this land, traditional territory named Tkaronto, 'Where The Trees Meet The Water'; 'The Gathering Place.' We do not support colonial forces that undermine, distort or erase the vital role of Indigenous people in our world."

David and I sat in the back row at the final perform-ance of Marcus's play. Its three-week run had been extended an extra three shows. It was the artistic director himself who spoke tonight, offering up the land acknowledge-ment, and thanks to various funders. When he reminded everyone of the closing night party afterwards, half the audience started whooping and hollering. As the house faded to black, David nudged me and pointed. Professor Frederic and his wife Rebecca were sitting just a few rows below us.

Thirty seconds later, five screens gently glowed,

framing the back of an empty stage. A single piano note sounded. A close-up image of an embryo appeared on the centre screen. "A human face," Marcus's voice said, "becomes recognizable at eight weeks gestation."

A hundred minutes later, the show was over. The audience surged to its feet. The lights came back on and Marcus reappeared to whistles and renewed applause. On this occasion, he summoned his director, and then his entire production team up on stage. They clasped hands, forming a rough line-up, and bowed in unison. When a stagehand presented him with a bouquet of roses, he looked genuinely surprised. This moment, I thought to myself, was forever, quintessentially Marcus. When he blew a kiss to someone in the first row, I felt a pang of jealously.

"That," David shouted in my ear, "was incredible."

Later, in the adjoining Cabaret space at the post-show party, I searched the crowd for Charles who'd said he and Megan would meet us. Instead, I spotted Marwa behind the bar filling up an ice bucket.

"Daniel!" She waved me over. "Patricia, this is my friend Daniel, he's in med school. Daniel, this is Patricia." The bartender, an older, tough-looking blonde in a leather vest and black bracers nodded in my direction, methodically assembling a tray of shooters.

"Patricia used to be a welder," Marwa said as I followed her to the food table. "Now she plays in a rock band called Crackpuppy. Is your musician brother still in that band of his?"

"Three Dog Run? Yeah, they just got back from Burning Man last month. But Pat, he's kind of gone missing."

"Missing?"

"Yeah, well, after Burning Man he emailed to say he was heading into the desert. And now no one's heard from him."

"How long ago was that?"

"Two weeks. His girlfriend's pissed."

"Are you worried?"

"Yeah, kinda. I mean, I'm used to it. It's my brother Pat. But yeah, a bit. Look, we can talk about this later. Is there anything I can help you with?"

"You can help me carry in the cake."

Someone tousled my hair. "Yo, Dan-the-Man," Trevor Fang said striding past. Jonathan, following behind in a red dress and heels, smiled and waved.

Marwa had her assistants Youssef and Brody setting out platters and trays of foods, all three wearing pink and purple T-shirts featuring an exploding cherry logo.

"Normally I'd be sticking to baking these days," Marwa said, as I followed her outside to the loading dock. "But Marcus really wanted me to cater my old menu. The Ta'meya is Youssef's mom's recipe. I also made my garlic yoghurt cucumber salad, which is one of his favourites. I know he loves that. I'm not charging him for the cake. That's compliments of Cherry Bomb Bakery." When she opened the back of her van, I stepped back in shock.

"Do you think," she said, "I made it too big?"

"Well, I mean. Go big or go home, right?"

"Exactly." The cake was in the shape of a gigantic yellow smiley face resting on a square sheet of plywood lined with tin foil. It had been one of the central images in Marcus's play.

"Maybe," I said, "we should get someone to help us?"

"We can do this. C'mon."

Together, we slid the cake out of the van. For someone so small, Marwa was strong. "So, where's your boyfriend?" she asked, as we manoeuvred our way back into the building.

"Um. I dunno. He went to the washroom earlier. Excuse us, coming through. So, did you make your Egyptian meatballs tonight?"

"Is the Pope Catholic? I am the Meatball Queen, I'll have you know. In case you've forgotten."

"No. Definitely haven't."

Finally, we reached the table where Youssef and Brody had cleared a spot for us.

"There," Marwa said, "now that wasn't so hard, was it? Thanks for your help." Standing on her tiptoes, she planted a kiss by my ear. "Let me know if you need anything."

By now the Cabaret space was filling up shoulder-to-shoulder. I couldn't find David anywhere. Just as I was heading down to the washrooms, I spotted him coming up the stairwell with Rebecca and Frederic.

"Daniel." Rebecca beamed, taking my hands in hers. She looked radiant in a black-and-white paisley dress with accents of silver jewellery. "It's so good to see you again. David has been telling us all about his summer in Sicily. You must have missed him terribly."

"Um." I glanced at David. "Yeah, I did."

Frederic clapped me on the shoulder. "You two boys are looking well."

"Thank you, sir."

"They're young, Frederic," Rebecca said. "Youth always looks well."

"Very true, dear."

"Although I admit," she said, "I did especially enjoy their formal attire last Valentine's Day."

Frederic squeezed my arm. "Darling, you just preferred them without any undergarments on."

"Did you know," Rebecca said, "there were a number of Popes in the Vatican who considered nudity in artwork indecorous? They went so far as to have genitalia painted over and statuary covered with bronze fig leaves. Can you imagine that? Not women's breasts, mind you. Those remained exposed."

"In the Middle Ages," David said, "the damned were portrayed naked, and only the saved were given clothes."

"Did you know," I said, clearing my throat, "the classical Greeks considered big penises unattractive? They were equated with being animalistic or decrepit or uncivilized."

David and the others stared. Rebecca released my hands. "Well," she said momentarily. "If that is the case, I suppose I must be married to quite the old and vulgar man-beast."

"I suppose so," Frederic said, eyebrows raised. The two regarded each other soberly, before bursting into laughter.

I spotted Charles coming in and excused myself. "Hey," I called out, "nice haircut."

"Thank you, Daniel." Charles stood with his arms at his side, sporting a neatly trimmed goatee. "Megan discovered this new barber shop for me."

I grabbed his arm and led him past the box office, back outside through the pink doors. I didn't know why

Frederic and Rebecca made me so nervous. David had said it was because they weren't much older than what my own parents would be if they were still alive. We stood by the railing overlooking the Alexander Street Parkette.

"It's called Blood and Bandages," Charles said, "out in Little Portugal. I was a little uncertain about the taxidermy-themed decor. But they do an excellent job. My own head is somewhat square and thus challenging for most stylists. They also sell their own hair pastes and pomades."

"Charles, I always thought you got your haircuts in Chinatown."

"I did. This is new for me. Megan says it's all part of a lifestyle makeover. I do feel more attractive now that I've started to pay more attention to my personal grooming. Except I've discovered my feet are extremely sensitive, and pedicures are not something I'm able to tolerate."

"Sorry to hear that."

"Mind you, this has led to some quite invigorating tickle torture sessions with Megan."

"Really? Where is Megan?"

"Parking the car. How was the show?"

I leaned against the brick wall. The show had, in fact, given me a hard-on. The show had made me laugh so hard I cried. The show had made me want to rush on stage, fall to my knees and hold Marcus as he wept wailing. The show had made me want to shout from rooftops my love for this mad, mad, mad world. Marcus had found the right words and they were simple. I drew a breath, my hands in my pockets. "It was sold out. There was a standing ovation at the end."

Charles nodded. "That was to be expected."

"I'm guessing most of his friends are here tonight."

"Did everyone participate in the sing-a-long?"

"Oh, yeah."

Across the parkette, I could see Megan approaching in a tight-fitting, tasselled dress. "So, Charles, how are you and Megan doing?"

"Very well. Thank you for asking. Our recent misunderstanding over the Duchess has brought us much closer. There is some news I wanted to share with you."

"Daniel!" Megan called out, stumbling in her red heels before scurrying up the ramp to the entrance. "Charles and I, we have an announcement. You'll never guess."

"You've set a wedding date?"

"What? No."

"You're pregnant?"

"Oh my god, no. Not at all. Why would you say that? No! In fact, we're going to get a vasectomy. Charles saw his doctor, and we've set a date in a couple weeks."

"Oh." I was taken aback. "I thought ... I thought you wanted to raise a family together."

"We do," Charles said, "eventually. Just not now."

"It's a reversible vasectomy," Megan said. "There's no snippety-snip. They just go down there and put in these tiny little clamps. We'll still use protection when we're playing with others. You can't be too careful about those nasty STIs. But Charles and I wanted to be more intimate. It's not the same wearing condoms all the time."

"I get it."

"Do you and David still use condoms?"

"Uh, no. We stopped a while ago."

"You're lucky. Same-sex couples never have to worry

about birth control. But are you still having sex with other people?"

"Who says we were ever having sex with other people?"

"Oh, I just don't assume people in relationships ever are monogamous," Megan said. "Not anymore. I mean, these days, really, monogamy, it's like, oh, poopsie, how did you put it?"

"Anachronistic," Charles said.

"That's right. Agonistic. What he said. But if you and David really are exclusive, that's wonderful too." Megan gripped my arm. "I mean, if it works for you, all the more power to you."

"I remember," spoke a gravelly voice, "when we used to do Dungeons at Buddies years ago." We all turned our heads. It was the bartender Patricia, perched on the railing finishing a smoke, wearing dark sunglasses. "The truth is, you kids are pretty tame these days." She glanced over at us. "Now Wittenbrink, he's a crazy shepherd of rebellion." She took a final drag off her cigarette before butting it out. "It's people like him who're gonna change the fucking world."

David stuck his head out the front door. "Hey, there you guys are. Marcus just showed up. He's going to cut the cake. C'mon, you're going to miss the toast."

We followed David back inside. But when I held the door open for Patricia, she just shook her head. Her body language said it all: *Been there, done that.* I wondered what a woman like that might've seen or accomplished in her lifetime. To someone like her, we were all still just kids.

I hurried after the others, wondering just how much growing up I had left to do.

CHAPTER TEN

Superman is Dead

My brother Pat was missing.

None of his band members or any of his Facebook friends knew where he might be. Carolina Sanchez had parted ways with him in Roswell. Eventually, Blonde Dawn and I filed a report with state troopers in New Mexico but they didn't seem too concerned. They told us kids like that go "missing" all the time, only to turn up a few days later in some Mexican bordello or broke, hitching a ride into Vegas. I was furious at their attitude, but Blonde Dawn kept the cooler head. "Look, Dan, what more do you expect them to do? Launch a manhunt into the Chihuahuan Desert? They said they'd put out an APB and keep us updated. He's going to turn up. It's Pat. He's resourceful."

"You called him a man-child, Blonde Dawn. He's a fucking idiot. When he does show up, I am going to kill him."

A few days later, we got a call from State Indian Affairs. They'd picked up one Patrick Garneau, broke, hitching a ride out of the Mescalero Apache Reservation. When I finally got him on the phone, he asked if I could send him some money, and assured me he'd be home for Thanksgiving. When I reminded him that Thanksgiving had come and gone three weeks ago, he seemed genuinely taken aback. In that case, he replied, I wouldn't mind if he stayed on a little longer, would I?

Apparently, after rescuing a little barefoot girl from a five-foot diamondback in the parking lot of a Mexican bordello, he'd been taken in by the family of a Chiricahua medicine man who was a direct descendant of Lozen herself. I took a deep breath, before asking Pat who Lozen was.

"Dude! Lozen was this legendary badass warrior woman who fought alongside Geronimo, totally outnumbered against Mexican and U.S. troops. Lozen, she was like the Apache Joan of Arc."

During his time in Roswell, Pat told me he'd had dreams of being probed by interdimensional alien beings, and that the medicine man had offered to guide him on a peyote vision-quest to help interpret them. As it turned out, the money he needed was to pay off a fine for criminal trespass into Area 51, and for a plane ticket out of Vegas.

He said he'd brought one book to read: Kerouac's *On the Road*. Marcus had quoted Kerouac in *Face*.

I told Pat to come home and hung up the phone.

I sent him the money he asked for.

⌒ That November, I met up with Parker Kapoor at Fran's Restaurant at College and Yonge. It was a cold, rainy afternoon and I huddled beneath the brightly-lit, marquee-styled entrance. Once Parker arrived, we found a booth in the back of the retro diner, all bright chrome and red vinyl seating. Old menus dating back to the 1940s were displayed under glass. Parker ordered the chocolate milkshake, while I had a cup of coffee and a slice of coconut cream pie.

Parker had just come out of a hot yoga session, and his skin was glowing.

"Daniel, I felt like I was going to barf," he said. "My sister Charita's gotten me to come to a few of her classes over the years. But really it's just not my thing, especially Bikram. I get dizzy and nauseous. It is not a pretty sight."

"Parker, then why did you go today?"

"Well, this time it was different. I was intrigued. It wasn't something I'd ever tried before." He leaned forward and lowered his voice. "It was naked yoga."

"I beg your pardon?"

"Naked yoga, Daniel. I had no idea women could be that hairy. But I'm not judging."

"This was for men and women?"

Parker nodded. "All body types, people in their twenties to their sixties. The class was packed. At first, it was terrifying. All those people ogling me? What if I had to fart? What if some creepy person tried to hit on me? Well, probably not if I fart. But after the first few minutes, it just didn't matter anymore. It was exhilarating. I felt transported. I've never felt so connected with my body in my life."

"So, did anyone hit on you?"

"No, it's not sexual at all. It's like how your grandpa is a nudist. It's all about honouring and accepting your body. And the bonus is you don't have to spend a fortune on a new outfit from Lululemon or anything."

"Right."

Parker sipped from his milkshake. "So I was talking with this older gentleman after the class. Did you know, up until the mid-70s, it was actually the requirement in public pools that boys and men swim naked?"

"The requirement?"

"In high schools and at YMCAs everywhere, it was de règle. Something to do with hygiene and wool fabrics clogging up the filtration system. I know, I was sceptical too, until I looked it up."

"Wow. That's really weird."

Parker's eyes widened. "Exactly. That's what you and I are taught to think today. But back then, that was the expectation and the norm: Mr. Cleaver, Beaver, Wally and Eddie, all frolicking together poolside with their dangly bits in full view."

"Who?"

"Never mind. The point is, in our generation what do we equate nudity with? Sex, perversion, and impossible standards for the human physique. These days, it's all about body-shaming. I'm as much a victim as anybody else. Look at me: too skinny, too short, too brown. But if I've learned to be so self-judgmental, then I can unlearn it. Naked yoga helps us get over this. Daniel, I am so totally going back."

I'd never thought of Parker as someone who had body-image issues. But then, who didn't? I tried to imagine a room full of men and women stretching and posing with their bare butts in the air, liberating themselves from the humiliating shackles of a body-shaming society. I remembered reading how ancient Olympic athletes would rub themselves all over with olive oil and compete naked in front of the crowds. Just that idea itself had fuelled jerk-off fantasies for years.

"I know what you're thinking," Parker said.

"What am I thinking?"

"You're wondering if the men ever get erections."

"Maybe. Okay, yes, I was."

"They talk about this on the website. Yoga moves a lot of energy though the body, and yes, it sometimes happens. It's normal and healthy, and nothing to be embarrassed about. But it never lasts long. Frankly, Bikram is so intense, really, I'd say it's next to impossible."

"You were never concerned?"

"Me?" Parker sat back with a funny look on his face. "No, not at all."

"What is it?"

"The biggest concern I had was squashing my nut-sac during Vakrasana."

"Okay. And ...?"

"Well." Parker shifted restlessly and looked past me. "The truth is, Daniel, I've been wondering lately if I was ace."

"What?"

"Ace. Asexual."

"A sexual what?"

"Daniel, you're in med school, you should know these things. Asexual, as in, I really don't have any sexual attraction to anyone."

"But, Parker, you're gay."

"I know, I thought I was, for the longest time. I remember my parents sitting me down and saying if I was gay then that was perfectly fine, and that they'd always love and support me no matter what."

"That was decent of them. How old were you?"

"I was five. That made a big impression on me. I grew up with four big sisters. They'd dress me up in their clothes, I'd play with their dolls. After watching Brian Orser in the Calgary Winter Olympics, I begged my parents for figure skating lessons. When I was twelve, I came in second place at the pre-novice men's Central Ontario sectional. My mom made me this fabulous white cowboy outfit with tassels and rhinestones. Daniel, it was glorious. In high school, I just thought Madame Valdez had really nice hair and nails."

"What? Who's Madame Valdez?"

"Oh, she was The Spanish Teacher. Every boy in high school fantasized about Madame Valdez. She had the body of a *Penthouse* model."

"The Spanish Teacher."

"Me, well. I was in love with Madhubala and Judy Garland. My fantasies were all about Bollywood and Broadway. Ergo gay. It just made sense. At least at the time it did. People were just waiting for me to come out. My parents even threw a party for me when I did. I became president of my GSA. I built a LGBT YA section in the school library which they named after me: 'Kapoor's Corner' ('Parker's Pit' didn't quite sound kosher). Everyone welcomed me with open arms."

"So, why are you saying you're not gay?"

"Because." Parker made a pained expression. "I don't think I'm attracted to men."

"But you've had sex with men."

"Sure, and I've also tried Christmas fruitcake, more than once even, but that doesn't mean I like it."

"Okay."

"Look, the truth is, I can count the number of times I've had sex on one hand. It never did very much for me. When I look at porn, it's sometimes interesting, but mostly boring. I'd rather watch cooking shows. I practically never think about sex. When I do, it's only because people expect me to. It's a lot of pressure, Daniel."

I thought about sex all the time. Not an hour went by when I didn't think about sex. I'd talked about sex often with Parker, just assuming he'd get it. "Parker, I don't know what to say."

"You don't have to say anything."

"Weren't you making out with that friend of yours, Kyle, last New Year's Eve?"

"Well. He was kissing me. That was interesting. Since then, I've told him I think I'm ace. He's okay with that. Kyle and I, we're still good friends. We still cuddle a lot. He still thinks of me as his boyfriend."

"So you two are boyfriends?"

"I'm not sure. By default, I guess you could call us that. But can I be ace and still be someone's boyfriend? Kyle seems to think so. I want to be his boyfriend, I really do. I want to be somebody in his life. Except Kyle, he's not ace. I caught him masturbating once, and then I felt so bad I wanted to break it off. I even suggested it. But ..."

"But what?"

"He said he loved me. It's been just over a year since we met. Don't you think that's a little soon to tell someone you love them? Especially if that person can't love you back, at least not in the way you want them to?"

For once, Parker was looking directly at me, searching my face. Except I had no idea what to say. "Parker." I wanted to reach out and hold his hand, but I didn't because we were men, and in Fran's Restaurant. I thought of Betty watching my family visit the nursing home, year after year. It was Betty who'd asked me to help move a couch into Grandma's room just so us kids could all be a little more comfortable. It was Betty who'd bring two cups of tea every day Grandpa visited, long after Grandma stopped drinking hers.

"People love each other for all sorts of reasons," I said. "There's never too soon. And there's never too late. You and Kyle are friends already. There's no need to hurry. You don't have to be anybody. Just be yourself."

"Daniel."

"Yeah?"

"You just quoted Virginia Woolf."

"I did?"

"Kind of."

"Oh. That's just what a friend told me once."

"I like to sparkle."

"You're the most sparkly person I know."

"Really?" Parker's face lit up. "Thank you. Well." He drew a deep breath. "Thinking of myself as ace is what works for me right now. It's kind of a relief, really. I'm definitely queer. I've been queer ever since I can remember.

I'm pretty sure that's never going to change. Why don't you just think of me as queer?"

"Works for me." I sat back and rested one hand straight-armed on the table. "Parker, I didn't know you were a figure skater."

"I never knew I'd be into naked yoga. Daniel, you really should try it."

To my surprise, I was just the tiniest bit intrigued. I'd never had much issue with my body image. As an athlete, I was used to public showers. I'd gone skinny-dipping often with my brothers, and Karen and Anne. I felt I was in decent shape, although I'd never tried yoga before in my life. "When are you going next?"

"I'm not sure. Look, here's their card." Parker pushed a slip of paper toward me. "There are drop-in classes. But if you are going, tell me when just so I can avoid that time. I'd hate to run into you. That would be mortifying. With strangers, it's one thing, but I could never do this in front of my friends. Be forewarned: there will be balls, in your face, and penises and vaginas. Oh, and be especially care-ful, Daniel, with Child's Pose."

"Child's Pose?"

"It's an eye-opener."

⌒ For Christmas, David and I decided we'd get every-one socks, which sounded boring except these ones had wacky, colourful patterns and prints, inspiring lengthy debate over which socks best suited which individuals. Some were no contest: The purple pair covered in crazy cats was for our neighbour Liz who'd started fostering kittens from the Toronto Cat Rescue; a dark pair with a moose motif had Liam written all over it. Others were tougher: Should the pink cupcake socks go to Nadia or Marwa? The pair lined with musical notes could go to any number of people. "Not to your DJ lover Fang?" David asked.

"He's not my lover," I said. "He never was. He was Marcus's lover."

"Then what about your special friend Sean?" David winked at me.

"He's not my special friend."

"Fuck buddy, then."

"David. Jesus. He's not my fuck buddy. Like I said, until Parker's party I hadn't seen him in years."

"No sockies for Seanie?"

"No. Look, I'm not getting Fang or Sean anything. I hardly know those guys."

We were rummaging through cardboard boxes in the back of a warehouse outlet in Kensington Market. Big plastic bins brimmed over with discounted toques, thermal underwear, and lacy bras. David was convinced half the stock in the store was stolen merchandise. "Except," he remarked, "you'd still have sex with them."

I took a deep breath. I knew he was teasing me. Karen always said I was too easy to tease. "David, you," I said, "made out with Silvia Sabatini."

"Yes, I did. It was situational heterosexuality. I hated every second of it. But I was lost and alone, a stranger in a strange land, far from my French-Canadian lover. How was it with DJ Sean?"

I thought of Sean's pale legs spread wide, his feet in

the air, the small, chirping-gasping sounds he'd make, and the way his round toes would curl. He'd brought his own condoms, and I'd wanted badly to fuck him, but I hadn't. That was the agreement David and I had made.

"It was okay."

"Just okay?"

"I dunno. David, that was months ago. We've talked about this."

"No, not really. Not in detail. Life is in the details. It's Seurat in the park."

"What?"

"Never mind. Oh, these are fun." He held up a pair of socks with psychedelic swirls. "For Pat?"

"Hm. Maybe."

The storeowner was watching TV by the front register, eating noodles from a Styrofoam box. Every now and then, he'd glance over, making sure we knew he had his eye on us. Big signs hanging from the ceiling read: YOU ARE ON CAMERA. SHOPLIFTERS WILL BE PROSECUTED.

After a moment, I replied: "It was okay."

"You used to really like the guy."

"Years ago. Not anymore, not that way. Anyway, I'm with you now."

"So, would you ever have a threesome with him?"

"What, with Sean? The three of us?"

"Yeah."

"Seriously?"

"Just asking." David shrugged.

"I don't know. Look, why are we even talking about this?"

"Daniel, you've been in a threesome. I've never been

in a threesome. We're just talking. It's no big deal. I thought he was cute."

After David got back from Italy, I'd told him about Sean and shown him a photo from the Drake Hotel website. Sean was more than cute. There'd been a (very brief) time in my life when I thought he was the most beautiful man in the world.

"You know," I said, "he has this thing for ears."

"Ears?"

"Like as in an ear fetish."

"Really, there's such a thing?"

"Sure. Charles says anything can be a fetish."

"True. Interesting. Okay, well, tell me yours."

"Tell you what?"

"What's your fetish?"

"Who says I have any fetish?"

"Daniel, everyone's got some kind of fetish. It's just something particular that turns you on. Feet, leather, redheads, whatever."

"Okay, um …"

"Hello?"

"Okay. I guess I used to be really into jock straps."

David's eyebrows rose. "I did not know that. Is that from your hockey days?"

"Probably."

"Guys in locker rooms, all those steamy showers together. Sure, I get it."

"Alright. Okay." I wondered if the security cameras could pick up our conversation. I turned to another box. "So what about you?"

"Superheroes. Totally hot."

"Really?"

"All those tight outfits and masks, secret identities, and masculine angst. Definitely super sexy."

"Is that why you still read those comics of yours?"

"Maybe. Did you know the first gay superhero was Canadian? Northstar from Alpha Flight. Jean-Paul Beaubier, he was French-Canadian. His parents died in a car crash when he was young. And he has a twin. You two have a lot in common."

"The similarity is uncanny."

"For a while there he was a member of the X-Men."

"So, you'd have sex with Jean-Paul?"

"Oh, no. He's been brainwashed and switched sides too many times. He's way too messed up."

"So it's not just the tight outfits."

"Hell no. It takes a lot more than that to turn my crank. Oh, check this out." Sea-green socks covered with golden starfish.

"Who's that for?"

"Silvia."

'You're sending Silvia Sabatini a Christmas gift?"

"Sure, why not? You got that Canadian beaver one for Antonio. I think you're secretly in love with Antonio."

"Yeah, that's exactly right." I rolled my eyes. "Sicilian farm boys, totally hot."

"Salt-of-the-earth, sun in their faces, sweaty limbs and hairy pits, all smelling like hay."

"You wanna box of Kleenex to go with that?"

"Antonio's cute."

"When your mom gets married again, he's going to be your cousin, you know."

David sighed. "Then I guess I'll just have to settle for Silvia Sabatini."

"David, are you sure you're not bi?"

"I've told you lots of times, I'm not. I'm just … homoflexible."

"Homoflexible?"

"Making out with people is fun. Boys and girls."

"Now you sound like Pat."

"You and Karen never fooled around?"

"No, never. I'm pretty sure I'm a six on the Kinsey scale. Parker told me he thinks he's asexual."

"No kidding? Good for him to figure that out."

"You're not surprised?"

David shrugged. "Why should I be? It's the 21st century. This is the next evolution of Homo sapiens: gender and sexual fluidity, and that includes ace. Although 'renaissance' is probably a better word. Hey, what about these for Anne?" He held up electric blue socks covered in gorillas.

"Karen's sister, Anne?"

"She's family, isn't she? I bumped into her, by the way, last week at Silver Snail. Did you know she's a collector? *Runaways*."

"What are *Runaways*?"

"They're these super-powered teens, mostly girls. They run away from their evil parents and form this kind of dysfunctional family. Their leader's a Japanese witch; another one's this alien lesbian who ends up dating another member who's a bi-gender shape-shifter."

"Oh. You're talking about comics again."

"Daniel don't be so judgmental. Comic book writers are modern day myth-makers."

"Really?"

"There's a reason they killed off Superman back in the day. There's a reason that antiheroes are so popular now. The industry used to be totally patriarchal, misogynist and heteronormative, but that's changing."

"Those are some pretty big words there."

"Comics, mister, are touchstones for our collective consciousness."

"And," I said, "superheroes are sexy."

David grinned. "And some supervillains too. Yum. Oh, and don't even get me started on *yaoi*. Hey would you be interested in going to ComiCon this spring?"

"No, not really. Why don't you go with Anne?"

"I just might." David counted through the socks we'd set aside. "You wouldn't mind?"

"No, go for it. How many pairs do we have?"

"Eighteen."

"Whoa." I took a step back. "That's a lot of socks."

"Yeah, and these are Christmas gifts for pretty much everyone we know."

"Do we really need to get that many?"

"Daniel, how much money do we blow in one night out at Sneaky Dee's?" He had a point. "C'mon, it's fun to get gifts for people. We can figure out who gets what later. This is a sweet deal. People are going to love these."

Ever since David got promoted to assistant manager last summer, he'd been making a lot more money. Instead of fixing up our old broken couch, he'd insisted on buying a new one. I figured it'd be the 22nd century by the time I paid off my student loans. But if my boyfriend wanted to get all our families and friends socks for

Christmas, who was I to say no? I remembered getting clothes for Christmas as a kid, and how underwhelmed I'd be. I'd just wanted toys. When did socks suddenly start becoming cool? Somewhere along the way, I'd grown up. Now I had bills to pay, debts to manage. I wasn't even twenty-five yet and I felt I'd passed a milestone in my life, leaving some younger part of me behind. The truth was, I secretly loved that David still loved his comic books. I'd turned my back on my childhood long ago. No more secret tree house club meetings with Pat and Liam. No more toboggan races with Mom and Dad. No more snuggling up with Grandma to watch back-to-back episodes of *The Golden Girls* until one in the morning. No more toys for Daniel Garneau.

꙰ For Christmas, David got me a vibrating dildo.

He had me unwrap it in advance in Toronto, before I headed up to Sudbury. He tried to keep a poker face but couldn't stop giggling.

"What is it?" I asked.

"Just open it."

When I did, I was stunned. "Oh. My. God." I gingerly took it out of the box and hefted it in my hands.

"It's The Cherry Scented Vibro-Dong," David said. "It has two speeds. The batteries are already in there. You turn it on with that knob at the bottom."

I turned the knob and the thing started vibrating like some anti-tank stick grenade about to blow.

"It's huge," I said.

"It is pretty big. So? What do you think?"

"I ... I don't know what to say."

"Do you like it?"

"How much did you pay for this?"

"Not that much. C'mon, it's fun. I can't wait to play with it when you get back. Unless you want to try it out now."

"David, there is no way I'm putting this up my bum."

"We don't have to put it up your bum. We'll just explore, and experiment, and see where it goes. When you come back, we can have a date night. Have a little wine. I can smoke a joint. Maybe you can test it out on me."

"You want me to put this up your bum?"

"I dunno." David bit his lower lip. "Maybe." He was grinning like a kid in a candy store. "Like I said, we'll see where it goes."

"Yeah, literally."

"C'mon, it's fun to have toys. Merry Christmas!"

I thought of the G.I. Joes my brothers and I used to play with as kids, the Autobots and Decepticons, Super Soakers, and Nerf blasters. It was fun to have toys. Except I was sure this was meant for a lot bigger boys than me.

"This isn't a toy. This," I said, "is a weapon of mass destruction."

"Daniel." David leaned into me and arched one eyebrow. "Don't disrespect the Cherry Scented Vibro-Dong."

The first time I'd ever tried an actual dildo was on my first date with Marcus. That toy had been a lot smaller but no less intimidating. From an early age, I'd put a few things up my bum: fingers (I'd eventually work my way up to three), my thumb, the end of a toothbrush, a few select vegetables using a whole lot of body wash. It was all secretive, a little bit shameful, and a total turn-on. I learned later that pretty much every guy had tried sticking things up their bums. (ER doctors removed foreign objects from rectums all the time.) But even after I moved to Toronto, it never occurred to me to walk into a store, slap down my credit card, and purchase something designed and manufactured for that singular purpose.

You had to be eighteen to walk into a sex shop, but in Ontario, a twelve-year-old could get a license to own a gun. In Sudbury, I'd grown up knowing a lot of classmates who'd gotten real guns for Christmas. Why was it so much more shameful to own a dildo than a gun? Not every family in Sudbury had guns in the house, but I figured most of them did. Grandpa would regularly dismantle and clean his rifles at the kitchen table. By the time Liam, Pat and I were in middle school, Grandpa had taught us all how to shoot. If Mom had been alive, things might have been different. But she wasn't. If child welfare had ever caught wind of our shenanigans, the three of us would've been taken away for sure. But Grandpa also taught us respect, even Pat. I'd been to enough bush parties since to know not everyone had respect for guns. It wasn't like David had brought a firearm into the house. The truth was, no one ever died from a dildo accidentally going off.

⌒ Christmas Eve afternoon. Flecks of icy snow drifted down out of a luminous sky.

Liam told Pat and me he'd started working for the Greater Sudbury Police Service. Earlier that fall, he'd gotten into the local news. A three-year-old had wandered away from a campsite in Killarney close to the North Channel. There was a lot of fresh bear scat in the area, and Liam Garneau had joined the desperate manhunt. He'd pointed out how clearly the authorities were searching in the wrong area, but no one listened. After that he set out on his own and walked out of the woods four hours later with the kid in his arms, hungry but unhurt. Since then, he told us, he'd been helping law enforcement track down missing persons on a half-dozen occasions.

"You're a fucking hero," Pat said. "That is so totally awesome."

"There's something else," Liam said, stacking wood. He took off his gloves and pulled a splinter from the palm of his hand. "There's this detective constable."

"Okay?"

"We've worked together on a couple cases."

"Yeah. And?"

"She's invited me to dinner."

Pat and I both looked at each other. The three of us were working out by the garage. A month ago, Grandpa had bought himself a splitter, and a buddy of his from the lumberyard had dropped-off off a ginormous load of roundwood, at least four cords worth. Grandpa with his chainsaw had already cut the logs into half-metre lengths. Now the three of us were loading the splitter and stacking the firewood. Pat had dumped a two-four of Northern Ale in a nearby snowbank. To his credit, Liam stuck to a thermos of hot tea. Jackson lay close by gnawing on a beef shank bone.

"Invited you?" Pat said. "Like, as in, on a date?"

Liam's brow knit. "I dunno. That's what I was wondering." He took out a pin joint and lit it with a wooden match. "A while back, I was telling her about the salmon stocks on Manitoulin." He exhaled two thin streams of smoke through his nose. "Her dad's a District Marshall with the Knights of Columbus and heads up their annual spring fish fry." He took another puff, before passing the joint to Pat. "Then she suggested going for fish and chips, so we did."

Grandpa and Betty were out delivering tourtières, but they'd be home any minute. We were in full view of anyone pulling up the drive.

"Hey guys," I said, "you're going to finish that before Grandpa gets back, right?"

Liam looked at me strangely. "What?"

"That." I pointed at the joint.

"Daniel, that's from Betty."

"Our Betty, the nurse?"

"It's medical grade. She recommended it over what Pépère and I'd been smoking."

Pat took a swig of his beer and savoured a drag. "How d'you figure this holds up?"

"It's okay." Liam observed Pat. "It's a pure indica. Eighteen percent. Mellow body buzz. Pépère says he still prefers the Blue Dynamite."

"That's cuz it's Canadian, man." Pat laughed, and he and Liam high-fived.

I stared at them. After that, I concentrated on working the splitter. They knew enough not to offer me any. I'd just end up puking all over the driveway. Back in Toronto, David, Liz, and our building manager Rick would sometimes smoke up together on the rooftop. I'd had no idea that Grandpa and Betty smoked. There were a lot worse things, I tried to convince myself, than Grandpa being a pothead.

"Guys," Pat said, "we need to start planning our twenty-fifth birthday."

Before Liam or I could answer, Jackson barked and jumped up. A dented, blue four-door pick-up pulled up into the drive. I powered down the log splitter, brushed the sawdust off my jacket and took off my gloves. Karen and Bob clambered out of the front. In the backseat, I could make-out three figures.

"Hey," I called out.

"Hey," Karen shouted. I gave her a hug and shook Bob's hand. Bob and Liam clapped each other on the shoulders.

"Bob," Karen said. "I don't think you've met Pat. Pat, this is Bob."

"Hey, man," Pat said. "You're Karen's new boyfriend, right? Merry Christmas Kwanza Hanukkah Solstice." He pointed. "What happened to your eye?"

"Well." Bob stood back. "Well, it just so happens I got mauled by a bear some years back."

"No kidding? Holy shit. How'd that happen?"

"I was rescuing my dog."

"Is that your dog there?" Pat peered toward the truck.

"Yeah, that's her. Gracie."

"Those your kids?"

"My daughters."

"What're their names?"

"Zephyr and Sky."

Pat made a beeline for the truck. Karen plucked a

piece of bark off my toque. "We're just dropping off something for your grandpa." Bob opened the tailgate and Liam helped haul a generator and a couple gas canisters into the open garage.

Two girls jumped out of the cab followed by a gigantic German Shepherd. Gracie sniffed noses with Jackson, tail wagging. Pat and the girls huddled around both dogs.

"Zephyr and Sky?"

Karen nodded. "Yeah. That's them."

The two girls were round-faced and dark-eyed, bundled up in colourful winter jackets. I didn't say it out loud, but they looked just like Karen and Anne when they were younger.

"Should I make some hot chocolate?" I asked.

"Sure. That'd be nice."

"Your mom dropped off her shortbread cookies earlier today."

"Where's David?"

"In Toronto, at home with his mom and Luke. It'll be their last Christmas together in that house."

"His mom's really moving to Sicily?"

"Sicily's always been home for her. As far as she's concerned, she's just been living abroad these past thirty years."

"Well. Good for her."

Pat unbuckled his belt. "Now check this out," he exclaimed, pulling it from his pants. "I had this custommade by an Apache medicine man. See there was this evil rattlesnake and this little girl out in the desert ..."

"How're you doing, Karen?" I asked.

"Alright. Better." We observed Liam and Bob in the

garage: two hulking unshaven men, one in a plaid Mackinaw coat and the other in a fur-lined bomber jacket, kneeling over the gas generator. Liam's hair was growing long again, Bob's was cropped short. If there ever was a zombie apocalypse, I'd have them both on my team.

These were the kind of men I'd known all my life. Growing up in Sudbury, I didn't know people like Marcus or Fang or Parker or Sean. As far as I knew, I was the only gay guy in the world.

Karen's hand slipped into mine. Our breath formed frosty clouds in the air. Bob's girls were screaming and giggling now, chasing Pat through the snow, twirling his snakeskin belt over their heads. The dogs bounded past in pursuit. Months back, when I'd accompanied Karen to her abortion appointment, we'd agreed we'd say I was the father. It was just easier that way.

"This morning," Karen said, "he asked me to move in."

Grandpa's truck pulled in off the road. He honked his horn as Betty waved open-mouthed at us through the windshield.

I squeezed Karen's hand. "It's all good. Karen Fobister, Merry Christmas."

"Merry Christmas, Daniel Garneau."

CHAPTER ELEVEN

Taking Care of Business

I lay on my mat in Savasana.

I focused on my outbreath, listening to the instructor's steady, modulated voice. I let my shoulders and jaw soften, my eyes quiet down. My state of mind did seem calmer. After the class, everyone scattered, chatting in small groups, mats under their arms, water bottles in hand. Others were talking with the instructor and I waited by the exit until they were done. When we were the only ones left in the room, she gathered her belongings and walked over to me. I noticed a small rose tattooed on the top of her left foot.

"So," Nadia said, "how was that for you?"

"It was great. I feel really good. You're really good. Thank you for inviting me."

Nadia's eyes were bright and reflective. "I'm glad you came."

"And how long have you been teaching?"

"Not quite one year. I'm just starting."

"Well, you're a natural."

"Thank you. You have good core strength, Daniel. But you are in your head a lot."

I drew a deep breath and exhaled. "That sounds right."

"Let's see your Mountain Pose."

I put down my bag, took some space and adopted Tadasana. Nadia circled, making subtle corrections to my spine, my hips. Standing back, she observed my form. "Better." She adjusted the angle of my head. "Much better flow than when you began."

"I've been told I could use more flow."

Nadia picked up her bag. "Everyone, Daniel, could use more flow."

After changing, we met in the lobby of the studio where Nadia signed a clipboard and exchanged a few words with the receptionist. Leafy bamboo framed a gurgling fountain in one corner. Outside, February snow fell gently, blanketing downtown Toronto.

"So where are you taking me this time?" I asked, as we strolled side-by-side down the street.

Nadia raised the wide, fur-trimmed hood of her overcoat, and slipped on matching calfskin gloves. "There's a special place, in the east end."

The last time we'd met in November, I'd taken Nadia to The Necropolis, a secluded cemetery in Cabbagetown. I'd brought rum balls and cinnamon croissants from a Sri Lankan bakery on Parliament, and a thermos of hot unsweetened chai. We'd sat on a blanket beneath the centuries-old trees, among the lichen-stained headstones. Most of the leaves had fallen, and the ground was a fiery sea of amber, yellows and gold.

It was fall when we had scattered Grandma's ashes up at the Good Medicine Cabin. Mom and Dad were buried at Maplecrest Cemetery up by Onaping. Every Christmas, we'd visit them. Cemeteries were peaceful, reassuring places for me, reminders of a bigger story than just our own.

When I told Nadia about Parker's hot yoga experience, she revealed she'd been practicing herself for some years, and invited me to one of her classes.

On this occasion, in the heart of winter, we took the Queen streetcar eastbound. Crossing into Leslieville, I gazed across the Don Valley where the deep snow lay unbroken on the frozen riverbanks. When we disembarked, Nadia led me into a spacious patisserie called Bobbette & Belle, its front counter resplendent with fragrant bouquets of artisanal pastries. Portraits of wedding cakes decorated the pale, cream-coloured walls. We sat by the expansive windows, savouring an assortment of macarons, washed down with sips of latte. Nadia's favourite was the white chocolate passionfruit, mine the black current cassis.

"I've been thinking," Nadia said, "about what you told me about Marcus's play."

"How so?"

"About how he used personal photos and film footage from his own life."

"There were clips of shows he'd put on as a kid in his parents' backyard."

"Where your friend Marwa would videotape him."

"Those two have been a pair since middle school. They'd call each other Tweedledum and Tweedledee.

Apparently, he'd make all his own costumes, perform these elaborate magic tricks, stage all sorts of experimental art pieces."

"Apparently?"

"He never told me any of this. I learned it all from Marwa. Then all through high school, he had these two personae: The Marvellous and The Maleficent. He'd talk about them like they were real people in his life. It'd be like: 'Oh, sorry, Dee, I can't hang out tonight, I've got a project to work on with The Marvellous.' Or: 'Hey Dee, it's Dum. I'm going with The Maleficent to the Poetry Slam tomorrow, and we'd like you to join us.' He was documenting himself before anyone ever starting blogging."

"And he used this footage in *Face*."

"Bits and pieces of it. It was a little bit meta, the whole thing. The *NOW* reviewer called it a memory play."

"But it wasn't autobiographical?"

"No, not in the sense that he was telling you his life story. But Marcus is really good at that: drawing you in and making you feel like you're his most intimate confidante, while hardly telling you anything about himself at all. Toward the end, I felt like there was this invisible glass barrier between us. I took it personally. I thought he was keeping me at a distance. But now, thinking back on it, I suppose he brought me in as close as he could."

"That's kind of you."

"Is it? I thought I was being cynical."

Nadia folded her gloves. "Yet you said this was his most personal play yet."

"That's what all the reviewers said." I searched for the

right word. "It was … intimate. Charles called it voyeuristic. The director wrote how *Face* explores the ways we document and remember our lives."

"And give meaning to who we are."

"There was this one reoccurring sequence where Marcus kept taking selfies in front of the mirror. It was really funny at first; each time he'd take off more clothes, but then it got more and more desperate and sad. Finally, these strobe lights kicked in and it turned into this kind of nightmare moment."

Nadia closed her eyes momentarily. "Everyone wants to be seen. Being witnessed makes us feel alive."

"Everyone, you think?"

"Yes, I think so. Even people like myself."

"What do you mean by that?"

"I'm a student of comparative literature, Daniel. I live in academia, tucked away in my secret walled garden of books."

"You make it sound like you're a hairy little hobbit."

Nadia laughed in surprise. "Now that's a fine literary reference."

"Hardly. It's David's influence. He's got this nerdy inner fanboy I'm just discovering."

"Well, I don't mind at all if you think of me as a hobbit. I shall consider it a compliment."

I studied Nadia's face. The truth was, of course, she was beautiful. I found myself undressing her in my mind. It wasn't difficult. I'd just spent an hour in class observing her body, her limbs and breath, syncing my own to hers. I imagined the curve of her breasts, her rose nipples, the cello lines of her shoulders, back and buttocks. I imagined cupping my palm over the furred mound of her *mons pubis*, the folds of her vagina beneath my fingertips.

"What is it?" Nadia asked over the rim of her coffee cup.

I looked away but not because I was embarrassed. My hand rested over my own knee. Outside, a streetcar trundled past through the trembling silver-grey light. A cinematic quality illuminated its movement, anticipating the intersecting stories of its occupants, shadowy figures within its haloed interior.

I pushed my saucer and cup away. Finally, I said: "Did you know, the first time I met Luke he was naked, at least from the waist up. He knew I was out in the hallway, and he made a decision to walk out without his shirt on. He had these scars left over from his double mastectomy. He wanted me to see them."

"What was your first impression?"

"Well, I didn't actually notice the scars at first. I just saw this shirtless guy wearing a pair of my boyfriend's jeans. So I was like: Who the hell is this shirtless guy wearing my boyfriend's jeans?"

"You thought he was David's lover?"

"I'm not sure what I thought. I'd just gotten back from the holidays. So, I must've. I remember feeling jealous, like someone had just pressed a scalpel, hard, against my throat."

"That is a visceral description."

"It just happened really suddenly. I figured it all out within a few seconds. But still."

"Is your friend Parker still going to naked yoga?"

"Oh, regularly. He's also told me he's asexual. Did I mention that? When he first told me that, I felt sorry for him. I used to think sex was everything. But then it occurred to me Parker Kapoor has more life in him than anyone I know. Parker's on medication for ADD, and he's also convinced he has Asperger's. But I just think he's a joyful, fun-loving human being."

"Naked yoga can be quite freeing."

"That's what Parker said. He also said men sometimes do get erections, but that it's no big deal. It's still a big deal for me. That's why I don't think I could ever go myself."

"Although?"

"What?"

"There's an 'although' written all over your face."

Okay." I leaned forward. "Remember that guy Antonio, the one who came to visit Toronto?"

"The photographer."

"Who?"

"Antonio from Torretta. The boy who lost his arm in a motorcycle accident." Nadia sipped from her latte. "The one to whom David's mother gave her plane ticket."

"Oh. That's right. Well, near the end of his summer in Sicily, David and Antonio, this girl Silvia, and a few others road-tripped to a place called Balestrate, which is famous for its nude beach. They spent the day there and had a great time. After Antonio arrived in Toronto, he was wondering if we had anything like that here. So the next weekend, we head out to Hanlan's Point on the Toronto Islands. Do you know it?"

"Hanlan's is the clothing-optional beach."

"We'd heard about it, but never been before. It's

pretty secluded. The three of us get off the ferry and have to walk a bit. I'm nervous but excited, for a whole bunch of reasons. We follow this boardwalk through some dense trees, and then suddenly we're there, standing in front of all this white sand and sparkling water. There're hundreds of people, lounging under umbrellas, sunbathing, drinking, listening to music. I'm shocked at how busy it is. I even see a family with kids. Not everyone's naked, but there're enough."

"And how was that for you?"

"Strange, at first. You can't help but look, right? People strip naked in doctors' offices but not usually in public."

Nadia repositioned the doily on her plate. "And did you?"

"Me? No, I couldn't do it. I mean, I'd just started clinical rotations. What if I met a patient? Maybe if I was on vacation somewhere. But David and Antonio did. Antonio had his arm and his clothes off before I'd finished putting on my sunblock. David and I mostly lounged on our towels, but Antonio spent the whole afternoon splashing in the lake, exploring the beach, talking to strangers. He even got himself invited onto one of the dozen party boats anchored offshore."

"Sounds like a sociable fellow."

"Antonio's not the brightest apple on the tree. But he's really, genuinely the nicest guy. I thought seeing him naked would be a total turn-on, but it wasn't like that. He has a great body, he's hot. When he was climbing up and over into that sailboat, I think half the beach was, well, enjoying the view. But David and I agreed he's more like a kid brother."

I recalled observing Antonio's round butt and his furred balls bobbing between his thick legs. His penis was almost obscenely large but he seemed unaware of this fact. Or if he was, he didn't seem to care. It occurred to me I wasn't entirely telling the truth to Nadia. I blushed, wondering if she could tell.

"Your grandpa's a nudist."

"Yeah, Grandpa and Liam. I'm pretty sure Betty is too. The three of them spend a lot of time up at the cottage. Ya gotta wonder."

"I wonder if 'naturist' might be a more apt description."

"Probably. Naturist then. Well, if Liam is hanging out *au naturel* with Grandpa and Betty, good for him. I couldn't do it."

"You had sex in front of Pat once."

"Ooh." I buried my face in one hand. "My brother Pat with the Three Amigas, yeah. Although"—I drew a breath—"I used to try my best to forget that ever happened. But now, I dunno. I don't really mind anymore. It happened." I straightened in my chair. "Last fall, when Pat missed Thanksgiving, I was so angry. But that's because I was so worried, y'know? Blonde Dawn's got the patience of a saint. She's good for him. I'm glad they didn't break up."

"Loving someone, it's like Tadasana. It's the simplest pose there can be."

"You also told us it's one of the most difficult."

"So I did. Tadasana is everything, but it's only just the beginning." Nadia observed the wedding cakes on display, elaborately ornamented with flowers and leaves. "You'd think it needn't be so complicated."

"Here," I said. "This is for you." I set in front of her a small package.

"What's this?"

"It's a Christmas gift. Better late than never."

"When have you and I ever exchanged gifts?"

"Never."

Nadia picked up the package and held it in both her hands. "I haven't gotten you anything."

I shook my head, "That's okay."

She pursed her lips. For a moment I thought she might not accept it. I was about to reassure her it was just a pair of novelty socks and didn't mean anything. But then she said: "Thank you."

"You're welcome."

"At least, let me pay the bill for both of us today."

"Alright."

And so she did.

∿ "We're going as Tank Girl and Booga," David said, poking at the tandem bike frame suspended over his cluttered workstation. He'd been working on this bike for two years. So far, he'd installed the handlebars and suspension seatposts. At this rate, I figured it'd be another two years before he was done.

"That's great." I rummaged through the front closet on my hands and knees. While David was away at ComiCon, I was looking forward to a full-blown spring cleaning.

"Ai Chang's been helping with the costumes."

"Supercool," I said, setting aside rusted cans of paint and hauling out a box of cleaning supplies. *Bingo.* I found my bag of rags, old throwaway socks and underwear I'd been hoarding all year just for this occasion.

My annual spring clean was a personal tradition. Pat called it "Daniel's Day." I'd given up long ago trying to recruit allies to the cause. Grandpa was never any help. His idea of tidiness was keeping a week's worth of dirty dishes confined to the kitchen. I was twelve when I snuck a peek at our social worker's report and read how the three Garneau children were living in "squalor." I didn't know what squalor meant, but I felt right away it was a dirty word, and I was mortified. I was also old enough to understand "squalor" meant we were in real danger of being taken from our home.

David, on the other hand, had grown up in a home that was pristine and perfectly ordered. Of course, in our Kensington loft, he was almost as messy as Pat. I was constantly picking up after him. But because he did all the cooking and laundry, it worked out just fine.

On the morning of ComicCon, David left to meet up with Karen's sister Anne. They'd be gone all day at the Metro Toronto Convention Centre. I made an extra large pot of coffee, put BTO's "Taking Care of Business" on the stereo, and cranked the volume. I rolled up my sleeves, put on my rubber gloves, and hefted my bucket and mop.

It was D-Day.

By mid-afternoon, armed with a bottle of Windex and a roll of paper towel, I climbed up onto the rooftop to wipe down the filthy skylight window. Two pigeons humping nearby flapped indignantly at my intrusion. After that, I hauled five bags of garbage to the dumpster.

In the evenings, I had to be careful not to startle the ill-tempered raccoons who regularly patrolled the alleyway. Coming back inside, I bumped into Liz, dressed in a floral muumuu with curlers in her hair, chasing one of her foster cats down the hallway. "This little girl," she said, scooping up a tiny tabby, "is an escape artist, aren't you, my little hairy Houdini?" When she put the kitten on her shoulder, it promptly climbed up onto her head. "You know," she said, "a lot of people call those wife-beaters."

"Pardon me?"

Liz pointed at my stained, ribbed undershirt. "Wife-beaters. Such an awful name." The cat on her head meowed at me disapprovingly.

"Well, I just call it a white tank-top," I said, lying.

"Make sure you do." Liz wagged a finger. "It all started with Stanley Kowalski, you know."

"Who?"

"He played such violent, dangerous characters, but Brando, he had affections for other men. So did Tennessee Williams. You're about the same age James Dean was when he died. Tsk, so tragic. Now, you two boys remind me just a little bit of James and Sal. It really is a sad and queer world we live in, don't you think?"

I wasn't quite following what she was saying. It also occurred to me Liz wasn't entirely sober in that moment. Her rather overpowering perfume smelled suspiciously like cherry brandy. One of her eyelash extensions was coming loose. She'd left her own door open and now the hallway was beginning to fill with cats. Her Pomeranian crept out last, bug-eyed and full of teeth (like a prop, David once observed, from John Carpenter's *The Thing*).

I spent the next ten minutes helping Liz herd them back into her loft. At the end, she picked up Lucille.

"No, but you're not like Stanley," she said outside her doorway. "You can't always judge a book by its cover. You're a good boy, Daniel, I can tell that about you. Did you know, my mother named me after Elizabeth Taylor in *Cat on a Hot Tin Roof*? If I'd been a boy, she'd have named me Paul. My ex-husband, he was a Brick Pollitt. He left me for our wedding photographer. I still love him though. Those two operate an ice cream parlour in Provincetown now, but we still talk sometimes." She rested her hand on my chest. "Boys like you are the future. No more mendacity, I say!" She wrinkled her nose, leaned in and sniffed. "Daniel, if you don't mind me saying so, it's high time you took yourself a bath."

She patted my arm and shuffled back into her loft. I smelled my armpit and realized she wasn't kidding. I'd been moving furniture, vacuuming, and running up and down three flights of stairs doing laundry all day. When I opened my own door, Hairy Houdini darted inside. She jumped up onto the kitchen table, sat back, tucked her tail over her paws, and regarded me expectantly.

When I pointed to the hallway, she only meowed.

"Out," I said. *Meow.*

"Out." *Meow.*

When I went to pick her up, she retreated behind my giant palm. Then when I crept toward her, she fled underneath David's worktable and peered at me with round shining eyes, one blue and the other green. "Fine. You win."

I set out a saucer of milk and a bowl of water and went to take a shower. When I finished and drew back the curtain, Houdini was perched on the vanity watching me. I spent the next three hours tidying our closets and shelves while she prowled around the loft. As I was sitting on the floor organizing the contents of our junk drawer, Houdini crept into my lap and licked my chin. *Meow.* Then I realized she was hungry and also probably needed to poop. I stepped out for supplies. When I got home, Houdini was pacing, I swear. *Meow.* I poured litter into a plastic tote, and she promptly and neatly did her business.

"Good girl."

Meow.

"Food. Right."

I set down a bowl of kibble, which Houdini sniffed and nibbled at. While I cracked open a beer and wolfed down two gyros I'd bought, I kept waiting for Liz to knock on my door asking for her cat back, but she never did.

"You need to go home."

Meow.

"She doesn't even know you're missing, does she?"

Forty-five degree head-turn.

"Did your parents abandon you too?"

Houdini yawned and strolled off. Eventually she curled up in a patch of sunshine on the kitchen window ledge. I cleared away a spider plant and our collection of Kinder Egg toys and set down a tea towel for her to rest on.

After that, I opened a second beer and sprawled out on the couch. David had left *Teenage Mutant Ninja Turtles* in the DVD player but I was too tired to get up to change it. I was done. D-Day accomplished.

I fell asleep just as Splinter revealed he was the pet rat of his ninja master murdered by The Shredder. When I woke up, I discovered a kangaroo leaning over me. It had big floppy ears and was wearing an army cap and aviator goggles. I knew it wasn't a gigantic dog or rabbit because of its long, plush kangaroo tail. It clambered up onto the couch and straddled me.

"You have got," I said, "to be kidding."

The kangaroo took off its camouflage vest and tossed it aside, revealing a red-white-and-blue bullseye painted on its bare chest. "Hey there." It grinned and pawed at me lustily.

"Whoa," I said. "Excuse me, but I have a boyfriend."

"Yeah," the kangaroo (obviously a mutant, since it could actually talk) said, "but I don't think he'd mind if you got it on with Booga."

"Booga?"

"That's me." It raised its goggles. "I'm Tank Girl's boyfriend, but we're open. We're an inter-species couple. Ai Chang's friend Jayden did my makeup. What do you think?"

"Honestly? It's freakin' amazing."

"I know. He's a professional makeup artist. Everyone kept stopping us to take our pictures."

"Did he paint your chest too?"

"Yeah."

Scalpel nick against my throat. "Where's Anne?"

"Anne went home. Her Tank Girl outfit totally rocked."

"I didn't know you were dressing up."

"Yeah you did, I told you all about it. You just weren't listening."

"Was there some costume event?"

"It's called cosplay, Daniel. Fans have been doing it forever."

"Oh, alright. Did you have a good time?"

"It was awesome. Anne's hilarious. She stayed in character practically the whole time we were there. You should've seen her. I can't remember when I had so much fun. Next year, we're getting the whole weekend pass, and you're coming with us. Oooh, I have something for you."

"What's that?"

David straightened, and slowly unzipped his cargo shorts. He pushed down the front, just enough to reveal he was wearing a pair of athletic jockstraps. I could also tell he was super excited to see me. "Ta-daa. Now if you're really good, mister, Booga might serve you tea and crumpets."

Houdini jumped up next to my head. *Meow.*

"Holy shit," David said.

"Booga, meet Hairy Houdini."

"That is a cat. Why is there a cat in our loft?"

"I'll tell you in a moment. But first," I said, pulling the big mutant kangaroo down on top of me, "let's see about those tea and crumpets."

⌢ Years ago, on my first date with Marcus, I'd run into Gary Kadlubek, the bully from my high school days in Sudbury. He'd been in a costume then too, an elaborate drag queen get-up complete with a fox stole and fishnet stockings. Since we were kids, Karen and I'd dress up for Halloween together, long after we'd given up trick-or-treating, well into university. I was always fascinated (and turned-on) to see how certain super masculine jocks would regularly get drunk and deck themselves out in women's clothing this one night of the year. At Vazaleen,

Pussy Pierogi was more alive and joyful than Gary Kad-lubek had ever been. Later that evening, I made a point of introducing Marcus to Kadlubek. By then, it was closing in on 2 a.m. and the whole crowd was rip-roaring drunk and high.

I was holding my dick in my hand at the washroom urinal when I heard gasping and grunting coming from one of the stalls. I couldn't help but crane my neck. It wasn't hard to figure out some guy was getting fucked. An empty condom packet lay on the floor by the toilet. I shouldn't have been shocked. I'd gotten a blowjob from a complete stranger once in a public washroom. Still, I felt like an intruder, finished my business and retreated as quickly as I could.

I found Marcus by the DJ booth along with his circle of friends. I was pretty sure he'd introduced me already to most of them. The guy in the shaggy mohawk was Mitz; he'd won the Bobbing-for-Butt-Plugs contest earlier that evening. The beauty queen in the sparkling corset was Julia.

"Daniel." Marcus waved me closer. "It's Reginald's birth-day today. We're going to celebrate at Julia's. You'll come join us?"

"Of course he'll come," Julia said. "We're all coming back to my place. Isn't that right, Reggie?"

Reginald scowled. "It's my birthday. I gets to say whether anyone comes or not." His Limp Wrist T-Shirt had a wet stain all over the front.

"He can come all over me if he wants," Mitz said, grin-ning.

"Our love," a girl in a furry Tigger onesie said, "is all-encompassing."

Reginald grasped me by the shoulders. "The Lady Julia has baked a cake. Let us all eat cake. May I compel you, comrade, to come?"

"It's compulsory he not be circumspect," a tall redhead said, draining her beer bottle.

"Um, sure." I hugged my chest and peered about, wide-eyed. "Thanks for inviting me."

Reginald flung his hands in the air. "Oho, he succumbs completely!"

"He shall receive his comeuppance," Big Red said.

"I," Tigger Girl said, "am craving a kumquat."

"Have you seen my cummerbund?" Julia said.

"Why, I do declare," Mitz said, "I have been circumcised!"

"With mirth," Marcus said, "and laughter."

Reginald stabbed a finger at him. "Let old wrinkles come!" he shouted.

Marcus nodded in approval, eyes bright. "Wild Things," he said, "gather yourselves." He put on a tattered top hat. "I've received news from the Maleficent: The wild rumpus is about to begin."

After that, we abandoned Vazaleen and piled ourselves into two cabs. Someone thrust a flask into my face and I took a swig. Somehow we were on a sidewalk, and then clambering up a crooked flight of stairs where we huddled beneath a single red light bulb while Julia searched for her keys, during which time someone shared their Jolly Ranchers and I was so happy to get orange tangerine. Then we all tumbled inside and I was sinking into a purple couch that was the softest, most comfortable couch I'd ever sat in in my entire life. I counted seven people in the tiny apartment. A cork popped loudly, someone handed me a glass of bubbly, then everything went dark (except for a tangle of fairy lights and a blue and pink lava lamp glowing in the corner). And a sparkling birthday cake floated into the room buoyed by jubilant singing, and I was singing just as loud if not louder than anyone. After that, someone put on a scratchy mixtape of punk rock, and people were dancing, pouring drinks, eating cake and smoking outside on the fire escape.

Marcus sat down next to me and squeezed my knee. "You okay?"

"Yep."

He took the paper plate of unfinished cake from my lap and set it aside. "You want to go home?"

"What? No, I'm — *burp* — great time!" I searched Marcus's face in horror. "You want me to go home?"

"Of course not. I'm just checking in." He wiped my chin with his hand. "I'd like you to stay. We're just getting started." He licked the frosting from his thumb. "But I can also call you a cab anytime you want, alright?"

"Alright."

"I just want to make sure you're feeling taken care of."

I felt a lump rise in my throat. Tigger Girl and Big Red were shrieking with laughter in the washroom. Ever since my parents died, I'd never felt taken care of, not by Grandpa or Grandma, not by anyone. Except maybe Karen. I had the impression that Marcus and all of his friends were at least three or four years older than me.

"What is it?" Marcus asked.

"Nothing." I wiped at both my eyes. "What's that smell?"

"I believe our Reginald and Mitz are doing hot knives in the kitchen."

"Oh."

Julia bent over us both, hands on her knees. From this angle, I had the most magnificent view of her cleavage enthroned within her rhinestone-studded corset. "Marcus, does your boy need a pick-me-up?"

"Daniel," Marcus said, "would you like a pick-me-up?"

"Huh?"

"You're falling asleep, sweetie," Julia said. "How about a little bump?"

"What?"

"Something to get you back on your feet."

"My feet?"

"Jules." Marcus made a face. "Would you be a darling?"

Julia winked. "No worries. Marwa's taken care of everything. One moment, please." She tapped me on the nose and strutted out of the room like a cocktail hostess.

"Who's Marwa?" I asked.

"A special friend." Marcus brushed my bangs aside. "Except, she's out of town this weekend." His mouth continued to move, but I was no longer listening. I was just wishing he would kiss me. I was wishing it as hard as I could in case I had dormant psychic powers and could influence the thoughts and actions of other human beings around me but only if I wished it hard and long enough. I supposed if I was religious one might call it fervent prayer, but I'd stopped believing in higher powers long ago.

Marcus stopped talking and still I kept wishing. The corner of his mouth turned up and still I kept wishing. And then, to my astonishment, he did. First he kissed me on my forehead. Then he kissed me on my lips. It was a wonderful kiss. Warm and not too wet. It was a perfect kiss. He tasted like watermelon. How could the inside of Marcus Wittenbrink Jr.'s mouth taste so good and delicious at this late hour of the night? He drew away, still smiling.

Julia poised above us. "Et voilà." She leaned over, presenting an elegant round mirror with three lines of white powder, and held out a rolled bill. This was blow, I realized. This was cocaine. I'd seen how this was done in the movies. I'd seen *Scarface*. I sat up and hiccoughed.

Then I sneezed.

"Oh." I blinked and swallowed. "Shit." Julia and Marcus stared. "I'm, I'm so sorry." I opened and closed my mouth. "I can pay for that."

Julia shut her eyes and bit her lower lip. "Not to worry, sweetie."

"Jules," Marcus said.

She breathed deeply through her nose. "Yes?"

"That," he said, pointing with his baby finger, "really shouldn't go to waste."

She looked down at herself. "You think?"

"Should it, Daniel?"

I winced. "No?"

I was still snorting blow off Julia's boobs when someone shouted from the kitchen. A large cat padded through the living room with a white square of rolling paper stuck to its tail. Reginald and Mitz, both shirtless now, stumbled in pursuit. I was beginning to feel more awake.

"Better?" Julia asked.

"Better," I said. "Thank you. And really I'm, like, I'm so sorry about that."

"Well." Her brow furrowed. "You can make it up by bringing me a coffee in the morning. There's a Timmy's around the corner. Extra-large double-double." Then she winked and walked away.

"What did she mean by that?" I asked.

"She means," Marcus said, "you get to stay overnight."

"I do?"

"Only if you want to. Everyone else is."

"They are?"

Marcus nodded. "And to cure your hangover, Lady Julia will make you the most superlative Caesar you've ever had in your entire life."

I sniffed and wiped my nose on the back of my wrist. "I can crash on this couch?"

"No. Reginald's called shotgun on the couch. I've got Marwa's room. You and I can share her bed if you like."

I raised my eyebrows, slack-jawed.

"Marwa lives here. She's Julia's roommate."

"But she's gone for the weekend?"

"She has."

"She wouldn't mind?"

"Marwa? No." Somehow, magically, Marcus produced his top hat, which he carefully set down atop my own head. "I don't think she'll mind at all."

CHAPTER TWELVE

Queen of the Broken Hearts

On the first day of May, Parker Kapoor's mother fell and broke her hip. This was Parker's birthday, and he cancelled our dinner date in a text message while on the GO Train to Brampton. When I asked him if there was anything I could do, he said no thank you. His father and two of his sisters were already at the hospital, along with an auntie and three cousins. Another auntie was booking a flight from Vancouver to spend a month to help with caretaking. Surgery was scheduled for the following afternoon. A third sister remained in Calgary working on a case in the Federal Court of Appeals. They were still trying to reach Parker's fourth sister who was somewhere outside Inuvik studying Canada's melting permafrost.

"We Kapoors," Parker said a few days later, "are not your typical Indo-Canadian family. We grew up on Christmas sleigh rides and moshing at the Sarnia Bayfest. We love our poutine as much as our pakora."

We were sitting by the fountain in the Toronto Eaton Centre, at the midpoint of the vaulted, glass-ceiling galleria. On this Sunday afternoon, hundreds of tourists and shoppers milled around us, brand-name bags, Frappuccinos, and cell phones in hand. Five storeys above, Michael Snow's sixty geese soared suspended in perpetual glorious flight.

"Parker, I always thought your family was from Brampton."

"My parents moved to Brampton after I left for U of T. But my sisters and I, we were all born and raised in Sarnia, Ontario."

"Sarnia? How was that for you?"

"You mean how was it growing up in a community that was ninety percent white?" Parker sipped from his Booster Juice Breezy Banana smoothie. "Well, I never quite got along with the other kids playing in the sandbox; I was that boy off by himself dropping bits of potato paratha on an anthill. I didn't mind. My closest friend was this little girl named Karenjit whose parents were Sikh Punjabi. In a town that small, you get to know the other brown people pretty quickly."

Water jets formed a ring of glimmering parabolas filling the massive, turquoise fountain bowl. A woman in an African headdress sat nearby, her three kids clearly fascinated by the entire process.

"Karenjit actually went to a Catholic school but she and I got to know each other through skating practice. When she was thirteen, her family moved away to the States. I miss her a lot. She's really famous now, but we still keep in touch."

"She's famous?"

Parker nodded. "Although now she goes by her professional moniker. A couple years ago, she was named *Penthouse* Pet of the Year."

The glass elevator nearby descended, and two men pushing a baby stroller emerged. "Parker, your childhood best friend is a porn star?"

"Her name's Karenjit," said Parker. "Or you can call her Karen if you ever meet her."

"Sorry."

"It's okay. She was a tomboy and loved her G.I. Joes as much as I loved my Barbies. I think the two of us really bonded over that. She was also afraid of bugs and I'd protect her from them. I remember we had the same lime green fanny packs. She was small but tough and always stood up to the bullies. Really, it was Karenjit who helped me get through my childhood. I owe her a lot."

"She sounds like a great friend."

"She was my best friend. I wish her all the best, whatever she does. She deserves it. She even sent flowers to the hospital after I told her my mother broke her hip. I love my Karenjit."

The splashing fountain abruptly fell still. The bowl of water was filled to the rim.

"How is your mom doing?"

"She'll need five to six weeks to recover, but knowing her, she'll probably manage it in four. She takes on a lot of responsibilities. Honestly, the hardest part for her will be just resting."

"Both your parents are doctors, right?"

"Well, mother's Chief Medical Director of Ob Gyn

at Brampton Civic. She also chairs the Board of the South Asian Women's Centre. Father just sticks to his family practice. He used to give all of us kids our flu shots every year and then take us out to Swiss Chalet. He's Guy Ritchie to her Madonna."

The water drained out of the bowl. Teenagers in backpacks pointed. Strolling past, an old man in a *kippah* paused and watched expectantly.

"Parker, you haven't started your blog yet, have you, the one about your family?"

"No. I meant to, I just can't seem to get organized. I've got a plethora of ideas and notes written down. But I doubt it's going to happen, not in this lifetime." Parker sighed and hung his head. "Maybe you can publish them for me posthumously, like *The Diary of Anne Frank*."

"Parker, your mom's going to be okay. Everything's going to be fine."

"Oh, no, Daniel. It's not that at all. I know she's going to be fine. I'm just upset. Maude died."

An enormous plume of water shot twenty-five metres straight up, causing the littlest kids to jump in delight.

"Maude?"

"It's all my fault. When I heard about Mother's accident, I panicked. I packed a bag and headed straight to the train station. I was only gone three days, but when I got back, Maude was belly-up in the fishbowl. I forgot to leave any food and I think she starved to death. How awful is that? Can you imagine how traumatizing that must've been for Harold? Now he just sits on the bottom of the bowl and barely moves. How do you console a goldfish who's just lost his life partner forever?"

I pinched the bridge of my nose. "Parker, I'm pretty sure a goldfish can't starve to death in three days. She probably just reached the end of her natural life. I think it was just bad timing."

A second and then a third powerful jet of water shot into the air. Parker raised his head. "You think?"

"I'm sure of it. I'm sorry about Maude. For what it's worth, she lived a good life."

Parker's big eyes widened. "Daniel, you predicted this."

"I did?"

"In my betting pool, three years ago, you predicted Maude would die in May."

"I don't remember that."

"Do you know what that means?"

"No."

"Daniel, you get to come with me to the pet store to help find her replacement."

With a sparkling rush the fountain started up again, and the empty bowl began to refill itself. "We'll need to go to Big Al's Aquarium Supercenter," Parker said, "out in Scarborough. Can you come on a Tuesday? They have a live Shark Feeding Frenzy every Tuesday evening at 7 p.m. sharp. It's really quite thrilling. I can come pick you up. Oh, do you think I should bring Harold?"

"What? Bring your goldfish to the store?"

"OMG, you're right. The shark feeding would probably terrify him. I suppose we can find him a suitable partner on our own. I don't know. What do you think?"

"Yes, Parker. I think we can."

"Of course we can. I mean, my parents met through

an arranged marriage, right? And look at them. They've been together thirty-five years."

"Your parents had an arranged marriage?"

"And two of my sisters, or at least both their husbands came highly recommended. Mother and my aunties always were the biggest fans of *Shaadi.com*. Of course, Charita and Mona, they had the final say."

"Of course."

"Daniel, arranged marriages can be quite successful. You were the one who introduced me to Kyle."

"There you go."

"Thank you for doing this. I feel better already. You've been a big support. I don't know what I'd do without you. Sometimes I feel I can barely take care of myself."

"Parker, you help handicapped people in their own homes. You take care of people all the time. You have a lot of responsibility."

"Tell that to my parents. I'm their only son, and what have I accomplished? In their eyes, I'm the ultimate underachiever."

"They've said that to you?"

"No, of course they haven't. But I know that's what they're thinking. I mean, how could they not? My sisters all have their own successful careers and where am I? I was my high school valedictorian but how far has that gotten me? Look at me, I'm a mess. You and Karenjit have been my two best friends. You're on your way to becoming a doctor, she's already made it to the cover of *Penthouse*. I can barely get over the fact that my goldfish just died. My psychiatrist says I could benefit from more structure in my life."

"What do you think?"

"Maybe. I dunno."

"Parker, would you ever get a cat?"

"What?"

"A cat. My neighbour fosters cats from Toronto Cat Rescue. David and I took one in, kind of by accident. Except since then we've discovered David's allergic. We can't keep her, but we don't want to give her back because she's really cute and amazing. We've been calling her Hairy Houdini. She's already gotten all of her shots and everything. Would you be interested in adopting a cat?"

"Daniel." Parker stared at me, his eyes bulging. "You know my parents never let us have pets when we were growing up."

"Oh, right. Maybe not, eh?"

"I'd love to."

"Really?"

"Yes. Definitely." Parker sat bolt upright, gripping his thighs. "You have no idea."

"Okay. Well, I mean, you'll probably want to meet her first and see what you think after that."

"Alright. But I'm telling you now, Daniel, my answer is absolutely yes. The honest truth is, I've been thinking about getting a cat for a while now." He slurped down the remains of his smoothie. "I mean, this is kismet. This is meant to be. I've always dreamt of starring in a Raj Kapoor love epic with a Bengal tiger at my feet. Karenjit would be so proud of me. She's a big supporter of PETA. When can I meet her?"

"Hairy Houdini? Anytime you want. How about to-day?"

"Can Kyle come too?"

"Sure. In fact, why don't we have you both over for dinner? We can order pizza and wings, and you can spend some time with her. If it works out, you can take her home tonight."

"Daniel?"

"Yeah?"

"Thank you."

"Hey, well. You're the one doing us a favour."

"You can come visit her anytime you want. You'll be Uncle Daniel and Uncle David. We can all be one big happy extended family together."

"Parker," I said, "we're counting on it."

∿ Luke was accompanying his mom back to Italy. Isabella De Luca's fourth marriage, to Nicoli Badalamenti, was to take place on the family farm in an intimate ceremony with a dozen guests, Her eldest son was to walk her down the aisle. David was staying back in Toronto to manage the sale of the house. I asked him how he felt about missing his mom's wedding.

"It's alright," he said. "I've hung out with Nicoli, he's a good guy. He's a lot like Antonio. I don't mind Antonio's uncle being my stepdad. He's worked for the family his whole life and practically been like a son to my grandparents. My aunts couldn't run the farm without him. I wrote a little speech Luke will read at the wedding. It's all good."

We stood at the bar of The Cameron House on Queen West, waiting for Three Dog Run to take the stage.

Constellations of blue fairy lights glimmered overhead. Baroque, gilt arches and faded murals decorated the walls and ceiling, recalling the venue's more glamorous past as a hotel in the 1920s.

"Nicoli and my mom," said David, "were childhood sweethearts. When I first heard this man had proposed, it just seemed crazy and totally impulsive. But my *nonno* took me aside and reminded me: This romance goes back to when they were kids. It's been fifty years in the making."

I observed the galloping horse-drawn chariot carrying young lovers over our heads. "Okay, here's a question. If your dad was your mom's third husband, and Luke's dad was her second, who was her first?"

"Ooh." David perused the drinks menu. "In my family, we don't talk about that."

"Your mom's first marriage?"

"All I know is, back in the day there was some rivalry for her affections, and she couldn't decide between two suitors."

"She told you this?"

"No, not even. But my *nonno* did. Last summer, we'd go for long walks around the olive grove. He told me a lot of things."

"So, what happened?"

"Well, on the day she turned eighteen, apparently she did marry one of her suitors. But then someone challenged the union and there was some kind of annulment. It was all really scandalous. After that, she left Italy on her own to start a new life for herself. That's when she immigrated to Canada."

"Sounds dramatic."

"I think there were a lot of broken hearts all around. Like I said, Ma doesn't talk about it."

Whistles and clapping signalled the band's arrival onstage. Tonight, Pat was sporting suspenders and a ruffled shirt, his shaggy hair pulled back in two ponytails. Rob had shaved off his beard, leaving only an enormous handlebar moustache. Bobby hefted his saxophone, wearing a flat cap and a tweed vest. A heavyset kid in glasses settled in behind the drums; he was probably twenty, but in his Pokémon T-shirt, he looked closer to twelve.

"Hey," I said, "where's Blonde Dawn?"

"Maybe it's her night off?"

A tall ginger guy in a black V-neck and a pierced lip wiped down the bar in front of us. "What'll it be, gentlemen?"

David ordered a Boneshaker off the menu, just for the hell of it. It sounded like a concoction a lumberjack might throw back. But it turned out to be a delicate, floral cocktail of lemon juice, cream and gin. The bartender winked at the two of us. "Enjoy."

It'd been a while since we'd seen Pat on stage. The band was performing two or three times monthly now to small but devoted crowds. Since coming back from Burning Man last year, Pat was different, more focused on his song writing and I didn't recognize half their set. After an hour, Bobby, Rod and the drummer stepped off the stage. Alone, Pat pulled up a stool and adjusted his mic. "Glad you could make it out. We're Three Dog Run. You've been a phenomenal audience." More whistles. Someone shouted: "Take off your shirt!" Pat mopped his brow and took a sip from his beer. "We'd like to do one last number before we go, something I wrote recently. See, a while back, I lost something, something really good, something really important to me." He plucked at a ukulele in his lap. "This is dedicated to all the fuck-ups out there, to anyone who's ever regretted anything, who's ever felt truly sorry. This one's for you."

He strummed a chord, then paused to untie his ponytails and shake out his hair. He rested his lips against the mic. As he sang the opening two verses *a capella*, the hair prickled on my arms. After the first chorus, Pokémon Kid marched back onstage playing a snare drum. After the second chorus, Bobby joined them with his accordion. Last to make an entrance was Rod on a gigantic, booming sousaphone, by which point everyone in the room was singing along, belting out the song's final rousing refrain.

There was enthusiastic applause long after the band had left the stage. Pokémon Kid walked around with a plastic bucket which people filled with change and small bills.

David leaned against me. "Do you think that last song was about Blonde Dawn?"

That song had been about a lot of things. But yeah, I nodded. In Pat's case, it probably also had to do with Blonde Dawn.

"That's too bad. I wonder what happened."

"Me too."

Pokémon Kid stopped in front of us. It was obvious he had no idea who we were. He was pale and pudgy, his big brown eyes made bigger by his thick glasses. I put a twenty in his bucket for both David and me.

"Oh, wow. Thanks a lot," he said. "Thanks. Thanks for your support. Guys, y'know, like, you can always go to our website if you want to follow us."

I looked at David who'd helped design the website for Three Dog Run.

"You're new," David said.

"I am. Yeah, I know. I am."

"What happened to Blonde Dawn?"

"Their first drummer?"

"Yeah."

"I'm not sure. I dunno. I never asked. I mean, I just auditioned three weeks ago. Tonight's my first gig, my first time out with these guys."

"Well, you were great," I said.

"Wow, thanks." The kid actually blushed. You might've thought I'd given him a gold star sticker and patted him on the head. "Thanks a lot."

"Tell Pat, David and Daniel say hi."

"You friends with Captain Pat? Hey, you wanna come backstage, meet the band?"

"Um, no." David glanced at me. "Tell Captain Pat we had to go. Big voyage ahead of us. Gotta weigh anchor, set sail."

I elbowed David in the side. "The show was awesome," I told the kid.

"Really, you think? Thanks, I'll tell the band, for sure. Have a great night, guys. And thanks again."

"You too."

On our way out, the bartender raised his hand, displaying an octopus tattoo on the inside of his bicep. "Have a good night, gentlemen."

David clapped me on the shoulder. "Hold on a sec." He strode over to the bar, and I waited two minutes while he chatted with the guy.

"What was that all about?" I asked when we hit the sidewalk outside.

"I told him," David said, "I really enjoyed his Boneshaker."

"Really? And what did he say?"

"He said thanks. Then he asked if you were my boyfriend."

"And what did you say?"

"What do you mean, 'what did I say'? I told him yes you were, we'd been together four years, and that you were the best lay I've ever had in my life."

"You said that?"

"I did."

"And then?"

"He said the two of us should come back sometime and try his Red-Headed Slut."

"Are you kidding me?"

"You heard me. It's a shooter."

"Oh my god."

"It's all good."

"You sure he said 'the two of us'?"

"He definitely said 'the two of us.'"

"Oh jeez."

"Relax, lover." David wrapped an arm around my waist. "We got all the time in the world."

Later that evening, long after midnight, drowsy and comfortable, thinking we might have sex but okay if we didn't, I flopped down on our bed.

"David. You know how you said there were those two guys in Sicily who were both in love with your mom?"

David paced the room, laying out his work clothes for the next day. "I don't know if they were in love with her. But yeah, okay."

"Do you think," I asked, "one of those guys was Antonio's uncle?"

"Yeah. I thought about that too." David set his alarm. "I dunno, the way my *nonno* told the story, it'd make sense if one of them was Nicoli. Maybe one day it'll all come out." He turned off his lamp and crawled into bed. "Time heals all wounds, they say, right?"

"What's important is that your mom's happy."

David snuggled up against me. He was quiet long enough I thought he might've fallen asleep. But then he spoke. "Last year, when Ma and I arrived on the farm, we sat down for supper with my grandparents and the rest of the family and it was a real homecoming. By the end of that summer, it was like she'd grown ten years younger. It was as if my whole life she'd been holding her breath, and in Sicily she could finally breathe again."

David's hand rested between my legs. I stroked his back and his hip, thinking about the bartender, his thick neck and freckled, muscular arms. I thought about what it'd be like to pull the guy's V-neck over his head, to kiss him, or to watch him kiss David. Or maybe he and I could make out while David blew us both, the way Marcus had done once with Fang and me. I wondered how it'd feel to be on my hands and knees deep-throating David while the big guy fucked me from behind.

Then I thought about what home meant in my life,

what it meant for me to finally truly breathe. It was sharing a loft with my lover, this man called David Gallucci.
It meant shopping together in Kensington Market,
spooning him on crisp autumn nights, sitting side-by-side
on the family couch as Betty lit the Christmas tree. If he
and I had sex with other people, that didn't mean we
loved each other any less. If anything, I told myself, it
meant we trusted each other enough to do so. Opening
a relationship wasn't for everybody. We were just starting
out. I'd already hooked up with another guy while David
was away last summer. All he'd done was kiss a girl. We
had a whole new summer just ahead of us. It was only a
matter of time before David had sex with another man.
Softly, like bees buzzing against my skin, David began to
snore. I wondered if I'd still be able to breathe then.

⌒ Late in May, the Toronto Alliance for the Performing
Arts announced its annual Dora nominees. *Face*, written
and performed by Marcus Wittenbrink Jr., received six
nominations, including Outstanding Male Performance
and Outstanding Production. Marcus was no stranger to
the Dora Awards, having been nominated three years ago
for *Philophobia*. I congratulated him with a perfunctory
but polite Facebook message. Within minutes, he replied
with a rambling thanks which I figured he cut-and-pasted
in response to all his adoring fans. However, at the end,
he did add a P.S.: "Daniel, I hope you and David are well.
I'd love to have you both over for dinner if you're free at
all this summer." After that, he cited a few quite precise
dates and times he was available.

When I mentioned Marcus's invitation, David shrugged, concentrating on tightening a bolt on his tandem bike. "Sure, why not? It has to be later though. Right now, I'm totally swamped."

"You really don't care," I said, "that Marcus is my ex-boyfriend?"

He tossed aside his wrench and picked up a drill. "We've been through this before. Everyone has a past. You can't go through life tip-toeing around the past." He straddled the bike frame clamped to his repair stand. "All that's important is that I'm your boyfriend, not him. Here, check this out."

He handed me a cycling magazine opened to a full-page ad. In the glossy photo collage, I recognized David and the rest of his bike store team, all wearing matching T-shirts. The owner was opening a second store, and David had just been promoted to manager. He'd be working long hours all through the summer helping train new staff. "Very nice." I studied David's colleague Arthur crouched between two kids in helmets. I'd been soaking wet when we first met at the climbing gym. I hadn't realized how good-looking the guy actually was. "Arthur's really handsome."

"What?" David powered down his drill and raised his safety glasses.

"Arthur, he's an attractive guy."

"Yeah, he's a DILF." He squinted at his bike frame, picking away metal shavings. "That's his real kid in the photo, the one on the right."

"No way."

"He gets him most weekends. He brings him into the

store all the time. Art Junior is kinda like our mascot. By the way, I just hired Anne."

"What?" I put down the magazine. "Karen's sister?"

"Mm-hm."

"What does she know about bikes?"

"Not bikes. Skateboards. She showed me a couple longboards she'd built. Totally sick. Then she showed me her OCAD portfolio, and all these graphics she'd done for skater friends. I was blown away."

Back during high school in Sudbury, I vaguely recalled Karen's kid sister skating around with her torn jeans, toque, and army rucksack on her back. I hadn't thought twice about what it might've meant to her. "She's that good?"

David loosened the clamps and flipped the frame over. "Yeah, well, Duncan's the guy who handles all our skate gear. Anne came into our shop a while back looking for some truck parts. They got to talking. Now that we're hiring, Duncan was the one who suggested her. And yeah, she's that good."

"Wow. I'm happy for you both. I hope it works out."

"Duncan seems to think it will."

"You and Anne have really hit it off."

"Yeah, for sure. Except now, I'm her boss. But I don't think that'll be a problem."

"Does Karen know?"

"I haven't mentioned it. Look, Daniel, I know you're best friends with Karen and everything, but Anne Fobister, she's her own person too, y'know."

"Okay."

"She's pretty cool once you get to know her."

"Well, I'm glad you're getting to know her." I set the

magazine aside. After a moment I said: "And you're right, she is part of the family."

David wiped his hands on a rag. "I'm going to have to bring this into the shop." He tossed the rag aside and cracked his neck. "I don't have the right equipment here to work on it."

"Alright."

"So." David plopped himself down on the couch next to me. "This is it."

"What?"

David extended his arms. "This is it. This is all I've got. This is my home now, here with you. Ma's shipped some of her belongings to Italy. Luke took a few things. All the rest she's sold. The house goes on the market next week."

I pointed at two stone lions flanking our TV. "And that's all you wanted to keep?"

"Yep. I think they're badass. I grew up with them. Oh yeah, and him."

The glass-framed print of Michelangelo's *David* leaned against the wall by the front door. "Where," I asked, "are you planning to put him?"

"We'll find some place."

If Grandpa were to ever sell the Garneau family home in Sudbury, I wasn't sure what I'd feel. Probably panic. Maybe Liam could inherit the property when the time came. This was a discussion the family had yet to have. I squeezed David's thigh. "How is all of this for you?"

"I'm okay with it." David opened his hands. "I wasn't expecting this, but hey. Life moves on, right? I'm supposed to bury a statue of St. Joseph in the yard upside down."

"What are you talking about?"

"When you're selling a house, apparently that's what you do, for good luck. Ma says I should bury it by the rose bed in the front."

"You're actually going to do this?"

"Daniel, never mess with Sicilian superstitions. Always look people in the eye when toasting and take your first sip before you set your glass down on the table. Otherwise, it's seven years bad sex."

"Whoa. Harsh."

"Recognize this?" David slipped from under his T-shirt a small amulet on a chain, a twisted, horn-shaped piece of gold.

"Sure, you brought that back last summer."

"My *nonno* gave it to me. But do you know what it is?" I shook my head. "It's called a *cornicello*. In Italy, it's a symbol of virility and strength. It's a talisman to guard against the evil eye. Specifically, it's meant to protect my junk."

"How's that work?"

"You ever wonder why an Italian man grabs his crotch? It's to protect against bad luck. The next time you see a hearse drive by, or if any bad omen comes up, watch who grabs their balls. It's the Italians. It all has to do with protecting our most valuable asset: the future fruit of our loins. Family's everything in Italy. You can't be too careful with the *Malocchio*."

"What," I asked, "are you talking about?"

David lowered his voice. "The evil eye. Look, you know I'm not religious. I'm not even really superstitious. Except we Sicilians, we don't mess with the *Malocchio*." He arched one eyebrow and grabbed his crotch.

"Seriously?"

"Okay, like I said, I don't really buy into that stuff. Still." He examined the *cornicello*. "There's all sorts of phallic amulets and effigies dating back to Roman times. Sexual symbols are supposed to distract the person trying to cast the evil eye. Ever see someone do this?" He thrust out his fist with his thumb pinched between the index and second fingers.

"Isn't that kind of like a 'screw you'?"

"Sometimes. Lots of cultures use this one. But in Italy, again, it's a sign to ward off evil. It represents you-know-what."

"What?"

"C'mon.' He wiggled his thumb. "Take a guess."

I made a face. "Really? That?"

"Bingo."

"Good to know."

"Daniel, Italians might be obsessed with sex, but we're not the only ones. The Greeks the Japanese the Bhutanese, people all over the world attribute supernatural powers to the penis."

"The Bhutanese?"

"In the mountainous Kingdom of Bhutan, the symbol of an erect penis is seen as good luck, driving away evil forces and spirits. Go to Bhutan, my young Padawan, and you shall see paintings and statues of hard-ons everywhere."

"Pray tell, and how do you know this?"

"Because I used to run D&D campaigns, and you come across this stuff in your research. You wanna know about the *Kanamara Matsuri*?"

"No, I don't. Oh my god, you are such a nerd. And you and your whole family are obsessed with penises."

David lay back with his head in my lap and crossed his legs. "Would you love me if I wasn't?"

"Maybe," I said, "we should mount the Cherry-Scented Vibro-Dong over our front doorway to ward off negative energies. After all, this is your one and only home now."

"That," David said, "is a fantastic idea. Hook it up to our downstairs buzzer. Anytime someone rings, the Vibro-Dong goes off."

"Better than garlic or a horseshoe. Do you think we can get Rick to jerry-rig that?"

"Rick can jerry-rig anything."

"I'll ask him the next time I see him."

"Better put it in writing, just to make sure. There's a Maintenance & Repairs Request Form you can fill out."

"I'm on it."

"Liz might want one too. She's convinced she sees dead people."

"Like your mom."

"Yeah."

"She'll need her own Vibro-Dong."

"Maybe we should order one for every tenant in the building," David said. "Get a discount rate."

"That, Dr. Venkman, is a brilliant idea," I said. "I'll start a collection."

"Just trying to be a civic-minded citizen. It's the least we can do."

"How very Bhutanese of you."

CHAPTER THIRTEEN

Wondering Where the Lions Are

"**Y**ou all packed?" David asked, frying up eggs, bacon, and homemade hash browns.

"Pretty much."

"I'm going to miss you."

"It's just a weekend." I sat at our kitchen table going over a list of items to bring. Extra socks, check. First-aid kit, check. Chlorine tablets, check.

"Are you going to have fun?"

I considered my answer. It'd been years since I'd gone camping with my brothers, and there was a reason why. For months, Pat had suggested ideas for how we'd commemorate our twenty-fifth birthday. Liam was mulish. He wasn't coming into the city. He wasn't going to Vegas or New York. And definitely, neither Liam nor I were interested in flying to South America to take *ayahuasca* in the Columbian jungle with Carolina Sanchez.

In the end, it was Karen who suggested the three of us go back to Killarney. Apart from the Good Medicine Cabin, Killarney was where we'd spent much of our childhood, backpacking La Cloche Silhouette Trail, canoeing and fishing. Back in the day, it was members of Canada's Group of Seven who'd petitioned to preserve Killarney as a provincial park. The land's white quartzite and pink granite cliffs, jack pine forests and sparkling lakes were memorialized in their artwork. After Mom and Dad died, I'd turned to hockey while Pat immersed himself in his music. But it was Killarney that saved Liam.

"Everyone thinks," I said, "because we're triplets we're best friends. But we're not. We were always too different."

"Blonde Dawn," David said, "says she'd heard about you guys long before she ever met Pat."

"Oh. Sure. Those poor kids whose mom and dad got killed in a car crash."

"No, it was more like those three brothers who grew up wild, who never quite fit in. You were all dark and athletic, and you had a rep. Nobody messed with the Garneau boys. You always had each other's back."

We did always have each other's backs, despite our differences. "What do you mean 'dark'?"

David shrugged and refilled my coffee cup. "Ask Blonde Dawn."

The truth was, I already knew what Blonde Dawn meant.

"People," I said, "think tragedy is romantic."

"Tragedy," David said, "is romantic." He leaned over the stove seasoning the contents of his frying pans. "What if Thelma and Louise never drove off that cliff? What if Romeo and Juliet never offed themselves?" He threw me a knowing look. "What if Patroclus never died?"

I had no idea what he was talking about and it must've shown on my face.

"Look." David turned off the stove. What if," he said,

"King Kong never got himself all shot up and swan dived off the Empire State Building. Let's say he was captured and taken back to Skull Island where he lived happily ever after. How would the story be then?"

I remembered watching the original black and white movie at the Starlite drive-in with Liam and Pat when we were just kids. I couldn't believe how it ended. Our parents hadn't warned us. Why hadn't they warned us? I remembered bawling my eyes out afterwards. In that moment, I was inconsolable. Mom and Dad drove us to the Dairy Queen all the way out on the Kingsway just to make us feel better. It was the last movie we ever saw at the Starlite together. The drive-in closed the next year.

"That story," David said, "wouldn't be the same, would it? People love it when tragedy is thrown into the mix. That's what makes for great romance."

I thought of Bambi's mom. I thought of Simba's dad. I remembered being ushered out of our beds by Grandpa and gathered in the living room while uniformed officers waited outside. Mrs. Milton would watch over us while Mr. Milton and Grandpa went with the police. I didn't understand what had happened. None of us did. It was true. That story wouldn't have been the same at all.

"Pat," I said, "would use it to pick up girls. Ever since we were teenagers, he'd 'confide' in them how our parents died, and then girls would want to sleep with him."

"How do you know that?"

"Because," I said, "he told me. He used to practice in front of the mirror. I watched him do it once at a party, sitting on a couch looking all sad with all these girls draped over him, telling his fucking sob-story."

"You were the angry one."

"What?"

"Blonde Dawn said everyone thought of Pat as the happy one. Liam was the sad one. You were the angry one."

"The angry one?" I was genuinely taken aback. "I was the only one who kept my head. I never ended up at the police station or the hospital psych ward."

"You did your best."

"You're damn right I did my best. Why would people think I was the angry one?"

"Hey." David piled his frying pans in the sink. "I'm just telling you what I heard."

"From Blonde Dawn. Dawn Singer didn't know us. She didn't even go to our high school." Bear banger, check. Emergency whistles, check.

"No, she went to a different school across town. But she'd still heard about the Garneau brothers."

"Sudbury's not that big. People talk. Why are we even talking about this?"

David set two plates on the table and sat down across from me. "Look, I just asked if you were going to have fun camping with Liam and Pat. We don't have to talk about this if you don't want to."

I concentrated on scraping butter on my toast. I might not have been suicidal or on a first-name basis with the police, but I did manage to get myself kicked off my hockey team. I should've been team captain. Finally, I said: "I should talk about this though, shouldn't I?"

"It's up to you."

"Maybe," I said, "I was angry."

"You had every right to be."

"Sure." Growing up with Pat and Liam had been an

endless string of crises. It was putting out one small fire after another, sometimes literally. I was constantly vigilant, constantly in rescue mode. Grandpa already had his hands full taking care of Grandma.

"Daniel. Your family's safe now. Everything's okay. Pat and Liam are both doing good. You can relax and enjoy this trip. You deserve it."

I stared at David. I had a million come-backs. I wanted to believe him. I wanted to believe him so badly my body ached. I felt like I'd spent my life hiking up a mountainside hauling my brothers after me and now I stood at the highest precipice, frost-bitten, breathless and dazzled, at the edge of the world. All I needed now was to take just one more step.

Maybe it was the truth, finally, after all these years. Pat still hadn't paid me back the money I'd loaned him when he was stuck in New Mexico. I took a bite of toast, and dumped ketchup on my hash browns.

"Or," David said, "suggest something else to them. No one's forcing you to go on this trip."

"I can't cancel now. Pat's picking me up tomorrow. Anyway, I want to go. We're going camping. We agreed to this. Karen thinks it's a great idea. She says it'll give us a chance to reconnect."

"Absolutely. Some long overdue brotherly bonding."

"Right."

David sipped from his coffee. "So are you gonna have a good time?"

"I am going to have," I said, "a very good time."

"You don't sound convinced."

"I'll do my best."

⌒ I wanted to punch Pat in the face. "You did what?" I shouted, jumping up.

Pat scrambled to his feet, making sure to keep the campfire between us. "I put shrooms in the chili?"

"You're saying that," I said, "like it's a question."

He crouched and splayed his hands, *Ta-daa!* "I put shrooms in the chili."

I pointed at Liam who was sitting cross-legged on a log still finishing his second helping. "He," I said, "is on Zoloft. Did you ever think about that?"

Pat blinked. "I don't think he minds."

"That's not the point."

"Actually," Liam said, licking his spork, "I've been off my meds since last fall." He scraped at his empty bowl. "I thought something tasted funny."

"It was just a little bit," Pat said, "a couple caps. Maybe a few stems. You probably won't even feel it at all. It's all good. Right, Liam?"

Liam raised one eyebrow. "What's done is done."

A log crumbled, sending up a shower of orange sparks. Stars beyond the trees twinkled in the twilight sky. Pat was back on his feet, waiting for my next move. I actually considered sticking my finger down my throat, but what would be the point? So I could spend the rest of the evening watching my brothers get high while I sulked in my tent? A mosquito whined and I slapped the side of my head.

"Alright, look," I said. "I am not the angry one."

"What?"

"I just wish you hadn't done that without telling me. If you'd told me you wanted all three of us to take shrooms, then, then I would've considered it."

Pat made a face. "Really?"

"Well, we'll never know now," I said, "will we?"

"I guess not. So, does that mean you're cool?"

"I am always cool. Just talk to me, alright? I'm cool." To prove the point, I sat back down. "Hey, I can be a fun guy." Pat's face twitched. "I'm down with this. We're good. We can do this."

"So," Pat said.

"So, what?"

"So, are you going to finish that?" He pointed at the half-empty bowl of chili I was still holding. "Cuz if you're not, man, I'll finish it."

"No," I said. "It's my chili."

Pat sat down. "Okay, sure thing. Just asking. Just didn't want it to go to waste."

"It's not going to go to waste."

"You're the boss."

"I am not the boss."

"Okay, boss. If you say so."

Later, after we'd washed all our dishes and strung up our food packs, Pat took out his ukulele and he and I sat on the edge of a rock ledge overlooking Lumsden Lake. The moon was out, huge and luminous, and the water shone like it was made of silver and glass.

"*Gumusservi*," Pat said, whispering.

"What?"

"That's the Turkish word for 'moonlight-on-water'."

"It's making love," I said, "to the shoreline." Everything seemed so peaceful, radiant and in sharp, glittering focus. Details stood out as if in broad daylight.

Pat strummed his ukulele. "Slow passionate love."

Through my cargo shorts, I could feel the warmth of the stone, charged with the energy of the sun. And now that energy was moving, flowing up into me through my butt and spine. It was like that with all living things; with shorelines, with words, with sex, with the accretion of memories. It was like that with all the relationships in our lives. Everything was connected, everything in flux, vibrating. I pressed my palm against the rock.

"Can you feel that?" I asked.

Pat splayed his hand next to mine. He locked eyes with me and nodded.

Liam stepped up between us. His blackened toes flexed, gripping the stone flecked with starlight. Scars covered his shins and thick knees. His legs were like ancient tree trunks.

"Dude," Pat said. "You're naked."

Liam was stark naked, smoking a roach. A dense tangle of pubic hair framed his pendulous genitals. Like Pat and me, he was uncut. Unlike Pat and me, his belly button was an outie. Grandma on his wide chest smiled down at us. From this angle, Liam was a giant towering over the ragged pines, his stance the perfect Mountain Pose, his brow brushing the heavens. He took one last long hit, swallowed the roach and exhaled, an intractable but benevolent forest god. "Yippee ki-yay," he said. He stepped back, his muscles tensed. Then he surged forward, leaping high into the air.

"Motherfucker," Pat said.

When Liam hit the lake five metres below, the sound was symphonic.

Within seconds, Pat and I were both on our feet,

stripping off our clothing as fast as we could. We left the overhang simultaneously. The air against the inside of my legs was electrifying.

Growing up, we must've jumped off this ledge a thousand times. Liam knew all 585 square kilometres of Killarney like the back of his hand. This particular campsite was hardly more than an hour's hike from the parking lot, but it was the first campsite we'd gotten to know as kids.

After a few more jumps, we decided we'd swim out to the middle of the lake. It wasn't far and only took a couple minutes. We gazed around us, treading water, breathing heavily, full of strength and awe. Night had fallen, and overhead the Milky Way blazed like crushed diamonds. I tasted the subtle odours of loam, stone and algae in the clear water. I was reminded how salmon could find their way home, after years travelling in the deep ocean, through geomagnetic and chemical cues at the mouths of their native rivers and streams.

"Ooh that feels good," Pat said.

"What?"

"I'm pissing right now. It feels really good."

A silky warmth brushed my side. When I glanced at Liam's gleaming head bobbing a metre away, his smile flashed in the dark. Then all three of us took a moment in silence to pee together.

Bubbles broke the surface next to Pat.

"Oops," he said. "Must be the chili."

That's when I had my vision.

Back on the shore, in the shadows of the tall pines, stood two figures. Others might regularly see visions of their dead loved ones, but this was new to me. Just beyond the banked campfire, I could see Mom and Dad holding hands, watching us.

Speechless, I pointed, but Pat and Liam each seemed to be lost in his own world. I left them and swam toward the shore. When I clambered out of the water, what I thought was Mom and Dad turned out to be our packs hanging against the tree trunks. I stood dripping wet and shivering a little bit, the pine needles soft and brittle beneath my feet. I focused on my breath until my heart was no longer a jackrabbit in my chest. Then I stoked the embers and added fresh wood. By the time Liam and Pat returned, I'd gotten the fire blazing.

We dried ourselves off and put on our shorts. After that, we roasted fat Amish sausages from Manitoulin on sticks Liam sharpened. Pat and I shared a mickey, while he and Liam shared a joint.

"Dude," Pat said. "What is that?"

"This?" Liam weighted his knife on the palm of his hand. "This is a Norwegian Helle Temagami, triple-laminated ten-centimetre blade with a Masurian birch handle."

"Whoa. Can I see it?" Pat asked.

"No," Liam said. He sheathed the knife.

"Why not?" Pat asked.

"Because," Liam said. He set another piece of firewood onto the embers. "Oh, here." Almost as an afterthought, he rummaged in his cargos. "These are for the both of you." He took out two small packages tied with twine and handed one to each of us.

He watched as we unwrapped our gifts.

"No ways," Pat said.

"It's a Recon 1 Spear Point," Liam said. "5.3 ounces with a 3.5-millimetre Japanese stainless-steel folding blade. Super-light, sharp and tough. Just right for EDC duty."

"EDC?" I asked.

"Every day carry."

"Oh, okay. EDC. For sure." EDC for a lot of gay guys was a lubricated condom in their wallet, and casual sex was a matter of course. It was never so easy for me. Now I had my own personal killing instrument. Yippee ki-yay.

"Liam, thanks," I said. "This is really amazing."

Liam turned his roasting stick propped over the fire. "Your names are on them."

When we looked more closely, we saw our individual initials engraved on the hilts.

"This is so totally wicked," Pat said. "I lost my last knife in the desert." He jumped up and gave Liam a hug. "I absolutely love it. Thanks, bro."

"Happy birthday, guys," Liam said.

"I guess now's as good a time as any," Pat said.

"For what?"

"I also have something to share. I'm really excited. I'm a little nervous about this. I hope you like it."

"What is it?"

"I wrote," Pat said, "a song." He picked up his ukulele. "About us." He strummed a chord and adjusted a couple tuning pegs. "You ready?" We nodded. He cleared his throat, turned his ball cap backwards, and told us the name of the song.

Five minutes later, he sat back down. The fire quietly crackled. "Pat." I picked at a twig in my hands. "Sing it again."

Obligingly, he sang his song again. Just beyond the

circle of firelight, as before, I saw Mom and Dad. This time, I remained as still and as quiet as I could so as not to frighten them away. After Pat was done, he turned his ball cap back around, and set his ukulele aside. I tossed my twig into the fire. "You rhymed," I said, "'tree house' with 'Brussels sprouts.'"

"Yah, I suppose I did."

"That's Karen and Anne in the second verse."

Pat nodded.

My brow furrowed. "The 'monkey on the tracks.' Are you talking about the time we rescued Anne's stuffed animal?"

"Yep."

"That was when," Liam said, "the three of us almost got hit by that train."

"You almost broke your arm."

"We never did tell Grandpa the truth."

"We were what, twelve?"

"Eleven-and-a-half," I said. It'd been a stuffed giraffe, but I didn't say anything. That detail wasn't so important.

"I know it was a giraffe," Pat said. "But 'monkey' works better."

Liam sighed and clasped his big, callused hands. "Mom and Dad always called us their little monkeys."

"I know," Pat said.

Firelight played across the faces of my two brothers. In them I saw my own. Boys now inside the bodies of men. It was true, we had grown up wild. But we always had each other. Liam bowed his head. The long, low wail of a loon echoed across the lake.

"Pat?" I said.

"Yeah?"

"Your song. I love it. Thank you."

Liam nodded.

"It's our song," Pat said.

⌒ Late June. Nadia and I sat on the patio of the Rectory Café on the Toronto Islands. It was a blustery afternoon, whitecaps speckling the expanse of Lake Ontario, but a luminous canopy of young and old trees sheltered us. Today my companion was draped in a sheer, floral dress that bared her shoulders and back. A translucent disc of agate rested beneath her throat. I wore a faded Rush concert T-shirt that had once belonged to my dad.

"I heard," Nadia said, "Marcus's show swept the Dora Awards."

I nodded, stirring my tea the way Charles taught me (the way the Duchess of Grey had taught him: back and forth from twelve o'clock to six o'clock). "*Face* won for Outstanding Production and New Play, and Outstanding Male Performance. He's going on tour with it this fall."

The waitress returned with our orders: Apple Peach Crumb with salted caramel sauce, and Citrus Raspberry Cake. Our silverware flashed in the shifting sunlight.

"Where is he going?"

"He's opening in Vancouver, then he's got a show in Seattle. He's throwing a launch party next month."

"He's certainly making a name for himself."

"David and I are supposed to be having dinner with him next week."

"Oh?" Nadia glanced up at me.

"He's been asking to get together for a long time."

"Is that so?"

"Normal ex-boyfriends are supposed to fade into the past. Marcus just has to stay relevant."

"You'd prefer not to have him in your life."

"I didn't say that."

"But you feel he's intruding."

"I didn't say that either." I studied a beetle crawling in the moss between the flagstones at our feet. "I broke up with him, I'm the one who's moved in with a new boy-friend. I should be the confident one."

"What do you mean?"

"I mean, I just feel nervous when he's around, you know? I feel so threatened anytime anyone even mentions his name. What's that about?"

"I think you know the answer."

"No, I don't."

"Isn't it obvious?"

"Nadia, just say what's on your mind."

"You're still in love with him. Or at least a part of you is. You're not threatened by Marcus. You're threatened by your feelings for him. You believe it puts your relation-ship in danger. I don't doubt you and David love each other very much. But we're more complicated than that. We can love many people at the same time. Until we under-stand that, we'll always endure guilt and shame. Marcus Wittenbrink Jr. was your first great romance. Nothing in our lives will ever compare to that. He'll always be with you. He'll always be a part of you."

I might have argued with her, or at least pretended to be shocked at her words. Except I'd confessed long ago to Karen I still wanted to sleep with Marcus. A flock of birds circled and settled in the swaying tree tops. "Did you know," I finally said, "he still sends me birthday cards? Most people just post, 'Hey, happy birthday!' on Facebook. Don't you think it's a little inappropriate, mailing hand-written birthday cards to your ex? I don't even get birthday cards from my brothers."

"No." Nadia sipped from her water glass. "I don't think that's inappropriate at all."

"Gee. Thanks."

"Your brothers prepared gifts."

"When we went camping? Oh, sure, this time around. But most birthdays we just call each other up."

"Pat surprised you."

"He did. Pat's a goofball. But his music, it's … I dunno. Sometimes I'll hear one of his songs and, well, it's absolutely amazing."

"Pat's very talented. He puts his heart into his songwriting."

"I never thought he'd get this far. I have to admit, he's really good at what he does."

"He was quite a good lover."

I blushed, startled. I'd half-forgotten Nadia and Pat had hooked up briefly years ago. "Really?"

Nadia savoured the raspberry sauce drizzled over her plate. "He was," she said, "attentive. He took his time. That's more than I can say about most of the men I've known."

"Okay."

"I was very attracted to Pat."

"Until you found out he was also sleeping with your best friend."

"That changed things."

"Whatever happened to loving many people at the same time?"

"Loving is not the same, Daniel, as making love." Nadia met my eye. "Or fucking around on someone." I blushed again. "Do you know why he and Blonde Dawn broke up?"

"No. Pat just said they were taking some time apart. He insists they're still friends."

"I see."

"They're still living together, just in separate rooms now. She's also not in the band anymore. They've already gotten a new drummer."

"Is she still managing the band?"

"Oh, I don't know. I didn't ask." I observed the waiter clearing a nearby table, a handsome, burly fellow with a shaved head. I imagined the size and weight of his dick in my hand. "The truth is," I said, "I think things started going downhill for them ever since Burning Man."

"And Liam, how is he doing?"

"Liam? Great. He's been dating this police constable in Sudbury. Her name's Joan. They've gone fishing and turkey hunting. He's been teaching her how to use a crossbow. They had dinner with Grandpa the other night."

"How did that go?"

"I assume it went well." The waiter departed back inside the restaurant. "I mean, Grandpa and Betty aren't the classiest people in the world. But they're super easygoing, and they both love to have a good time."

"They're good people."

"They are."

"May I see this knife Liam gave you?"

I took out my pocketknife and handed it across the table. "Joan introduced him to an instructor at Laurentian University," I said. "Liam will be helping teach a course this fall."

"A course?"

"Wilderness survival."

Nadia opened the blade. "Impressive."

"It comes in handy."

"Does it?"

"Good for slicing cake."

"Apparently." Nadia cut both her cake and mine in halves and exchanged pieces.

"Look, Nadia," I said. "I'm not still in love with Marcus. I can see why you'd say that, but I'm not. It's true, I still think a lot about when we were together, about the way he made me feel, or at least the way I used to feel when I was with him. But that's not the same thing. Being with Marcus, it was like riding a roller coaster, or stepping into a casino for the first time. You know what I mean? And sure, I'd love to have sex with him again. But I'm not in love with him."

"I have a confession to make."

"Okay."

Nadia set Liam's gleaming knife next to the sugar and cream. "I saw you and your boyfriend David at The Cameron House."

"You were there, at Pat's last show? Why didn't you say hi?"

"I was incognito."

A gust of wind bent the treetops, sending pale leaves

cascading across the patio. I picked up my fork, then set it down again. "Really?"

"My best friend and I," said Nadia, "we agreed we'd both stop seeing Pat, to save our friendship. Boys in rock bands are dangerous. They're also usually clichés. But there was always something different about your brother."

"You make it sound like you've known a lot of boys in rock bands."

"Maybe I have." Nadia pursed her lips. "Maybe this girl's not all just about dusty books and dead poets."

"Does Pat know?"

Nadia shook her head.

"Are you seeing anyone now?"

"I am."

"And? Tell me more."

"He's someone from school, in my department. He taught me how to use a fountain pen. He's someone who admires the same authors I do, who understands why just the smell of old books sometimes makes me cry. Someone who actually knows how to properly use a semi-colon."

I observed the corner of her mouth turn up in a half-smile. "It's not the same," I said, "is it?"

"No," Nadia said. "It's not the same."

"Pat's a poet."

"Yes, he is."

"What about your best friend?"

"Sam? She moved away this spring, to study abroad. It may be some years before she returns."

"Ah. Okay, I get it."

"I'd like to ask your permission."

"You mean, you want to see my brother Pat again."

"I do."

"Nadia, you don't need my permission."

"I feel I do."

"Well, look, of course you can see Pat again. I mean, that wouldn't change anything, not between us. Honestly, I wouldn't mind. But be careful. Boys in rock bands can be dangerous."

Nadia searched my face, before leaning across the table to kiss me on the forehead.

"What was that for?"

"Just for being you." She reached out and held my hand in both her own. She stroked my fingers and the skin of my wrist. "This man David's mother just married, how long did you say they waited?"

"Fifty years."

"What were their names again?"

"Isabella de Luca and Nicoli Badalamenti."

"Do you think Isabella and Nicoli were destined to be together?"

"Destined? What do you mean by that?"

"Do you believe their coming back together was part of a natural order?"

"A natural order?" I sat back in my chair. I imagined the flow of the Great Lakes into the Saint Lawrence River out into the North Atlantic Ocean. Where did it all start but with that single tiny stream in the forest, a drop of dew on a mossy bank. "I'd like to think so."

"*Komorebi*," Nadia murmured.

"What's that?"

"It's the Japanese word for 'sunlight-that-filters-through-the-leaves-of-trees.'"

"*Gumusservi*," I said.

Nadia's eyes crinkled. "Come again?"

"That's Turkish," I said, "for 'moonlight-on-water.'"

"Now where on God's green earth, Daniel Garneau, did you learn a word like that?"

"From Pat."

"Ah." Nadia clasped my hand. "Of course, you did."

⌒ I was only twenty when I went on my first date with Marcus, when I filled my lungs with air, eyes wide open, stretched out my arms, and stepped off the edge of a cliff. Late that night, we ended up at his friend Julia's party in a dim, ramshackle, third-floor apartment over a Queen West fabric store. A purple couch and a frayed loveseat crowded the tiny living room. A standing chandelier illuminated a colourful Georgia O'Keeffe print. Patchouli burned in an incense holder on a glass coffee table strewn with rolling papers, shot glasses, and Red Bull cans. The fire escape was the de facto smoking area.

We'd left Lee's Palace before last call to celebrate Reggie's twenty-fifth birthday. I learned Reginald was the oldest of the gang, grad students who'd argue over Marshall McLuhan and Douglas Coupland while hot knifing in the kitchen. It was 3 a.m. when Reginald suggested everyone drop E. Earlier that summer I'd tried Molly for the first time at a gay bar on College Street. It didn't matter that I was a lot younger than everyone else. I was with Marcus.

Marcus's childhood best friend Marwa was roommates with Julia, except Marwa was away in Burlington visiting her cousin in the hospital. (I wouldn't meet Marwa until months later at Marcus's New Year's Eve party). The dimpled blonde in the Tigger onesie was Claire, and the tall redhead was a black girl named Madison. I learned Mitz and Reginald had gone to the Etobicoke School of the Arts, and that Reginald and Julia used to be an item. Both Reginald and Mitz had lost their shirts by this time. Mitz's pale torso was covered in random tattoos, from Looney Tunes characters to Celtic crosses. For years, apparently, Mitz had secretly been in love with Reginald. "That bromance," Marcus said, glancing over at the two arm-wrestling in the kitchen, "is a ticking time bomb."

At some point, Claire knelt in front of me and slipped into my mouth her very last Jolly Rancher because she knew how much I liked them. Then Reginald insisted on putting on Moby's newest album which Julia had gotten him for his birthday. Just as the E was kicking in, Madison folded herself into the couch, offered me a sip of her ginger beer, and asked about my family. Then I had to explain how I was one of three triplet boys and that when we were ten our parents died in a car crash, after which we were raised by our grandpa.

"And how," Madison asked, "do you feel about that?"

She had enormous rings on her hands, tiger-eye and black onyx bound in silver. I pulled both my knees up beneath my chin. In my entire life no one had ever asked me this question before. I felt like a sinkhole was crumbling open in the middle of my chest. "I feel," I finally said, "grateful."

"Grateful?"

"We had exactly ten years together as a whole family."

"What were they like?"

"My parents?" I drew a shaky breath. "They were happy. I don't ever remember seeing them fight. I mean, they must've had arguments, right? Everyone does. But I only remember Mom and Dad as always laughing and cracking jokes. They'd let us do pretty much anything we wanted: stay up all night, have ice cream for breakfast. In the middle of the day, they'd pull us out of school and take us on road trips, up to the cottage or out to some farm to go apple picking, stuff like that. They'd tell us we were ephemeral, and that they didn't want to tame us."

"Ephemeral?"

"I figured they meant us as kids living out our lives. It only comes once, childhood. That's something special, right?"

"That is something very special," Madison said.

"So, yeah," I said. "I'm grateful."

This was the hugest epiphany for me, sucking on my sour apple Jolly Rancher. The truth was, for years after they'd died I'd resented my parents for leaving the three of us and Grandpa and Grandma the way they had. For a second, I thought I might just burst into tears. But then Madison took my hands and somehow she had me up on my feet dancing with the others, and the world was dizzy and loud, and beautiful and good. Reginald clapped me on the shoulder and said he was glad I was there, man. Then he messed up Mitz's mohawk and kissed fiercely the side of his head. Nearby, Claire had her eyes closed with a huge smile on her face, her pigtails bouncing up and down as she twirled her tiger tail.

It felt wonderful to dance with these people. Somebody had moved the coffee table and furniture to make more room. My vision kept going blurry but inside of me, something else was coming into sharp focus. Apart from family (which included Karen and the Miltons), I'd never felt this connected with anybody in my life. Even with family there was history which shadowed all the good: betrayals and disappointments, resentments and slights. But with these people, total strangers to me until just hours ago, the slate was clean. In this evolution of us, we'd just crawled out of the sea and were basking in sunshine and drawing air for the first time into our moist and pink, newly-formed lungs. There was no competition for resources, no battle for dominance and power. There was only this single-hearted communion beneath a magical sky.

Just as I was starting to wonder where Marcus was, two figures strolled arm-in-arm out of the bedroom: Julia wearing Marcus's velvet dinner jacket and top hat with a thin moustache pencilled with eyeliner on her upper lip, and Marcus in her rhinestone-studded corset and ruffle skirt. They made a spectacular couple and everyone whistled and whooped. After that, somehow I ended up trying on Claire's Tigger onesie, which everyone insisted I keep on, even though it rode up my crotch and was really hot. Eventually I unzipped the front and took off my own T-shirt. By the end, all seven of us had our arms around each other, forming one shining circle like a halo fused from glowing and indomitable alloys. And I felt nothing but love and ridiculous gratitude for the messed-up, insufferable joy that was my entire ephemeral life.

CHAPTER FOURTEEN

I Will Give You Everything

David and I weren't the only people Marcus had invited to dinner. When we knocked on his door, Marwa answered, wearing a black and gold lamé cocktail dress and Cleopatra-styled bangs.

"Oh thank god you're here," she said, grabbing both our arms and pulling us in.

Little had changed since I last stepped into Marcus's east-end condo at Carlaw and Queen. The building was a refurbished printing warehouse, all gleaming concrete floors, exposed brick and rafters. Marcus's décor remained spare bordering on ascetic. Above a leather-bound sofa, a black-and-white print featured Andy Warhol surrounded by partyers at The Factory.

"Youssef's in the hospital again," Marwa said. "I thought I could manage with just Brody, but he just got rear-ended on the Gardiner and can't make it. I am so desperate, I need your help."

"Yeah, sure, Marwa. Anything you need."

"What do you mean, 'Youssef's in the hospital again'?" David asked.

"Youssef has an underactive thyroid." She took the wine bottle we'd brought and set it aside in the kitchen. "He takes these pills, but sometimes things still get out of whack. He's been exhausted all week. Yesterday he collapsed and was admitted for more tests."

"Is he going to be okay?" I asked.

"Of course, he's going to be okay," Marwa said, peering into the oven. "He's my Youssef. The question is: Is my *fatteh* going to be okay? I've got my *mise en place*, I just need a sous chef and a server. I was counting on Brody to roll the *dolma* while I prepped the rabbit. David, Daniel, have either of you ever rolled *dolma* before?"

Marcus emerged from the bedroom in a brocade vest with his hair styled back.

"Marwa," he said, "my guests are here to be regaled, not enslaved."

"We don't mind," David said, rolling up his sleeves. "This will be fun."

"Hello, Marcus," I said.

Marcus opened his arms. "I'm so glad you've come. The others won't be arriving for an hour." He hugged both David and me and kissed us lightly on the lips. "Marwa, your *molokhiya* can wait. Come join us for some bubbly."

"This is impressive," David said, observing a dining table set for eleven. Silverware and crystal gleamed beneath the brushed steel lamps.

Marcus pulled a Veuve Clicquot from an ice bucket.

"I wanted some time alone," he said. "Just the four of us, to celebrate." The citrus fragrance of his cologne lingered. He wiped down the bottle and peeled off the gold foil. "Daniel, I remember when we'd order in Chinese and I'd help you study. Now look at you."

I compressed my lips into a smile. As usual, I had no idea what Marcus was talking about.

Marcus untwisted the wire cage over the cork. "We spend our lives working to become something better, something worthwhile. It's important to witness these moments. So, how does it feel?"

"How," I said, "does what feel?"

Marwa brought out a tray of four Champagne flutes. Marcus wrapped the towel around the bottleneck. "To finally graduate?"

"Graduate?"

"Medical school. You're a doctor now. Your grandfather must be so proud."

"Wait, stop."

Pop. The cork came out.

"Marcus, look. I mean, thanks for all of this, but I'm not graduating."

The oven dinged.

Marwa blinked. "What?"

"What I mean is, I haven't graduated yet."

"I distinctly recall," Marcus said, "helping you study for your MCAT."

"You did."

"And?"

"I didn't get in that year. Marcus, we broke up, remember, before I found out. I guess no one told you."

"Ah." Marcus lowered the bottle. "The dreaded med school rejection."

"But Daniel," Marwa said, "you told me you were in med school."

David pointed a finger at me. "He's definitely in med school."

"I am in med school. I mean, I got into med school. I reapplied the next year. I just have another year before I graduate, alright?"

Marwa blushed. "Alright."

Marcus raised a hand. "We understand."

"We do."

I shrugged. "Sorry."

"Oh, sweetie," Marwa said, "don't be sorry."

"I'm not sorry. That's not what I meant. I mean, what do I have to be sorry for?"

"Oh." Marwa squeezed my arm. "Nothing. No, of course not. You don't have to be sorry for anything."

"That's right."

"This," David said, "is awkward."

"Hardly," Marcus said, pouring the champagne. "Life is a celebration. Let us live without apologies, and with gratitude for every moment we have." He handed out three glasses. "To our beautiful muse Marwa. To our beautiful compatriot David. And to our beautiful physician-to-be, Daniel Garneau."

This was more than awkward. David raised his glass. "And to you," he said. "Congratulations on your show. To our beautiful Marcus."

"To us," Marcus said. "To the glorious precipice of now."

As it turned out, Marcus had invited to dinner his entire production team as well as his director, agent and publisher. Conversation was brisk and business-like, centred on preparations for his up-coming tour. David and I spent the evening in and out of our seats, helping Marwa prep and serve dishes. Toward the end, the stage manager, a tall, soft-spoken fellow named Gee, insisted on helping David and me clear the table.

Just before dessert, Marwa beckoned me to the front door. "What's going on?" I asked.

"The band's here. They're downstairs at the loading gate."

"What band?"

"The band, for the party."

"What party?"

"Daniel, the pre-launch party tonight. You knew that."

"What? No, I didn't know that."

"We're celebrating Marcus's up-coming tour."

"Tonight?"

"Look, Daniel." She pressed a key into my hand. "This is for the freight elevator. Can you just help the band load in? Everyone will be arriving in forty minutes. I really need to prep my baklava. I owe you big time, thanks so much."

I arrived at the elevator just as my brother Pat walked out carrying two amps. His hair was green and he was sporting a tight T-shirt that said "MR. DRESSUP" in disco-styled lettering. "Hey Dan! Good to see ya!"

"Pat. What are you doing here?"

Rod shouldered past in dark sunglasses, hauling mic stands and a mixer. "Dan."

"Hi Rod."

Pat set down his amps. "We're playing Marcus's pre-launch party."

"He's booked Three Dog Run?"

"Technically," Pat said, unwrapping a pack of gum and shoving its contents in his mouth one by one, "he's called in an IOU."

"An IOU?"

"Well, you know how he lent us his loft to record our EP, right? We couldn't pay him, but we all agreed we'd owe him a private gig. When the time came, he said he'd let us know. This is it, man. It's payback time!" Pat clapped me on the shoulder. "By the way, congratulations, big brother."

"For what?"

"For finishing med school."

"I'm not finished, Pat. I have one more year to go. Who told you I was finished?"

"Oh, shit. I dunno. I just thought you were done. I've been telling everyone you were done."

"Including Marcus?"

"I think so."

"Well, I'm not."

"Oops." Pat shrugged. "Okay, well, I guess next year then. Hey, can you help Rod load this gear in? Bobby and the Egster are still parking." He jumped back into the elevator and flourished two hang-loose signs. "Tonight, we is gonna bring da house down!"

That night following dinner, three dozen more guests arrived, a whole case of sparkling wine was opened, and Three Dog Run brought the house down. I was acquainted with many of the people present, including Fang and Jonathan, and others from Marcus's closing night show. Gee, David and I helped Marwa pack away all the table-ware and haul it downstairs to her van. "This stuff," I asked, "doesn't belong to Marcus?"

"Oh no," Marwa said. "It's all rented, and so are the table and chairs."

"I didn't know you could do that."

"Daniel, you can rent anything you want. There's so much stuff in life we can't afford or don't have the space for. But we can still enjoy them."

"I suppose so."

I helped Marwa load the last box and we closed the doors to her van. Gee and David had already gone back up to the party. Marwa sat on the rear bumper and lit a super slim menthol. Violet clouds glowed in the west. Across the parking lot, a three-storey mural depicted giant robot insects dancing amidst colourful flowers.

"Can I tell you something?" Marwa asked. "But you can't tell anyone."

I sat down on the sidewalk curb. "Sure."

"I've been making some money on the side, working for a company called RentAFriend."

"Rent-a-friend?"

"I've been doing it for a while now. It's not what everyone thinks. The service really is platonic friendships only."

"The service?"

"There are a lot of lonely people out there in the world, Daniel. People appreciate having some real company."

"People hire you to be their friend?"

Marwa nodded. "Mm-hm."

"Like, by the hour?"

"That's right. Although I might lower my rate if they're paying for dinner or tickets or something. A client might want company shopping, or someone to show them around town. I had this one older guy who just wanted me to help with his scrapbooking."

"And you said this is all platonic?"

"Totally. There are very strict rules. I don't even normally hold hands. I might give you a hug at the end of the evening, but that's it. Women and men from all walks of life are doing this. We're just really friendly people, looking to make a bit of extra cash."

"Wow."

"Once I did have this boy take me to a family barbecue and pretend I was his girlfriend."

"How did that work out?"

"Oh we planned it all out in advance. It was fun."

"Was he gay?"

Marwa nodded. "He was tired of people asking him why he wasn't with anyone. He was the one I let hold my hand. He was sweet. I really felt sorry for him. I've been a bridesmaid twice. I've still kept one of the dresses. Then there's this one woman up in Markham who's hired me to visit her mother in the nursing home every week."

"Marwa, how much time are you spending doing this?"

"A lot more than I expected. More than most, I think." She handed me her cigarette and I took a puff. "I've discovered, Daniel, I'm really good at it. People like me. I've had to cut back on other things in my life."

"Like what?"

"Like the special catering."

"Really?"

"It's not the same income, of course, but it still covers

the overhead for Cherry Bomb Bakery. I figure I've been supplying favours long enough. I don't miss it."

"Wow, Marwa. I don't know what to say." If Marwa had cut back on drug-dealing so she could spend more time scrapbooking and socializing with seniors, who was I to judge? "I'm proud of you."

Marwa turned to face me. "That means a lot. Thank you. I mean, I'm still making people happy right? Now it's just different. Some people think it's next to prostituting myself. But I know I'm doing a good service. People can always find another dealer. But my RentAFriend clients, they really need me. If I can help them feel a little less alone, if I can give them advice, if I can make them feel a little more confident about themselves, then I'm doing good, aren't I?"

"Yes, you are."

Marwa bit her lower lip. "You surprise me sometimes, Daniel Garneau."

"Why do you say that?"

"There are times when Marcus makes you out as someone who's, well, just a little conservative."

"Is that right? Well, I don't blame him. The truth is, a lot of the time I think I am."

"Maybe on the surface. But who was that boy who showed up at a burlesque show wearing a kilt?"

"Oh jeez."

"Without any underwear, might I add."

"You want to know the truth?"

"What?"

"I just did that to make Marcus jealous."

"I don't think that's true. Not entirely at least. You were having too much fun."

"It was fun," I said. "I'm glad you invited us."

"Oh, Gee likes you, by the way."

"Why do you say that?"

"He's been watching you both all evening. You and David are really sweet together. Do you think he's cute?"

"Um, he seems like a nice guy."

"He's very organized. He's also really talented. You should get to know him. This is for you, by the way." She held out an envelope.

"What's that?"

"It's what I would've paid Brody and Youssef if they'd been here."

"Oh, Marwa, thanks. But you don't need to do that."

"You earned it."

"We were happy to help out. Gee helped out too. Seriously, put that away. Really. I appreciate it. Look, why don't you bake us a cake sometime?"

"Oh." Marwa's face lit up. "I can do that. When's your anniversary?"

"David's and mine? It just passed in June."

"How long have you been together?"

"Four years."

"That is a long time."

"I suppose it is." I scratched the back of my head. "You know what they say about gay relationships: They're just like dog years."

"Excuse me?"

"Dog years. You multiply it by seven. So that means we've been together twenty-eight regular years."

"Daniel." Marwa stared at me like her puff pastry had just collapsed. "That is so demeaning. Don't say that. Dogs have a life expectancy built-into their DNA. You can't say the same thing about people's relationships."

"Marwa, it's just a joke."

"It's not funny."

"Okay."

"Really, it's not."

"Alright."

An elderly couple passed nearby, walking two schnauzers. Marwa worried at the hem of her dress.

"You know," she said, "people used to call me Marwa the Mutt."

"Oh. That sucks."

"It was fucking shitty, that's what it was. In high school, there were these assholes who'd bark at me every time they'd see me: *woof woof woof*. I tried to pretend I didn't care. But it got to me. Back then, meeting that special someone, it was always this end-of-the-rainbow, this unicorn in the forest. Sometimes I'd think I was getting close. I'd get a tiny glimpse of it. But then. It's hard not to get hopeless or bitter. I used to keep telling myself, one day my prince would come. But after so many disappointments, you can't help but start wondering if there really is something wrong with you."

"Marwa, you don't seem like the kind of girl who'd ever wait for some prince to come."

"Oh." Marwa laughed. "I'm not, not anymore. Fuck that shit." She butted out her cigarette. "Marcus would say to me: 'Dee, you're royalty, you're magnificent. Don't ever let anyone tell you otherwise.' He helped me turn

my life around. I owe him my life. There came this moment when I really didn't love myself anymore, you
know? When I lost sight of everything that was good and
beautiful. I'd hide behind this badass goth persona, but
really I was dying inside, every day. Marcus saved me. I
don't expect you to understand. You have a loving family.
I never had that. My parents were divorced alcoholics, I
had no one."

"I'm sorry to hear that."

"You asked me once if Marcus was my best friend. I
said no, because he's more than that to me. He's my
family. We've been each other's family."

"He's lucky to have you."

"For a while, Daniel, I hated you. You really hurt him
when you broke up. I know people break up all the time.
I know that. But you walked out on him on Valentine's
Day. Marcus is sensitive. He still loves you. I remember
offering to throw a brick through your window or something. But he made me swear to forgive you. It's important to Marcus he stays friends with all his lovers. You're
his family too. He'd never say that, but it's the truth.
Please don't tell him I've told you all this. I mean it. But
Marcus, he's trying really hard."

I didn't know what to say. I wasn't sure what shocked
me more: Marcus's feelings toward me, or Marwa's pro-
tectiveness of him. Maybe if Marcus had shown some
hurt, some upset of any kind, I would've stayed to work
it through. But it was his aloofness I couldn't stand. I
wanted to speak in my own defense, but there was no
recrimination in Marwa's tone.

"You know those guys," Marwa said, "who'd call me a mutt, and woof at me in high school?"

"Yeah?"

"Well, Marcus and I, we got our revenge. The Maleficent formed this plan. These assholes were all on the football team, see. So just before this big game, we filled their equipment bags up with dog shit. I mean, a lot of dog shit. We'd spent days collecting it. It was spectacular. They figured out who it was, of course, and a week later came after us. But Marcus was ready. He'd cashed in a savings bond and gotten his hands on photos of a couple of them at a college party. Someone had taken pics of them sucking off frat boys. That's what you had to do, apparently, if you wanted to get in with some fraternities: something horrible like getting down on your knees and putting anther boy's cock in your mouth. These assholes were still seniors in high school, but I guess if you're that ambitious. Straight guys will do some really strange things to feel connected with each other. After that, well. They left me and Marcus alone. No one ever called me Marwa the Mutt again."

By this point, the party was in full swing. There were people on the rooftop calling down to us. I spotted Pat's green hair. "Hey Dan!" he shouted. "C'mon up here, we're doing body shots!"

"Your brother's cute," Marwa said.

I started to say: "He's an idiot," but caught myself. Pat was an idiot, but he'd always accepted and loved me no matter what. I observed the green saplings growing along the edge of the parking lot. "He's a popular guy."

"If you want to head back to the party," Marwa said, lighting another cigarette, "I'm okay out here on my own."

"No, I'm fine."

"You don't have to be all chivalrous and keep me company."

I sat in silence while Marwa enjoyed her second smoke. Blocks away, a police siren wailed. After a moment, I asked: "So, what happened to those guys?"

"The ones from the football team? I have no idea. I haven't thought about them in ages."

The siren grew louder. Abruptly, we saw the flashing lights of the cruiser speeding past. Seconds later it dimmed and vanished back into the darkness of the city.

"In Toronto," I said, "I bumped into an old bully once, from Sudbury. I hadn't seen him in years. He'd changed, a lot. He was a lot happier, a lot nicer. He actually apologized to me. I wasn't expecting that. It really affected me. I dunno. I was glad for him."

"You were glad for him?"

"Back then, everyone knew his dad was a real hardass. His parents put him through hell. He described to me how, his whole life, it was like he had this gigantic bear trap clamped around his chest. Then one day, he'd had enough, and he just pried it off. It took all his strength, but he did it. It was really scary and painful, and there was a lot of blood. For a while, he didn't know if he could survive it. But soon after that, he said, everything got better. That weight off his chest changed everything. He could finally breathe for the first time in his life."

"When people are feeling trapped, they cope in all sorts of ways."

"Sure."

"Most people live their whole lives wearing their bear traps. They get used to it."

"Oh? What's your bear trap?"

Marwa held up her cigarette. "These. Devil sticks, that's what Marcus calls them. I smoke like a fiend, I know. But I'm not sure how I'd live without them."

"Here." I got up. "Give that to me." I took her cigarette and butted it out.

After that, we went back upstairs arm in arm. Three Dog Run was between sets, and the band was throwing back flaming sambuca shots with Marcus's tech crew. I found David and Gee in Marcus's bedroom sitting side by side, bent over a laptop in Gee's lap. I poked my head in the door. "Hey guys."

"Daniel," David called out. "Come here. You have to take a look at this."

The room was familiar and dark, lit only by a single spotlight on a disco ball in the corner. Feist played on a tiny CD player. I sat next to Gee and peered at the glowing screen. They were looking at photographs, fantastical images of bizarre, half-human figures: a mermaid stranded on a stony beach, a snake in a floral garden, a winged maiden clutching a broken bottle in a neon-lit alleyway.

"You'd think these were photoshopped," David said, "but they're not. It's all body paint and prosthetics."

I looked at Gee. "This is your work?"

He nodded. "It's how I met Marcus. He asked me to be his makeup artist for *Philophobia*."

I studied an image of a young black man with horns and goat's legs, golden eyes red-rimmed, his torso covered in bruises, hands tied, bent over the tailgate of a pickup truck in a field.

"I can see," I said, "why Marcus would want to work with you."

"I asked Gee if we could model for him," David said.

"Really?" I said. All of the figures in the photos were at least partially nude.

"I'd be happy to do it," Gee said quietly.

"You said you wanted to do something more compositional," David said, sipping from his wine glass, "involving multiple figures in tableau."

"I did. But I'm not making any money off these. I can't pay anyone."

"Are you kidding?" David leaned into him. "People should be paying you."

Gee's face was precise and narrow, with large, thoughtful eyes. "I've done a few commissions. I get a lot of calls around Halloween." This close, I noticed a small scar bisecting his left eyebrow, and on the upper cleft of his lip.

"Too bad you won't be around this fall," David said.

"Oh, I'm not going on tour with Marcus," Gee said. "I can't afford to take the time off work."

"What do you do?" I asked.

"You mean what's my real job? I work at Loblaws. I'm a produce manager. It pays the rent. I'm the person they hire to squeeze the cantaloupes."

"Well. Like you said, it pays the rent."

"Did you know," Gee said, "the old scientific name for banana was *Musa sapientum*, which meant 'fruit of the wise men'?"

"Did you know," I said, "the word for avocado comes from the Aztec word for 'testicle'?"

Gee regarded me sidelong like I was some serious sideshow freak. "Awesome."

"Superheroes," David said.

"Pardon me?"

"Then you can do us up like superheroes," David said, "for Halloween. We'll pay you. Whaddya say?"

"I don't do superheroes."

"You don't do superheroes?"

"I've been asked to paint people like superheroes," Gee said. "But I prefer to do my own creations. I'll body-paint you both for Halloween, but I get to do whatever I want. That way, you don't have to pay me. Can I show you something?" He searched through his files and opened a photo album titled, "Marcus ROM."

An antlered figure in a leafy thong stood alone centre stage. Beneath a narrow spotlight, the contours of his torso and limbs stood out in sharp relief.

I stared at the image. "That's me."

"It is."

"Holy shit." David squinted. "That's you?"

"I was an animistic spirit."

"I thought you were a forest god."

"That's my mask you're wearing," Gee said. "I hand-made all the masks for that show."

"Did we meet?"

"No. That December I was in Turkey visiting my family."

Gee scrolled through the rest of the production shots.

"These," David said, "are from that fundraiser for the

Royal Ontario Museum, isn't that right? That multi-media show Marcus was commissioned to create."

"That's right." I recognized a few of the photos from Marcus's own website. "Gee, you don't work in theatre professionally?"

"I'd like to. Right now, mainly, it's still just my hobby."

"I remember your masks. They were all auctioned off later that evening. They were really popular. They raised a lot of money. You're really talented."

"Thank you."

"I know someone who's a professional makeup artist," David said. "I could introduce you."

"Sure, that'd be cool."

"Whoa." David pointed. "Daniel, are you showing your bare ass there?"

A wide shot captured twelve actors on stage. Gee centred and enlarged the image of me, slowly zooming in on my naked butt. "Gee!" I shoved him.

"Clench those cheeks," David said, laughing.

Marcus and I had only been dating three months when he convinced me to be in his show. "Just hit your marks and strike a pose," he said, "that's all you have to do. You'll be wearing a mask, no one will even recognize you."

Before then, I'd never done theatre in my life. What on earth had I been thinking? I couldn't possibly have been in my right mind. But of course, I knew where my mind was back then. It was no mystery what had overcome me: I'd been drunk on Marcus.

Gee paused on a close-up image of me crouched on a boulder reaching for the stars. The Feist CD came to an end. The disco ball glimmered.

"That," David said, "is spectacular."

Gee nodded. "The lighting designer did a good job."

"That's my boyfriend."

"Technically," Gee said, "Daniel was Marcus's boyfriend when these were taken."

David and I exchanged glances. Gee looked up at us both. His Adam's apple rose and fell. "Sorry."

David squeezed his shoulder. "Don't worry about it. Look, can you send these to us, the ones with Daniel in them?"

"Um, legally, I'm not supposed to distribute these. But, well, sure. Just the pictures of you, right?"

His face was earnest, his long fingers hovering over the keyboard. "Yeah," I said. "Just the pictures of me. Thanks for letting me wear your mask."

"You look really good in it."

"Daniel," David said, "I'd let you fuck me wearing that mask."

"David," I said, "we already fuck."

"True. But I've never been fucked by a forest god before."

For the next minute, Gee hunched over his laptop assembling select photos into one folder. David stroked my cheek with his knuckles and put his thumb in my mouth. After that, he rested his hand on the back of Gee's neck and emptied his wine glass.

I pressed my nose against Gee's head. His hair smelled clean, like ginger mint. I could feel my heart thudding in my chest.

"Thanks," I said. "I hope we're not getting you into any trouble."

"I don't mind," Gee said, "getting into trouble." I caught a glimpse of his computer's wallpaper, a mosaic of a naked youth being carried skyward in the talons of a gigantic eagle. He closed his laptop lid.

"I'm glad," David said. "Daniel, what do you think? Do you mind getting into trouble?"

"No, I don't mind," I said. I'd lost track of the amount of times I'd had sex in Marcus's bed. I wondered if he still kept his lube, condoms and toys in a box in the bottom drawer of the nightstand to the left. The first time I'd ever had a threesome was with Marcus and Fang in this bedroom, up against the dresser, next to the Alex Colville print of a shirtless man and a gun. We'd left stains on the wall.

I traced the edge of Gee's ear with my lips, and then with the tip of my tongue. Hesitantly, his hand moved to rest on top of mine.

"Is this okay?" David asked.

Gee nodded. After a moment, he turned his head and kissed David, open-mouthed. The bedroom door was wide open, anyone could walk into the room.

I straightened. "We should go," I said. "David, let's go."

David's eyebrows rose.

I took Gee's laptop and set it aside. He made no motion to conceal the unmistakable erection inside his pants.

"And you," I said, "are coming home with us."

⌒ When I woke up the next morning, Gee was already gone. My fingertips and the tangled sheets smelled musky. The faintest hint of ginger and mint lingered on the pillow case. I also detected the familiar odour of dried semen. The tacky residue of lube remained on my hands and between my legs.

"I saw him out," David mumbled against the back of my neck. "He left twenty minutes ago."

I was surprised. Usually I wasn't such a sound sleeper. "Was he okay?" I asked.

"He was fine." David draped an arm across my chest. "He just has to work today. I told him he could shower here, but he needed to go home."

After last night, I'd asked Gee to stay, and the three of us had fallen asleep together.

"Are you okay?" David asked.

"Me? Yeah."

"Are you sure?"

"Yeah," I said. "I'm sure."

Hairy Houdini jumped up onto the bed, padded across our legs, and climbed onto my chest. *Meow, meowr.* She head-butted me in the face. *Mreowr.* Translation: *Feed me, amuse me, serve me.* I reached out and rubbed her belly. Parker was visiting family in Brampton, and we were watching Houdini for a week.

"Do you think," I asked, "he had a good time?"

My phone on the nightstand buzzed. It was a text from Gee: *Thanks for last night, I had a good time. You're really nice guys. I'm glad we met. Let me know if you ever want to hang out. XO Gee.*

I showed David the text. "'Nice guys,'" David said. "That's us. Do you think we're 'nice guys'?"

I rolled onto my side to face him. Houdini meowed and jumped away. "I think so."

"'Nice guys.'" David smiled sleepily. "I can live with that."

I remembered last night watching David and Gee kissing in bed as I stroked Gee's chest and the taut muscles of his stomach. Gee's body was lean and hard, silky to the touch. I massaged the inside of his thighs, the warm mound of his perineum. When I pulled back his foreskin, the head of his penis glistened with precum.

Earlier that night, during our cab ride home, Gee had directed the driver along a shorter route. Before we left the party, he'd insisted on saying goodbye to at least a dozen people. While David and I waited for him, Marwa and Marcus met us at the door.

"I heard you boys were leaving," Marcus said. Down the hall, Three Dog Run was back on stage and people were dancing and having a good time.

"Can you tell Pat we said goodbye?"

"Of course." Marcus held out the Verve Clicquot cork. He'd cut a deep slit in it and inserted a loonie. "This is for you."

"Thanks." I gave him a hug. "Best wishes with your tour. Break a leg."

"Good luck in your last year of medical school."

"Gee mentioned," Marwa said, "you might model for him this fall?"

"Hopefully," David said.

"You must send pictures," Marcus said.

Gee arrived carrying a battered briefcase and backpack. Marwa clasped his arm. "Gee, sweetie, if you ever need someone a little more curvy than these two boys,

I'd be happy to have you body-paint me again." She twirled and struck a pose.

"I'd love to," Gee said.

"It looks like I'm going to be missing all the fun," Marcus said.

"Marwa," Gee said, "dinner was fabulous, as usual. Thanks for hosting, both of you. Marcus, you'll call if you need anything?"

Marcus nodded.

Gee gestured toward David and me. "Um. We're sharing a cab."

"I'm sure you will," Marcus said.

"Be good, boys," Marwa said.

Then I figured they both knew David and I were taking Gee home with us. I searched Marcus's face as he wrapped his arms around Gee and hugged him from behind. "This one's special." He winked at me. "Take good care of him."

"We will," David said.

We rode the elevator down to the lobby in silence. Gee wasn't Marcus's boyfriend. David and I could sleep with anyone we wanted. In my jacket pocket, I clenched the cork Marcus had given me, feeling the hard edges of the golden coin bite into my palm. The sex columnist Sasha Von Bon Bon had been among the guests tonight, as well as the Cree painter Kent Monkman. (Rumour had it he and Marcus had dated a number of months earlier this year.) If Marcus surrounded himself with his beloved, chosen family, it was also an incestuous one. In addition to Fang and Jonathan, I'd also spotted Joseph the dancer. He'd seemed cozy with Marcus, sitting in his lap for much of the evening, laughing a little too loudly, looking gaunt, his makeup not quite concealing the dark circles under his eyes. The last time I saw Joseph, he'd been performing in drag as the nurse in Marcus's burlesque number. I wouldn't have been surprised if those two were lovers again.

Deep down I knew, if I truly desired it, David and Marcus and I could be lovers. David had let me know long ago he was open to that prospect. I just needed to walk us through that door. But it was Gee we were taking home tonight. And from the look I'd glimpsed in Marcus's eyes, I knew I wasn't being a nice guy at all.

CHAPTER FIFTEEN

Life is a Carnival

L ate in August, David and I took a streetcar to the
Ex where we met up with Pat and his date Nadia in
the early evening. Thrusting out a bag of Tiny Tom's
donuts, Pat asked if I remembered Nadia; we'd all met
years ago at Sneaky Dee's. Beneath the kaleidoscopic
Zipper, Nadia and I regarded one another. Why yes, Pat,
I replied, taking a donut, we did remember each other.
Nadia and I shook hands, and I introduced her to David.
Nadia was wearing a ball cap, torn jeans, and a black T-shirt
emblazoned with Ashley MacIsaac's fiery golden face. It
wasn't quite so dramatic as Olivia Newton John's trans-
formation in *Grease*, but it was still remarkable to me.

We roamed the colourful chaos of the midway, amidst
the bells, screaming and whistles, the whirling lights, the
smells of caramel corn, waffles and cotton candy. We
rode the Polar Express (David crushed into me), the Siz-
zler, and Crazy Mouse Roller Coaster (which left my
shoulder bruised). It was only after being rear-ended re-
peatedly by kids driving bumper cars that Nadia and I
opted out of the rides. As David and Pat ran off to

line-up for the Mach 3, I heard someone shouting my name. It was Megan and Charles in matching Blue Jays jerseys on the Sky Ride passing overhead. Nadia and I both waved back.

"Do you think," Nadia said as we settled on a bench to wait for David and Pat, "Pat and Blonde Dawn might get back together again?"

"I have no idea," I said. "She's agreed to stay on as manager of Three Dog Run until they find a replacement. Pat's writing a lot of new music and the band's really starting to get popular. But no, I don't think they're getting back together. He's on a date with you, isn't he? How'd you manage that, anyway?"

"I went to his workplace."

"His workplace?"

"I waited until one of his classes ended," Nadia said, "and we 'bumped' into each other. I told him I was looking into doing some teaching myself."

"One of his classes?"

"At the Hansa Language Centre. He teaches English as a second language. Daniel, you knew that."

"Um, yeah. For sure." I vaguely recalled Pat had been certified years ago as an ESL instructor. He'd mention teaching off and on, along with some private tutoring. But Pat seemed perpetually broke so I'd never thought it amounted to much. Conversations with Pat always turned to what was happening with Three Dog Run. "How did you know he worked there?"

"It's on his band's website," Nadia said. "He writes about it in his biography."

I handed her my whiskey flask. "Right."

"Pat's been a teacher at Hansa for years. He's quite popular. His students love him."

"He told you that?"

"He didn't have to." Discreetly, Nadia took a sip and returned my flask. "I saw the way they interact with him. I think half the girls are in love with him, and half the secretarial staff."

"Okay. That sounds like Pat."

"He wears a shirt and tie."

"What?"

"Pat, when he teaches, he wears a shirt and tie."

"Is that the dress code?"

"No, not at all. I saw some of the other instructors, and they were all dressed more casually. I asked Pat about it and he said he just likes wearing a tie and carrying a briefcase."

I was at a loss for words. I tried to picture Pat in a tie with a briefcase. This was the same guy who'd wear nothing but a sock performing with his high school band Krypton back in the day. This was the same guy who got picked up wandering barefoot through the Chihuahuan Desert after Burning Man.

Pat and David appeared, dishevelled and laughing. "That," David exclaimed, clutching my arm, "was awesome! You guys are totally missing out."

Pat still had a long string of tickets left over, and Nadia suggested we meet up in an hour at the Food Building in front of the 99-cent spaghetti stand.

"You sure about that?" Pat asked. "You don't mind?"

"I don't mind," Nadia said, hooking her arm around mine. "Do any of you boys mind?"

"Ooh," David said, "can we all get BeaverTails later?"

"Yes, David," Nadia said, "we can all get BeaverTails."

Pat and David stared at each other. "You know what this means?" The two high-fived and fist bumped. "It's Mega Drop time!" The two ran off again through the crowd.

"Did you know," I said, "one of the most popular events at Burning Man is The Great Canadian Beaver Eating Contest?"

"Is that," Nadia said, "what I'm imagining it is?"

"Only couples are allowed to participate."

"Did Pat tell you about this?"

"You know he did."

"Did he take part?"

"He never went into much detail and I never asked. That and something called The Orgy Dome." I looked at Nadia. "You sure you want to be dating my brother?"

"Your brother," Nadia said, "has many sides to him. Doesn't David?"

We strolled arm-in-arm toward the Food Building around a line-up of people buying corn dogs and candy apples. A girl in a wheelchair passed by with a gigantic yellow Pikachu twice her size in her lap.

"David's not that complicated," I said. "I think that's why we get along so well."

"Daniel, people are always complicated. Some are just more open about it than others. Pat's open. He'll answer any question I ask, as honestly as he can. That's worth something to me."

It was true Pat was unfiltered. If he said or did things that seemed outrageous, it was only because others were afraid to say or do the same. Once in high school, he'd told Mr. Van Dyck right in front of the entire chemistry class to stop staring at Janet Leibowitz's boobs.

"David and I are honest with each other," I said.

"I never said you weren't. I apologize if it came across that way. All I'm saying is, I can trust Pat."

"My brother Pat?"

"That's right. I can trust Pat to be himself."

"Hey buddy," a voice barked. "Hey, buddy!" A greasy-haired carny was waving me over to his game booth. "Win your girlfriend a prize! Five-bucks-three-throws. Hey little lady, y'think your boyfriend here can win ya a prize? C'mon, buddy, five-bucks-three-throws."

I kept walking, but Nadia opened her purse.

"Whoa, Nadia," I said, "I play hockey, I don't shoot hoops."

"Daniel." Nadia made a face. She passed a bill over to the carny and positioned herself in front of the basketball nets.

"The trick is," she said, "a high arc with a lot of back spin." Her first throw rattled off the rim, but her second was a perfect swish. Coolly, she handed me her third ball. "Don't try rebounding; the backboard's made of plywood and extra springy."

Taking aim, I tossed the ball high as instructed. To my own shock, it dropped in neatly.

"And we have a winner," the carny announced. "Two out of three, we have a winner!" He winked at me and handed Nadia a large orange monkey. "Who's gonna be getting some tonight?"

"Um, we're not together," I said. "We're just friends." But the carny had already begun roping in other passers-by.

After that, Nadia asked if we could take a detour and I followed her through the crowds. When I asked how she knew so much about the midway games, she took out some tickets. "I'll tell you if you come on one last ride with me." I looked up, following her luminous gaze. We were standing in front of the Ferris wheel.

We joined the line and eventually took our seats. With a lurch, the earth fell away. All around us, the CNE grounds pulsated and sparkled, a thousand points of light. As we lifted skyward, the tumult of humanity took on a distant, ethereal quality.

Nadia pointed. "See the new BMO Field? That's where the CNE Grandstand used to be. Back in '93, Pearl Jam opened for Neil Young there. I'd have loved to have seen that concert."

"No kidding."

"The story goes, after the show Mr. Vedder and Mr. Young rode the Ferris wheel together. I always wondered what they spoke about while they were up here, taking in the sights."

"Nadia, how do you know all this?"

"I follow rock bands." Nadia held the monkey's hand and gazed across the midway. "It's something of a hobby of mine." The stars and faraway carnival lights illuminated her face. "Also, I used to date a carny who worked for Conklin Shows. I met him here at the CNE. He was the most beautiful boy you could imagine, like a young Hayden Christensen or Taylor Kitsch. The first time I saw him, he was wearing a crop top and a ball cap, with a cigarette tucked behind one ear. He just smiled at me and asked if I wanted to shoot a gun. It was only an air gun, but I was sixteen and I'd never held one, so he hopped the counter and showed me how. It was that game where you shoot out the star on the paper. I didn't come close, but he gave me the biggest prize anyway. I was there with my girlfriends and they teased me about it the rest of the night.

"The next day, I went back on my own. When he finished his shift, he invited me to his trailer where he had cold beer in a cooler. I gave my virginity to that boy. After that, we saw each other every night for a week. It was the single great romance of my life. Then the Ex packed up and he left town. For a while, I'd receive postcards every few months, but then they stopped coming. I went back the next year and asked about him. Eventually, someone took me aside and told me he'd died in a bar fight out west, at the Calgary Stampede."

"Oh shit, Nadia. I'm so sorry to hear that."

"A few years later, I spotted him operating the Duck Pond Game."

"What?"

"When I went up and spoke to him, he pretended he didn't know me. He said he'd hit his head a while back and didn't remember a lot of things. That may well have been the truth. But I knew he remembered me. What I couldn't understand right away was why he kept insisting he didn't. It was humiliating."

"That was an asshole thing for him to do."

"You misunderstand. He didn't mean to be cruel. He was ashamed. He was humiliated to be seen by me. He knew he wasn't beautiful anymore. He was missing teeth and he'd gained a lot of weight. His nose looked like it'd been broken more than once, and he had a limp. But in that moment, if he'd asked me to go back with him to his trailer, I would have. He couldn't understand what I still saw in him, because he could no longer see it in himself."

"So, what happened?"

"I asked when his shift was done, but he wouldn't tell me. He told me to leave him alone. I only left after he threatened to have security escort me out."

"Whoa."

Nadia bowed her head. "I never saw him again."

"But you still come back to the CNE."

"Of course I do." She smiled. "I've been coming to the midway since I was a little girl. It's magical here. One day I'll bring my own daughter or son. It's always held a special place in my heart. It always will. I even fell in love with a carny once."

After a few more turns, the ride ended and we disembarked. When we reached the Food Building, we sat outside the entrance on the wide steps with the big orange monkey between us.

"I can't say whether I'll be with your brother the rest of my life," Nadia said. "But for now, it's what I desire, and I'm happy to be here. I'm walking into this with eyes wide open. You don't have to worry about me."

A vendor passed by pushing a cart piled high with gaudy plastic toys blinking and flashing in the dark.

"You should come up," I said, "for Christmas in Sudbury. It's not that far. David will be there. You can meet Grandpa and Liam. I can introduce you to Karen."

"Well, if Pat invites me, that would be something to consider."

"I'm counting on it."

"That's not for many months, Daniel. Let's just see where this fall takes us."

I stood up and held out my hand. "My turn. You're coming with me."

"Where are we going?"

"Inside. We'll have BeaverTails with the guys later. But right now, Nadia, we are paying a visit to the Cake Shack."

And so we did.

⌒ Late one evening, I sat down to study at the kitchen table. I was working my rotation in emergency medicine, and it'd been a gruelling thirteen-hour day on my feet. One patient shouting "nigger" and "faggot" at the top of his lungs assaulted a nurse (and spat in my face), security had called 911, and I'd needed to file an incident report. I'd drunk way too much coffee and I could feel a headache coming on, like a crack forming in an ice sheet. I heard the rattle of keys and David walked through the door. He'd been out for dinner with Luke, just back from Italy.

David kicked off his shoes, said hi, sank into the couch and started perusing a magazine. He knew not to interrupt me when I was studying, but this time I set down my highlighter and pushed away my textbook.

"So how's Luke?" I asked.

"What?"

"How was Luke's time in Italy?"

"He had a good time." David picked up another magazine.

"And how's your mom settling in?"

"Great. Ma and Nicoli just opened her new art gallery. It's a big success. Luke says everyone's doing great. Antonio says hi."

"Your mom was going to exhibit some of his work, wasn't she?"

"Yeah, she did. She also got him to take a photography course. Now, everyone's getting ready for the olive harvest. Antonio's good."

Something wasn't right. I closed my textbook. "And how was Ai Chang's visit?" Luke's girlfriend had gone to visit him in August. Over the course of their relationship, it seemed those two spent more time apart than together, but somehow they made it work.

"Ai Chang's been to Italy before. Luke says the whole family made her feel really welcome. Apparently, her Italian's better than mine."

"What? Really?"

"She's been taking classes for years. She can speak four languages: Mandarin, Cantonese, English and Italian."

"I'm impressed."

"Daniel." David put down the magazine. "There's something I need to tell you."

Then I knew something was wrong. "What is it? What happened? What's going on?"

"It's complicated."

"Okay." I sat back in my chair. "Tell me."

David's eyes were puffy. "I'm not sure where to start."

"Just tell me."

"Remember Silvia Sabatini?"

"The girl you made out with in Balestrate?"

"You remember that."

"The neighbour's granddaughter. Of course, I do. A bunch of you visited that nude beach last summer. It was supposed to be a day trip, but you ended up renting motel rooms. Antonio had a crush on her."

"Yeah, he did."

"Did something happen to her?"

"No. I mean, she's fine. She's okay."

"Alright."

"When Ai Chang visited this summer, those two really hit it off. They became like best girlfriends."

"Okay."

David pulled his knees up under his chin. "Ai Chang's leaving the ballet school. She's signed a contract with Club Monaco. It's only an entry level position for now. But she's set to be making a lot of money."

"No kidding. Good for her."

"Once her career gets going, she and Luke are hoping to raise a family."

"Wow. They're really that serious?"

"Yeah, they are. So, at some point Ai Chang and Silvia get to talking about kids. Then Silvia takes her to this church and shows her a gravesite. It's tiny. It's just a small plaque in the ground."

"Okay."

"She tells her she had a miscarriage, back in January."

"Oh. I'm sorry to hear that."

"Luke says miscarriages are common." David picked at a tear in his jeans. "Is that true?"

"I guess you could say that." I didn't quite entirely grasp yet where this was going. But my hands were starting to feel numb.

"People," David said, "don't talk about these things."

"No, they don't."

"She really wanted to have this baby. That was her plan."

"David."

"She was already nineteen weeks in when it happened. She wanted a proper burial. It was important to her." His cheeks were flushed, his eyes wet. "Cemeteries have areas set aside for these kinds of things."

"David. What are you saying?"

"She was ready to be a single mom. She wasn't ever going to tell me. That's what she told Ai Chang."

"And Ai Chang told Luke."

David nodded.

"David. Last year, when I asked if anything had happened in Italy, you told me you'd kissed a girl."

"I did kiss a girl."

"Did you have sex with Silvia Sabatini?"

He nodded.

I drew a breath. "Holy shit." I sat back in my chair. "You had sex with Silvia Sabatini." I closed my eyes. My headache was suddenly a spasm in the front of my skull. "David, when I told you about Sean, I told you everything. I told you everything. We'd agreed on this."

"I know." David wiped his nose on his wrist. "I'm sorry."

"When were you going to tell me?"

"I'm telling you now. I'm sorry. It was wrong. It was a stupid mistake. It just happened. I didn't plan it."

"What's that supposed to mean: 'It just happened'?"

"That weekend in Balestrate, after we booked into the motel, we decided we'd step out for something to eat.

There were six of us, we'd been drinking all day. It was close to midnight, but people in Italy eat whole meals at that hour. Except Silvia forgets her purse and asks me to come back with her.

"When we get to her room, she's all over me: She pushes me onto the bed, and she's on top of me, and she's got my belt off, and before I know it ..." David buried his face in his hands. "We caught up with the others at the restaurant. We couldn't have been gone thirty minutes. But, I dunno, there must've been lipstick on me or something. The next day, after we get back to the farm, Antonio asks me if I'd kissed Silvia. He's really nervous about it, but he asks me flat out. So I tell him. I told him I had. I knew he liked Silvia, so I wasn't sure how he'd react. For a few seconds, he doesn't say anything at all. But then the guy congratulates me, and it's obvious he's making this genuine effort to be nice about it, you know what I mean? He insists I tell him everything, so I tell him about the 'kiss.'

"After that, I couldn't bring myself to tell him what actually happened. I mean, Antonio had liked this girl for years, and I'd known her just a few weeks, right? I also told him it was personal and private, and not to mention it in front of Silvia or anyone, and he was honestly really good about that. That's also when I came out to him, that's when I told him I was gay. The guy's like stunned. He doesn't know what to make of it. He has a hard time understanding this and believing me, so I end up showing him pictures of you and me to prove it.

"After that, he finally seems to get it. He makes a point of giving me a big hug, and he tells me we're like family and nothing will ever change that. Then he and I come back to Toronto and all three of us, Daniel, hang out and we have this great time, right? And I guess I was already feeling guilty about what had happened, so that's the story I stuck with: that yeah, I'd made out with Silvia Sabatini. Except, I know that wasn't all of the truth, Daniel, I know that. And I'm sorry I didn't tell you sooner. I really am. I know after Antonio left I could've told you, but I didn't. By then, I dunno. I guess, maybe by then I half-believed the story myself: that it had been just a kiss."

"A girl," I said, "doesn't get pregnant from just a kiss."

"Jesus." David stood up. "I didn't know she was pregnant, alright? I had no fucking clue! She never told me. She told me I didn't have anything to worry about, that she was on the pill. Luke thinks she was never on the pill, that she lied, and that she actually wanted to get pregnant." Tears were streaming down his face. "Silvia told Ai Chang she'd always wanted to have a baby, and that she never wanted to get married, that she didn't need any man in her life, and that she didn't give a fuck what the Church thought."

"And that you were the father?"

David nodded.

David's face was contorted, and he was sobbing. But I couldn't bring myself to get up and comfort him. Instead, I just said: "She shouldn't have told him."

"Who?"

"Ai Chang, she shouldn't have told Luke."

"Well, Daniel, she did. She did, and I'm glad she did. Luke figured I had a right to know."

"And what is it that you know?"

"That there's this cemetery," David said, "in a village in Sicily, with my kid buried in it."

On our very first date, strolling through the hushed corridors of the Art Gallery of Ontario, our hands sometimes brushing each other, David had told me he wanted to be a father. Poised before a portrait by Paul Peel, he told me how he felt it was the most important thing he could ever see himself doing. If he could help bring a child into the world and raise it well, then he believed his life would be well-spent and complete. In this moment, in some part of my mind, I understood what this news from Sicily meant to David and how painful it must be. But my headache was a haze in front of my eyes.

"David, and now you're telling me because, what? You want my sympathy? Is that, I mean, is that really what you're expecting from me right now?"

David looked taken aback. "I'm sorry."

"You're not sorry. That's bullshit. You are not sorry. Yeah, you're sorry it turned out this way. But you're not sorry for what you did." Now I was also standing. "David, you were in Sicily, you were horny and you were drunk and you fucked a girl behind my back. There's nothing complicated about this."

"Daniel."

"No. You kept this a secret from Antonio, and you kept this a secret from me. You covered this whole shitty thing up this whole past year. What's the chance you were ever going to tell me, seriously?"

"Daniel. I'm telling you now."

"And are you telling me now because you've been feeling guilty, because you think I deserve to know? I don't think so. This is about you. This is about you wanting something from me. Am I really supposed to say: 'I'm sorry, I'm so sorry this, this girl you knocked up, this girl you cheated on me with, lost her baby'? Seriously? Well, right now, I don't have it in me. I'm tired. I'm tired of having to take care of people. I'm tired of always having to be the bigger person. I'm tired of putting other people's shit ahead of my own shit, my whole entire fucking life. I'm sick and tired of having to deal with fucking selfish shit. You're just like Pat, and Liam. You're just like Marcus."

"Daniel."

But I wasn't done. I turned and pointed a finger. "You know, David, you're a lot like your brother."

"Daniel."

"You ever think about that? You're a lot like Luke. Think about that, okay?" Then I was done. I concentrated on putting on my shoes. My hands were shaking. David was talking but I wasn't listening. I grabbed my jacket and walked out the front door. When I hit the alleyway outside, I kept walking.

My vision was blurry. I scraped my knuckles across my eyes. Why was I crying? The truth was, David and I had never fought. Not in four years. Not really, not about anything important.

I could've fucked Sean the DJ and how would David have felt about that? I took out my phone and texted Sean. Part of me did feel bad this girl had lost her baby. At nineteen weeks, its bones would have been starting to form, its limbs lengthened in proportion to its body, it would've been starting to grow hair and beginning to hear its mother's voice. I'd seen real life miscarriages during obstetrics and gynaecology last year. Hell, I'd helped deliver a newborn baby once. Experiences like that stay with you the rest of your life.

Sean texted back. I told him I was coming over and asked for his address. I knew he lived in Liberty Village not so far away, and I started walking in that direction. David was calling me, but I didn't answer. It was only when I'd reached Trinity Bellwoods Park that Sean replied. I hailed a cab and got in.

Mom and Dad hadn't been married when she got pregnant. It wasn't until years later that they decided to throw a party and get hitched in our backyard. As Mom walked barefoot across the lawn with flowers in her hair, Pat played his concert ukulele and sang Leonard Cohen's "Suzanne." Dad wore his favourite leather vest and a long feather in his top hat. Up in our pirate ship tree house, Liam leaned out scattering flower petals down onto the bride and groom. When Mr. Milton signalled me to present the rings, they had blazed in the honey sunlight, made of true and honest gold.

Sean had moved since we last dated and this condo building was new to me. A sign warned trespassers off the manicured lawn. A security camera blinked over the entranceway. As I was about to buzz up, a man with a Doberman Pinscher exited; I caught the door and entered the lobby. A brittle metal sculpture, flanked by two black ottomans, looked like it might cut me if I stood too close. When the elevator opened, a woman in a cardigan emerged carrying an empty casserole dish. In that instant, she saw in my face all my weariness, my anger and my lust. Her gaze followed me as I passed her by.

At the last moment, she turned. She put out one hand and stopped the doors from closing. We stood facing each other.

"Are you," she asked, "Sean's boyfriend?"

My heart skipped a beat.

"Um. No."

"But you are Sean's friend?"

I didn't know how to reply to this. My hesitation was enough. The woman's eyes narrowed. "I don't know who you are, or who you think you are. But right now, he's needing a friend. D'you understand me?"

I nodded.

"Sean is my son. I care for him very much. He may not understand this, but it is the truth."

Her lips compressed into a thin line. Her eyes were hard and rusted as iron nails. I became acutely conscious of my own unshaven and dishevelled appearance.

"Why don't you have your own boyfriend?" she whispered. "Why're you coming here?"

I was the proverbial deer in headlights. I was an escaped convict pinned down by the helicopter searchlight. It was all I could do to muster a simple shake of my head.

"Is it that confusing for you young men? Is it truly that confusing? Are you all that lonely? Are you all that lost? D'you think you're the only ones who are suffering? We all suffer, all of us. But we get on. We get on. Or is it that you boys think you don't deserve to be happy? Is that what it is? Well, hear it from me: you do." She released her restraining hand. "You have as much right to happiness as anyone in this world. You tell that to him. Maybe he'll listen to you." The elevator doors closed and she was gone.

I stood with shoulders raised, my fists clenched in my jacket pockets. If someone had accosted me at knifepoint and stolen my wallet, I would not have been in more shock. I didn't know what to think. I stood alone in a windowless box made of cold steel and darkened glass. The rows of square glowing numbers waited for me.

When I broke up with Marcus, I'd left him by way of an elevator. That had been one of the worst moments of my life.

I had compared David to Marcus, and to Pat and Liam. I had absolutely no idea why I'd said David was like his brother. Maybe it was because Luke had hurt him, and David had hurt me. Was I really so lost and confused? Even when Karen was thinking of moving in with Bob and his two daughters, I'd never judged her for having sex with Liam. At the abortion clinic, when I stated I was the father of Karen's unborn child, I had held Karen's hand and looked the physician in the eye. People kept secrets all the time. They just didn't talk about it. If there was anything I'd learned in my quarter century of life, it was that loved ones hurt each other. Inevitably, without exception. Fifteen years ago, my parents died in a fiery car crash. How many people had they hurt? How many people, I wondered, never heal from such things?

I remembered to breathe. I unclenched and lowered my hands. I opened my eyes.

I reached out and pressed a button.

CHAPTER SIXTEEN

Boy Inside the Man

Julia and Reginald, Mitz, Madison and Claire.

I'll never forget them.

I'd met them on my first date with Marcus, at a party called Vazaleen. Back at Julia's apartment, we celebrated Reginald's birthday with a white chocolate raspberry trifle cake Julia had baked just for the occasion. After that, we all dropped E and danced until dawn. The others were older, but that didn't matter. Everyone took care of me, each in their own way.

Mitz made a point of approaching each one of us and asking for a hug. His eyes were bloodshot and he'd mumble: "I love you man." When he caught up to me on the fire escape, he took a drag off my cigarette, blinked blearily and asked what my name was again. When I told him, he gave me a bear hug, kissed me hard on the cheek and mumbled in my ear: "Daniel Garneau, little buddy, I love you man." When Claire pointed out that she was a girl, Madison replied: "That boy's speaking his language, Claire, just close your eyes and listen to the boy, honey."

After that, everyone took to saying "I love you man" at every instance they could. For one night, it became our own beautiful private language. When I asked Reginald if Vazaleen was his favourite scene, he shook his head: "Club 56 I love you man." When Reginald commented how a Senate committee had just ruled in favour of legalizing marijuana in Canada, Claire rubbed noses with him: "I love you man." After Claire mentioned the Queen was arriving next week to celebrate her Golden Jubilee, Madison shouted from the kitchen: "That's fifty fucking years of fucking white colonial oppression I love you man." Then Marcus stopped the music entirely to declare that Switzerland had just become the 190th member state of the United Nations, whereupon everyone responded in unison: "I love you man!"

In the end, Marcus and I crashed in Marwa's room. Marwa was out of town visiting her cousin Youssef. Years later, I learned Youssef had a hormone condition which kept landing him in the hospital.

I had a condition with my hormones, too.

Earlier that night, a moment came when Marcus went to the washroom. I followed him in and closed the door.

"I have to pee," Marcus said.

"That's okay," I said. "I don't mind do you mind?"

Without waiting for an answer, I ran the cold water, drank from the faucet and soaked my head underneath. I leaned dripping over the sink. My vision had stopped going blurry, but now my jaw ached and I was having a hard time talking.

"Holy shit," I said. "What is that?"

"This?" Marcus said.

"Yeah."

"This is a Prince Albert." He finished peeing, wiped himself with toilet paper, and zipped up his pants.

While he washed his hands, I gripped his arm and pressed my nose into his shoulder. Caramel-scented candles glowed golden over the sink. Jars of cotton balls and pink plastic razors, perfumes and shiny bath soaps cluttered the shelves. Next to a hair dryer lay something else, sleek and gleaming. Marcus held out a towel.

"You having a good time?"

I nodded.

He dried my hair for me. "Are people being nice to you?"

I nodded again. More than nice. "What's that?"

"That?" Marcus followed my gaze. "That is Marwa's vibrator." When I only stared blankly, he added: "That was my graduation present."

"You bought that for her?"

"For Marwa, yes, I did. I even had it monogrammed."

"So how does it work?"

"How does it work?" Marcus looked me in the eye. "Daniel Garneau, really now." I was shirtless, wearing Claire's Tigger onesie around my waist because I was so hot. Setting the towel aside, Marcus splayed his hand over my sweaty chest, and pushed me up against the wall. He bent and kissed first one nipple, taking his time, and then the other. If this had been a Harlequin romance, my bosom would have been heaving. I wondered if he could feel my heart pounding. As it was, I reached out, picked up the vibrator and held it up. "Can you show me?"

That night, Marcus fucked me. He did it with Marwa's vibrator in the shower, on his knees with my dick in his mouth. At first he was gentle, using his fingers and a lot of soap. When he finally slipped it in, thrumming and buzzing, the sensation was indescribable. Between Marcus' thighs, the thick steel of his Prince Albert kept bobbing up and down. The curtain was drawn, but I could hear others in the washroom, talking and laughing, using the toilet. "You guys okay in there?" someone called out. "Yeah," I replied, clutching the shower rod. Then Marcus was less gentle, and within moments I could feel myself getting close. The toilet flushed. I started to come. The water turned scalding hot. I must've made a sound because someone exclaimed: "Oh shit so sorry guys my bad I love you man." My eyes rolled back. I had visions of King Kong thrashing atop the Empire State Building as roaring Helldivers circled pumping bullets into his massive, heaving body; Neo shot at close range again and again by Agent Smith, staggering back into the wall; Rocky Balboa, bloody and drenched in sweat, clinging to the arms of Apollo Creed, gasping and utterly spent.

These were the unforgettable moments of our lives.

Marcus turned his head and spat. When he pulled it out of me, I slid and crumpled down next to him in the tub. He leaned forward, gripped the back of my head and locked his mouth to mine.

"Marcus, sweetheart," Julia said, "you wouldn't happen to have Marwa's vibrator in there with you, would you?"

When she repeated herself, Marcus sat back on his heels and replied: "Yeah." He peeled the condom off of it and drew back the curtain. "Why, yes in fact, we do. Here you go."

"Oh my." Julia averted her gaze. She took the vibrator between thumb and forefinger. "Now, would either of you be wanting any more cake?"

We shook our heads.

"Well, then." She reached in and turned off the water. "It's bedtime. The girls and I are saying good night. Sherlock and Watson are out on the couch. Daniel, I'll see you, young man, when we get up."

"Julia?" I said.

"Yes?"

"Thank you," I said. "Thank you for having me in your home. Thank you for inviting me. Thank you for everything. Thank you."

"You're welcome, darling." She glanced at Marcus. Gently, she pinched my nose. "You are very welcome."

When I woke up the next day, it was late-afternoon and everyone was gone, even Julia who had some wedding rehearsal to attend. They had let me sleep in and only Marcus had stayed behind.

On my streetcar ride home, I wore my sunglasses and sat in the back, my hood drawn down low over my face.

I hadn't even had a chance to say goodbye.

They were all Julia's friends and not long afterwards, I heard she and Marwa had some kind of falling out. Of course, Marcus's loyalty was to Marwa, and my tie-in was with Marcus. Marcus had no shortage of people in his life. He was perfectly okay to move on.

I never saw them again.

My first date with Marcus happened in September. In December, I let him dress me up as a masked, half-naked forest god in his ROM gala fundraiser event. At Marcus's New Year's Eve party, I met his best friend Marwa, and found myself in a threesome with his ex-boyfriend Fang. Then on Valentine's Day, we broke up. Five months. Marwa told me later that five months was the longest Marcus had ever been in a relationship. At the time, it was also mine.

A few years after that, I was riding the subway. Across from me was some guy wearing headphones, in a toque and a bomber jacket. We made eye contact and he looked away, the way any stranger might. Except I thought it might've been Mitz. If I knew for sure it was him, I would've said something. But the funny thing was, I wasn't sure. Two stops later, he gathered his stuff and got up. He glanced back just as the doors opened. I was sure in that second he thought he recognized me. But then he was gone. I wanted to shout; I wanted to leap up and run after him. But I didn't move. The doors had closed. Today, if I were to bump into Julia or Reginald or Madison or Claire, I honestly couldn't be sure if I'd recognize any of them. I no longer had any clear memory of how they looked.

But what remained crystal clear for me was that for one night, we were each other's best friends and soulmates. That it had been glorious. For nine hours, we were a family. We loved each other. We were in love with each other. We were shameless, united and full of brazen wonder. Then it was over. When I met Marcus, that was the world he lived in.

And as far as I could tell, Marcus was still living in that world.

⌐ Sunday night Skype date with Karen.

Bob's wife had returned to Manitoulin.

She'd written to Bob first, saying she wanted a second chance, that she was better now, that she'd been clean over twelve months. She said she wanted to be the mother to her two girls that she couldn't be before.

Her name was Elsie.

Two weeks later, she showed up at Karen's work. She was pretty and soft-spoken, wearing just a bit of make-up. She asked if they could meet for coffee. The next day, they sat down at the Kagawong Main Street Café, an old school house on the hill on Highway 540. She kept thanking Karen for taking care of her kids. In the end, they talked for two hours. After that, they agreed to meet again.

"We have a lot in common," Karen said. "She could've been me."

"What do you mean?"

"I mean, in a different time and place, I could've been her."

I didn't know what to say. But this time, Karen wasn't asking for advice. She just wanted to let me know. "And how are you and David doing?" she asked.

"We got into a big fight last month."

"What about?"

I hesitated. "A lot of things."

"Are you guys okay?"

"I think so. We're working on it. We're talking it through."

"These things take time."

"Look, Karen." I set aside my unfinished bowl of ice cream. "You didn't tell me Bob's wife was still in the picture."

Karen sighed and gazed somewhere past the computer screen. Eventually she drew a breath. "Bob told me. She'd left him and the girls three years ago. He went to pick up Zephyr and Sky from hockey practice one day. When he got home, she was gone. It was early in the fall. Dinner was on the table, the girls' favourite: spaghetti and meatballs. There were fresh cut flowers. But she was just gone. He called everywhere, but no one knew anything. He was about to file a missing persons report but then he found a letter saying how sorry she was. He hasn't heard from her since. He told me."

"What? She left just like that?"

"Bob says she had a past. It caught up to her."

"Where's she been all this time?"

"Away. On the road. Figuring things out. She told me Bob was the best thing that ever happened to her. He was good to her. But she wasn't ready for anyone to be good to her. She needed some time to figure things out."

"Three fucking years?"

"Don't be angry with her."

"Really?"

"She's a decent person, Daniel. Bad things happen to decent people. Elsie, she's put herself through rehab and counselling, and done an awful lot of soul-searching."

"How can you be defending her?"

"Because," Karen whispered, "she's what they need."

"She's what who needs?"

"Zephyr and Sky, the girls. They need a mom." Her lips were trembling. Tears rolled down her cheeks. "They need their mom."

"Oh. Karen." If I could've reached through the computer screen, I would've held her. "I'm so sorry." All I could do was cradle my laptop in my arms. "Are you sure about this?"

"Yeah. You'd be too, if you met her."

I tried to imagine the kind of woman who'd leave her loving husband and small children. I tried to imagine the kind of woman who'd come back.

"You should see Bob," Karen said. "He's a mess. He's worse than me. The girls have no idea. We haven't told them yet. I spotted her once, across the schoolyard watching them. But she's been keeping her distance. She's been really respectful. Elsie said it herself, they probably wouldn't even recognize her if they did meet her."

"And what does Bob think of this?"

"A lot of things. For a while, he wasn't even ready to meet her. He's having a hard time saying what he feels. He's like Liam that way."

"So how does he feel?"

"He says he doesn't know. But I know he wants to get back together with her. I know he wants her back. He won't admit it yet, not even to himself. But I can see it. I watch him when he sleeps. I can see it in his face."

"You know this?"

Karen nodded. "Did I ever tell you, Gracie used to be her dog?"

I shook my head.

"Elsie really wanted a puppy. She picked her out from the litter."

"Didn't he save that dog's life?"

"He did, two years ago. Bob says it was the stupidest thing he'd ever done. He and the girls were in the back-country. Somehow a bear cub ended up in their campsite. Of course, mama bear was right behind it. He got Zephyr and Sky into the canoe first. By then the mama bear had Gracie pinned down; she was also on top of the pack with the bear spray. Bob went back and fought her off with a paddle. But then she turned and charged. He says he remembers seeing his own blood in that bear's teeth. He finally got his hands on the bear spray. After that, Zephyr was the one who called 911. He had to get forty stitches in his head and arm."

"Oh my god."

"The girls saw it all happen right in front of them. He could've died. But Gracie's alive because of it."

"Shit."

"That family, they've been through a lot."

"What happened to the bear?"

"She and the cub took off. She was just protecting her baby. That's what mama bears do."

Obviously, I thought to myself, not all mothers were mama bears. "What," I asked, "are you going to do?"

Karen looked away, her eyes wide open. "The right thing."

"Fuck."

"You're telling me." The tears were coming again, and she wiped at her cheeks with the back of one hand. "And I thought I'd finally found him, y'know?" She shook her head. "For a moment there, I thought I'd finally found my guy."

"Karen, you deserve better than this. You deserve so much. You deserve the world."

"I do, don't I?" Karen said, laughing. "Look, after this, I'm not so sure I can stay on the Island anymore."

"What do you mean?"

"I can't be here. Not with Liam and Bob here, not seeing the girls at the Centre every day. I can't be here. Elsie's asked me to stay, but I can't."

"Okay."

"I think I might go north."

"Why north?"

"It won't be right away. I'll finish out my year. But there are a lot of teaching gigs up north. They need teachers."

"Your old schoolmate Derrick, wasn't he from North Bay?"

"Yeah. But I was thinking, farther north."

Something in Karen's tone alerted me. "How much farther?"

"I have a friend who works in Fort Albany. I thought I could start looking around there. Maybe Nunavut."

I straightened. "Nunavut?"

"Hey, world." Karen's eyes sparkled. "Here I come."

I wanted to protest. I wanted to shout. Why couldn't Karen move back to Toronto? Why did she have to move so far away?

"Or," Karen said, "I could try moving back to Toronto maybe. I don't know. Daniel, what do you think?"

"Come to Toronto." I drew a shaky breath. "Karen, come to Toronto. You know this city. You have friends here, you have family. You'll be close to Anne. There's so much we can do here. It won't be like the way it was before, but we can make it work. You told me once we've barely scratched the surface of this ridiculous city. Karen, come back to Toronto. You have every reason to come back."

I was standing on my feet, holding my laptop in my hands. I had no idea how much I'd missed Karen until this moment. My heart was pounding in my chest. "Karen Fobister?"

"Yes?"

"I'm your guy. I'll always be your guy."

"You promise?"

"Yeah. I promise."

⌒ On the last day of October, crowded into a booth at Sneaky Dee's, Pat, Nadia, Luke, Ai Chang and I ordered another pitcher and a second plate of nachos with extra guac on the side. Tegan and Sara's newest album played on the sound system: off-kilter, grief-stricken and dark. Anne had introduced it to David who had introduced it to me. There were moments when the twins sounded out of tune.

"Ma thinks," Luke said, "there's a Sicilian curse on our family."

"Your ma," Ai Chang said, "thinks you'll be cursed if a broom touches you."

"Your ma believes in curses?" Nadia asked.

"They say if someone's sweeping and they brush your feet," Luke said, picking at a jalapeño pepper, "you'll stay single the rest of your life. But that's only if you're already single."

Pat put down his beer. "Who says that?"

"Italians." Luke tossed invisible pizza dough in the air. "Hey, we have a lot of superstitions about sex and love."

"So what's this family curse?" I asked.

"That every man she marries will drop dead," Ai Chang said.

Pat's eyes widened. "Whoa."

"But she just got married again," Nadia said, "to her fourth husband."

"Yes she did," Luke said, "and now it's been five months, and she's starting to get worried."

"Why would she marry someone," I asked, "if she really believed that marrying them was going to kill them?"

"Hold on, look," Pat said. "Everyone's going to drop dead at some point. That's life. Each one of us is going to die one day. Did you guys ever think about that?"

"Yeah." Ai Chang made a face and regarded him sidelong. "Sure. I think about that all the time."

Pat jabbed the tabletop. "The point is, life is short. We make the best of what we have in the time that we've got. I figure, Luke, that's what your ma is doing."

"Does Nicoli know about the curse?" Nadia asked.

"Yeah," Ai Chang said, "did she even tell him?"

"Oh, he knows about the curse, alright," Luke said. "You might even say he's the one who's responsible."

"Wait a second," I said. "You're all talking like this is real."

"My grandmother," Luke said, "was advised by a high-ranking Church official to take a vow of silence to break the curse."

Ai Chang turned to Luke. "But your *nonna*, I've heard her talk."

"Yeah, but did you notice it's only after sundown? Except she thinks the family's cursed because she had a child out of wedlock with a Canadian soldier. She blames herself for a mortar shell blowing up the old parish priest. She also blames herself for her first daughter running off with a *mago* and for her second daughter being a lesbian."

"A what?" I asked.

"Oh, Dan," Pat said, "that's when a woman does, you know." Surreptitiously, he wagged his tongue at me between two fingers.

"A *mago*," Luke said, "is a male witch. Except at the time, he was in disguise, and Ma thought she was eloping with a Romani prince."

Nadia rested her arms on the table. "A prince?"

Luke looked us all in the eye. "This boy comes through the village and claims his father's king of the gypsies. He's dark and handsome. All the girls swoon over him, but it's Ma's hand he asks for in marriage. Of course, nonna and nonno don't approve of this at all. But Ma's smitten and she runs off with this guy on the night of the full moon. So then Nicoli Badalamenti, who's passionately in love with her, chases after the two, riding on horseback for three days and three nights. Except by the time he catches up to them, some ceremony's already been performed. Nicoli challenges the outcome and defeats the *mago* in a kind of ritual contest. After that, the union's reversed." Luke leaned forward and whispered: "But it led to the curse. Henceforth any marriage in their families would be followed by death."

"Harsh," Ai Chang said.

"Totally," Pat said.

I looked at the others. "Seriously?"

"That's why Ma left Sicily," Luke said. "She thought that by crossing an ocean she could escape the curse." He shook his head.

"And you believe all this?"

"Hey." Luke shrugged. "I just heard all this from my eighty-four-year-old Sicilian grandfather who's half-blind and half-deaf." The fresh pitcher arrived and he refilled all our glasses. "Nonno always liked to tell a good tale. You can believe it if you want. He's also hinted there's stolen Nazi gold buried some place on the farm. But that, my handsome little devils and wicked angels, is a whole 'nother story."

A while back, we'd all agreed to show up at Sneaky Dee's tonight either as a devil or an angel. It was fun to see what costumes people assembled. The plan was to head out later to the Halloween block party on Church Street.

"Is your whole family Catholic?" Nadia asked.

"Absolutely," Luke said. "We're Sicilian. Except the De Luca family, we've always had a bit of a shady reputation." He winked at her. "If y'know what I mean."

"So it seems," Nadia said.

Luke raised his glass. "*Salute*! Happy Halloween."

We all toasted, mindful of our plastic pitchforks, haloes and tails. I thought of Michele Moretti who'd died of a heart attack, and Tony Gallucci who'd died of a drug overdose. Neither Luke nor David ever had a chance to get to know their fathers. At least Pat, Liam and I got to know ours.

"Maybe," Nadia said, "this *mago* meant 'the little death.'"

"What's that?" Ai Chang asked.

Nadia sipped from her pint. "*La petite mort.* That brief feeling of melancholy or euphoria you experience after an orgasm, a sense of loss or transcendence."

"Holy shit," Pat said. "I get that all the time."

Luke turned to Nadia. "The little death?"

"She means," Ai Chang said, "the afterglow."

"These kinds of foretellings," Nadia said, "needn't always be taken literally."

Ai Chang leaned into Luke. "*La petite mort, signore.* Perhaps that is the curse that has haunted your *famiglia* all these years."

'What, that we have a lot of sex?" Luke said.

Then Ai Chang spoke into his ear in rapid-fire Italian, ending with something that sounded like a question, and Luke Moretti actually blushed. Ai Chang sat back and smiled, while he downed half his pint.

"You're not going to share that with us," I said, "are you?"

Ai Chang shook her head.

"Something's different about you," Pat said. "Did you do something? Your face looks different."

"She finally got her braces off," Luke said, knuckling the foam from his lips. "Show them." Now it was Ai Chang's turn to blush.

Pat knocked his glass against mine. "Well, on Thanksgiving, our grandpa announced he and his lady friend Betty are getting engaged."

"Your grandpa?" Ai Chang said.

"They've been dating over two years. He says at their age there's no time to waste; who knows when you might keel over and kick the bucket."

"He said that?" Nadia asked.

"His exact words."

"Good for him," Luke said. "There's never time to waste. Like I always say, ya gotta grab life by the balls."

"You should meet him," Pat said to Nadia. "Maybe you can come up to Sudbury for Christmas."

Nadia glanced at me. "I'll think about it."

Luke raised his pint. "Here's to great sex, and a whole goddamn lifetime of little deaths."

We all knocked glasses.

"Hey, I have another announcement," Pat said, wrapping his arm around Nadia. "Three Dog Run has found a new manager." I looked at Nadia in surprise. But Pat continued: "His name's Marcus Wittenbrink Jr. He's the guy who helped us cut our first demo tape. He's super connected and totally cool. Right now, he's on tour out west, but when he comes back we are kicking into high gear. Dan here knows him, don't you, Dan?"

All eyes turned toward me.

"Daniel?" Luke said.

"Who's Marcus?" Ai Chang asked.

"Oh." I stared at her. Then I stared at Pat. "Just my ex-boyfriend."

Nadia caught my eye and pointed outside. On the far corner across the street, I could see David waiting for me. I got up and walked out.

Fiery leaves swirled across the sidewalk. The sky

glowed, a cool blue expanse, streaked with gold and pink. Jack-o-lanterns flickered in alcoves and in front windows all along the wide avenue. David had said he'd be working late at the shop. Except now I could see the real reason he'd stayed behind. A streetcar rumbled past. I crossed the intersection.

"I see you finally finished it," I said.

"Yep, I did. Finally."

"Wow."

"Yeah."

Awkwardly, we stood facing each other. "Your costume," I said, "looks great, by the way."

"Yeah, I'm happy how it turned out." David adjusted his shoulder straps. "Anne helped me make my wings. It's all that cosplay she's into."

"Is she coming too?"

"Naw, she's off to some house party. But Gee's already on Church Street and says he'll meet up with us."

I studied the man before me. "The nail polish is a nice touch." I remembered how the first time I met David, he'd been wearing nail polish.

"Thanks."

"Well, you look great."

"So do you."

"Parker did my hair. I think he might've used too much glitter."

"You can never have too much glitter."

"That's what Parker said."

"Is he coming with us?"

"He's on his way to some dance on Ward's Island."

"Okay."

A bat skittered overhead. Stars glinted in the deepening sky. "So look, Marcus is going to be the new manager for Three Dog Run."

"Marcus? No fucking way. When did that happen?"

I folded my arms. "Pat just told us."

"Did he talk to you first about it?"

"What do you think? Hell no. But that's Pat for you."

"So, like, how are you feeling about this?"

"I dunno. Shocked, I guess. But okay." I rested my hands on my hips and sighed. "Actually, I'm surprisingly okay."

"Surprisingly okay?"

"Yeah. I mean, life goes on, right? We just have to deal with it. If you and I get to sleep with Marcus's stage manager, I suppose Marcus gets to manage my brother's band."

"Yeah, well, I guess we're all just one big happy extended family."

I drew a deep breath. "Sure." That David would even suggest that Marcus was a part of our family was frightening and magical. I could smell wood smoke on the air. Peals of laughter rang out in the distance.

"So, when's Karen moving back to Toronto?"

"She hasn't decided yet. She won't be making any decision until the new year. Liam just broke up with that police constable."

"Really? What happened?"

"They were just too different."

"Detective Joan, right? I thought those two had tons in common."

"Well, Liam said her family said some pretty stupid things over Thanksgiving and she didn't disagree with them. One thing led to another. And, well, that was that."

"What kind of stupid things?"

Gingerly, I shook the glitter from my hair. "Homophobic stuff."

"Really?" David squinted at me. "That's why Liam broke up with her?"

"Apparently."

"Wow. Okay. Well, that's too bad. Her loss. How's Liam?"

"I dunno. With Liam, it's always hard to tell."

"Are you worried about him?"

"I used to be, all the time. But no. Not anymore. I think he's going to be okay."

David glanced at Sneaky Dee's. "Hey, is Luke here already?"

"Yeah, he and Ai Chang were the first to arrive. Why?"

"He said they had something really important to ask me. Did they mention anything to you?"

"Nope."

"I guess I'll find out."

I observed David's face, strange in his make-up. But his eyes were the same, steadfast and bright. I could feel the weight of his gaze upon me. "Have you eaten?" I asked.

"Not yet."

"Well, we're just having a few drinks. You're right on time."

"I was thinking," David said, "you and I could go for a ride first." He stood holding the handlebars to his tandem bike: sleek and gleaming, freshly painted. Since he'd taken it into the shop last spring, I hadn't given it a thought.

"I didn't know you were actually still working on this thing."

"Yeah, well. I wanted to surprise you." David extended his arm. "Surprise."

"I'm surprised. Congratulations."

"The rear wheel bracket was too low and I had to refit the whole frame. That was my problem. Arthur helped. I got it fixed now."

"Alright."

"I think she's magnificent."

"She's a beauty."

"*Rocambolesco.*"

"She is *rocambolesco*. She's a girl?"

"Definitely," David said, "although I haven't named her yet. I thought we could do that together. I still have to take her for a road test. I walked her here from the shop. So, mister, how about a spin around the block?"

"Right now?"

"Yeah, right now. You up for a ride, Daniel Garneau?"

"David Gallucci. You want me to go for a ride, right now, with you?"

"I do. Now check this out." David flicked a switch and the whole bike lit up, sparkling with white fairy lights.

"No ways." I laughed out loud, despite myself.

David flashed his lopsided grin. "Pretty neat, eh?"

By now my vision had adjusted to the dark. I gazed past him, across the smoky cityscape, brimming with shadows, thresholds, and a thousand undiscovered avenues. Of course, Tadasana was everything and just the beginning.

"Alright, then." I looked my lover in the eye. "Let's do this."

EPILOGUE

Golden Hour

On a rainy Sunday autumn afternoon, in the mountainside village of Torretta in the province of Palermo, on a small side street named Via Maiorana just off Piazza Vitorio Emanuele III, down the block from Maria Concetta's cake shop Di Maggio and steps from the Speciale Filomena tobacco shop, Isabella de Luca opened her art gallery.

Her husband Nicoli had completed all the renovations an entire day ahead of schedule, calling in every favour he could. No detail was too small or insignificant: from the Gessi bathroom faucets to the lovingly handcrafted olive wood sign, to the selection of elegant stationery font. This was, after all, the extraordinary wedding gift Nicoli Badalamenti had promised: that he would build Isabella De Luca an art gallery if she were to ever move to Sicily and marry him. How could he otherwise entice her? As her fourth husband, he was also wise enough to insist that she keep her maiden name.

Because this woman had received the Order of Canada for her lifetime contribution to the arts, her repatriation had not gone unnoticed. At the urging of friends, colleagues and her publisher, Isabella crafted a two-part article documenting her return: beginning with an excerpt from an Emily Carr biopic she'd screened during her transatlantic flight and ending with philosophical reflections on the Greco-Roman archaeological site of Rosa-Columbrina. In response, her editor at the *Globe and Mail* suggested she expand her essay to a twelve-part series.

That suggestion, Isabella replied, would have to wait. Since the wedding in May, all her efforts had been poured into preparations for this *grande apertura*. Her eldest child Luke Moretti (a *furbo* if there ever was one), had spent the summer assisting. It was critical her first exhibition exclusively showcase local artists. For months, she and Luke had scoured the countryside, visiting the surrounding villages of Cavallaro, Orioles, Bellolampo, and the town of Carini. They were not disappointed. The influences of Sicily's florid history were unmistakable: European, Greek, Arabian and African forms, colours and motifs revealed themselves before her discerning eye. In the end, she settled on five artists: two potters, a ninety-year-old jeweller, a blacksmith who sculpted the most intricate ironwork, and a photographer.

The photographer was closest to home. It was in fact her twenty-three-year-old nephew, Antonio Badalamenti. Entirely self-taught, the boy had been documenting his world ever since his sister died. "She is no longer with us," he said. "She has no eyes to see. I shall see the world for her. Every photo I take is a love letter I am sending to her."

His work, of course, was immature, even childlike. It focused on the corporeal: faces and hands, skin and scars, moisture, and sexuality. He had spent years photographing the humanity of the rural working-class around him, including his employers on the De Luca farm, Isabella's own family. After some weeks of conversations, Antonio shyly shared with his new aunt a series of self-portraits depicting his own burned and dismembered body. In these raw images, Isabella saw the numinous aura of artistic genius.

The boy was uneducated with no insight whatsoever into his own talent. Years ago, he'd saved enough to acquire a vintage DSLR Nikon D1. Isabella insisted she pay for his first photography lessons in Palermo, and purchased him a far superior, more durable Nikon D2H. "Consider it an advance," she said. "I expect you will be making some money for the both of us."

Isabella De Luca was not wrong. With Carina as her assistant, she had invited dealers and journalists from Palermo (and one writer friend from as far as Rome) to a private view a week before the public opening. All five artists were present, even the scarred blacksmith Carollo in a suit that likely dated to the Second World War. The guests found the pottery charming, the jewellery intriguing, and the ironwork dazzling. One critic complained Isabella had packed too much into the little space. Her sisters Bianca and Romy catered the event. Thank God the gallery boasted a small courtyard out back, where patrons might enjoy a glass of wine and a cigarette.

Everyone wanted to meet Antonio Badalamenti.

Of the hundreds of images he'd shown her, Isabella De Luca had eventually selected seventeen to exhibit. Four were self-portraits, twelve others were of family, neighbours and friends. The last was a photograph of

Isabella's own son David Gallucci and his companion Daniel Garneau.

This particular image was shot at a high shutter speed with a wide-open aperture, capturing an instant just as the two were about to embrace. The color rendition was slightly off, its depth of field thin. But the figures themselves were mesmerizing.

Ever careful of nepotism, Isabella initially passed over this photo in her long-list of selections. But days later she returned to it. She studied it closely. All her other selections were shot in Sicily: Toretta, Palermo, Balestrate. This one was taken at the arrivals gate of the Toronto Pearson Airport. Daniel's back was turned, compelling the viewer to focus fully on David's face: his exuberant smile and chipped front tooth, the unruly facial hair (so fashionable among young men these days), the musculature of his (too thin) bare arms. The sheer joy and vibrancy in his body was palpable. David's expectant embrace of Daniel was Italy's embrace of the world. This image was more than Italian, she concluded. It was lightning in a bottle.

One afternoon, three weeks after the grand opening, a Canadian couple arrived at the De Luca Gallery. The girl was pretty with long colourful hair. She carried a magazine in her hand and asked (as had so many others) about "David e Amico." If only the young lady had called in advance, she might have saved herself a trip. Unfortunately, the limited edition 27x40 platinum prints were sold out; the one remaining on the gallery wall was an artist's proof and not for sale. The girl explained she'd come all the way from Mexico, and tomorrow she'd be travelling on to Germany. Was the gallery certain it couldn't part with this one copy? By way of a reply, Isabella showed a nude self-portrait of the artist (then aged nineteen) with his three-legged puppy Pepi in his lap. The girl was more than enamoured. Immediately, she had her husband settle the transaction as she signed the guestbook. He gave an address in California where the piece could be shipped. "But you are both Canadian?" Isabella asked.

"Yes." The young man glanced at his wife. "She also has her French citizenship. But yes, we are."

After the couple departed, Isabella checked the guest-book. As suspected, she recognized the name. The buyer had left behind her magazine, opened to an English-lan-guage review of the De Luca Gallery. It featured a wide-angle photo of Isabella leaning against the entranceway, arms folded, a cigarette in hand. The article began: "On a Sunday afternoon, not far from Palermo in the rolling foothills of Mount Canalicchi, on the feast day of Sergius and Bacchus, an extraordinary event took place in the village of Torretta."

The writer went on to extol the virtues of the country-side and its history, and the quality of the eclectic pieces assembled for display.

"Of course, the two stars of the exhibit were the gal-lerist De Luca herself, and the photographer Antonio Badalamenti. While not the centrepiece of Badalamenti's work, the insouciant sensuality of 'David e Amico' (the gold *cornicello* dangling suggestively about the young subject's neck) tested most the imagination, captured in the lim-inal space of a Canadian airport, daring the viewer to cross a threshold into the 21st century where same-sex love was

celebrated as it had once been centuries past. De Luca
was to be applauded for her contemporary vision. Her
curatorial statement was a gauntlet laid down, a challenge
to the old regime."

Isabella smoothed the creased pages of the magazine.
She had already read this review many times over since
its publication. She had, in fact, posted a carefully com-
posed letter thanking its author, a famous colleague of
her friend in Rome. She closed and set the magazine
aside, jotting down a note to include it in the shipment
to California.

After that, she made herself an espresso and retired
with her laptop to the courtyard. Her London editor had
requested a review of a new biography of Johann Joachim
Winckelmann. The deadline was close at hand and Isabella prided herself on her punctuality. She settled in her
Carollo chair, observing the computer screen, and lit a
cigarette.

Smoke curled. Ivy wreathed the little stone fountain
in the corner (a wedding gift from the Sabatinis). The
sound of flowing water always soothed her senses. But on
this occasion, she could not concentrate. The great German master Winckelmann had spent the last thirteen
years of his life in Italy, studying the homoerotic in classical art. How had she herself not seen it in this single
photograph of her son?

She rose and left the courtyard, returning to the gallery
to stand before "David e Amico."

When she confronted Luke, he confessed he'd known
for years that David was gay. Very little ruffled Isabella's
composure (her world had been turned upside-down long

ago; life was an *opera buffa*), but this was news she never imagined. She had always assumed one day she would have grandchildren. That, Luke declared, was still a possibility. In fact, he assured her, it was something he and Ai Chang were working on. Then Isabella wondered if this was all the influence of yet another Sicilian curse. She had dealt with so many over the years. She considered her own tumultuous life: born a bastard, self-exiled overseas, three husbands buried. She considered the Chinese girl Ai Chang Cho, and the French boy Daniel Garneau.

"At least your sons," Tony said, "have taste in lovers."

"Hush," Isabella said.

Tony shrugged. "All the early Roman emperors kept male lovers."

"Not Claudius." Her second husband Michele chuckled. "That one slept only with women."

"Strange man," Tony said.

"Isabella, *mi amore*," Michele said, "your children and your family are healthy and happy. That is all that matters."

Isabella nodded, gathering her resolve. As usual, her first husband said nothing but hovered at a distance, ephemeral light over the fountain basin.

She herself had known a great many men in her time. Nicoli had been her first. She recalled their inexpert fumblings forty-five years ago in the shadow of Carini Castle (where, in 1563, the Baroness of Carini and her lover were infamously murdered after being discovered in the throes of passion). To his credit, Nicoli was far more skilled now than he had been then; certainly his stamina was much improved. Now almost every day at the lunch hour, he would come down from the farm to visit her.

Then she would close the gallery, and they would retire to her apartments above, where they would make love with the windows wide open. Then each evening they would repeat the ritual.

Fuck the classical Greeks and their tiny phalluses.

How little did they know.

The truth was, of all the men in her life, Nicoli was always the one she had loved the most. Still, if he were to drop dead tomorrow, she could not promise he would be the last.

Isabella De Luca reached out, resting her fingertips upon the *cornicello* about David's neck. The gold wedding ring glinted upon her own hand.

She bowed her head, and began to laugh.

ACKNOWLEDGEMENTS

This book was written on the traditional lands of the Haudenosaunee, the Anishinaabe, and the Huron-Wendat, and on the treaty territory of the Mississaugas of the Credit.

I'd like to acknowledge use of the following Canadian song titles as chapter titles: "Somewhere Down the Crazy River" by Robbie Robertson; "The Limit to Your Love" by Feist; "Magic Carpet Ride" by Steppenwolf; "Lovers in a Dangerous Time" by Bruce Cockburn; "The Spirit of Radio" by Rush; "The Grand Optimist" by City and Colour; "Where Have All the Good People Gone?" by Sam Roberts; "You Ain't Seen Nothing Yet" by Bachman-Turner Overdrive; "Miasmal Smoke and the Yellow-Bellied Freaks" by Wintersleep; "Superman is Dead" by Pouya; "Taking Care of Business" by Bachman-Turner Overdrive; "Queen of the Broken Hearts" by Loverboy, "Wondering Where the Lions Are" by Bruce Cockburn; "I Will Give You Everything" by Skydiggers; "Life is a Carnival" by The Band; "Boy Inside the Man" by Tom Cochrane; and "Golden Hour" by Sam Roberts Band.

I'd also like to acknowledge the liberties I have taken in this work of fiction to respectfully represent actual persons including Avril Lavigne, Patricia Wilson, Sook-Yin Lee, Will Munro and Xavier Dolan.

Lastly, I'd like to express my heartfelt thanks to the dedicated staff at Guernica Editions for their support and inspiration, and for their hope that the books they publish will make this world a better place in which to live and love.

ABOUT THE AUTHOR

David Kingston Yeh is a counsellor and educator in Toronto's LGBTQ community. He has written four plays produced in Toronto, and his short fiction has appeared in numerous magazines. David holds his MA in sociology from Queen's University, is an alumnus of George Brown Theatre School, and attended Advanced Graduate Studies in Expressive Arts in Saas Fee, Switzerland. David lives in downtown Toronto up the street from a circus academy, with his husband and a family of raccoons. *Tales from the Bottom of My Sole* is the sequel to his first novel, *A Boy at the Edge of the World*.

This book is made of paper from well-managed FSC® - certified forests, recycled materials, and other controlled sources.